The new Zebra Regency Romance logo that you see on the cover is a photograph of an actual regency "tuzzy-muzzy." The fashionable regency lady often wore a tuzzy-muzzy tied with a satin or velvet riband around her wrist to carry a fragrant nosegay. Usually made of gold or silver, tuzzy-muzzies varied in design from the elegantly simple to the exquisitely ornate. The Zebra Regency Romance tuzzy-muzzy is made of alabaster with a silver filigree edging.

Silver Moonlight

We stood together, admiring the glitterand sparkle of the ocean, and listening to the low crash of the waves on shore. "Not at all like the night we met, is it, Miss Maudsley?" Lord Dayne asked.

Mozart, the moonlight, something in the tone of his voice, spelled danger. I replied lightly. "I wonder if one can call a struggle in the water and a douse in the chops a *meeting?*"

"It has a certain *cachet.*"

"Yes, exactly the way I like to meet gentlemen. Balls and routs are so terribly ordinary, don't you think?"

"I don't believe, Miss Maudsley, that in whatever circumstance we might have met it could have been ordinary."

ZEBRA BOOKS
KENSINGTON PUBLISHING CORP.

ZEBRA BOOKS

are published by

Kensington Publishing Corp.
475 Park Avenue South
New York, NY 10016

First printing: June, 1991

Printed in the United States of America

Chapter One

Lia

I was twenty-one years old and thinking about marriage. Although the gentleman had never actually spoken to Papa, he was attentive enough to make anyone think he was a serious suitor. I, at least, thought so, and I also thought he was prodigiously handsome. And then Papa died. And I grew up.

We were a big, loving family. Besides Mama and Papa, there were five of us children, although I could have said, like the child in Mr. William Wordsworth's poem, that we were seven. That means that two of us did not survive childhood, but that the ghosts—or the memories—of Adam and Star are still vividly with us. In fact, Mama sometimes hears them speak to her; they tell her that they are happy and sometimes even relate to her their adventures in a place that they call "Here," which we suppose means Heaven. They sometimes come to Mama in dreams, and when they do, Mama can see them; but usually it's when she's sitting alone, quietly sewing, that they visit her and she speaks to them. Adam and Star were seven and five when they were taken from us (both the same day from a lung congestion), but they were old enough to speak well and had some understanding of the world. We don't tell people that they visit Mama, of course, because Communications with the Beyond are not quite the thing among people of our class.

As I was saying, we were a big and loving family, and despite the loss of two of us, and of Papa, we are still a big and loving family. I should also say that this will not be a sad story, although we had our share of tribulations after Papa died.

I am the firstborn, and little Irene is the last born of eight, which I will explain later. (Or we remaining six, as my sister Sunny prefers. Sunny is quite precise, very down-to-earth, and is the only one of us who won't believe that Mama receives Communications.)

Perhaps the best way to introduce the numerous progeny, as Papa used to call us, is by name and age at the time of his death, which is when my story begins.

Benjamin Rousseau Maudsley is the second born. He was sixteen, completing his studies at Winchester and soon to be going up to Cambridge. He was named after a famous American republican, diplomat, and scientist, Benjamin Franklin. Papa was an ardent republican himself, until the French gave the word a bad name. The famous French philosopher, Jean-Jacques Rousseau, who as I understand was more democratic than republican, was all the rage in Papa's salad days. That's where the Rousseau in Ben's name comes from.

In any event, Papa had been very much impressed by Dr. Franklin when he was introduced to him as a boy. Dr. Franklin proved something about colors by lying pieces of different-colored cloth on the snow to see whether it would melt faster under one color than another. I think it was the simplicity of the experiment that intrigued Papa, who could never quite fight through his complex ideas to the simplicity he longed for. Incidentally, Dr. Franklin demonstrated that snow melts faster under a piece of black cloth than under a white one.

The rest of us have easier names to explain. Sunny, or Summer, comes next. She's named after the season in which she was born. Ben began calling her Summer Sunshine when she was old enough to know she was being teased and to cry about it. Somehow, though, it stuck, perhaps because of her somewhat cranky disposition. So we call her Sunny. She was thirteen when Papa died.

Adam would have been ten had he not already Gone Before, as our Great-Aunt Edula says. He was named after Mr. John Adams, an ambassador to the Court of St. James from

America and a recent president of that country. Papa spent some years in diplomacy. . . .

My readers may have noticed that we older children arrived at rather lengthy intervals. Papa would be away for two or more years at one post or another, or one mission or another, and then he would be home and Mama would be increasing again. I wasn't supposed to know about the Facts of Life, but it wasn't hard for an intelligent child, as I was, to draw certain conclusions.

Papa gave up diplomacy after Adam was born, so Chunk—whose real name is Brook—was nine the year Papa died . . . that is, he was only a year younger than Adam. I believe there was also some private association between Mama and Papa, having to do with Chunk's conception, a fact I have surmised from certain significant glances between them when the brook at High Oak was mentioned. In any event, he was a square, burly baby and surprisingly heavy. One day Papa picked him up and exclaimed, "What a chunk you are!" He's been called Chunk ever since.

Star would have been seven. Papa saw a shooting star at the very moment he calculated that Star first opened her eyes on our world. It was an appropriate name, for she was in life a veritable shooting star, as bright and elusive as quicksilver. And, as Mama says, she shot across our firmament, brightening a small moment of time for us, before she Went Before.

I suppose it is becoming clear at this point that Papa was eccentric and Mama a trifle unworldly.

Nonetheless, although as sweet as a woman can be, Mama could put her foot down when she was pushed too far. She must have been pushed too far after Star, for Angela was given her name because Mama liked it. But as things turned out, it was as significant as any of our names. Angela is a perfect angel, and she was born with the pretty manners that most children must be taught. Perhaps that's why she remains Angela, the only one of us, except for Irene, to be commonly referred to by her proper name (although Papa always insisted on the Greek version of her name, Angeline). She was six when Papa died.

And then there was our surprise. Mama had discovered she

was increasing again just before Papa's death. So when the new baby was born, Mama felt that we should return to his system of significant names. Since Papa died only a week before we received the news of Lord Nelson's success against the Baltic powers in the Battle of Copenhagen, and since Irene was born in October of that same year, 1801—which was when the news of the peace agreement between England and France reached London—the baby was called Irene, for the mythological Greek goddess of peace. Mama said that if Papa had been living, he probably would have wanted to call the baby Copenhagen or perhaps just Peace, but she wouldn't have permitted it.

Irene made us eight, or—as Sunny would have it—six: Ben, Sunny, Chunk, Angela, Irene, and myself. And Adam and Star, who are Beyond.

Looking over what I've already written, I discover that I have failed to mention my own name. I was born at sunrise, so my name is Aurelia, which is Latin for *dawn*. My family calls me Lia.

Papa's death was unexpected. We believe now that strain from the worry over money and the plight he had pitched us all into contributed to the apoplexy that carried him off. Mr. Price, a very sensitive and worthy gentleman who attended Papa's affairs—or tried to—waited for nearly two weeks after the funeral before seeking an appointment to apprise us of our financial position. Even then, knowing how shocked and overcome we were by Papa's sudden death, he would have waited had he been able to hold our creditors off any longer.

Ben and I have often wondered how Papa managed to hide from the world the straightened circumstances into which he had wandered, but we were not long in ignorance of *how* it had happened. Mr. Price, with profuse apologies, explained to us that it had been impossible to control Papa's expenditures. Papa was too much inclined to give beggars pound notes and to distribute largess to what he considered worthy causes. (Papa believed, like Mac of the Mint in *The Beggars' Opera,* that money was made for the freehearted and generous.) And although he never kept an opera singer or anything like that, he did like luxury, magnificent clothes, and to cut a dash.

And, of course, he belonged to the gaming and jockey clubs. Papa liked horses and the races, but he didn't know a thing, really, about horses. One of his cronies, who called on us to express his sympathy in our bereavement, told us that Papa had a geometric system for judging a horse's capacity to run. If one drew a series of straight lines from various points in the horse's anatomy and then calculated angles, and how near the parallel certain lines were . . .

"Whit won now and then with his system," the gentleman told us, "although can't say I ever found it useful. Worked for him recently, though. I've been holding his winnings from the last race the two of us attended together. . . . Said he wanted me to place it for him at Newmarket. Said he didn't think he'd be able to attend. . . . But it's a rather tidy little sum. Thought perhaps you, Lady Maudsley, might like to decide whether or not . . . That's to say . . ."

Mama smiled graciously. "Why, how kind of you! And of course you must place it, if that's what my dear Whitney wanted."

"Oh, no, Mama!" I exclaimed, horrified at the thought of this rather tidy little sum escaping our grasp. "We mustn't ask this kind gentleman to go to such trouble! Really, Mama, it just wouldn't do!"

Mama might just as well not have heard. She smiled her beautiful smile again and said, "Your dear Papa obviously received a Communication, and that does relieve my mind. I did so hate to think of him going Unprepared." She held out her hand to the gentleman in such a gracious gesture that he actually popped up to kiss it. "I can't thank you enough, sir," she said as she gracefully withdrew her hand. A faraway look came into her eyes. "I wonder if it was Adam and Star who told him. They certainly didn't tell me, and I shall scold them for it."

Ben, the first to recover from Mama's revelation, said hastily, "Lia's right, Mama. We mustn't impose on this gentleman's kindness."

"But, my dears, your dear Papa knew he was Going, and he

wished his winnings disposed of in this way. . . ."

"*Disposed of* is right," Ben muttered, for only me to hear.

The kind gentleman threw us an anguished glance. I am certain to this day that he knew our circumstances and had hit upon this means to save our pride, while contributing to our support from his own pocket as Papa's muddled affairs were sorted out. In any event, he took the money away, and after the July meeting at Newmarket, we received by messenger a sum very close to the first, in which he described how some horses won and some lost, and he was sorry that the sum had been so marginally increased, etc., etc., etc.

Papa had also contributed a good deal of our worldly substance to the support of two astronomers named Herschel, to a Mr. Priestley who did experiments with gases, and to others who were making serious contributions to science, as well as to some scientific gentlemen who as yet remain obscure—and who Ben says will forever remain obscure. We received heartfelt letters from those who could not attend Papa's funeral, and two of the scientists sent us money, saying that although Papa had never expected repayment, they no longer needed subsidy themselves and that we might like to redistribute the money to other needy persons. We managed to persuade Mama that, unfortunately for science, we were the needy persons.

Papa had remodeled and enlarged the house at High Oak, and had purchased elegant furnishings worthy of its new grandeur. Great sums were also spent on scientific agricultural schemes for the estate. But for all the science, the schemes didn't increase income as they ought to have done. Mr. Price explained, with barely concealed disapproval, "Your father was not a man to be bothered with checking the books, and the management at High Oak was left entirely in the hands of a steward who should have been dismissed years ago."

"Yes," I replied, "Mr. Boggsworth. His family has served at High Oak for three centuries, and his father was steward before him. I'm sure Papa—"

Mr. Price observed me over his glasses. "I have been much struck, Miss Maudsley, with your good sense, and I am forced to say—and I hope you will excuse me for saying it—that your understanding is of a higher order than your father's. You will understand me, I'm sure, when I say that one cannot introduce new schemes and expect a man whose knowledge of management is confined to the methods of a previous century to succeed. I told your father: High Oak has always rendered a satisfactory, although not a large income; therefore, either continue as before and keep the man, or introduce your new schemes and pension him off."

I bowed to the good sense of this statement, and Mr. Price continued with his enumeration of Papa's failings.

Ben later had the ill grace to remark in front of Mama that it wouldn't have been so bad if Papa had managed our High Oak estates better, since with all those improvements it was at least one investment that should have paid off.

Mama directed a rather severe look at us. "I know you are terribly worried, children, because we must face straightened circumstances. But your Papa was not an *ordinary* man; you must always remember that." Her severe expression softened. "Life was too small for him, I believe." Then she added, as we digested that remark, "Don't fret, my dears. Something always comes along. The Lord provides, you know."

If that wasn't just like Mama! Ben and I could only exchange hopeless glances.

Other expenditures that had brought Papa to ruin were in support of our extravagant way of living, for he had never intimated once to any of us that we couldn't afford whatever we wanted. We found also that he had invested money in business endeavors and industrial inventions with an uncanny sense of what wouldn't succeed and what wouldn't work. Only one business venture had netted an income worth mentioning, and unfortunately that business failed soon after Papa died. Finally, there were some investments that Mr. Price couldn't identify and some expenditures that he could never trace even when Papa was alive—substantial cash withdrawals for purposes that Papa never revealed to his lawyer and man of business. Papa was very poor at saving receipts and that sort of thing.

The result, however, was clear: he had gone through his

own fortune and Mama's dowry, and had mortgaged almost all the property he hadn't already sold.

To make a long story short, we found it necessary to sell our London house and the land at High Oak—the latter for a respectable sum because of Papa's scientific improvements. We realized enough from those sales to pay off almost all of Papa's debts and to cover those mortgages he had taken out over the years to finance his extravagance. High Oak itself—the home farm, coverts, gardens, and woods, which we did not sell—was rented to a retired naval officer, a Captain Metcalf. Luckily for our former steward, Mr. Boggsworth, Captain Metcalf kept him on. Mr. Price was most disapproving, remarking that if the naval person depended on income from the home farm for the rent, we should soon be searching for another tenant. But it's been three years now, and the naval person is still in occupancy.

"Someday," Mama said soon after the lease was signed, "we'll move back to High Oak. Just be patient, children, and you'll see."

Ben and I exchanged one of our usual hopeless glances, but Sunny, who at thirteen was much too disrespectful of her only remaining parent, said with a great deal of exasperation, "Mama, for goodness sake, why can't you realize that we're *poor!*" And then she burst into tears and ran out of the room. Thirteen is a difficult age at which to be cast from riches into rags.

We also remained in possession of our villa at Brighton, which I mention last because it figured largely in our future, as the reader will shortly learn.

The villa was the one piece of property that Papa had not mortgaged, so we owned it, and some land with it, debt free. Mr. Price counseled us to keep it, in order to derive income from rent. (Mr. Price always favored Rent over Interest.) In the summer we rented it to Londoners seeking sea air and refreshment, and in the winter it was rented to people who didn't own country houses and who retired instead to Brighton.

The Prince of Wales, the king's oldest son and heir, had taken a fancy to Brighton several years before, which made it one of the most fashionable and popular of watering places. We never had a bit of trouble renting. Even though our villa was farther than most people preferred to be from the Stein, Brighton's favorite promenade ground—the villa is west of the town on the Shoreham road, a little past Belle Vue—there were always those who would accept the inconvenience for the comfort of a detached villa and a garden, rather than being crammed into lodgings or one of the narrow terrace houses on the developed streets east of town. I could also offer a marquis and marchioness at nearby Belle Vue, and of course there was a wonderful view of the sea. Papa had loved the sea.

Mr. Price found us a cramped but adequate house just outside Lewes, which wasn't far from Brighton and where we could live more cheaply than in London. And we fared pretty well, although of course we had to give up the social circles in which we had once moved. A few friends remained, but pride prevented us from accepting invitations that we couldn't return. Little by little our social life began to be confined to local Sussex gentry.

The gentleman I mentioned in the first paragraph of this story was never got to the post, as Papa would have said. In any event, I would have refused him. I had fancied myself in love and had made rather much of myself, anticipating the sacrifice I was preparing for the moment he threw himself at my feet. Well, the fact is that he had his own feet too firmly planted on the ground to throw himself at mine. The gentleman, a third baron who shall go unnamed, was perfectly willing to marry the daughter of a baronet (have I mentioned that Papa was a baronet?), in apparently good pocket, but was not willing to marry that same daughter when she was discovered to be—at least by his lights—poverty-stricken.

That was when I began to grow up and to think about something other than parties and pretty dresses, novels and romantic poetry. I am ashamed to say that I was quite empty-headed when young, but then neither Papa nor Mama ever expected any of us to be anything else. But perhaps impractical parents automatically create practical children, and when the hard times came, we turned out—at least we older ones, Ben and Sunny and I—to be very practical indeed.

Even before the third baron drifted away I had known that I couldn't marry, what with all that brood of younger brothers and sisters, and being the head of our family. Although Mama *can* put her foot down, she seldom *does,* and she is just terribly unworldly. There is a belief that idiots are the special province of God. Mama, of course, is blessed with all her faculties (in fact, extra faculties), but in any event, I have come to believe that the gloriously impractical and unworldly may also claim a portion of grace. And, as Mama herself says, she has Adam and Star to speak for her Up There.

We lived comfortably enough during the following three years, chipping away at Papa's remaining debts. Ben went to Cambridge as a gentleman scholar, since we were fortunate enough to have an ancestor among the founders. We of course had to dismiss the governess, and so I undertook to complete Sunny's education. A very stubborn girl, Sunny, when it came to being educated. We nearly drove each other to distraction. Angela, on the other hand, was a lamb, and Chunk was at a school in Lewes for young gentlemen, which taught by the Eton system. He didn't like it at all, so he wouldn't have liked Eton either, and, as I told Ben, if he was going to hate school, better he hate it in a cheaper place.

In the summers we went to Brighton for two weeks, living in lodgings. It was a vacation for Mama and the children, and an opportunity for me to consult with the rental agent about the villa—necessary repairs, whether or not to raise the rent—the usual tiresome things. Then Mama decided—and would not be persuaded otherwise—that we all needed a long summer holiday ourselves . . . that we shouldn't rent our Brighton villa to others, as we had been doing, but should spend the summer there and even think about living there permanently.

"I was just speaking to Mrs. Yewdall," Mama said, "who has a sister-in-law in Brighton—a dressmaker by trade, I believe. . . ." Mama must have caught Sunny's disapproving expression—Sunny is always scolding Mama for conversing too freely with the tradespeople—for she added hastily, "A very *fashionable* dressmaker. She keeps her shop open all year, now that Brighton has Society year round. And Sunny, you may remove that *very* disagreeable frown. Please remember that frowning induces wrinkles that are terribly disfiguring and age one remarkably."

Sunny's frown disappeared, to be replaced by the blank, stupid look that she employs when the children play at Smiles. Her eyes become slightly unfocused as she stares at someone and her mouth sort of droops open, so of course her opponents always smile first. Chunk once tried to call that blank stare against the rules, but it only resulted in Sunny gazing at him across the dinner table with exactly the same offensive expression.

"But in any case," Mama was saying, ignoring Sunny, "Adam and Star visited me yesterday, and they have counseled—I'm sure they're speaking for your Papa, for of course they're too young for such judgments. . . ." She broke off again, and her eyes took on that faraway look that they always did when she was thinking about the Beyond. "I wonder why your Papa never speaks to me? Do you suppose that only the very young and the very innocent—for of course your dear Papa could never have been described as innocent . . . such a man of the world. . . . But never mind. Adam and Star suggest that we spend the summer in Brighton, perhaps live there permanently."

"Just what, exactly, did they say to you, Mama?" I asked, not bothering to look up from the book I was mending for Angela.

"Well . . ." Mama is always truthful when pressed. "They asked why we weren't spending the summer there. In fact," she added, a little defiantly, "they said it is *very* important that we do so, and, furthermore, that they would love it!"

"Oh, piffle!" Sunny said. "How can dead people enjoy the seashore?"

"I'm sure I don't know," Mama replied tranquilly. She doesn't mind if Sunny questions her relationship with Adam and Star. It's only when Sunny frowns—at the risk of acquiring wrinkles—or misbehaves in some other fashion that Mama scolds her.

I stopped listening. Mama and Sunny enjoy their bickering, so I left them to it. I just couldn't see our way clear to the education of Chunk and a modest presentation for Sunny, who by now was sixteen, without the rent from the villa. And it was so expensive in Brighton! Even simple foodstuffs would cost us more. Besides, we had recently suffered a financial reversal—and just as we had about cleared the last of Papa's debts, too. Those business and mechanical investments Papa had made sometimes brought in small sums, which were always nice surprises, but sometimes they resulted in demands for payments, and we had just been presented with a rather staggering one for Papa's share of the debts of a dissolved partnership. It's all so terribly vulgar, this talk about money, but when people are just barely making ends meet, they do think about it rather more than others may. And then Great-Aunt Edula, who was the only one of our relatives who condescended to help us—aside from an occasional brace of fowl or a pot of honey—had written that she had suffered financial reversals herself and was forced to reduce the small sum she sent us every quarter. The sum had never been large, but on our budget we missed every penny.

The season before, 1803, had not been the best year at Brighton, and I'd had to lower the rent on the villa. The war with France had started up again; Bonaparte was threatening invasion and people were afraid to go to the south coast. That winter the girls at the boarding school had kept "Napoleon Kits" under their beds, should they have to take flight in the night. I've always wondered why they couldn't just snatch the covers from their beds and make off. It all shows how silly people can be . . . as if the soldiers would have time to bother with a few girls or with frightened sea bathers, either, when they had England to conquer!

Anyway, Brighton was full of officers and enlisted men, with an infantry regiment out toward the Lewes road and a cavalry regiment near the Prince's Marine Pavilion. And of course there was always Brighton Camp in the late summer, when the militia took the field. The soldiers were one of the reasons I hesitated to go to Brighton for the summer. Sunny was at a very impressionable age, when a uniform has more importance than the qualities of the man inside it.

When I mentioned this to Mama, she replied with annoying placidity, "Sunny is a sensible girl and her head is not about to be turned by a scarlet coat."

"Mama, she's sixteen. All girls of sixteen are fascinated by scarlet coats. And military camps are always an attraction to the sort of female that—"

"Lia, I think sometimes you are too wise by far. You must be careful, dear, for being too wise is often mistaken for an unfeminine nature."

I had to admit that sometimes I felt like Mama's guardian, but what would have happened to us if I hadn't been "too wise by far?"

In favor of a summer at Brighton, we had all noticed that Mama was pale and even somewhat peevish of late, which was not like her at all. The winter people at the villa weren't staying on, and I'd had no really good offers for the summer. Ben wrote that he could forego the spring term at Cambridge to help us move, for it would be necessary to give up the house in Lewes. We both thought we could find ways to reduce our own expenses, and Sunny—who is a dear girl, really—agreed. And Mama had always seemed to thrive in Brighton. . . . The upshot was that we did just as Mama wished, which somehow we always did seem to do, one way or another.

I find it hard to describe my emotions when we arrived, valises in hand, at the gate of the villa, knowing that it was ours for a whole summer. All sorts of memories flooded back of other summers spent there, and of one Christmas when we didn't go to High Oak but came to Brighton, and I fell in love for the first time. He suffered from spots, but love is blind.

Our villa, as I've already explained, is one of the few detached houses in fashionable Brighton. Papa inherited a house in town, but he sold it to build the villa on some land he had also inherited on the western cliffs and which he eventually named Xanadu, from a strange poem that Mr. Coleridge, the poet, wrote. The poem hasn't been published or even finished as far as I know, although Papa thought it had the potential to be as great as *The Rime of the Ancient Mariner.* Papa and Mr. Coleridge were great friends, but we haven't seen him since Papa died. I believe he is presently in Malta.

The house Papa sold is on West Street, and it is now a profitable lodging house, which is just one more example of his bad business judgment. Sunny says it's not such bad judgement, really, since if we still owned it, we'd have to be cooking for the lodgers and cleaning their apartments.

In any event, Xanadu is what's called a *cottage orné*—rambling, fanciful, with seashell trim in some kind of plaster, and painted a merry shade of pink. There's a small, rather scrubby garden in front, for the shoreward side receives the full force of the wind from the sea, but there is a walled garden at the rear and southeastward side of the house, where we and our local caretaker have over the years achieved some small degree of success. Marigolds and daisies and other hardy flowers bloom along the walls, tamarisks give us some welcome shade, and a few inland trees are making a noble effort to adjust to the seashore sun and salt and wind. There's a covered arbor and a rock garden, and a terrace, opening onto the garden in the rear, is green with potted plants.

Mrs. Oliphant, an amiable lady from the town who had been our housekeeper in happier days, having secured the key from the estate agent, had been watching out for us. She came hurrying out the door, a housemaid behind her. She hugged us all and wept, and so did we—at least the females. Ben and Chunk just stood about stiffly, frowning and looking very sober and owlish. The new housemaid, Jane, was introduced, and then Mrs. Oliphant took Irene from my arms. And although Irene is past the age to be cooed at, Mrs. Oliphant nevertheless still had to do so, before coaxing Mama upstairs to rest. The house was sparkling clean bright with flowers. The wagon with our baggage had arrived the day before, so the rest of us could set right to work unpacking. By evening, we were well on the way to being settled.

Then what should I do that first night of our holiday summer but fall in the ocean!

After the children were in bed, my excitement at being in Xanadu once again began to dissipate and I started to feel sorry for myself. Ben, who is my confidant, declared himself exhausted and went heartlessly to bed. Sunny, after much complaining, had rocked baby Irene for perhaps fifteen minutes (traveling always upsets Irene), then had gone off to write a letter to her very best friend back in Lewes. Why was it my fate, I thought petulantly as I at last put the sleeping child in her baby bed, to be mother to a brood of children not my own? I loved them all dearly, of course, but they were my brothers and sisters, and in the natural way of things they should have had two parents, and I should have been married and thinking of raising my own family. A terrible vision rose up before me: I saw myself, stricken in years, a lace cap perched on my thinnish grey locks, with a batch of great-nephews and nieces quarreling about my feet.

I believe that even the best of us fall into such moods, and I, certainly, had far to go to achieve perfection. I thought that if I could just go down to the beach, where I could contemplate the stars and listen to the rhythmic splashing of the waves, out of reach of my family, my spirit would be soothed. The freshness of the breeze, reaching me from across those long stretches of ocean, unsullied by the noxious poisons of towns and manufactories, would clear my "badness glands", just as Papa had always assured us the sea air would do for every one of us, including himself, as we set out for Brighton each summer.

It was nearly midnight and pitchy dark when I slipped away from the house, but the stars were bright in the black sky and shed sufficient light for one who knew the way as well as I. My destination was the wharf on the beach below Belle Vue Field, where boats are drawn up for repair and bathing machines pulled to safety when the seas are up. The cliff above the beach is about thirty feet high—not nearly as imposing as the cliffs to the east of town, but high enough for a nasty jolt if one should fall. So although there are wooden steps down to the beach not far from the villa, I decided to follow the road to the foot of West Street, where a gap in the cliffs gives easy access to the sands. It meant I would have to backtrack along the beach for some distance, but after all, I had no idea what the condition of the wooden steps might be after a year of winter storms, and I am not a foolhardy sort.

All was quiet as I walked slowly along the road, savoring the freshness of the air. I drew my warm shawl more closely about me, for the Brighton air is not only fresh but also exceptionally bracing, and it was only the middle of April. I was descending the gap to the beach when a man's voice called out, "Who is it there?" I recognized the gravelly, gritty voice immediately as that of Mr. Scruggs, one of the men who attends the fire in the fire cage that hangs over the West Street Cliff as a guide to fishermen and sailors.

"It's just me, Mr. Scruggs, Lia Maudsley," I answered. "How are you?"

"Miss Lia, is it?" He held his lantern closer. "Well, you're a sight for sore eyes. Prettier every year." Mr. Scruggs, who fancies himself rather gallant, makes the same remark to every young lady.

"You're looking very well yourself, Mr. Scruggs. I hope Mrs. Scruggs is also well."

"Couldn't be better. We've moved out to the crofts north of town. Healthier out there, and she's got her a cow and some chickens. You and your family all here? Your good mother? All well, are they?"

"Yes, we're at the villa. We just arrived today."

"Mrs. Oliphant mentioned you was coming. Good woman. I've always said it was a pity she married such a brawler. Never could understand what she saw in him! Left her well fixed, though. Will say that." Mr. Scruggs shook his head, to indicate that the world was full of mysteries, before narrowing his eyes to regard me suspiciously. "But what might you be doing out alone at this time of night? Young ladies better be in their beds now that some of the summer folks are coming down. Never know what kind of lowlife will show up, hanging around the gentry and the swells, looking for some kind of advantage."

"I'm just going down to the beach for a very little bit, Mr. Scruggs. I couldn't wait until morning to feel the sand under my toes."

Mr. Scruggs shook his head again as he contemplated another mystery. "Well, I'm sure I don't understand it, but Mrs. Scruggs always says that young ladies is fanciful. Just be sure you don't go far. You stay close enough I can hear you call if there's trouble."

I had no intention of staying within calling distance, but I agreed to do so, and after all the proper farewells were said on each side, I set out once more. The trouble with small towns where you've been known all your life, and your father before you, is that people assume a proprietary interest in your welfare. I'd only gone a few steps when Mr. Scruggs called after me. "Oh, Miss Lia. Forgot to tell you. The two young gentlemen staying at the Old Ship are out again tonight. So just in case you meet them . . . One with the gimpy leg always takes a swim about midnight. Funniest thing you ever saw. Goes down to the beach in his dressing gown . . . Swims at night 'cause he doesn't want anyone to see that gimpy leg, or I miss my guess. . . . Wouldn't get me in the water at this time of year, I can tell you, no matter what!"

Mr. Scruggs had a way of going on at length with his opinions. I interrupted him to ask if I had anything to fear should I encounter the two young men, which I knew would please his fatherly heart.

"No, no. Perfect gentlemen, they are. But what they'll think of a young lady like you, Miss Maudsley, well brought up like you was, out there alone at this time of night, I couldn't say." A thought suddenly entered his mind that had eluded him previously. "Does your mother know you're out here?" he asked. "I'll lay odds she don't."

"Mama was asleep when I left the house," I said, avoiding a direct answer. "Well, I just want to go down to the beach for a minute, and I've lots to do tomorrow, so I'd better be going."

"Like I said, Miss Lia, you stay close. You've always been too independent by far, and what your mother would say if she knew . . . Why, I remember the time . . ."

"Yes, Mr. Scruggs," I assured him again. "I won't go far."

So I set off once again, Mr. Scruggs watching my progress and muttering to himself.

It was high water, and I walked along close under the cliffs. I stopped for a minute to contemplate the dark distances and the stars, picking out the constellations that Papa had taught us to recognize. I could no longer see Mr. Scruggs's lantern; he had apparently returned to add fuel to the fire in the fire cage, which was now blazing up with great vigor. Nor did I see any sign of young gentlemen.

As I stood on the beach, I was reminded that until I was eleven, there had been a magnificent yacht anchored offshore. But Papa had sold it, saying that he just didn't like sailing and that it was too dangerous for children. I suspect now that it was sold to pay for Papa's extravagances. That made me feel a surge of resentment toward my father. And then I felt guilty, because Papa had been as extravagant with his love as with his money, and as Mama says, he wasn't an *ordinary* man.

It was really as black as the inside of a pocket, and even though my eyes were well adjusted to the dark, I made my way cautiously along the wharf. The tide was coming in, and although the waves rolled with a kind of tranquil majesty, the sea was high. I was pondering the many aspects of the ocean and perhaps was distracted from close attention to what was under my feet. Suddenly I heard a shout from somewhere to my left and automatically directed my gaze toward the source—or toward where I thought the source was—and walked right off the wharf. As I hit the water, I heard an exclamation, something like *"Hey!"*

I rose, spluttering. My skirts, which had caught the air as I descended, floated around my ears, and my shawl was wrapped uncomfortably about one arm. But although it inhibited my movement, I was in no danger. I have been able to swim since I was a child. Papa made certain that we all learn to swim so we could play freely on the sands without supervision. Nonetheless, I was disoriented from so abruptly finding myself in the cold water rather than on the wharf, and furthermore entangled as I was in my shawl. Then someone—or some*thing*—grabbed me from behind. I drew breath to scream, which caused me to choke, for I had taken on some seawater. In a perfect panic, I began to kick furiously and flail about with my free arm.

My ears heard an obviously human voice yelling, "Don't struggle," but my brain had conceived the notion that I was in the grasp of a sea monster, and I fought with the fury of the damned. The monster and I went under, I still struggling and the monster trying to confine my flailing arm with its tentacles. The water was blacker than the night. I was certain I would drown, be dragged to a watery lair, and be eaten. Even in my panic, I was thinking what a disgrace it would be to drown in only seven feet or so of water, within no more than twenty yards of dry land! Then the monster at last released me. I broke surface again and saw a man's face appear directly in front of me. "Stay away from me!" I gasped. And then I was forcibly struck on the jaw.

Chapter Two

In the distance, I heard a male voice saying, "Come now, wake up. I didn't give you that much of a knock." And I felt my cheeks being gently slapped.

I said, "Stop that this instant, Irene. I'm just getting up." This may seem a strange remark for one who had just miraculously fought off a sea monster, but my sadly confused brain now suggested that Irene was patting my cheeks to wake me up, one of her new tricks and one that I very much disliked. I opened my eyes and found myself lying on the pebbly beach, staring up at the stars. I had been wrapped in what I later discovered was a gentleman's dressing gown, and I had a gentleman's coat thrown over me. Two men knelt beside me, one of whom—the one who was patting my cheek—was in a rather shocking state of undress, as I perceived instantly. I turned my eyes to the other, who was more fully clothed.

"How do you feel?" the clothed gentleman questioned.

"What happened?" I asked.

The unclothed gentleman said to his companion, "We'll need some blankets. Chaff, why don't you—" One's eyes tend to automatically turn to a speaker (how else had I managed to walk off the wharf?), but I quickly turned mine away again as he moved, awkwardly but just as quickly, out of my line of vision.

The clothed gentleman replied in a deep, quiet voice, "Yes, I'll go immediately. Won't be more than a few minutes."

I had recovered my senses sufficiently by this time to deduce that these two young gentlemen were undoubtedly the ones Mr. Scruggs had spoken of, and that they were under the misconception that they had rescued me. Dark as it was, I had also seen enough in those two quick glances to realize that the unclothed gentleman was as totally undressed as a man can be without being stark naked. He had apparently pulled a pair of underdrawers over his wet skin, and they were clinging revealingly to his manly form. I had also seen that one of his legs was scarred and shrunken. The most tactful thing to do under the circumstances would be to sink back into a faint until his friend returned, which, with a little cough, I immediately pretended to do.

It was tactful but thoroughly ineffective, for the gentleman uttered a strong oath and, immediately grasping me from behind, sat me up and doubled me over, one hand on my midsection. Air swooshed from my lungs.

"Sorry, didn't mean to . . . uh . . . be so rough. Just keep your head down," he instructed, "and you won't feel so faint."

"Stop it," I gasped. "I'm all right. And stop that cursing."

He was still kneeling behind me. "Sorry. Now lie down again. Chaff will be back in a few minutes with some blankets and some smelling salts."

"I p—prefer to sit up, if you don't mind. And I d—d—don't need sm—smelling salts." The coat that had covered me had crumpled into my lap, and the dressing gown had fallen from my shoulders. My teeth were chattering from the cold. I tried to pull the coat around me again.

The gentleman once again draped the damp dressing gown over my shoulders. "Hand me the coat and I'll wrap you in it also," he said.

Although I couldn't see him, I could sense that he, too, was trembling from the cold. "Please, sir, take your dressing gown. The coat will be s—sufficient."

"No, no, I'm a regular polar bear. Let me wrap you in the coat."

"I don't know if polar bears—whatever they m—may be—can catch cold, but gentlemen surely can. Please take the dr—dressing gown. I assure you I need only the c—coat."

"I insist you keep it. Chaff will be back shortly with blankets. He'd have gone immediately, but we were concerned that I'd injured you. . . ."

"Well," I said, "I b—believe I'll be going along then. I find it uncomfortable conversing with a person who is sitting out of my sight."

I made a move as though to rise, but the effort called my attention to my throbbing head—the result, no doubt, of the blow to my jaw. I automatically put my hand to my head.

"No, no, you're not at all well enough. And you're freezing. If it will make you more tranquil, I'll do as you ask."

I had to get to my knees to divest myself of the dressing gown, and as I tried to remove it, while at the same time pulling the coat around me and revealing more of myself in my wet gown than I cared for the man to see, he said, "I'm not looking."

I handed him the dressing gown over my shoulder. My eyes were carefully fixed on the dark horizon, but I was very much aware of naked masculinity immediately behind me. I had an image of his form in my head, as clear as a picture in a book. I forced my mind to practical matters. "You really should walk around a bit to warm yourself. The ocean is terribly cold at this season, and after your exertions . . . I have this warm coat, but your dressing gown is damp. . . ."

"What an authoritarian young lady!" He ignored my advice and sat down beside me. "Are you warmer now? Perhaps we should introduce ourselves. I'm Breverton Dayne."

He also seemed to be exactly what he claimed to be a regular polar bear. (I discovered later that polar bears inhabit the Frozen North.) In any event, he no longer trembled from the cold. I was conscious that a good portion of my legs were still in view, outlined under my wet skirts, and I drew them up under me. I hugged the coat more closely about me, trying to relax inside its shelter so my teeth would stop chattering. "I'm Aurelia Maudsley. How do you do?"

To my surprise, he uttered a short laugh. "I'm doing very well, it seems."

He left me to consider for several minutes what that statement might mean, since I couldn't think of any kind of reply. Finally, doubtless feeling, as he certainly should have, that he had been discourteous, he asked, "Do you live near here, Miss Maudsley?"

His silence had irritated me, and despite his attempt to rally up his manners, I found it hard to quell my annoyance. He was no doubt thinking me terribly ungrateful. After all, I should have been thanking him fervently for saving my life. Or perhaps my irritation was because I was the head of my family—there was no use pretending Mama filled that role—and that I couldn't bear to be thought in need of saving. Or perhaps it was because my jaw was beginning to hurt and my head ached. However, I answered politely, "Yes, we have a villa up on the cliff. Not far from Belle Vue."

"I hope you won't think me forward, Miss Maudsley, but what were you doing out on the wharf alone at this time of night?"

Indeed I did think it forward, and had I not earlier encountered Mr. Scruggs, I could have asked very much the same question of Mr. Dayne. But I answered calmly, "I was taking a walk and thought I'd sit on the end of the wharf awhile. Then someone shouted, and I just walked off."

"You just walked off!?"

There was *that* in his tone that suggested disbelief. It's true that a young woman of my social class—even the reduced social class into which we had fallen—would not be allowed to walk alone on the beach so late at night, but most young women of any class had not had to pull a family together with no help except for a very young brother, confer with lawyers, haggle with creditors, and just generally do everything. This man sounded as though he thought I had been trying to put an end to my earthly existence. "Do you think I *intended* to walk off the wharf?" I asked, the irritation in my voice undoubtedly as obvious to him as it was to me.

"I have no idea what you *intended* to do, but I do know that you very well might have drowned if my friend and I hadn't happened to be there. As it was, you nearly drowned me." There was some irritation in his voice, too. I suppose nearly being drowned by a person one is attempting to save does put one in bad humor.

"I'm very sorry for it, Mr. Dayne, but you frightened me. . . ."

"Of course, very understandable," he replied, with renewed but irritating graciousness, and a complete misunderstanding of my words. "Those who can't swim can hardly help but panic in deep water."

That did it. "I didn't panic! My father took me into the water with him before I could walk, and I was swimming perfectly well by the time I was three years old. I was *terrified.* First someone—you or your friend, I suppose—yelled at me and I looked back, and then there I was in the water, and something grabbed me from behind. . . . How was I to know that it wasn't a . . . a . . . sea creature of some kind?"

He actually shouted with laughter. "A monster! What kind of a monster, pray?"

I stared at him. "Well . . ." I couldn't help smiling. He had a rich, full laugh, and his teeth flashed white in the dark. "My first thought was that you were an octopus. . . ."

His laughter rang out again, and so I laughed, too. And just then the large figure of his friend loomed up out of the darkness. "Friends already?" he panted. "I take this laughter to mean that the young lady has fully recovered her senses. And her spirits." He handed a blanket to Mr. Dayne, dropped others on the sand, and unfolded the one he still held. He knelt and draped the blanket around me, with the help of Mr. Dayne on my other side. Until that moment, I hadn't realized that I had been tense with cold. I relaxed inside the warm shelter, and my headache (although not the ache in my jaw) began to subside.

I reached up out of my blanket to rub the affected part, and Mr. Dayne asked sympathetically, "Does it hurt much? I am sorry."

"You may be one of a very few ladies who've ever been given a douse in the chops," his friend said.

Mr. Dayne was wrapping himself up in one of the blankets. He paused to gesture toward the other gentleman. "Miss Maudsley, this is my friend, Stuart Chaffinch."

There was an almost imperceptible pause before Mr. Chaffinch replied, "I'm most pleased to meet you, Miss Maudsley."

"We'd better be getting Miss Maudsley home," Mr. Dayne remarked.

"I have a question first, Mr. Chaffinch. Why did you shout at me? I presume it was you who caused me to miss my footing on the wharf."

"Indeed, Miss Maudsley, the guilt lies at my door, but the wharf is in rather bad repair after the winter storms, and I feared for you to proceed further. Had I seen you sooner . . ."

". . . Miss Maudsley would have been spared a struggle with a sea monster and a . . . er . . . douse in the chops. Shall we escort Miss Maudsley home now?"

"A sea monster, you say!" Mr. Chaffinch feigned astonishment.

I sniffed. "If Mr. Dayne chooses to call himself such."

Chaffinch laughed, but as nearly as I could tell in the stygian darkness, Dayne merely raised his eyebrows. "As you say, Miss Maudsley." An argument then ensued between Mr. Chaffinch and Mr. Dayne. Mr. Chaffinch urged Mr. Dayne to return to their hotel, since he was clad only in a robe and a blanket—and his underdrawers, which of course neither man mentioned. Nor did they mention that when Mr. Dayne walked, he was required to lean on a cane, as I shortly discovered. It was diverting to have two gentlemen so concerned about my welfare—considering, of course, that they had been the cause of my need for welfare—but my patience was soon exhausted. I stood up, clutching the blanket about me, and said, "Thank you, but I do not need an escort."

They expostulated.

One must often speak as firmly to male adults as to children. "I walked to the wharf by myself, and I can walk home by myself. I'm uninjured—unless I should suffer aftereffects from being struck on the jaw. I am not faint. And if you'll give me your direction, I'll send someone tomorrow with this blanket, which I presume you are willing to lend me."

They were both equally determined that I should have an escort home, but Mr. Chaffinch was also determined that Mr. Dayne should not be the one to escort me. At last, I lost all patience.

"If you hadn't shouted at me, Mr. Chaffinch, I would be walking home at this moment, alone and in dry clothing. And if you hadn't tried to save me, Mr. Dayne,

I should also be uninjured."

"It seems that Miss Maudsley is a swimmer and was in more danger from me than from drowning," Mr. Dayne remarked to his friend.

"Are you indeed a swimmer, Miss Maudsley?"

"Yes," I snapped. "A very *good* swimmer." I started off down the beach at as fast a pace as the blanket would allow, but had only gone a short distance when Mr. Chaffinch caught up with me. He was an enormous man, well over six feet I was sure, with something about him that reminded me of a great friendly bear.

"Brev's returning home, but with apologies for having caused you grief. He asked me to tell you he'll call tomorrow with more suitable apologies. And if you'll allow me, I'll escort you to your door. It's the least I can do after sending you pitching off the wharf."

"As you wish."

Mr. Chaffinch was not easily daunted. "Suppose you noticed." He cast a quick look behind him to make sure that his friend, who was making his way slowly forward in the same direction we were walking, was far enough behind not to hear. "Brev—I suppose he introduced himself as just Breverton Dayne. That's his real name, of course. . . ."

So I learned that Mr. Dayne was not a Mr. at all but a Lord—in fact, a sixth baron, which perhaps in some mysterious way explained our unpromising introduction, for the reader will recall that it was a third baron who decamped once I was stricken by reduced circumstances.

And I learned also that Mr. Chaffinch was very fond of his friend. They had been together in Spain as very young men, Mr. Chaffinch with the diplomatic service and Mr. Dayne—or Lord Dayne, for such he was formally styled—as a young naval officer. "Suppose you noticed that old Brev isn't too steady on his pins. His leg was shattered. . . . Two operations, but he'll walk again, with a cane. . . . Worst of all, it happened in a minor engagement. Brilliant, but hardly significant enough to make the textbooks in years to come. That's what's chewing at his pride. I hope he wasn't . . . discourteous."

"No, he wasn't discourteous."

I also found out that Lord Dayne swam every night because he was determined to walk properly again. He'd already graduated from crutches to a cane, which the doctors hadn't had much hope of. I didn't ask why he swam at night. Mr. Scruggs had already put his finger on it. Lord Dayne wanted to take no chance that anyone would even glimpse that scarred and mangled limb. I couldn't find it in my heart to condemn his vanity.

And speaking of Mr. Scruggs, I won't even attempt to recount what *he* had to say as we climbed up the West Street gap. His silence, however, was promised—possibly with the help of a small sum from Mr. Chaffinch, although I saw nothing actually change hands.

Sunny woke up when I came into our shared bedroom. I'd left my dress and petticoat hanging on the clothesline to dry, and entered the room in my drawers and camisole, which of course struck her as unusual. So while I brushed the sand and tangles out of my hair, I had to tell her the story, from start to finish. She immediately pounced upon one of the points I had been neglecting to consider.

She sat cross-legged on the bed, squinting at me in the dim light. "When they pulled you out and laid you on the beach, they must have seen *everything*, Lia, with your wet clothes clinging to you! Until they covered you up with that coat. I *do* hope they were gentlemen and averted their eyes until you were decently covered. How will you ever face them again? For they will call upon us tomorrow, I promise you! That is, if they are truly gentlemen." Although her mind often strays to thoughts about the opposite sex, Sunny can also be very proper.

"I believe they wrapped Lord Dayne's dressing gown around me the minute I was out of the water," I said. And it did seem to me a likely possibility. "And it was very dark, you know."

Sunny seemed satisfied with that and went off to sleep again, so I was now free to indulge in girlish blushes at the thought that they had probably had a fairly good look at my maidenly form, not to mention that, in the struggle in the water, Breverton Dayne—Lord Dayne—had actually laid a hand on various portions of it. I felt my face grow hot just at the thought. But then, it was sauce for the goose as well as the gander, if that old saying can be said to apply. I had managed to lay a hand on him during our struggle in the sea, and although he undoubtedly had a lengthier and more leisurely vision of my form than I of his, nonetheless, I did see rather *more* of his, all things considered. He certainly stripped well, as Ben would say.

Ben had been much enamored with boxing even before going up to Cambridge—"the Fancy," he calls those who practice the art and patronize it. He affects a Belcher neckerchief rather than a proper cravat, much to Mama's distress, and sprinkles his conversations with boxing cant. So I knew what Mr. Chaffinch meant when he said I'd received a "douse in the chops." And that's why I could say of Lord Dayne that he stripped well. Very, very well, I was thinking as I slipped gently into the arms of Morpheus, as Papa used to say.

Sunny was right. Lord Dayne and Mr. Chaffinch did make their call promptly the following day, so promptly in fact that I had hardly had time to recount to Mama and Ben the events of the evening before, what with Sunny making her usual comments.

All of us were at the breakfast table except for Chunk and Angela, who were already at the beach. Papa had taught them to be easy in the water at an early age, just as he had Ben and Sunny and me, and during our short summer holidays in the three years since he died, we had made certain that they continued their education. Also, Ben and Chunk often swam in a squire's pond not far from Lewes, and now and then Sunny and Angela and I slipped away with them to enjoy a refreshing dip. Mama says I am too old for such things, but I pay no attention to her.

Even though only twelve, Chunk is the strongest swimmer among us. He's not as fast as Ben, who always wins races, but his endurance is phenomenal. Ben is tall and slender and graceful, like Papa; but Chunk is constructed on the general lines of a large, strong cart horse. He's already taller than Sunny and me, and according to Mama, he resembles Great Aunt Edula in both figure and physiognomy.

Sunny and I resemble Mama in being quite ordinary in both shape and height. Fortunately, we both have her wonderful complexion and her long-lashed greenish-bluish eyes (it depends on what colors we wear), although only Sunny inherited her tawny curls. My hair, like Papa's, is dark brown, almost black, and has not the hint of a wave, let alone a curl. It is so fine, but at the same time so abundant and heavy, that it just continually falls out of pins. And the minute there's a hint of dampness in the air, what curl has been crimped into it immediately disappears. Last year I called quits (another bit of Ben's cant, I'm afraid) and started putting it up in braids. Ordinarily, I wind the braids around my head in a sort of crown, and on special occasions I wear them coiled over my ears, which is really the best effect. But sometimes, when I am especially busy, I don't even bother to put them up. Mama disapproves of braids, for she says they make me look like a maiden aunt, or—when they're down my back—like a French peasant girl. But I am just simply too busy to spend time attending to my hair, so I don't listen to what she says. As the reader may have guessed by now, I don't often listen to what Mama says.

But as I was saying, Chunk and Angela were already at the beach, and although Angela is only nine, we have no need to worry about her safety when Chunk is with her. Angela and Chunk are the only early risers among us, and so they have usually breakfasted and are about their private pursuits by the time the rest of us, by ones and twos, get to the table.

Today we late risers were all at table together. Irene was in her baby chair, spooning gruel into her rosy little mouth, stopping every now and then to listen to our conversation with an intent gaze that at times could be downright disturbing in a child so small. Irene doesn't speak English. She is past two and a half (you will remember that Mama had only begun to suspect she was in the family way again when Papa died), but other children begin to talk properly by the time they are her age. She understands perfectly what is said to her and we know she's not mute, for she speaks in some unknown tongue to her dolls and to herself, and even to us. One would almost believe that it's a foreign language, for she speaks with all the variations of voice and tone and expression that people speaking real languages use. I have been told by a very experienced nursemaid that although it is unusual for her to be clinging so long to her own language, it is not unknown, and she will eventually begin to speak English quite as well as the rest of us.

Mama and Sunny had just finished their comments on my adventure, Sunny repeating her suggestions that my modesty had been sullied, and Mama remarking tiresomely on how unladylike it was to be on the beach alone at night, and that I must learn to curb such hoydenish—not to mention ill-bred—behavior, and so on in like vein. Mama is a dear, but she has no conception of how inappropriate her ideas are for a woman of twenty-four who is the head of a large family. She would have me, I think, retire into a proper spinsterhood, sitting around and doing fine needlework. Mama herself is a skilled needlewoman, and it affords her such immense enjoyment that she cannot comprehend why she has been so unsuccessful in her attempts to teach Sunny and me. Only Angela, who of course is a perfect angel about everything, has shown any promise of having Mama's talented fingers. And I must add, in all fairness, that Mama does not confine herself to pretty lady-work; she also fashions new chair cushions, and darns and repairs linens and draperies in the most frugal, housewifely way. She has always made her own gowns, and all of us are better dressed than our income would allow because Mama is so skilled with the needle.

In any event, it was nine o'clock in the morning, with the sun slanting in the long French windows that open out onto the terrace, with its many potted plants. Five of us were still at the breakfast table when Mrs. Oliphant, a disapproving expression on her face, entered to announce that two gentlemen, offering apologies for the early hour, were asking the privilege of calling on us. "They say that they only wish to assure themselves that 'Miss Maudsley' has recovered from her 'misadventure' last night." Mrs. Oliphant's voice dripped sarcasm and disapproval. (Unfortunately, before I had managed to recover my still-damp garments, our venerable housekeeper had come upon them and demanded explanation. And that any such hoyden should be rewarded by such notice as a respectfully intoned "Miss Maudsley" was not to be believed.)

Mama said, "But of course we will see them." Then to my immense surprise, I realized she intended to entertain them at the family breakfast table, for she added, "Please ask Jane to clear the table of our plates and, when she has finished, to show the gentlemen in. At this early hour they would no doubt enjoy a cup of your excellent coffee, Mrs. Oliphant."

Mrs. Oliphant departed, looking even more disapproving, and Mama said, "Very proper of the gentlemen who rescued you last night, Lia, to call in order to ascertain that you had no ill effects. We must show them every courtesy."

"Mama, they did not rescue me! If it hadn't been for them, I wouldn't have stepped off the wharf, and—"

"Shhh, shhh, my dear. Details are never of consequence in such situations."

And so we were all sitting like sticks when the two gentlemen were shown in, both of them looking slightly surprised at being received in the breakfast parlor with the family still at table. I rose to greet them, conscious that although I was wearing a respectable enough dress, my braids were not yet up and I must indeed look like a French peasant girl.

Ben was also very properly on his feet, but looking absolutely awestruck. He had never met Mr. Chaffinch, although he knew the name to be that of a famous amateur of the Fancy. Ben recognized the man instantly, having seen him at a distance at various famous mills. It seems, as my brother told us later, that Mr. Chaffinch is reputed to have been one of the very first to recognize Mr. Jem Belcher's pugilistic talents (Mr. Belcher is slight of build, but strips well), and that Mr. Chaffinch is himself not only a skilled practitioner of the art, but also a wrestler.

Mr. Chaffinch had the powerful look of a wrestler, while his friend more closely resembled the hero of a romantic novel. Lord Dayne was a good height, although not as tall as his mountainous friend. And—as I well knew and tried not to remember at that particular moment—his physical attributes were manly and . . . shall we say . . . virile? His limp, the cane on which he leaned, his dark hair, and his finely chiseled features, which still bore the clear traces of pain, impressed the susceptible mind—which I have to admit mine was. Sunny, who has very little imagination, was much more impressed by the sheer bulk of Mr. Chaffinch and thought Lord Dayne's expression somewhat haughty. And so she said when they at last departed.

I introduced the two gentlemen to Mama, who held out her hand graciously and murmured, "But how can we ever thank you enough for rescuing Aurelia? The foolish child should never have been on the beach at night, and I am quite overcome with shame. You will think me a very bad mother indeed!"

Lord Dayne and Mr. Chaffinch bent over her hand in turn, both protesting that they thought no such thing, Lord Dayne adding that I had given them to understand I was quite old enough to make my own decisions and that they would never presume I had been about so late at night with my mother's permission.

Mama looked ever so slightly routed and said, "Yes, she is a very naughty girl. Now, may I introduce another of my daughters, Miss Summer Maudsley, and my oldest son, Sir Benjamin Rousseau Maudsley."

Ben, unable to contain himself, burst out, "I've seen you, Mr. Chaffinch, at the mills. Wasn't it a great go last winter? When the Game Chicken fought Burke, I mean . . . Do you know him, Mr. Chaffinch—the Chicken, I mean?"

"You're an *aficionado* of the Fancy also, Sir Benjamin?" Chaffinch inquired politely.

Ben, suddenly realizing that he was perhaps too forward with his opinions in addressing such a great personage, and having no more idea than the rest of us what an *aficionado* was, said with becoming modesty, "Oh, I'm not such a great swell as you, sir!" and then blushed crimson. He'd properly put his foot in his mouth, and I had to bite my tongue to resist commenting that I'd told him a hundred times to stop such heavy use of what he calls "lingo," or his tongue would slip in the wrong place sometime.

Mama to the rescue said, "But won't you both join us? I've just ordered fresh coffee."

Mr. Chaffinch smiled kindly at Ben, and Lord Dayne proffered their excuses for calling at such an early hour. "We'd like very much to join you for a cup of coffee, Lady Maudsley. But we must first apologize for this early visit. We've been suddenly called back to London and couldn't delay longer. However, before we departed Brighton, we desired to assure ourselves that Miss Maudsley suffered no ill effects from our errors last night, due to our mistaken belief that she could not swim." He turned an inquiring glance at me.

"No, no ill effects," I replied coolly, rewarding his inquiry with one of my imitations of Mama's gracious smile. "But thank you for your concern," I added, with a great effort, as I met his gaze, not to remember how well he stripped. For all I knew, he was laboring under the same effort I was.

"Please do seat yourselves," Mama said. "Ben, make more room for Mr. Chaffinch." With that simple statement, she admired Mr. Chaffinch's great height and at the same time directed him to one of the two empty chairs that would have caused Lord Dayne, leaning on his cane, a good deal of difficulty. "And you, my lord, that chair beside Lia."

Since I was not sitting down, Lord Dayne was given no clear indication which of the three empty chairs was to be his. And so it was with great perversity that he sat not in the one closest to Mama, but to Irene.

Mama was informing our guests that she had two other children, Angela and Chunk, who were taking advantage of the early morning hours for sea bathing. Even Mama forgets to call Chunk by his proper name, although she had, to Sunny's ill-concealed disgust, just referred to my sister as Summer, a name she intensely dislikes.

After suitable comment on the advantages of early morning sea bathing and the wisdom of teaching children to swim when very young, Lord Dayne turned to Irene—whom Mama hadn't bothered to call to their notice—and said, somewhat conventionally, "I don't believe we've met this little girl." At least he didn't refer to the baby as a "young lady," in that precious way some adults speak of children.

I popped up from my chair again to remove Irene from hers, for she had begun to make one of those "baby messes" that so offend Mama and would in all likelihood also offend our guests. Wiping her mouth with her bib, I returned with her in my arms to my own seat. Lord Dayne now turned toward us both and reached out his hand to take Irene's. "How do you do?" he said. "I'm Dayne. And you are—?"

"Irene," I said. "She's the baby of the family." Talk about stating the obvious! Although, when I think about it, Mama looks so young that it might have been possible, I suppose, for an even smaller baby to be tucked away someplace upstairs.

Irene decided to be gracious, and she made a long statement in her own gibberish tongue. Lord Dayne listened politely, and then he replied in gibberish himself. (I learned later that it was Spanish, but since I don't speak that language, it sounded exactly like gibberish talk to me.) Irene's mouth fell open—have I mentioned that Irene still drools, especially after eating? In any event, her mouth fell open and she leaned more closely against me, slightly withdrawn but not frightened, and studied Lord Dayne. He said something else to her in Spanish, which I surmised meant, in effect, "May I present Mr. Stuart Chaffinch?" indicating at the same time, with a slight inclination of his head, his friend on the other side of the table.

"Tu servidor, Señorita," Mr. Chaffinch replied with a slight bow. Irene, on hearing this new language from Mr. Chaffinch too, squinched around a little, although still keeping herself securely pressed against me, and replied to both in gibberish. Both men looked attentive and rather grave. Neither laughed.

"Dayne," Mama said with a thoughtfully distant expression. "My lord, would your mama perhaps be the former Clara Calcott?"

"Why yes, ma'am. Are you acquainted?"

"No, I have never had the pleasure. However, I knew a sister of your mother's, Lady Sarah Pellett—or Sarah Calcott, as she was before her marriage. For a number of years I saw a good deal of Sarah, and she spoke more than once of your mother."

"So you are acquainted with my Aunt Sarah! She'll be

happy to learn that you are in Brighton. She's taken a house here for the summer. In the Pavilion Parade, I believe."

"Why, how very delightful! I shall certainly look forward to seeing her, although I haven't heard from her these many years. She never writes letters, you know, but she did write me a very short note about your father. I was sorry to hear that he had Gone Before."

"Gone before? . . ." Lord Dayne left the question hanging, as though Mama had not completed her sentence and it should have been "gone before" something—or somebody.

"Passed on," Mama clarified. "And so young."

"Oh, yes, of course. Yes, it was a sad blow for all of us. But I think it was hardest for my older brother, required as he was to take up his responsibilities so young."

The best said about that, Mama realized, the better, and she launched into a discussion of her own experience with respectable death, which Papa's had undoubtedly been.

Algernon Dayne, Lord Dayne's older brother, had disappeared several years before under mysterious circumstances. It was thought that he had been murdered, although a body was never found. He was a brawler, often ending up before the magistrates at one of the West End roundhouses. In fact, it was said that he sometimes took over the magistrate's stool himself, dealing out justice to the lowlifes who were brought in during the night. He had not only been a patron of the Fancy, but also of bulldog and cock fights, the latter of which Ben has fortunately never shown an interest in and for which we all give fervent thanks. Men may choose to be so foolish as to engage in bare-fist fighting, but I can't think of anything more disgusting than setting dumb creatures at each other, unless it is bull-baiting. If Mr. Edward Gibbon is correct, such spectacles were symptomatic of the decadence that led to the Fall of Rome, although two cocks fighting each other is perhaps not quite in a class with a bear fighting an ostrich or an unarmed man condemned to face a lion.

But to return to Lord Dayne's elder brother. Algernon Dayne's exploits in the less desirable areas of London were well-known, and it was because of those exploits that murder was suspected. It was thought that on one of his rookery adventures he had been murdered for his money—or even his clothes, which could happen in some parts of London, as Papa had said at the time. It happened so long ago that I had forgotten, but I thought Lord Dayne's right to the title to the barony could only be recent, for it takes a number of years, I believe, before a person is declared legally dead when there is no body discovered.

I could tell that Sunny, looking very small and shy sitting between the large Mr. Chaffinch and the tall Ben, was wishing she were miles away. And it was equally obvious that Ben was simply dying to talk about bruisers and mills. Nonetheless, they both sat quietly throughout Mama's expatiation on Papa's death, with not the slightest move that would distract our callers' attention from Mama. Irene, however, had not yet learned her manners, and she suddenly sat up and launched into a discourse in her own tongue, directed at Lord Dayne.

Mr. Chaffinch, taking advantage of the interruption, said, "I may have had a slight acquaintance with Sir Whitney, Lady Maudsley. I believe we met at the Foreign Office several years ago. I believe Sir Whitney was also an acquaintance of Lord Bagley. . . ."

Mama stated that Papa had never mentioned a Lord Bagley and that Mr. Chaffinch must be thinking of someone else. She, certainly, had never heard of any such lord. And was that Spanish the two gentlemen had been speaking to the baby? She had never had any ear for languages herself and only spoke French—and that rather badly, she had to confess, although she had been sent to Switzerland to live *en pension* at the tender age of thirteen. . . .

Mama was interrupted this time by our housemaid, Jane, who appeared in the doorway and, after dropping an all-inclusive curtsey to the company, said deferentially, "Excuse me, Miss Maudsley, but the men that's to repair the kitchen boiler are come."

"Thank you, Jane. Tell them to wait," was the best I could do, while reminding myself to have a firm talk with Jane about proper behavior in front of company.

Jane's rosy and rather stupid face took on a mulish look. "You said you was to be told immediately, 'cause you have to see the man about mending the carpet at ten o'clock, and not to let you forget—"

"Very well, Jane. Please tell them I'll be with them directly." If I hadn't given in, Jane would have gone through every one of my tedious appointments with tradesmen and repairmen. The poor girl had absolutely no flexibility of mind. Our guests were such swells, as Ben would call them, that it was unlikely they had ever heard of holes in carpets, and undoubtedly the tranquility of their breakfast parlors was never disturbed by leaky boilers. Jane's lack of propriety was what came of hiring cheap help. But it was all we could afford, and we would just have to do as best we could with her. Mrs. Oliphant refused payment of any kind, for which we were enormously grateful, but she graciously pretended that it was her privilege to be reminded of happier times when our "sainted father" was with us. If there was anything Papa wasn't, it was "sainted"!

Although Sunny avoids caring for the baby as much as possible, she had just pushed her chair back and was preparing to rise when Lord Dayne, with a smile at me, held out his two hands to Irene. "I'll hold her, Miss Maudsley, while you see to whatever it is that requires your attention." Irene stretched her arms toward him and tried to wiggle off my lap.

"Why, Lord Dayne, I believe that our baby has quite fallen in love with you!" Mama exclaimed. "She is never friendly with strangers."

Manifestly untrue; Irene is a very forward child, who will make up to anybody.

I surrendered her to Lord Dayne after mopping her up a little. He set her comfortably in his lap and she closed her eyes, apparently preparing to take a nap.

Mrs. Oliphant arrived with a tray containing clean cups and the coffeepot, which she set before Mama. Jane followed, bearing a tray with plates and a basket of small molasses cakes. And I went to the kitchen, where I soon dispatched my business with the two boiler repairmen. They were sitting in the kitchen drinking strong tea and feasting on molasses cakes (one of the men is Mrs. Oliphant's cousin, I believe), perfectly content and in no hurry at all to confer with me, or even to get down to business. I showed them the boiler and explained the problem, then returned to the breakfast parlor.

I must say of Mama that she can be quite grand when called upon. She was pouring the coffee and serving the cakes as though we sat in all the elegance of what was once Maudsley House in London, or the grandeur of High Oak in the country. The breakfast parlor in Xanadu is cheerful and pleasantly proportioned, but it is small, especially for a large family. There were crumbs on the table and all the disarray of a family recently at breakfast. But Mama's manner, together with the good breeding of our guests, seemed to make it all disappear.

So I forgot about not-too-bright maids and damaged carpets, and set myself to enjoying the unexpected early morning society of two most presentable swells.

Dayne

"Well, Brev, what did you learn from Miss Maudsley over there on your side of the table? Although I must say, appeared to me you devoted more time to the baby than to her big sister," Stuart Chaffinch said as he directed his sleek racing phaeton toward the London road.

"My approach, my good Chaff, is considerably more subtle than yours," Lord Breverton Dayne replied. "Time enough to get to know the charming Miss Maudsley, and I find babies so much more refreshing than their elder sisters. They accept one for what one is. And," he added, his voice taking on a derisive note, "now that Miss Maudsley knows my rank and her Mama my fortune, I doubt it will take much time to warm her up."

"Bit of a vinegar, I'd say."

"If I understand your lamentable boxing cant correctly, you mean she drives off one and sundry with a whip in order that they not get too close to the ring? Perhaps. But rather more like my brother, I think. Too much responsibility too young."

"Yes, knowing how it was with Algernon, you might detect something like that, I suppose."

A traffic jam requiring some exquisite driving halted the

conversation for the course of several minutes. When they were clear again, Mr. Chaffinch remarked, "Perfect opening with young Sir Benjamin. He's mad for the Fancy."

"You know, appalled as I was when the Foreign Office described the Maudsley family—such an alarming number of them—I begin to think we may enjoy this assignment. A young baronet named Benjamin Rousseau and a sister named Summer . . . but called Sunny, mind you. And a 'perfect little angel' named Angela, and Chunk. Chunk! An obviously elder and very managing sister, with braids down her back and whose name—if I haven't forgotten all my schooling—means *dawn* in Latin. . . . I presume we can be assured that her progenitors had a reason for naming her after the dawn!"

"No doubt. Certainly Sir Whitney, or so the legend goes, had his eccentricities."

"I suspect the whole lot of them. And we couldn't have asked for a better introduction to the family had we contrived it, could we? All because Miss Maudsley has a disgraceful penchant for wandering about alone at night without her Mama's permission. A true daughter of her lamented Papa, or I miss my guess."

The two gentlemen drove on in silence for a time, until at last Dayne said, "But seriously, Chaff, do you think it wise to start probing so soon?"

"You're referring to the remark about the Foreign Office and 'Lord Bagley'?"

"Look out! The cow!" Lord Dayne automatically braced his feet, then cursed as pain assailed him.

"Sorry," Mr. Chaffinch said as he brought his horses and vehicle back under control. "We should report the animal! Cows loose on the road are a hazard to traffic. Wonder why she wasn't staked?"

"We haven't time," Lord Dayne said in a tight voice. He willed his taut muscles to relax. "But, yes, I thought your mention of 'Lord Bagley' perhaps unwise, if not premature. Surely Sir Whitney wouldn't have revealed his code name to Lady Maudsley."

"No, not likely. Just a shot in the dark. The lady didn't even blink. Either she was kept in total ignorance, or she's a marvelous actress . . . likely the former." Chaffinch was silent for a moment, thinking. "We'll want to find out all we can about Sir Whitney's activities in Brighton—who he knew, where he went, his daily habits. All such details."

Dayne murmured an abstracted agreement as he tried to ease his leg into a more comfortable position.

"Now, which of your aunts is it that's spending the summer in Brighton?" Chaffinch asked. "Stroke of luck, that. Did you know she was acquainted with Lady Maudsley?"

"She's my mother's sister."

"We'll want to make sure the two ladies meet again. She can vouch for your character, I presume."

"I can't be sure of that."

"Well, you'll just have to convince her you've turned Quakerish. It's another opportunity to cultivate the Maudsleys. Although, truth to tell, suspect it'll be a waste of our time. Doubt they know anything useful."

"In any event, we're here . . . or I am. And unless the fabled salubrious air of this famous seaside produces a miraculous cure, I'll be here a good time more . . . or can be, for of course, I'm entirely at your disposal. Meanwhile, we might as well enjoy ourselves. It's something different, at least." Dayne's mouth drew down. "Nothing else to do until I get another command."

Mr. Chaffinch tactfully turned the discussion to other subjects.

Chapter Three

I was following Papa's principles and introducing Irene early to the watery element, as he called it. Although I hate early rising, I felt I should take her out before the sun was strong enough to burn her fair baby skin. And, of course, once I'm in the water, I wonder that I should have so dreaded getting out of my bed only a half hour before. There are a small number of us who enjoy the very early morning in the ocean rather than looking on it as a dose of medicine, as so many do who come to Brighton for their health.

When I swim alone or with the children, I swim far down the beach beyond the villa and never use the bathing machines. They cost a shilling, and we haven't any shillings to spare. Nor do I need a dipper to supervise my efforts in the water or to help me back into the machine. However, Sunny and I felt it best, when only one of us could spare the time to take Irene for a bathe, to use the machines in order to have a second person present. Irene is now acquainted with Elsie, the dipper I prefer. Although Martha Gunn is the most famous dipper, Elsie is more gentle with children, and that particular morning she had held Irene while I swam out for a distance. There were none of the floating streaks of coal dust from the barges that can sometimes make sea bathing so unpleasant at the ladies' bathing area below West Street, and I felt wonderfully refreshed and exhilarated from the exercise when I left the water.

As I descended to the beach from the bathing machine, a woman of advanced years, who was impatiently waiting to enter the same machine, gave me a severe stare and said, "Don't tell me you have taken that baby into the ocean!"

"Why, yes, ma'am," I said in surprise. "I or my sister take her out nearly every day, just as our father did us. It's quite safe, I assure you."

"I am not speaking of the danger of the child drowning, for I'm sure neither you nor Elsie here would be so careless, but of the danger of a chill. The ocean must be taken in small doses, and only by those with certain fortitudes. And particularly so early in the year."

The dippers, hardy wives of our fishermen, do not tend to servility, and Elsie spoke up vigorously in my defense. "Why, that baby, ma'am, is healthier than any one of us standing here. And you wouldn't believe it, but she started swimming just about the minute Miss Maudsley put her in the water. It's a rare thing, ma'am, but seems like it comes as natural to the human young as it does to the animals. I've seen it often."

"Miss Maudsley, is it?" the lady said, ignoring Elsie. "Lady Matilda Maudsley is your mother?"

"Yes, that is my mother's name."

"I am acquainted with her. Haven't seen her for . . . it must be years. I hope she's well."

"Yes, ma'am, thank you. Quite well." Who on earth? I wondered. I thought I knew all Mama's acquaintances.

"Been living in Naples, but heard about your father. Dreadfully sorry to hear it. He was a man of parts, whatever people may say. Extravagant, of course, but charming. Don't suppose he left you too many feathers to fly with, hey? And how is Tilly? Bearing up, is she?"

"Yes, ma'am, quite well."

"Is she with you in Brighton?"

"Yes, ma'am."

"If you will give me your direction, I'll be pleased to call on her and renew our acquaintance. In the meantime, you may tell her that Lady Sarah Pellett sends her regards."

Irene was squirming to be put down, which was uncomfortable; I'm terribly afraid she's another Chunk. It was even more uncomfortable because I was carrying a basket of fish in my free hand. The fish market where the fishermen unload their catch every morning is on the beach below the Little East Street Cliff. I had feared that if I waited until after our bathe, I wouldn't be able to find anything of merit, so I had visited the market before taking Irene into the water.

"Let me hold your basket, child," said Lady Sarah Pellett. "And so you can put the little girl down while we are speaking. What's her name?"

"Irene."

She fixed Irene with a stern eye. "Now you stand still, Irene, and mind your manners while your sister and I converse. Really," she addressed me, and in much the same tone, "you should have a maid attending you. I can't imagine what Tilly is thinking of. Surely your resources are not so straightened that a maid is beyond your means!"

I chose to ignore the latter remarks, which I'm sure my readers will agree were presumptuous. "My mother will be delighted to see you again, I'm sure," I replied politely. "We're occupying our villa, just beyond Belle Vue on the Shoreham Road. You couldn't possibly miss it, for it's the only pink villa between the Battery and Western House . . . perhaps the only pink villa in all of Brighton."

"A pink villa. That sounds like your father."

Irene was pulling at my hand. It was getting late and I had other errands yet to do—orders to place for provisions and a visit to the library for Mama. So I said, rather more hurriedly than was quite proper, "And thank you, Lady Sarah, for your interest in my sister's welfare, but truly, she comes from a family with the right fortitudes for sea bathing. However, I, like you, am most conscious of the dangers of chilling, so I must hurry along, if you'll excuse me."

"Well, see that you immediately get the child into something warm," she ordered majestically, then handed me back my basket of fish and climbed up into the bathing machine without even a by-your-leave.

Since I had already dressed Irene, as well as myself, in the confines of the bathing machine, I presumed that Lady Sarah's remark was intended to justify her own interference. "Well, Irene," I muttered as I picked her up, "I believe we have just met Lord Breverton Dayne's aunt! What a brazen old busybody! I can't believe she could be a friend of Mama's!"

Irene babbled her agreement, and we trudged on.

The morning was well advanced when I finished my errands at the vegetable and fruit market and in the shops in Great East Street, delayed as I was by greetings from local people I had known all my life. It would be two months before the season proper began, and shopkeepers do like a bit of a chat when business is slow. But Irene was getting tired and fussy, and I had yet to do my last errand at Fisher's Circulating Library on the south edge of the Stein. Thus, I was forced to cut old Mrs. Waxler short in one of her rambling stories about her son's success in London so I could hurry on. Mama wanted one of the novels that she had chosen from Mr. Fisher's catalog the first day after we arrived. It was my last errand.

Mr. Fisher was occupied when I entered, and his clerk was nowhere to be seen. I was waiting by a display of pretty trifles that I could point out to Irene and, after our fashion, discuss with her, when I became aware that a man was staring at me. I had never seen him before in my life, so I turned away, but he immediately moved so that he was once again in my line of vision. With a show of bored negligence, he raised a quizzing glass to stare at me more intently.

I was not about to be intimidated by one of the impertinent young bloods—Bond Street Loungers—who infest Brighton and think to entertain themselves by, among other incivilities, putting young women to the blush. I was not a frail and timid female to be ogled out of countenance, and I returned his stare, attempting to imitate Sunny's detached gaze. When I refused to respond to Irene's gibberish entreaties, she tried to turn my face in the direction she wanted me to look, giving the odious lounger the best of the exchange.

Fortunately, Mr. Fisher approached at that moment, and following polite queries after each other's health, he removed from the shelf the book Mama wanted and handed it to me, along with a number of best wishes for my mother and a pat on the head for Irene. As I moved to depart, the lounger intercepted me and, planting himself firmly in my path, silently raised his quizzing glass to his eye again and stared intently into my face.

"Sir, will you kindly let me pass," I said with hauteur.

He still did not speak, and I, with quick heat, said, "You impudent puppy! Let me pass."

That did break his silence, for his lip curled in a slow, insolent smile, and glancing down at my basket, now filled with vegetables as well as fish, he said, "Tell me, pretty li'l hothead, where you work? P'raps a gentleman caller'd be to your likin' some dark night."

At that moment, a cool voice drawled, "Good morning, Miss Maudsley. Miss Irene. How nice to see you again." Lord Dayne, his own quizzing glass to his eye, his eyebrows ever so slightly raised, and sighting down a haughty nose, looked my tormentor slowly up and down. Finally, in an aloof, bored voice and in very superior accents, he asked, "Have I had the pleasure, sir?"

"Uh, no, don't believe so," the youth muttered, his insolence suddenly evaporated.

Lord Dayne had placed himself so that the lounger had to back himself into a corner in his attempt to retreat, and although he looked right and left, and even—desperately—over his shoulder, he had no alternative but to stand his ground.

With a disdainful glance that would have withered a full score of impertinent young men, Dayne said in the same superior drawl, "You will excuse us, then." He took my arm and escorted me out the door. Irene was jabbering her greetings, fairly bouncing up and down on my arm in her excitement at seeing her friend again, and quite spoiling the effect of our exit. After several paces in otherwise silence, I couldn't help glancing up at my rescuer. And he, looking down at me, started to laugh, at which I, too, burst into laughter. Irene bounced and gurgled, and held out her arms to him. He took her hand and said (in English), "No, little pretty one, I can't take you now. But I promise I'll do so later, if your sister will permit. For now, I'll relieve her of the book and her basket."

"When did you return, my lord?" I asked as I surrendered the basket.

"Only last night. Chaff and I have decided to take lodgings and remain in Brighton for some time longer." Irene had pulled one of my braids forward over my shoulder, where it had made a damp spot on the front of my dress. Rather than taking the book, he reached out and lightly touched the braid. "Unless you have once again fallen in the sea, I surmise from these damp tresses that you have been bathing."

"Yes," I said. I continued to stare, hypnotized, into his eyes as he stroked the braid where it lay on my shoulder. They were clear grey eyes, rather more heavily lashed than those of most men, and even now, with the laughter in them, there was a suggestion that on other occasions they could be hard and commanding.

Recalling myself, I lowered my own eyes like a perfect maiden, to the vicinity of where gentlemen usually wear their cravats. However, Lord Dayne wore a scarf around his throat rather than a cravat. It wasn't a Belcher neckerchief, but fine silk, very much like the scarves favored by the artists one finds in locations of natural beauty, now that landscapes and seascapes are beginning to achieve some popularity.

And then he took the book from my nerveless hand, breaking the spell. "Do you approve of my seashore attire, Miss Maudsley?"

I glanced up at him quickly, thinking that he was deliberately reminding me of the scene on the beach in which he had been rather less attired. But a slight flush touched his cheek, and I immediately felt once again in command of myself. It had been a slip of the tongue, and he was not so very superior after all.

I realized that I hadn't thanked him, which I hastily did by way of changing the subject, and he said, *"Siempre a sus ordenes, Señorita."* That required an explanation, and then he observed that he was gratified to be able to effect a real rescue, which I acknowledged had been the case.

"He must have read Anthony Pasquin's *Twelve Golden Rules for Young Gentlemen of Distinction,"* I said. "I must look for him in a state of intoxication at the theatre, and tossing balled-up programs at the Cyprian nymphs in the green boxes."

"You find Mr. Pasquin's satirical pen amusing?"

"Very much indeed. I wish we knew who he is. I'm sure he's one of us . . . one of those who think of Brighton as home."

"Yes, I too enjoy him. He sees through all the sham and pretense in these fashionable watering places." We walked on in silence for a few moments, until he said, "I intended to take a cup of coffee in that pleasant little bun shop near here. Come and join me. Then I'll escort you home."

"Well . . ." I hesitated. There were so many things that needed doing at the villa. It had taken only a day or two to discover how hard renting can be on a house, no matter how good one's agent or how careful one's yearly inspections. The leaky boiler and the hole in the carpet I've mentioned just about as many times as I can stand, and then there was also the curtain rod that fell off the wall the minute we pulled the curtain back, the broken crockery discovered in the back of a closet, the stain on the rug over which someone had carefully placed a chair . . . But I needn't go on with descriptions of the mundanities of life with which I'm sure many of my readers are all too familiar. . . .

Lord Dayne was not to be diverted by any consideration of my responsibilities. "I know, Miss Maudsley, that you're thinking of all the many things that require your attention today. But you have at least twelve hours yet in which to attend to those surely very unedifying activities."

"How nice of you to give me an excuse to put them off for another hour!"

"That is an acceptance of my invitation?"

"Unless Cowley's Bun Shop has become very fine since last I knew. As you observed, we've just come from sea bathing and the morning marketing, and are not formally dressed."

"Nor am I. Shall we go on, then? And perhaps the child could walk, as she obviously desires to do. I must proceed so slowly that I, not she, will delay us."

There was just the barest trace of bitterness in his voice, and I said, without thinking, "I'm sure it won't be long before you'll be walking better. Swimming is marvelously strengthening for the legs . . . uh . . ." I scold Ben for blurting out inappropriately, but it's a lamentable case of the pot calling the kettle black. I truly try to guard my tongue, but there seems to be a fault somewhere in that part of my brain that restrains the tongue from immediately voicing a thought. To cover my confusion, I followed his suggestion and set Irene on her feet and took her hand, muttering something to her about going to have a pastry and that she must be well behaved.

But apparently, Dayne was not one to be shocked by too-wise females. He replied easily that it was exactly what he hoped, that swimming regularly would strengthen his limbs. "I have my general strength and health to recover, for I was convalescent for many months. But I must sound very ungrateful! I could have lost the leg had I not had the good luck to be attended by an excellent surgeon, and as you may know, there are few excellent surgeons on shipboard."

"You are in the King's Naval Service, I believe Mr. Chaffinch told me?" I was thinking that from what I'd seen, he had already pretty well recovered his strength, but my tongue's censor isn't entirely useless.

"Yes, a frigate with Jervis at the Battle of St. Vincent, with Nelson in the Baltic and then, after war broke out again last year, with the blockading fleet. Until my ship was ordered to the West Indies."

"You were in the Baltic? The Battle of Copenhagen?"

"Yes."

"You must know Nelson, then?"

"Yes, although not well. I was only a junior officer, you know, when with Nelson. I was given a new command with the blockading fleet when the war commenced again, and then, as I said, I was sent off on a special mission to the West Indies, where this happened." He had no need to say that he meant the injury to his leg.

"And Nelson, of course, is now in the Mediterranean."

"Do you follow the war news, then, Miss Maudsley?"

Well taught as I had been to avoid any hint of intelligence when within one hundred feet of a gentleman, the amused expression on his face was too much for me. "As a matter of fact, I do follow the war news, and furthermore, I've read Caesar's *Conquest of Gaul*—even if it was in translation!"

"Have you indeed?"

"Yes, I have. And I certainly enjoyed it more than Ben did."

"Perhaps because it was in translation. I never could abide reading Latin."

We were by now at Cowley's, which prevented further discussion of Julius Caesar. It took some time to get us settled and to place our order, for Cowley's is a popular spot. Irene sat on Lord Dayne's knee and converted a piece of sweet breakfast bun into crumbs, some reaching her mouth and the rest decorating Lord Dayne's well-tailored trousers. I drank tea and disposed of my pastry much more elegantly and neatly. Lord Dayne drank coffee, ate his pastry, fed Irene, jounced her on his knee while she drooled on his shirt, and talked about the blockade of French ports, which was the duty to which he had expected to return once the special mission to the West Indies was accomplished.

"Nothing important," he said of the latter. "Just an admiral who needed transporting to Jamaica, and some orders and official documents to deliver."

The blockading force, his regular duty, was another matter—essential to the immediate protection of the nation, although generally tiresome and wearying. A high degree of seamanship was required, I gathered, so that the officers and crews had to be constantly on the alert. But on the other hand, nothing much ever happened—by which it was clear that Lord Dayne meant nothing exciting like a battle. The blockaders got bored, it seemed, just fighting the sea and the elements, and every now and then, when the opportunity arose, made quick, swooping attacks on the French shore defenses. It was during one of those raids that Dayne was first injured. That was a "mere nothing" . . . simply a minor slice across the shoulder from a sword. Then it was the West Indies and a shattered leg. Had that not happened, he would at that moment have been off Brest, in command of a ship, blockading the French fleet.

Lord Dayne's description of blockade duty, together with his animation as he talked of it, was enough for me to guess that he desperately wanted to be back in command of a ship. We all know that Admiral Lord Nelson is missing one eye and has lost an arm, so surely a game leg wouldn't be a deterrent.

"And you, Miss Maudsley, you aren't afraid that Bonaparte's soldiers will eat you should they slip past our blockade?"

I sniffed. "Not in the least. I know that Bonaparte needs his battleships to cover an invasion and that Admiral Nelson has them immobilized in Toulon."

His eyes were amused as he countered with one of the wildly impossible possibilities. "And what if Bonaparte should find another way? . . . He has excellent engineers in his service, you know. Perhaps there's some truth to the rumor that he's constructing a tunnel under the Channel. . . ."

There were all kinds of notions about tunnels under the Channel and balloon-wafted troop transports, but sensible people didn't put much faith in those farfetched notions. "Any tunnels around Brighton one can be sure belong to the smugglers, not the French," I replied, with the disdain that his remark deserved.

We strolled slowly along the cliff in the general direction of Shoreham Road, Lord Dayne leaning on his cane. There were now several of the infirm about, making their way to the baths in Pool Valley, or to Mohammed's for a vaporizing, or just relaxing on the benches along the lower cliff streets, where they could enjoy the sun and the ocean view. Although there is not much society until the prince comes down in late summer, there are always people in Brighton seeking cures for their ailments.

We paused for a moment to gaze out over the ocean, which sparkled under the mounting sun. Yachts swung gently from their anchors beyond the bathing machines and the bathers. Maids passed behind us on their way to the market, as well as a few strollers who appeared in the full vigor of good health.

"Your father must have been an unusual man, Miss Maudsley," Lord Dayne remarked as we resumed our slow progress.

"Why do you say that?"

"He reared such an independent-minded daughter. . . ."

His teasing tone told me that he expected a riposte, but instead I said thoughtfully, "Papa never really expected anything from us, and pleasure was the reward for such efforts as we did make—or his own convenience. Even swimming." Papa had been more on my mind the last weeks than at any time since immediately after his death. To be resident again in

Xanadu had brought back so many memories of him for all of us.

"But unusual, nonetheless, to assure that his daughters learn to swim as well as his sons. Tell me about him. What kind of man was he?"

So I began to talk about Papa, but before I had fairly well launched myself into the subject, we encountered Mr. Chaffinch, just leaving the Old Ship Hotel. He joined our slow progress, and then as we approached the villa, we met Ben on his way to fish from our old rowboat, which led Mr. Chaffinch to say that he intended to engage a fishing boat at The Rising Sun for the afternoon and would Ben like to join them for some deep sea fishing. Ben, of course, was hard put to appear merely pleased rather than ecstatic.

Mama remarked later, much to my annoyance, that our new acquaintances were wonderfully condescending to invite such a greenling as Ben to join them. It wasn't like Mama to suggest that we deserved anything less that the respect due a baronet's family . . . and one of ancient and respectable lineage. After all, Mr. Chaffinch had no title, and Lord Dayne was a second son—a baron only because his elder brother had had the scandalous bad luck to be murdered. But I had to admit that they were very amiable and lively gentlemen, and it was vastly agreeable that they chose to distinguish us.

They began to make a habit of calling on us in the afternoons, and were soon on a first name basis with Ben and the younger children, and on the easiest of terms with the rest of us. By the end of two weeks, we had invited them to dine with us twice, and they had once entertained us at a sumptuous supper in the Castle Inn. Such was the state of our intimacy when Charlotte and Georgie came to us.

Mama and Sunny and I had just settled ourselves comfortably in the garden that morning, when Mrs. Oliphant appeared at the terrace door, a very strange expression on her face. "Miss Lia, may I see you a moment?" she asked.

I sighed. It was so pleasant there in the shaded arbor, and I felt absolutely languorous from a long swim. Not to mention that Mrs. Oliphant's expression suggested something out of the way and to which I would have to apply some thought.

"They're in the kitchen," she whispered as I joined her.

I looked at her questioningly. "What's in the kitchen, Mrs. Oliphant?"

"The children. They say they've been sent to live with Lady Maudsley, but they don't seem to know why or wherefore beyond that."

"Sent to live with Mama? Who on earth—?"

A girl who looked to be about the age of our Angela was seated in a chair by the kitchen table, holding a little boy on her lap. He was bigger than Irene, perhaps three years old, although he still had that baby look about him and he still sucked his thumb. He stared at us with big eyes, his thumb in his mouth and his other hand twisting one of his abundant yellow curls. He might have posed for a cherub in an illustration. The girl was not so cherubic in appearance. Her hair was dark brown and confined in two tight braids, and her face was disfigured by freckles—nothing like an enchanting scattering across a precious little nose, but rather masses of them. She stared at me with big frightened eyes. Her breathing was much too rapid and shallow, and her lips were pressed tightly together. She was trying so hard not to cry that my heart melted.

I smiled at her. "Hello. You look tired, my dears." (I had picked up the terrible habit from Mama of addressing those younger than myself as "my dears.") "Would you like a nice glass of milk? And a biscuit? Or, I believe Mrs. Oliphant made some of her wonderful molasses cakes this very morning." Molasses cakes were among Mrs. Oliphant's many specialties.

The little girl shook her head, but Mrs. Oliphant nonetheless set about pouring two glasses of milk and heaping a plate with cakes.

I sat down on another chair. "Will he sit on my lap?" I asked the girl, gesturing toward the baby.

She shook her head.

"Well, can you tell me your names?"

The girl licked her lips. "Charlotte," she said in a timid little voice. "He's the Wee Georgie." She thought a minute. "George."

As I soon learned, they had almost impenetrable Scots accents, but since they soon adapted their speech to ours, especially Wee Georgie—Charlotte never quite lost that little burr—and since I really do despise reading dialect—it's one of the reasons that I never read Robert Burns or Sir Walter Scott—I will not burden my own readers with it but will translate even these first communications into English. For several weeks we couldn't always understand what the children said, nor they what we said, so there was necessarily a good deal of repetition, which I will also spare the reader.

Charlotte shifted Georgie on her lap, and I noticed then that she had a paper pinned to the front of her dress. "What is that paper you have on your dress, dear?" I asked.

She put her hand up to touch it. "Mr. MacDougal put it there. It's with the name of your villa on it, so we wouldn't get lost." A look of resentment flashed across her face. "I wouldn't have got lost, but I promised Mam. But I didn't look at the paper once when I asked directions." Confession was required of Charlotte's Scottish spirit. "I didn't know how to say it, so I just spelled it."

"And who is Mam?"

The reminder of her own capability had animated the child. "She's my aunt. My *adopted* aunt. But she has so many bairns that now the money doesn't come she had to send us here."

Georgie had begun to squirm, overcome no doubt by his desire for one of the cakes. He reached his hand toward them, but Charlotte caught it back and gave it a light slap. Georgie's lip trembled. Mrs. Oliphant, who had been hovering nearby, said kindly, "Come now, child, let the babe eat a cake. And take a drink of milk. Miss Maudsley has offered, so all you must do is to say 'Thank you' and help yourselves."

Charlotte hung her head and murmured, "Thank you," but made no move toward the food. She still tightly held the squirming, and now sniffling, Georgie.

I took a cake from the plate and put it into Georgie's hand. "Now I'm going to hold Georgie while you eat your own cake and drink your milk," I told Charlotte firmly. I had learned very early in my responsibilities that with children one provides as little opportunity for argument as possible, stating one's intentions or desires clearly and matter-of-factly, then acting upon them.

Charlotte surrendered Georgie reluctantly, and I soon discovered at least one reason why. He was wet on the bottom. Although their clothes were neat, the children themselves were none too clean; they had traveled a long way and, as I subsequently learned, with only one change of clothing in which to introduce themselves to us.

"He's a good boy, miss, most times. He just does that when he's scared or—or nervy or sick. Let me have him back. I don't mind."

Georgie had crammed the whole cake into his mouth and was already demanding another. I stood him up on my lap, ignoring the odor as best I could, while he struggled to get within reach of the cakes. "Mrs. Oliphant, will you bring me something to put under Georgie? Then while he finishes his milk and cakes, will you be so kind as to look for a change of clothing for him? Do we have any nappies left of Irene's? Or some clean rags of some sort?" Irene, although only two and a half, and although she still drools, *never* has accidents.

Mrs. Oliphant folded some clean mop rags and laid them across my lap before departing on her errand. I sat Georgie back down, picked up his glass of milk, and held it to his lips. "Drink this now," I instructed, "and then you may have another cake." After the milk was down, I handed him the cake and turned to the girl. "Now tell me, Charlotte, why Mam sent you to us." Although I didn't really guess who these two children were, I had a sort of premonition of . . . not disaster, exactly, but certainly of complication.

"I've a letter, miss. Mam says Lady Maudsley is my—my stepmother, and she'll take care of us." She descended from her chair and unpinned the bundle that served as portmanteau. From it she took a crumpled letter, which she shyly handed to me. "I'm sorry it's like that, miss, but Mam didn't have any better paper, and I couldn't keep it flat in my bundle. . . ."

I hushed her apologies and unfolded the letter. The child

had obviously misunderstood this "Mam" person, but in any event, something would have to be done with the children. I began to read.

I doubt that many of my readers can imagine my shock, surprise, consternation, confusion, perplexity, and dismay as I perused that letter—a whole bundle of mental and emotional states that would require diligent consultation of Dr. Johnson's famous dictionary to describe in full. One can't comprehend in a moment that one's dear Papa—entirely unknown to one—has fathered another family.

Oh, I know that bastard sons and daughters are not uncommon among gentlemen of our social class, and that they are often recognized by their fathers, educated, and sometimes even legitimized, inheriting estates over the proper heirs. But the unexpected discovery that one's own parent has engaged in such activity just can't help but be shocking and a little overwhelming. I must say that considering the circumstances, I sustained it rather well.

I glanced at the signature and discovered that "Mam" was more formally known as Mrs. Margaret (Mamie) Clendenning. Mrs. Clendenning stated the facts, and certainly without mincing words. Papa had kept a mistress in Edinburgh by the name of Goodman, who owned an elegant hat shop in that city. The mistress was apparently endowed with the proverbial Scot canniness, for Papa had supported the children of the liaison.

Papa himself brought the barely six-month-old Charlotte to Mrs. Clendenning. Charlotte's mother, Miss Goodman, had little love for the child, Mrs. Clendenning wrote disapprovingly, and only visited her in the country when she came to pay the quarterly stipend. Mrs. Clendenning suspected that Miss Goodman paid her a smaller sum than she actually received from Papa, for she knew for a fact that the woman had lived exceedingly well. It was the Goodman woman, however, who brought Georgie to her, newborn. Mrs. Clendenning did not approve of that, either.

Mam described herself as an honest but poor woman with a good and hardworking husband, who provided her with as numerous a progeny as Papa had supplied Mama. She had not found it difficult to care for Charlotte and Georgie while the money came, but an addition to her own progeny about the time the payments stopped, and now still another bairn on the way, made it impossible to keep them any longer. The loss of funds for the support of the children, together with her large and increasing family, made it imperative that she find another home for them. Miss Goodman had run off with an Irishman, so it was said, and nobody knew where she went or where she was. Then, finally, the money stopped coming. So it was either an orphanage or us for Charlotte and Georgie.

I put the letter down on the table and absent-mindedly handed Georgie another cake. My brain was full of question marks.

"I say, Lia, Lord Dayne's brought us this smashing big fish. . . ." Ben halted in the doorway, and Lord Dayne, who was following behind with the smashing big fish, bumped into him. No one could have been less welcome at such a moment—unless, perhaps, a royal duke! "What are you doing?" Ben asked, frowning questioningly at the children as he approached.

Charlotte shrank in her chair. Ben doesn't mean to look ferocious but he does sometimes, especially when he frowns.

I hoped that my face betrayed nothing of the shock I had just received, although I managed to reply with at least some semblance of normality. "Don't pay any attention to his frown, Charlotte. It's just my brother Ben, and the gentleman with the fish is Lord Dayne. Gentlemen, may I present Charlotte and Georgie."

Mrs. Oliphant, bustling back into the room with some towels, dropped them on the table and hastened to relieve Lord Dayne of the fish.

"Oh, what a grand specimen!" she exclaimed. "I know just how to dress it. We thank you, my lord."

"I know how fond Lady Maudsley is of fish the way you prepare it, Mrs. Oliphant."

I looked up at Lord Dayne, who was regarding the scene somewhat inquisitively and certainly with amusement. "We do thank you, my lord," I said. "You must share it with us tonight, and Mr. Chaffinch also. Is he with you?"

"Yes, he's in the garden with your mother and sister."

"Please do join them. Ben, take his lordship to the garden, and I'll be along soon."

"Siempre a sus órdenes, Señorita," Dayne replied with a bow. That meant, as I had learned, that he was always at my command. I sniffed, as I always do, when he uses that phrase, for I am not so foolish that I don't know how ironically he uses it. In return, he managed to surreptitiously twitch one of my braids, which of course were down my back again, exactly like Charlotte's.

As they were leaving, I said, "Oh, Ben, after you've shown Lord Dayne out to the garden, could you come back for a minute?"

I picked the letter up from the table, folded it thoughtfully, and put it in my pocket. When I looked up again, Charlotte was staring at the door fearfully, as though afraid Ben might return to eat her. "Charlotte," I said, "Ben does not eat children, nor does the other gentleman. Now take a cake and drink your milk while I decide what's to be done."

Charlotte at last helped herself to a cake, apologetically and with a shy "Thank you," but was soon eating with as much restraint as hunger allowed. Her manners were rather pretty; she seemed a well-brought-up child. Georgie was now asleep in my lap, his little fist clutching half a squashed molasses cake. Crammed full of cakes and awash in milk as he was, he would most certainly soon relieve himself of his liquid burden if not hastened to the patented water closet that Papa had installed—although not paid for—shortly before he died.

Mrs. Oliphant returned from putting the fish away, so I sent her off with the still-sleeping Georgie to the water closet. I took the letter from my pocket and started to read it again, I suppose in the hope that it hadn't said what it had said. I was on the third reading when Mrs. Oliphant returned with Georgie, bare-bottomed and crying dolefully. He held out his arms to Charlotte. "Lottie, wan' Lottie," he wailed loudly.

"The poor dear," Mrs. Oliphant said. "He's tired to death, and so chafed and burned from those nasty nappies!" She looked severely at Charlotte. "When was he last changed, child?"

Charlotte's lower lip trembled and she gulped noisily as she tried to swallow a mouthful of cake and repress tears at the same time. But she held out her arms for Georgie, who wrapped his own tightly around her neck and reduced his wails to mere whimpering. She shushed him softly, then looked up at Mrs. Oliphant. "I—I didn't have any more clean ones, ma'am, Georgie was so nervous in that dreadful wagon, and the driver had such a dreadful face. . . ."

"You came by wagon?" Mrs. Oliphant interrupted, looking thoroughly shocked.

Charlotte answered the question respectfully. "Mr. Mac didn't have enough money for the coach past Lewes, ma'am, and he told us we could walk from there 'cause it's only a few miles, he said. . . ."

"A few miles!" Mrs. Oliphant exclaimed, outraged. "Eight if it's a foot!"

Georgie had quieted, so Charlotte unhooked his arms and sat him down on her lap. Encouraged by Mrs. Oliphant's obvious sympathy, she said, "But I had a bit of money, so I found a carter and he took us up. But there was another man coming to Brighton, too, and he had a terrible red scar all down his cheek and over his eye, and when he saw that Georgie looked scared, he made a terrible face. . . ."

Mrs. Oliphant and I immediately began exclaiming in indignation, which braced Charlotte up so much that she actually smiled.

Then Ben came back at last. I didn't want to reveal all to him in front of Mrs. Oliphant, and furthermore, the housemaid, Jane, had just entered and was staring tenderly at the children. Jane is overflowing with kindness and good will, which undoubtedly is a compensation the gods have granted her for her lack of intellect. So I said to Ben, "These children seem to be distant relatives of ours. . . ."

"No, miss," contradicted that wise little body, Charlotte. "You're our half sister and brother. Mam explained."

Mrs. Oliphant gasped, Jane screamed, and Ben frowned again at Charlotte, whose courage immediately failed. She clutched Georgie closer and shrank back again in the chair.

I said calmly, "For the moment, Charlotte, we will say that

you and Georgie are our cousins. It's very much the same as half brothers and sisters. Is that clear?"

Charlotte nodded, still either under the spell of Ben's frown or responding to my firm instructions.

"Do *you* understand, Jane?"

Jane nodded. She smiled at the children.

"Very well, Jane. Now please take our little cousins upstairs, get them bathed, and dressed in some clean clothes. If you have to buy something, buy it. But nothing expensive, and nothing that isn't necessary. Consult with Mrs. Oliphant and she'll give you whatever sum you need. And if you can find Angela . . ."

"She's out under the tamarisks reading her book," Jane said. "It's a true wonder."

Who knew whether Jane meant that the wonder was reading a book or sitting under a bush? In any event, I decided that I must find Angela myself and explain—as best as one can to a child of nine—before sending her off to help Jane with Georgie and to make Charlotte welcome. Other introductions, to Mama and Sunny and Chunk and Irene, could wait until the two little newcomers were cleaned up and Georgie deodorized.

It was not necessary to impress the need for mendacity upon Mrs. Oliphant, who was more jealous of our position in society than any of us, and so I could turn to other matters. "I suppose we should dine at six," I told her, "since I was so foolish as to invite Lord Dayne and Mr. Chaffinch to join us. Sunny and I will help you in the kitchen."

"Well, perhaps Miss Sunny . . ." Mrs. Oliphant said tactlessly. In the short time we had been in Brighton, she had come to admire Sunny's talents in the kitchen but did not think much of mine.

Which reminded me of something else. "And what do you mean, Ben," I said severely, "by bringing Lord Dayne right into the kitchen? It just—"

"Oh, come off it, Lia. He hates primosity. And so do you, and you know it. After all, if he insisted on carrying that fish out here himself . . . . And, anyway, just what's those little beggars' lay? I told Mama that two little beggar children were in the kitchen, and that you were stuffing them with cakes and trying to find out where they belonged. Mama was only kept from coming to your assistance by the fact that she had callers. She *dotes* on beggar children, she told Dayne. Now what in blazes is this business about half brothers and sisters?"

I handed Ben the letter, not bothering to reprimand him for using lingo. As he read it, the blood drained from his face. He looked up at me when he finished, with an expression that one might have expected if someone had struck him a blow on the top of his head. "Papa—Papa was—"

For all I know, I had had the same stunned expression myself after I had read the letter.

He gave me a rueful smile. "Fetched me up against the ropes, for a minute there." He looked down at the letter, which he still held in his hand, and then looked up again at me. "Do you believe it?" he asked.

"Well, Papa was always going to Edinburgh, remember? He had that friend—another one of his cronies . . . the one he played golf with. You know, at St. Andrews . . ."

The color was already returning to Ben's face. "This woman, Mrs. Clendenning, mentions blunt—"

We stared at each other. We were both remembering those substantial sums of cash that Papa had never explained to his excellent man of affairs, Mr. Price.

Ben said, with something close to awe in his voice, "Do you suppose we have French and Russian and American half brothers and sisters, too?" Those were Papa's posts during his diplomatic years.

I have said that Papa was extravagant with his love, but I simply couldn't believe that he had been *that* extravagant. And I didn't like the look on my young brother's face. Despite his fascination with pugilism and occasional use of cant, he had not, as far as I knew, dipped into dissipation. "If you're thinking, Ben, that there's one thing admirable or—or *smart* about a lot of bastard children . . ."

"Not for a minute. Especially when they arrive on my doorstep expecting to be taken care of." Observing my low opinion of his levity, he added, "Anyway, what do you take me for? Some sort of chucklehead?"

"Oh, Ben," I said, a fateful tear stealing down my cheek. "What are we to do?"

I know I have seemed very much in command up to now, but the truth is that I was not always able to maintain my equanimity or sustain my courage. It was only with Ben that I allowed myself to give way. Young as he was when Papa died and still was at the time of which I am writing, he was my only confidant about money matters and all the other worrisome things that burden a large family with meager funds. I don't know what I should have done if he had fallen into foul ways. There had been times after Papa died when the workhouse seemed our only possible future, and we had clung to each other in despair, so that the bonds that bound us were very strong. Somehow, together—and with Papa's man of affairs, Mr. Price, who must be given his due—we had managed. We had emerged not quite all to pieces, and we could live respectably enough to hold high our poor but proud heads. Even with the expenses of the move to Brighton, we could—with rigid economy—pay our bills. Now here we were with two more mouths to feed, and where the money would come from I just didn't know.

Ben helped himself to a molasses cake. Mrs. Oliphant had gone off after Jane and the children, to see that the housemaid got everything started right, and had not yet cleared away the children's repast. "Now that I think about it, it's a pretty rum story," he said judiciously, around his mouthful of molasses cake. "Can you really think that Papa—?"

"Oh, I don't know *what* to think!"

"Well, you'd better get out to the garden and at least say hello to Chaffinch, or they'll think there's some jiggery-pokery going on."

"But what will we tell Mama?"

Ben took the last molasses cake, frowned, looked thoughtful, and stuffed it in his mouth.

I flared up. "For God's sake, Ben! We have an *emergency,* and you sit there eating cakes as greedily as those two starved children!"

Ben swallowed and wiped the crumbs off his lips with his hand. "We'll have to tell her, unless we dismember them and pack them into a trunk and send them to Boney." Ben was recalling a famous crime that had occurred the winter before. "And even if we pretended they had nothing to do with Papa, do you think Jane or Mrs. Oliphant could keep their tongues between their teeth?" He went to the large stone container that purifies our water and keeps it cool, drew himself a glassful, and drank it.

The failure of the news to affect his appetite for sweets or the workings of his stomach irritated me, which was, of course, irrational. Just because I felt as though I would never be able to swallow anything again, solid or liquid, was no sign that Ben's emotions had to work on him in exactly the same way. And he was right. There was no alternative but to tell Mama.

Ben put down the glass and again wiped his mouth. "Make it quick and neat. Like the way you used to take slivers out of our fingers."

"But the shock . . . I mean, Papa . . ."

"Maybe Mama was wise to it. Or maybe they aren't Papa's brats at all, and she can clear up the mystery."

"And maybe she *doesn't* know, and the only mystery is how Papa managed not to let her guess!"

"Pluck up, Lia. Clean and neat's the only way."

"I have to find Angela first. . . ."

"You've got to do it, Sis. I'll help, but . . . well, you're—you're like the head of the family. . . ."

Chapter Four

When Ben and I entered the garden, Mama was languidly flirting her fan, cool and charming and the center of attention. Sunny looked bored but also slightly amused. Her romantic fancies did not lean toward gentlemen who had crossed the border between youth and age, which in her reckoning was somewhere in the neighborhood of twenty. When trapped by gentlemen callers such as Mr. Chaffinch and Lord Dayne, she looked on with a certain sardonic amusement. I thought perhaps Mama had started on one of her favorite subjects, such as astrology or animal magnetism or the possibilities of Communication with the Beyond, all of which Sunny regarded indulgently as long as Mama refrained from relating her personal experiences. Mama's subject, however, proved to be no more unfortunate than an account of an "endearing" incident from Ben's and my childhood, which naturally put us both to the blush. Her listeners were attentive and responsive, but Sunny sent us a wicked glance that she somehow managed to combine with a what-will-we-do-with-Mama look.

After Mama's story was concluded, her two attentive gallants arose to take their leave, but not, of course, without Lord Dayne remarking, "What a naughty child you were, Miss Maudsley! I would never have guessed!"

To which I sniffed and said, "All children are naughty, except stupid girls in romantic novels and Maria Edgeworth's instructive tales." Sunny and I never could stand Miss Burney's moronic Evelina, or Miss Edgeworth's revoltingly good

Simple Susan. Angela, on the other hand, being an angel herself, loves them both.

Lord Dayne smiled. "Your view of human nature, Miss Maudsley, would put a misanthrope to shame."

They each saluted Mama's hand, bowed to Sunny and me, shook hands with Ben, assured us how eagerly they looked forward to our dinner together, and were on their way.

And so the moment had come. Ben looked at me and I looked at him. Finally, Ben said, "Lia has something to tell you, Mama."

I cast him a desperate look, but of course he was right. As the eldest and the head of the family, such unpleasant duties had to be mine. "And you too, Sunny," I said. "So just sit down again."

Sunny looked at me curiously and even with anticipation, but Mama just picked up her sewing and said somewhat vaguely, "Yes, dears?"

"Well . . . uh . . ." I swallowed, cleared my throat, and began again. "Well, there are two children in the kitchen . . . that is, they were in the kitchen, but Jane is bathing them. . . ."

Mama looked up briefly from her sewing. "Oh, yes, the little beggar children." Her eyebrows were ever so slightly raised. It's Mama's method of frowning. As I have already remarked, Mama does not approve of real frowning. "Of course, you should have given them food, but do you think, dear, that it was *quite* necessary to bathe them?"

"The thing is, Mama, that they seem to be relatives of ours," Ben put in.

Both Sunny and Mama exclaimed, at the same time, "Relatives!"

Sunny's voice was eager with curiosity, but Mama was clearly puzzled. "I can't imagine who they might be. Of course, wayward relatives do have a habit of turning up from time to time, usually inconveniently, but—but children—unescorted by an adult?" She snipped off a thread without looking up. "And why did you refer to them as beggar children, Ben?"

"He didn't know what else to say, Mama, for there were

guests with you, and . . . well, the fact of the matter is that they say . . . the children say . . . or rather the little girl says . . . The girl is about ten, and the little boy is three . . ."

"Lia!" Ben said sternly.

I took a deep breath. "Well, the fact is . . . Mama, please prepare yourself. . . ."

She looked up then. "Yes, dear, please come to the point."

"Well, the fact is that they say they are our half sister and brother. It's probably some sort of trick. . . ."

"They have a letter from a woman in Scotland, a Mrs. Clendenning," Ben interrupted me. "Lia, give Mama the letter."

So I dug into my pocket and handed her the letter. Still with a slightly puzzled expression but without the least sign of distress, Mama took it and began to read.

Sunny was definitely frowning, primarily, it seemed, with the problem of working out how she happened to have an unknown brother and sister, for I saw the moment that the answer struck her. Her frown gave way to wide-eyed surprise, her hand flew to her cheek, and her mouth dropped open as she drew breath to voice her shock. I also saw that on the instant she thought better of it, as both hands covered her mouth, and her eyes, frightened and concerned, turned to Mama, then back to Ben and me.

"Sunny," I said, "perhaps you could bring Mama a small glass of brandy."

"No, dear." Mama looked up from the letter. "Just a glass of water, please." She returned to the letter, and when she finished it, she folded it carefully and then sat staring down at it. She had paled slightly, but her attitude was thoughtful. Sunny handed her the glass of water, which she took with a murmured, "Thank you, Sunny." She set it aside without touching it, still with that thoughtful, almost vague expression. At last she looked up. Her voice was calm. "Will you leave me for a few moments, my dears? I would like a few minutes alone. Then, when the children are clean and neat, bring them to me, please."

Mrs. Oliphant was waiting impatiently in the kitchen. Worthy as she is, and much as it must have tried her sense of the fitness of things, she had obviously been eavesdropping. "You have told her?" she asked anxiously.

"Yes."

"How has the poor dear taken it?"

I sat down in a chair, weak from the ordeal. "Of course, it's been a shock to her. But she's taking it very calmly."

"What did the letter say?" Sunny asked.

"A regular trooper!" Ben exclaimed, his face glowing with admiration. "Mama's got bottom, one has to say that for her! I was afraid she'd go into a fit of hysterics, or faint, or start to weep and denounce Papa, or go into a flaming rage and want to throw the children out. . . ."

"Lia, what did the letter say?" Sunny asked again.

Mrs. Oliphant, with a proud, approving nod, said, "Your mother's a lady, Mr. Ben." (Mrs. Oliphant has never conferred the baronet's title on Ben.) "A great lady. She's not one to give way under difficulty."

Sunny suddenly stamped her foot. "Well, *I'll* have hysterics and *I'll* go into a flaming rage if you don't tell me right *now* what you're all talking about! *What did the letter say?*"

So then we described to Sunny, and Mrs. Oliphant, too, the contents of the letter, and they repeated almost the same observations Ben and I had made: It must be a trick; it sounded suspicious. But, then, how did this Mrs. Clendenning get Mama's name and address? And there were those unexplained sums of money, and so on. We were still speculating when Jane and Angela returned with the children.

They looked neat and respectable. Jane was carrying Georgie, who smelled of soap and powder, his yellow curls shining like gold. Jane's tender if dim-witted goodwill had already won his baby heart, for he rested confidently in her arms and bestowed friendly smiles on us all. Angela and Charlotte were hand in hand, and I noticed for the first time how pretty Charlotte's eyes were, now that the fright and apprehension had lessened—thanks, undoubtedly, to Angela's sweet manner. She was wearing one of Angela's dresses, which was too big for her, for my nine year old sister is tall for her age. Charlotte's dark braids were neat and smooth, her face shiny with scrubbing. I realized that she was actually a very pretty little girl, freckles and all. She was not yet completely at ease, but she managed a timid smile at me, and to say "How do you do?" in a tiny voice when introduced to Sunny.

I took Georgie from Jane and sent her off to take care of Irene, whom we could hear jouncing around in her baby crib and loudly demanding attention.

"Now, my dears, you must meet—" I paused. Should I say "Lady Maudsley," or "our mama," or just "Màma"? I chose the latter.

Angela still tightly clasped Charlotte's hand in her own. "You'll love Mama, really you will," she whispered. "We all do."

Mama was at work on a piece of needlepoint when we returned to the terrace. She looked up, smiled, put it aside, and then held out her hand to Charlotte, "Come here, my dear."

Charlotte bobbed a wobbly curtsy and said rapidly, "How do you do, ma'am? I'm happy to make your acquaintance, ma' am."

I doubted that Mama understood the words, Charlotte's accent was so pronounced and her voice so low, but she ran her hand over the girl's hair and smiled her charming smile. "You have my dear Whitney's hair, my child. Soft and fine like Lia's. And although no one among my children has your freckles, I believe a distant cousin of your Papa was equally . . . had quite as many as you do. And what pretty eyes! Very reminiscent of that same cousin. Tomorrow I will make a lotion of lemon juice and spirit of wine to start bleaching the freckles away, and we'll buy a pretty little bonnet and parasol to keep the sun from your face."

Charlotte gulped and said, "Thank you, ma'am, but I—I—" She looked ready to cry. Sunny stepped forward to put her arm around the girl and Angela took her hand again.

"I know just the place to buy the *prettiest* parasol," Sunny said. "You'll adore it. We'll go tomorrow."

"And you can borrow one of my bonnets, until you have one of your own," Angela added.

Màma had not quite finished with Charlotte. "Also, my dear, since I am your stepmother, you may call me Mama, just as my own children do. And so you must instruct your little brother."

Mama now turned to Georgie. She did not offer to take him on her lap, but she did reach up to take his hand. "And you, my little man, are the very image of your dear Papa. Except for those golden curls."

And just then who should come clomping in but Chunk, back from some private expedition on the Downs or along the shore, demanding to know in a loud voice where everyone was, and then, in an even louder voice, who had eaten all the molasses cakes. The apprehensive fear immediately seized Charlotte again, but when Chunk appeared in the doorway, her face cleared. I could almost read her mind: just another big, loud, dirty boy. Although we hadn't learned the ages or extent of Mrs. Clendenning's numerous progeny up there in Scotland, it seemed likely that Charlotte would be familiar with that breed of humans called boys, as Papa used to say.

Chunk had stopped abruptly in the doorway to the terrace, staring first at Georgie and then, more closely, at Charlotte. Sandwiched by his birth between Sunny, who teased him, and Angela, who refused to be teased, Chunk was for his part familiar with the breed of humans called girls, and at the moment thought no more of them than he did of bugs. In fact, rather less, for Chunk has a bent for natural history.

I didn't think it was the moment to introduce the concept of half brothers and sisters and mistresses and all that, which I could better do later in private, so I said, "Chunk, this is Georgie and Charlotte, your cousins. Will you say hello to them, please?"

Chunk stepped forward reluctantly and, in one motion, seized and dropped Charlotte's reluctantly extended hand. "H'lo," he said, and Charlotte responded with a very superior, "How do you do?"

Mama intervened. "Chunk, come here. And please remember your manners."

So Chunk dutifully placed a kiss on Mama's cheek and was excused *just this once* for not having tidied himself before entering her presence. She then proceeded to explain to her twelve-year-old son that his father had two other children who were by rights his brother and sister.

"Mama, I do think . . ."

"There will never be a convenient time to reveal their relationship to us, Lia, and so we might as well begin now by acknowledging them for what they are."

Ben, trying not to speak too plainly in front of Charlotte, said in the most English of English accents, with the addition of some dandyish smirk and drawl, "Many things may be revealed in the course of time, Mama, that we are yet unaware of."

Mama ignored him. "Georgie and Charlotte are your brother and sister, Chunk, and I expect you to treat them as such."

Chunk began right then to obey Mama's command. "Another *sister?*" he asked, his nose wrinkled in distaste.

Charlotte, her own nose in the air, sniffed. Whether she had already learned to imitate me, or whether it was in our blood, handed down from some remote ancestor, I did not care to speculate.

Well, it was all very brave of Mama, but it made me uneasy that she hadn't fainted, or fallen into hysterics, or wept, or stormed and raged and denied the whole thing as a monstrous fraud. That's what I would have done. Not fainting or hysterics, of course, for I am very unfashionably not given to such demonstrations, but certainly rage. In fact, if I could truly bring myself to believe that Charlotte and Georgie were really Papa's, I should have been in a great rage at that very moment. And if I had learned that my husband—especially if I was as devoted to him as Mama had been to Papa—had had a mistress and fathered two children, I would have kicked up a frightful dust, no matter how unladylike. And if I were Mama, I'd tell him so, too. No reason Adam and Star shouldn't carry the message to Papa in the Beyond. After all, everybody else in the family knew about Papa's light o' love, why not Adam and Star as well? And I certainly hoped Mama would give him a piece of her mind, and I intended to tell her so.

But the confrontation with Mama had to wait. I'd foolishly

issued an invitation for dinner to Lord Dayne and Mr. Chaffinch, and we had a bare six hours to prepare for it. I suggested that we send a message saying that one of us had fallen desperately ill, but Mama wouldn't hear of it. Activity would be good for us, she said, and picked up her needlepoint.

As always, Mama insisted that Angela and Chunk present themselves in the parlor to greet our guests, before retiring to the kitchen where Mrs. Oliphant would give them their dinner. She also insisted that Charlotte and Georgie be presented to the gentlemen as our newly discovered half sister and brother. And that's the way it was. I must say that Mr. Chaffinch and Lord Dayne took it very well.

Angela and Chunk were the first to pay their respects to the gentlemen. Angela curtsied prettily, and when politely questioned by the gentlemen concerning her current interests, she said that she was writing a story about a little girl who was stolen by gypsies, which was the first I'd heard about any such activity. She answered some polite questions about the plot, then settled herself on a chair to quietly wait until she was excused. Chunk, who was incapable of such tranquility, was permitted to discuss briefly his archeological explorations, for which his enthusiasm never diminished, despite the fact that his adventures were almost invariably proved fruitless. He had already shown Mr. Chaffinch and Lord Dayne the giant elephant's tooth that was discovered when our well was being dug, and which he carried with him wherever his residence happened to be. He had currently given up hope of any other such find, but he scratched about on the Downs for Roman coins, which did turn up occasionally, and only lack of means and permission prevented him from digging into one of the ancient Saxon barrows.

Jane then brought Irene to us, and as he always, Dayne took her on his lap. She attempted to tell him something in gibberish and waited for his Spanish reply, which always delighted her, but he replied that henceforth he would only speak to her in English and asked if she understood. She frowned and looked as though she might cry, but he smiled, and—undoubtedly like numerous of her sex before her—she forgave him.

Mama then requested that Jane bring Charlotte and Georgie to her, explaining to our two guests that she wanted them to meet her newly arrived stepchildren, half brother and sister to her own children. Ben was studiously staring at nothing when Mama made this announcement, but both Sunny and I were too curious to risk missing the effect on the gentlemen. In fact, Sunny's face had that look of mischief about it that makes her such a trial sometimes. She didn't like this new discovery about her dear Papa, but she did seem to anticipate the consternation Mama's honesty almost guaranteed. As for the gentlemen, their faces were studies in quickly suppressed incredulity, replaced immediately by expressions of polite surprise suitable to the occasion—if there is such a thing as suitability for such an occasion. Lord Dayne turned his gaze on me with what I could only describe as a look of sympathy, and which I countered with a complacent smile. I was not about to let anyone feel sorry for us by guessing what a shock the discovery of Papa's deviations had been.

As we waited, Mama explained majestically, "The children have been living in Scotland, with a responsible woman who now finds it impossible to care for them longer. They will in the future live with us." Then, coming down from the heights, she added, "If I had known that they were developing such abominable accents . . . Well, I realize, Mr. Chaffinch, that your dear Mama was from Scotland, but she was educated in England, I believe?"

Mr. Chaffinch, looking only slightly bewildered, said that his dear mama had indeed been born in Scotland and that he was quite fond of the country. In fact, he had relatives in Falkirk, not far from Edinburgh. Was that near where Charlotte and Georgie had lived? He thought he recognized in the little girl's accent something reminiscent of that area. (Ben and I both exchanged significant glances, although what they signified other than that his relatives apparently lived close to Papa's sinful territory, we couldn't say when we later came to discuss it.)

Mama waived Mr. Chaffinch's question aside with a casual,

"Oh, yes, I believe it might be somewhere near there. A small village, of course, but since I really have not the slightest idea of Scotland . . . Geography has never been of interest to me, I'm quite ashamed to say."

Mr. Chaffinch then remarked that he intended to take Dayne with him sometime when he visited his relatives, to teach him something about golf, and that it happened he was going soon to Scotland, if she cared to send a message to the woman who had until recently cared for the two children. He was sure that—what was her name . . . had Mama said? . . . ah, Clendenning, was it?—that Mrs. Clendenning would be delighted to have a firsthand description of the children's new home and how they were faring.

Mama thanked him and was murmuring some nonsense about what an excellent woman Mrs. Clendenning was, when Charlotte, her hand in Angela's, and Georgie in Jane's arms entered the room to be presented. The gentlemen politely acknowledged the introductions, and then Mr. Chaffinch took Georgie on his lap and said, "Well, here's an infant that's more my size! Now both of us can have an infant to dandle on our knees, Brev" (which was, by all odds, the most fatuous statement made that evening). Georgie, who although older was not as forward a child as Irene, immediately made a fuss at being separated from Jane, so Mr. Chaffinch laughed and said, "Well, when he gets to know me better, then," returning him to the security of her arms.

Strangely enough, after a few innocent questions about the children, the conversation that evening tended to dwell on smuggling and war. Or perhaps not so strange, for fearing that the dinner might not be quite up to the mark, despite Mrs. Oliphant's wonderfully dressed fish, I served our best wine.

"What an excellent wine, Lady Maudsley!" Lord Dayne remarked after an appreciative sip. "French, or I miss my guess."

Mama smiled. "Lia chooses our wines, so you must congratulate her."

He turned to me. "Well, Miss Maudsley?"

Mr. Chaffinch intervened. "I suspect that the less said the

better, Brev, if indeed this came from across the Channel."

"Not at all," I said. "I buy from a reputable merchant . . . an old friend of Papa's, who advises me." I didn't add that what he advises is almost invariably smuggled, a fact that we are both aware of.

We all knew about the smugglers—in fact, in Brighton we *know* smugglers, although we never for a moment attempt to discover who among the people we know are actually engaged in the Trade. It is not wise to ask questions about any endeavor in which prison and death are the fruits of discovery. "The Gentlemen," as they are sometimes called, have been known to retaliate against suspected informers, so we all take care not to know anything.

"You have no compunction about breaking the law, Miss Maudsley?" Lord Dayne asked as he set down his glass.

"Come, Brev, she hasn't said that this wine is smuggled." Mr. Chaffinch, belying his words, was so audacious as to almost wink at me.

I thought: Just wait until you taste the brandy I'm going to serve you later, Mr. Chaffinch. Aloud, I said, "The smugglers see no reason why a war should interfere with their regular trade with France, any more than it does with other, more legitimate merchants. I've heard that Bonaparte's soldiers' uniforms are made from English cloth, which I'm sure isn't smuggled. And even the prince's intimates buy smuggled goods. I know perfectly well that half the great ladies who attended the prince at the Pavilion last Thursday were wearing French silk. Isn't that true?"

I happened to know that both Dayne and Mr. Chaffinch had been guests at the affair, which had brought the prince briefly to Brighton. Ordinarily, he doesn't come down to stay until July.

"Well," Mr. Chaffinch said, "possible. But I'm not such an expert on ladies' attire."

Ben, who found the idea of spies more exciting than familiar old smugglers, remarked that he had just read a newspaper report that Bonaparte had located guides in England to direct his invading soldiers to strategic points and to interpret for them. "What do you think, Brev? Chaff? Do you think the smugglers could? . . . Some of them must speak French."

"I should think more likely someone under the guise of a smuggler," Lord Dayne said.

It was obvious that they knew nothing about smugglers. "It's unlikely that anyone could fob himself off as one of the Gentlemen," I said. "Not, at least, if he tried to join them, and since smugglers don't acknowledge they are smugglers, it would be an unwise spy who tried to openly pretend he was one. He furthermore would no doubt be directly apprehended by' the riding officers."

"I agree with Miss Maudsley," Mr. Chaffinch said. "More likely such spies would be Irish, or to be found among the French émigrés. presume, Miss Maudsley, that you would agree that a spy could fob himself off as a refugee?"

Mama interrupted at that point. "Oh, I can't believe so, Mr. Chaffinch! When I remember the poor souls who we welcomed here in Brighton, my heart simply aches! In the beginning, you know, they came on the regular packet from Dieppe and they usually had money, but later, during the Terror and after the war began, they came by any means they could find—in stolen rowboats, with fishermen, even with the smugglers, although I think the Gentlemen prefer not to mix in politics. We did all we could for them . . . Sir Whitney and I often took them in. We both had connections in France, you know. I from my boarding school days—some of my dearest friends were French—and Sir Whitney from a continental tour as a young man and, of course, his years in France with our embassy . . ."

"And when was that, ma'am?"

"Oh, long before their revolution! Such charming people, the French, when one forgets they are French! But I just can't believe that any of those poor people were spies. They had lost their homes, everything they had, and many had been in danger of losing their heads as well."

I asked Jane to pour another round of wine before saying, "I should think that our government would keep too close a watch on the refugees for any of them to engage in spying."

"Yes," Chaffinch agreed. "Although I have little to do with that sort o'f thing. But as far as I know, the government does keep a sharp eye out."

"Are we discussing spies, or simply those illusory 'guides' that Ben first mentioned?" Lord Dayne asked. "A master spy, I believe, must either be an Englishman born, or one of those rare people who can assume a number of different roles . . . roles so completely different that even they must, from time to time, wonder who they really are."

Mama raised her eyebrows just a minimal fraction. "An Englishman born? Really, Dayne, your imagination runs away with you!"

Dayne bowed to Mama. "Undoubtedly. But tell us, Lady Maudsley, about the refugees. It must have been an exciting time here in Brighton, and I make no doubt strained the resources of the town to assist them."

Mama then launched into a description of the more colorful of the French who had found refuge with us in those early years of their revolution, now ten years and more past. "Of course, there are fewer émigrés since that man Bonaparte has declared himself First Consul and since he's compromising with the pope. . . . I always did say it was foolish of the revolutionaries to attempt to replace the pope and the bishops with some revolutionary council of riffraff." (Although Mama is rather democratical in real life, her politics are exactly the reverse. Papa, who was radical in his politics, and favored Mr. Fox and Mr. Wilkes, used to laugh at her conservative notions.) "If the French had had the good sense to make the king the head of the church when they threw off the pope, the way Henry VIII did here in England . . . But what must they do but guillotine their king! I've always been an open-minded person, but that was really too exaggerated, and I've never understood how they thought that they could undertake a successful revolution by destroying church and king, which are the very foundations of society. . . ."

Lord Dayne and Mr. Chaffinch were looking ever so slightly surprised, for they had never heard Mama when she gets going with her muddled notions about the French revolution. What she knows of that great event is what she learned from the French émigrés, whose views were naturally not pro-revolutionary. I couldn't help remarking, when Jane returned to the kitchen after passing the dessert, that the Americans had disposed of both a state church and a king, which set us off on another discussion of the possibility of a stable society under such casual circumstances, the advantages of republicanism, and similar subjects, about which we were just as ill informed as Mama was about the French revolution. And so I will spare my readers any further description of that discussion.

I knocked on Mama's door, and when she called to me to come in, I found her already in her nightdress and wrapper, but still working at the same piece of needlepoint. "Yes, Lia? Have you come to scold me?"

"That's exactly why I'm here. How can you be so calm about Papa's unfaithfulness—if, in fact, those children *are* his. I can't see any resemblance between Georgie and Papa, and as far as I know, there's never been yellow hair like that in Papa's family. . . ."

"We don't know what the mother looked like, dear. She may have been blond."

"And had freckles, too? I know perfectly well that the cousin with freckles is in your family, not Papa's."

"Perhaps you're right," Mama said vaguely. "Oh, well, we won't bother to set it straight. Charlotte needs to feel part of the family, too, for in truth, I couldn't see any resemblance to your dear Papa at all in her face. Her hair, however, is like yours—so abundant and so fine."

"Mama, how can you just accept that—"

"What would you have me do, dear?"

"Well, for one thing, I wouldn't so readily believe they're Papa's."

"Lia, you are a grown woman, and it's time you understood that men are susceptible to . . . to . . . adventures. I accept that Charlotte and little Georgie are your Papa's because . . . well, my dear, he was often away from home, even after he left the diplomatic service, and he was often in Edinburgh. I did sometimes wonder what took him there so often—if this game of golf could be so entrancing—but then, gentlemen do love their sports. Quite as much as they do their comforts, I believe. And had I in fact known of a liaison, why should I have deprived my own children of a loving father by making a fuss? Or myself of a loving husband? Your Papa loved me and he loved you children, but as you know, he always wanted to please, and he found it very hard to say no to anyone."

"Are you saying, Mama, that—that keeping a mistress was like buying me a pearl necklace just because I happened to say I wanted it?"

"Yes, I think that's what I am saying. What I don't understand is that he could have conducted an *affaire* with a Scotswoman. The Scots are . . . well, very advanced in their educational institutions, I'm sure, but I have heard that they aren't frightfully clean. And so terribly unimaginative. Although I suppose there are exceptions, as there are among all races and classes. . . ."

"Chunk must be Scots bred," I muttered, but the allusion passed over Mama's head.

Or she chose to ignore it, which is often the case. "Now that's all we'll say about the matter. When Adam and Star visit me again, I will ask some questions, but in the meantime, we will do our best to make the children happy here. Do you understand me?"

So, I thought, perhaps Mama was thinking about getting a message through to Papa in the Beyond after all.

Sunny and Ben poked their heads in then, however, and so we went through it all again. Mama was as firm with them as with me and had thought up a new argument in the meantime. "We have no choice but to keep them, as you could clearly see from Mrs. Clendenning's letter. It will certainly make them feel more at home to believe they belong here. And what harm does it do?"

We all admitted—rather sheepishly, for none of us had had such generous impulses as Mama—that indeed, we couldn't turn the children away, whatever the truth of the matter, and that it really didn't do any harm to claim them as our own sister and brother. If only we weren't so poor!

Sunny, who likes quibbling over fine points, then accused Mama of lying about Georgie and Charlotte, letting Mr.

Chaffinch and Lord Dayne think she had known about them all the time. But Mama said that she couldn't see how it was a lie to say that she hadn't known they were developing those abominable accents, for, in fact, she hadn't. That she hadn't known about the children, either, was irrelevant.

And so they were off on one of their bickering discussions, with Sunny holding forth on the absolute nature of falsehood, and Mama taking the position that little falsehoods to ease social situations were not falsehoods at all, but good breeding.

Dayne

"Well, Chaff, what do you make of this new development? Think they had any notion of the existence of those children?" Dayne asked as they strolled slowly along the Shoreham road in the direction of town and their lodgings in North Street.

"Not at all. I'll wager they were a total surprise. I must say, I'm rather disappointed in Sir Whitney."

"I, frankly, am more in awe of him every day that passes."

"This means a trip to Scotland—sooner than I expected, although we knew one of us would have to go sometime. Now it looks as if his affairs up there were more complicated than we'd suspected."

"Yes."

They walked on without further conversation, each puzzling over the new development and what it implied.

Lord Dayne broke the silence. "If it was only an *affaire,* there'll be little to learn. Sir Whitney was too astute to have confided in a mistress."

"And astute enough to also keep her at a great distance and to use a passion for golf as an excuse. But, on the other hand, more than one of the great have been induced by a woman to commit indiscretions. *Cherchez la femme,* as they say."

They each returned again to their private ruminations, until Chaffinch said, "We've never heard he was a philanderer. Unusual fellow—eccentric, spendthrift. A regular Sir Squanderall, but not a philanderer."

"Nothing surprises me when it comes to sin, so-called, but

aside from that, how would he have found the time? He seems to have been one of the busiest men of his day."

"Well, do we both go, or only one of us?" Chaffinch asked. "Lady Maudsley provided the opening for us with those remarks about my mother's Scots birth. We have the woman's name, the one who cared for the children . . . this Mrs. Clendenning. There'll be people who knew Sir Whitney, I'll wager, in Edinburgh and St. Andrews. We know he did indeed have a passion for golf. . . ."

"And horses and cards . . ."

"Well, if it hadn't been for those weaknesses, we wouldn't have even this opportunity to catch a very big fish." Chaffinch pondered a moment. "I've already told the Maudsleys that I was going to Scotland soon. . . ."

"Very clever of you."

"So I'll be off immediately—I do have some relatives near Edinburgh, you know—and you'll stay here and probe a bit harder. Agreed?"

"Agreed."

"I'll stop by the Foreign Office and the Admiralty, see what they have to say about any operations in Edinburgh, and then go on to poke around up there."

Lord Dayne stopped. "Hold up a minute, Chaff. My leg's giving me the devil tonight. Must be a change in the weather coming."

"Sorry. Your leg has strengthened so much these last weeks that I didn't realize—"

As they resumed their progress, Dayne said thoughtfully, "Why not check in at the Home Office as well; they handle internal security and may have something. Although I don't think we're looking for an Irishman, we shouldn't overlook the possibility. . . . They're always plotting with the French or plotting rebellion . . . not that one can blame them much."

"And always ready to betray each other," Chaffinch added cynically.

"Lamentably . . . Well, the Home Office should be able to tell us more than we want to know about the Irish. Also, we've never managed to get around to the Alien Office. They might have something interesting if our quarry is French."

"Good idea."

A few more minutes passed, each man deep in thought. Lord Dayne broke the silence. "What was the little girl's name?"

"Charlotte. Charlotte and George. I find those rather odd names myself. . . . If we presume the mother was a Scot, why choose names of the English royal family?"

"The little girl brought a letter. If we could get it . . ."

"Breaking and entering?"

"We have the means. . . ."

"You mean Henny?. . ."

"Yes."

Both men once again sank into thought, a silence that lasted until they reached their rooms. Mr. Chaffinch went to the dresser and poured two glasses of brandy. "This almost seems sacrilege," he said as he handed a glass to Lord Dayne. "However . . ."

"Yes, it's common stuff we've got here. Miss Maudsley's wine merchant rates higher with the Gentlemen than we do, I fear."

Mr. Chaffinch settled himself in his chair. "If we call in Henny, we'd have to have the family out of the house. Do you think it's worth it?"

"On thinking it over, no. Let's wait and see what you find in Scotland. I saw the address on the letter—Miss Maudsley had very carelessly left it lying on the table—when I was in the kitchen. I had only the hastiest look, but I think I remember it correctly." Dayne leaned his cane against the mantelpiece and eased himself into a chair.

"Well, how about this for a plan? I'll see about sending Henny down when I pass through London. Have him on hand when we need him."

"Good idea."

That settled, the two friends turned to other subjects.

Chapter Five

For the next week, Sunny and I were busy rearranging the household to accommodate Charlotte and Georgie. They also needed some new clothing, and so I wrote to Mr. Price to ask him to dip into our small capital in order to meet an emergency, and to instruct him to put off any new creditors as best he could. After some discussion with Sunny and Ben, I decided that Mr. Price was so familiar with our affairs that we could ask him what he knew about Papa's trips to Edinburgh, and if he thought it possible that those substantial withdrawals of cash had a connection with payments to a person in Scotland named Mrs. Margaret (Mamie) Clendenning. I also told him as much as we could learn from Charlotte about the children's mother, Miss Goodman, thinking that if Mr. Price had something to go on—an idea—he might see some part of Papa's muddled affairs in a new light.

We did not consult Mama. She had written to Mrs. Clendenning, assuring her of the children's safe arrival and that they would be as well cared for with us as if they were her very own dear little ones. Mama was clearly determined to accept Charlotte and Georgie as Papa's by-blows, and she had not the least curiosity about their mother or the circumstances of Papa's trifling. Perhaps it was easier for her than wondering or speculating, and certainly she had given not the slightest indication of distress once the first shock was past.

It had been so long since my encounter on the beach with Dayne's aunt, Lady Sarah, that I had just about given her up, but one morning we received a note from her that she would make her promised call that very afternoon. Mama is a social creature, for all she claimed to be retired from the world, and a call from an old friend was certain to hearten her.

As we had anticipated, Mama was delighted, and the two ladies sat for over an hour, gossiping about their friends and acquaintances and about the old times in Brighton, when Fanny Burney and Dr. Johnson had illuminated local society, and the only royalty who visited the town were the old dukes, the king's brothers.

Sunny and I were summoned to take tea with Mama and her guest, which reminded Lady Sarah of our encounter on the beach and the risks of sea bathing for babies. Mama answered complacently that Irene was the most vigorous of all her children. ". . . so robust that indeed, Sarah, I am at times concerned that she will grow up without the requisite female frailty. Angela will be much too tall, I fear, but she has a delicacy of form that compensates for her height. . . ." Mention of Angela reminded Mama that she had other daughters, and so Sunny was sent to find them, to pay their respects to our visitor after—it went without saying—suitable cleaning up. "And bring little Georgie, too," Mama instructed. So Lady Sarah was to receive her own introduction to our new charges. Sunny rolled her eyes at me and departed; we were both resigned now to the inevitable.

An interesting analysis, too racy for Sunny's sixteen-year-old ears, ensued on the character of Lady Hamilton, the *inamorata* of Admiral Nelson, and the remarkable complacency of Sir William Hamilton, her husband. Lady Sarah had known Nelson and the Hamiltons in Naples, and both Mama and I—although Mama refused to let it show—were agog to hear firsthand details of this scandalous romance.

Lady Sarah, to our mutual annoyance, took time out to add parenthetically, "Went to live in Naples to recover my health after Rob's death and stayed on. Lured by the sunny climate, you know, and the Italians. Interesting people, particularly the men." She tossed Mama a significant glance, in response to which my mother smiled. The removal to bonnier climes and interesting men had taken place when I was a child, apparently, and explained why I hadn't known Lady Sarah when we met on the beach, for the connection with our family had been ended. "I've never seen the day," she boasted, "including my schooldays, when I could put pen to paper without coming down with a monstrous headache. But I don't forget my friends."

Mama hoped to return the conversation to the more interesting affairs of Lady Hamilton and Lord Nelson, by remarking that she understood that there was a child.

"Yes, young Horatia, although they've some cock-and-bull story about the girl. . . . Nelson claims she was left in his charge by the Eskimos or something equally fantastic."

"My, my," Mama commented.

"Lady Hamilton was *indisposed* all this fall, you know, but the baby died. So Nelson hasn't had to conjure up another orphan to explain away what everyone knows anyway." Lady Sarah's expression was one of profound disapproval and something like disgust. "Lady Hamilton, you know, although one can't help being attracted by her energy and good humor, is not very clean. It does make one wonder about Nelson's taste, and one also wonders how a man who could loll around after a woman as though he were just out of leading strings could command such loyalty and adulation from his men. But there you are. Ever met his wife Tilly? Understand she spends some time in Brighton each year."

"Yes, I've met her, although I can't say I know her. A very well-bred woman, remarkably unselfish. She's been living with Admiral Nelson's father, who is extremely fond of her, but she's withdrawn from that relationship, I understand, in order not to make it difficult for Nelson's family."

"Well, there you are again. A worthy woman cast aside for thrill and tumult."

Further exposition on the recent affairs of the scandalous liaison had just gotten under way when Angela and Charlotte made their appearance, with Georgie and Irene toddling along behind, holding Sunny's hands. It put an end to the most interesting discussion of the afternoon.

Lady Sarah looked amused rather than shocked when our new little half sister and brother were introduced and explained, and after they were excused, she said, "So Sir Whitney left some pledges of his affection in other parts, hmmm? Well, Tilly, ain't the first time, as we've just been sayin'. Although don't seem to fit with what I remember of the man. A charming liar, but no philanderer, I would have said."

"Well, as you say," Mama replied, "it's not the first case on record." And then she added, with an altogether naughty flicker of her lashes and no concern at all for sixteen-year-old ears, "And it quite puts me in society, don't you think?"

"Sure enough, that's the spirit! Can't pretend to blue blood without a bastard or two around."

As soon as we had taken our tea, Lady Sarah prepared to depart.

"Hand me my cane," she ordered Sunny. Then, pointing the stick at us and fixing both Sunny and me with her bold stare, she said, "As for these young ladies, they should be getting about more. I'm giving a ball – nothing extravagant, since the season's not yet begun and society is thin. . . ." That gave her a new thought. "All the ninnies without the starch they were born with, jamming Scarborough or some other godforsaken northern watering place! Who wants 'em? Not I. As though Boney could get past the king's navy! Or if he did, as if full-blooded, meat-eating Englishmen couldn't fight him off! Well, you won't catch me running from any frog-eating Frenchman." Lady Sarah banged her cane on the floor for emphasis. "I'll expect you with these girls and young Benjamin Rousseau. He ain't foppish, is he? I don't take to these new manners. Where is that young gentleman, anyway? Need a strong arm to escort me to my chariot." Without waiting for an answer, she shook her finger at Mama, "And I'm ashamed of you, Tilly. A daughter twenty-four and not married! You always did need someone to look after you. Well, when the prince comes down to stay and the season opens, we'll do something about it. We'll find a plump pocketed fellow who'll suit her very well. Captain Wade called on you yet, Tilly?"

"Oh, yes," Mama said. "He waited on me the first day we were here. We're old friends, you know."

Captain Wade is the master of ceremonies at Brighton – rather old-fashioned and officious for my taste, but undeniably charming.

"Well, we'll get a start with my ball, but you can't stop there. An assembly every week, after the season opens, with a word in Captain Wade's ear about the kind of rich nob we're looking for.

And that reminds me, Tilly. Seems you're acquainted with a young relative of mine. I'll give him a hint on the matter, too. Got my eye on just the gel for him—no promises yet, of course . . . that's to say he's free to play the pretty where he will. If he gives your girl here some attention, it'll set her up. Nothing like a good-looking young fellow who's full of juice and with a name in society to help a gel's popularity."

"Yes," Mama said, "if you're speaking of Lord Dayne . . ."

Lady Sarah settled back in her chair again to discuss at length the sad case of Lord Dayne's brother, Algernon, presumed murdered in St. Giles. "Well," Lady Sarah sighed, "we'll never know why a young man bred up from the cradle to family interest suddenly takes to whoring and brawling. Rattled in his intellectuals, I've always said. Well," she sighed again and, planting one hand firmly on her knee and the other on her cane, prepared to rise. "But as for our plans for your gel, here, she should be seen at the assemblies, the theatre. . . ." She turned to me. "Have you your season tickets yet?"

Even aside from the woman's presumption in assuming the role of a bossy relative, she obviously had no notion as to the extent of our pecuniary embarrassment. "We do appreciate your interest in our family, Lady Sarah, and I therefore feel free to say that Papa left us without the wherewithal to—"

Lady Sarah charged on as though I hadn't spoken. "And this young lady"—she pointed at Sunny—"sixteen ain't too early to tie the knot. I always was a hand at matchmaking. Remember how I brought Georgianna and Nestor Wimpory together, Tilly?"

Mama didn't remember, and so Lady Sarah's departure was delayed for another several minutes, but at last she rose to take her leave. Lady Sarah was evidently among those dowager ladies whose position in society and their own self-esteem are sufficiently exalted to allow them full rein to any vulgarity they happen to fancy. I admit that I found her amusing enough to be able to overlook her meddlesome audacity. Sunny was shocked by her language, due to the excess of propriety stage she's passing through, and Mama pretended to be. Although Mama was herself a pattern-card of delicacy and correct behavior, Sunny and I knew perfectly well that she enjoyed Lady Sarah's old-fashioned gusto. It perhaps explained why their friendship had flourished despite the difference in their ages, and which by all appearances had survived equally well the years of separation.

In the absence of Benjamin Rousseau's strong arm, Lady Sarah chose mine. The minute we were out the door, she began to scold, "And what have you been up to, miss? Where's your sense of family responsibility? You should have a husband by now. How old were you when Sir Whitney died? Nineteen? Twenty?"

"Twenty-one. And I discovered then that rich gentlemen had a tendency to disappear as soon as our financial affairs were known."

Lady Sarah was as hard of hearing as she had been in the house. "Twenty-one! Too old . . . too old by far. I'm against late marriages. Tilly and I were both married in our teens. Well, there was excuse enough, I suppose, for waiting to marry while your Papa was alive. Rich gels can afford to fall in love. But once he was gone and money was needed, your duty was to find a rich husband just as soon as you could. . . . And there's only one way to do that, and that's to put yourself in the way of them."

"Really, Lady Sarah, Papa left us too short of funds to put myself in the way of anyone more prosperous than a country clergyman or squire, or perhaps an attorney of modest means. Certainly no one so prosperous that he could have taken on my family as well as me. Remember, there were six of us, including myself—seven with Mama."

"Ho!" the lady snorted. "If you ain't clever enough to put yourself in the way of a rich gentleman here in Brighton, you don't deserve a husband of any kind!"

She climbed into her chariot, ably assisted by a richly liveried footman with every appearance of being a Neapolitan import, and gave the order to the coachman to drive on without any effort to take polite leave of me.

Mama had a second caller shortly after Lady Sarah, a woman of whom Sunny did not approve and who caused me just a slight unease. It began when Mama asked the fashionable Brighton dressmaker, Mrs. Yewdall, to call to confer about ball gowns for Sunny and me. (She was recommended to Mama, the reader will remember, by her sister-in-law in

Lewes.) Mama had insisted, long before Lady Sarah delivered her lecture on the subject, that I should accept any invitations we might receive to balls in Brighton—any that didn't require reciprocal obligations we were too poor to afford—and that we would also attend some of the assemblies once the season was under way. By the time we had actually decided on a summer in Brighton, Mama had already run up two very nice gowns for me and one for Sunny. However, for the ball gowns, she said she needed expert assistance, which as it turned out had meant procuring some French silks.

Mrs. Yewdall, with a dressmaking shop in Great East Street, had acquired the silks, just as Mama had expected. We thought that would be the end of it but the intercourse continued, taking on something of a social tone. The two ladies, both of whom considered themselves to be almost natives of Brighton, gossiped about local people as well as the fashionable world, and they spent nearly as much time discussing needlework. Sunny had lectured Mama more than once on the subject of drinking tea and gossiping with Mrs. Yewdall, but Mama only smiled and said, "Really, Sunny, you must be more democratical in your attitudes. Mrs. Yewdall is a well-bred woman of good family, and that she has been forced into dressmaking and shopkeeping to earn her living is due to an unhappy series of events, including a gamester father and a ne'er-do-well husband. Had she had the same good sense in choosing her husband that she has in managing her shops, she would not have been reduced to such circumstances."

That there was something reminiscent of Mama's own plight in that story did not escape either Sunny or me. "I admit," I told Sunny later, "that it does cause me to wonder that Mama has become so intimate with a dressmaker, but isn't there a saying that misery loves company, which might apply here?"

"Oh, Mama hasn't the faintest notion that Papa was a ne'er-do-well. All *his* failings are due to his extraordinary character, not to any weakness for cards or horses or—or women," Sunny finished bitterly.

I gave Sunny a hug, but she pushed me away and stormed off to her room. Well, she was only sixteen.

In any event, Mama had been reminded, in recounting

Mrs. Yewdall's problems, that Brighton can be a dangerous place. "You girls must be exceedingly careful of any gentlemen who put themselves forward for your attentions," she remarked placidly as we lingered in the front parlor after our dinner. "One blessing attendant on straightened circumstances, of course, is that we need not fear fortune hunters. There are, however, men of another type. . . ."

Sunny snorted in an unladylike fashion and I felt like it, since the men of another type, along with soldiers in red coats, had been one of my objections to a summer in Brighton. However, I let it pass and, to divert Mama from a useless lecture, asked, "You said that Mrs. Yewdall has shops? I thought she only had the one establishment in Great East Street."

"Yes, she's opened a second shop in St. James Street, where she expects to sell objects of high quality—Wedgwood pottery, potpourri, prettily embroidered or needlepoint articles, japanned boxes. . . . Perhaps seashell decorations . . ."

"And where will she get the seashells?" Sunny asked. Brighton's beach was pebbly, with seashells scarce.

"Oh, I don't believe professionals search the beaches for seashells but rather buy them in job lots, just like they do their other materials."

Ben, who had been lolling in a corner reading a sporting magazine, looked up. "I say, Mama, when did you learn so much about the commercial lay?"

Mama said, "I will thank you, young man, to speak proper English."

We were interrupted at that moment by the announcement that Lord Dayne begged permission to wait on the family. Mr. Chaffinch had been gone two weeks, visiting his relatives near Edinburgh, and Lord Dayne, pining with loneliness no doubt, had come to ask our company for a concert on the Stein, the first one of the year.

Mama, knowing how much Sunny loves music, gave her permission for Sunny and Ben and me, but declined the invitation for herself, saying that she had become "quite the old stay-at-home." Mama likes to imply that our failure to participate in the social whirl may be charged to eccentricity rather than poverty. Lord Dayne, however, was not to be denied. He had ordered a sedan chair for Mama and would be devastated if she did not go. A band from a cavalry regiment would be playing Mozart that evening, and he had heard Mama say that Mozart was her most favorite composer.

Sunny said, "Oh, do come, Mama! Perhaps we'll meet Mrs. *F* dash *t.* I read in the paper that she's here for a few days."

"Mrs. *F* dash *t?*" Lord Dayne asked, intrigued.

"Mrs. Fitzherbert," I explained. "Sunny is being amusing."

"Well, that's what they call her in the papers," Sunny said. "Mrs. *F* dash *t.*"

It has always seemed curious to me that when there is gossip about people in high places, the newspapers use such devices as Mrs. *F— — —t,* or, when referring to a curse, something like *G— —d D— —n—d,* when we all know perfectly well who or what is meant. I stated as much, and Lord Dayne remarked that he also had always found such devices puzzling.

"She's building a house, you know, on the Stein. . . ." Sunny said, not to be distracted from Mrs. Fitzherbert. "Wouldn't you like to see it, Mama? They say that there'll be an underground tunnel to the Pavilion, so the prince may visit her whenever he wants without the world and all knowing about it. And you've always said that you like Mrs. Fitzherbert, and that she's discreet and a gentlewoman, not like the Duke of York's mistress. . . ."

"Sunny!!" Mama and Ben and I all exclaimed together.

Lord Dayne, nobly restraining a smile, intervened hastily. "Do come, Lady Maudsley. There'll be a moon, and the wind has died down. It should be a fine evening."

In the end, Mama was persuaded. And so we set out, Mama in a sedan chair with Lord Dayne walking beside her, while Ben escorted Sunny and me.

The band was just assembling when we reached the Stein. Lord Dayne dismissed the sedan chair and suggested that we take a turn around the grassy enclosure while waiting for the concert to begin. He offered Mama his arm and we set off slowly, for as Papa always said, a turtle with a twenty-five-yard handicap could beat Mama in a fifty-yard race. Lord Dayne was, of course, still handicapped by his game leg and the management of his stick, so Mama's slow pace no doubt exactly suited him. Ben and Sunny and I were still trailing along behind them. I couldn't help thinking that I could never entertain a fancy that Lord Dayne came to the villa to see me, for he seemed to enjoy Mama's company and baby Irene's—even Ben's and Chunk's—quite as much as he did mine. It was a lowering thought and was followed immediately by another one: Even though Brighton was thin of company, it was odd that two such rich and eligible fashionables as Lord Dayne and Mr. Chaffinch should spend so much time with us. I wondered if Lady Sarah had set them to their task of helping Sunny and me catch rich husbands even before her call on Mama.

Sunny was chattering to Ben as I fell to pondering, and I was so deep in thought that it took me a moment to recognize the lady who was speaking to Mama.

"Why, Lady Maudsley! My dear, such an age since we've met! I'm delighted to see you in the world again!"

"Mrs. Fitzherbert! It has been a long time, hasn't it? You're looking remarkably well."

"How good of you to say so. You must call on me. I'm leaving tomorrow, but I'll send you a card immediately on my return."

"How kind you are. But you must know that I have become quite the stay-at-home, as I was just insisting to Lord Dayne. You have met?"

So Lord Dayne took his bow, and then Sunny and Ben and I were presented, with the usual exclamations about how much we'd grown or blossomed since we were last seen. Ben was gallant, but I could feel Sunny's excitement radiating around her like heat from a stove, although to her credit—and to Mama's—she behaved very prettily.

The concert delighted Sunny, who is the musical one in our family. Her grand pianoforte had to be sold after Papa died—or rather, it was reclaimed, to be absolutely truthful, for Papa had never even paid for it. Although Sunny had been invited in Lewes to practice on the little pianoforte in our neighbor's parlor, she had refused, saying—with typical thirteen-year-old stubbornness and with many tears—that until she had an instrument of her own, she would play nothing but her guitar. Papa had given her a French guitar just before he died (fortunately paid for; Papa always managed the smaller expenses), and she taught herself to play it. Ben and I were determined to find a way to buy her another grand pianoforte, but every time we thought we might have sufficient funds, something came up for which the money was needed instead.

As the audience dispersed, Mama asked for Ben's arm. "His arm is certainly no stronger than yours, my lord," she told Dayne with her usual grace. "In fact, perhaps less so, but I am accustomed to it, and if you don't mind terribly . . ."

"But of course, Lady Maudsley. I will always surrender willingly to your wishes."

Lord Dayne now took Ben's place between Sunny and me, apologizing for having only one arm at his disposal, which arm he graciously offered to dispose on me, as the eldest and closest to infirmity. I suggested that he simply walk between us, saving his disposable arm for an emergency, should either of us meet with one. So we set out to promenade again around the Stein, for it is seldom deserted before midnight, especially on moonlit nights.

Sunny thanked him extravagantly for the concert, which had given her such pleasure.

"You are a lover of music, Miss Sunny?"

"Oh, yes!"

"We will come again, then, if your sister will accompany us as chaperone." He glanced down at me with a questioning look.

"I don't think Mama would permit it, my lord. Irene is much too young."

Lord Dayne sighed. "Well, Miss Sunny, I'm afraid no more concerts. You heard what your elder sister has said."

"Oh, she's just funning you," Sunny replied. Sunny has a dreadfully literal mind.

Although the season had not begun and the French invasion threat persisted, there were a number of the fashionable about, many of whom greeted Lord Dayne, while several young sporting bloods greeted Ben. There were soldiers in scarlet coats, young coxcombs smirking at all the girls, including at Sunny, a few of the detestable loungers such as the one I had encountered in Fisher's library, and—although Sunny and I weren't supposed to see them—the "little French milliners," as the prostitutes are sometimes styled.

The prince was not in residence, but the Pavilion windows were brightly lighted.

"They say that the new Chinese decorations are beyond anything fantastic," Sunny said. "That if the grand Khan of China should come to visit, he would think himself at home again. Is it true?"

"I've read that some call it vulgar," I observed.

"I don't think you would find it vulgar, Miss Maudsley, but rather beautiful. Miss Sunny's description is more apt."

"Do you go there often?" Sunny asked.

"Not often. I'm not of that set, but my brother Algernon was, and I've occasionally dined with the prince or been invited to a ball."

"He's very wicked," Sunny said disapprovingly. "Mama and her friends used to tell *such* stories about him, and a duke called 'Old Q,' and the Barrymores and Letty Lade and Lady Jersey . . ."

"Well!" I interrupted. "It's apparent to me that someone was listening at doors!"

Lord Dayne laughed. "The prince is also a man who appreciates good literature and fine art. And I expect that if he hadn't been the heir to a throne, he might have been a different man. You know, being a prince must be rather tiresome."

"I suppose," I said. "So many public duties required of one . . . and one's father always telling one to stand up straight."

He smiled down at me, and my heart gave a tremendous thump. "Yes," he said. "Standing up straight is no doubt the worst of it."

Mama interrupted this nonsense just then by suggesting that it was time we turn our footsteps toward home, but we had just stepped into Pool Lane when we encountered another acquaintance of hers, although hardly as exalted a one as Mrs. Fitzherbert.

"Why, it's the squire!" Sunny exclaimed. And sure enough, coming our way was the squire from Lewes, the same one who had so often kindly permitted us to swim in his pond. He was so kind, in fact, that I always felt ill-tempered for not liking him much.

"Lady Maudsley!" He bowed gracefully over her hand.

There is nothing of the hard-riding, hard-drinking squire about Richard Thurlby, Esq. – nor of a hearty John Bull in top boots, either. Mr. Thurlby likes to describe himself as a plain farmer, and it's true that he's not above lending a hand in the hay field or with the sheep shearing, but his manners are polished – one might say *highly* polished – and his wife – while she was alive to preside at his elegant table – had certainly never fed a farm laborer in her kitchen or undertaken any of the other homey tasks that fall to a plain farmer's wife.

"What great good fortune!" Mr. Thurlby beamed, once all the surprised greetings and introductions were over. "I intended to call on you tomorrow at the earliest acceptable hour, Lady Maudsley. Only staying a day, you know. Had to come down on a military matter having to do with the militia camp later this summer. I may call tomorrow, may I not?"

"But of course," Mama said. "You are such an old friend that our house must always be open to you."

"Must?"

Mama cast him a flirtatious look. "You know perfectly well what I mean, sir."

The squire was lodged at the White Horse Hotel, just off the Stein in Great East Street, and he invited us to join him there for a glass of wine. "And I hope you will also honor me, Dayne," he added. When we were all comfortably seated and the wine ordered, and following some discussion of uncontroversial subjects, Mr. Thurlby introduced the topic that I suspected had brought him to Brighton quite as urgently as any militia business.

My readers will remember that it was in 1803 and 1804 that Bonaparte concentrated troops and flat-bottomed invasion boats at Boulogne and other ports along the French coast, and they will also remember that Lord Dayne had commanded one of the blockading ships before his injury in the West Indies. Although everyone seemed to think Kent was the logical place for a French landing, some thought Essex or Sussex the more likely. The squire had opposed our plan to spend the summer in Brighton for just that reason – for, he said, that although Kent was so much closer to Boulogne, it's always a mistake to underestimate the enemy, especially a cagey fellow like Boney, who might just possibly be planning to land in Sussex or even, more specifically, on Brighton beach. Why an invading force should choose a spot where the soldiers would be required to climb cliffs from thirty to sixty feet high, I couldn't imagine and Mr. Thurlby couldn't explain, except that Boney was cagey and that the French had once successfully attacked and burned the town . . . sometime back in the sixteenth century! It was my opinion that he had designs on Mama and he didn't want his designs complicated by the ten or so miles between his ancestral hall and Xanadu, not any real concern for our safety.

But now he was telling Mama again that he "couldn't help considerable unease" at our residence in Brighton and had been thinking of removing there himself if we insisted on remaining . . . his militia duties "really did require" that he be in Brighton often. . . . And Mama, at appropriate intervals, was murmuring how kind he was. . . . Sunny and Ben and I, meanwhile, were busy exchanging significant glances, while Lord Dayne dispassionately observed us all.

It wasn't even as if the coasts were defenseless. The Army wasn't sitting on its thumbs, as Lord Dayne, no doubt weary of Mama and Mr. Thurlby's repetitive conversation, eventually pointed out. The Light Infantry was stationed at Shornecliff, "the spearhead of the force to repel the invasion," according to the newspapers—that is, ready to fight at a moment's notice. And there were also the Sea Fencibles, the corps of fishermen that the Navy was training to defend King and Country. "And the militia is in prime condition, I believe?" Dayne added, looking questioningly at Mr. Thurlby.

The squire admitted that as a militia officer he flattered himself that such was the case. "However, we must not underestimate Bonaparte—nor must we underestimate internal subversion. . . ."

"Internal subversion?" Dayne asked.

"Yes. I speak of the possibility of traitors. There are those among us, as I'm sure you are aware, Dayne, who have always sympathized with the republican and democratical views preached by the Americans and the French. And the Irish can *never* be trusted, of course. Disaffected Irishmen may be waiting—among other spies—to light signal fires when the French forces storm our beaches."

Everybody remembered that the French had nearly made a landing in Ireland in the winter of 1797, failing only because of the gales that drove the ships off the shore. Many of the Irish were French sympathizers, and it was only a year before, in 1803, that they had attempted to rebel and their leader been hanged. Actually, I didn't believe a word of all the talk about spies and traitors, any more than I thought Bonaparte could actually make a successful landing. But not so Mr. Thurlby, who still wished to impress upon us the foolishness of our removal to Brighton and lure us back to Lewes, where he'd heard of a spacious cottage to let, not far from the aforementioned ancestral hall.

Mama, remembering that Lord Dayne was a naval officer, asked if he had observed the French ship hovering off our shore, a sighting that we had apparently missed, for we only learned of it from the paper. "I thought," said Mama, "that Lord Nelson and the Channel fleet were keeping the French off the seas." In an aside to Mr. Thurlby, she said, "Lord Dayne is a distinguished naval officer, you know." Then turning back to the distinguished naval officer, she asked, "Have we been misled, sir? I, of course, wouldn't care to be in Brighton if there were any danger, no matter what Adam and Star may say."

"Adam and Star?" he asked.

"Two of Mama's advisors," Ben said hastily.

Mama knows perfectly well that we do not like her to talk about her Communications outside the family. "Yes," she agreed, just a hint of amusement in her voice. "Two of my advisors. They are very dear to me, and very close." Mama can be singularly sly when she chooses, and with her description of Adam and Star as "very dear," she was slyly poking fun at us for what she considers her family's unwontedly prim sentiments regarding her relationships with the Beyond and our little brother and sister who Went Before. She may also—and I wouldn't put it past her—have wanted to pique Mr. Thurlby's curiosity, who as far as I knew was unaware that Mama was parent to the two "dear advisors."

"Oh, I don't think you need worry about that particular ship, Lady Maudsley," Dayne reassured her. "The French have numerous privateers at sea. There are still neutral harbors that welcome them . . . America, for one. It was just one of those privateers sighted in the offing and which was reported in the paper. Every now and then a lone frigate's taken or an East India convoy attacked. But there's not much damage Boney can do against our warships—or our merchant shipping, either—without his fleet."

"Yes, I can well understand that, and I do thank you for explaining to me. Women are so foolish about such things, you know. I tell Lia that she had much better leave the war to the men, who I'm sure know very well how to manage it. Does she plague you with her opinions, too, Lord Dayne?" She then turned her sweet gaze on the squire. "Mr. Thurlby knows how decided she is in her opinions, don't you, sir?"

Richard Thurlby, Esq., rightly suspecting that Mama was gently baiting him, muttered something about it being true that he and Miss Maudsley had once or twice had a difference of opinion about the war.

Mama continued airily, "So unladylike of her, some would say, but to tell you the truth, I believe her Papa would have been proud of her." She turned to Lord Dayne. "Mr. Thurlby objected strongly to our coming here for the summer, you must know, but of course I was determined, for Adam and Star had been quite definite that they wanted us to come to Brighton. . . ."

Lord Dayne looked at me inquiringly. "No, Miss Maudsley hasn't plagued me with her opinions on the war. But I'd be happy to hear them. Perhaps if she will ride with me tomorrow . . . and Miss Sunny as well?"

Sunny, who had had no part in the foregoing conversation, almost jumped. "Oh! Oh, thank you very much, sir, but I don't ride. Horses are such great, intimidating creatures, and they like to bite and toss their heads. I'd be nothing but a burden to you both. Perhaps Ben?"

Ben shook his head. "Can't. Don't mean I wouldn't like to, but I promised to meet Dandy Rogers—old friend from Cambridge—for a game of billiards and perhaps some fishing, or—or something."

"Have you all forgotten," I said, "that I have no horse? I'm afraid that for that reason, my lord, if for no other, I must also decline your kind invitation."

"But I hadn't forgotten," Dayne replied. "You will allow me the pleasure, I'm sure, of providing you with a mount, just as though you were my guest at Brightling Hall. And as for a companion, I also have a solution, since neither Miss Sunny nor Ben can accompany us. There's a young man at Elmore's stables who tells me that he knows your family. My Aunt Sarah Pellett charged me with ordering her carriage the day she came to call on you, Lady Maudsley, and when I mentioned her destination, the young fellow was eager to tell me of his knowledge of your family. His father was employed by Sir Whitney, I believe?"

"Why, yes, of course," Mama said, her face lighting up with memories. "It must be one of the Battcock children. We employed Mr. Battcock as coachman and his oldest son as a groom when we kept a carriage, and Sir Whitney often stabled his hunters at Elmore's. Lia and Ben's own horses, too. I never cared for riding and quite agree with Sunny that horses are too large and formidable to be at all friendly. I always preferred a nice little donkey or the barouche, with an experienced driver handling the ribbons. . . ."

"I quite understand, Lady Maudsley, and my aunt would agree with you, I'm sure. However, as Miss Maudsley does ride, and I'm sure a gallop on the downs would give her pleasure, may I suggest that young Edgar Battcock accompany us? He is known to you and has impressed me as a responsible young fellow."

"Why, yes," Mama replied. "I think that an excellent solution. And Lia really should get out more. Fresh air is so good for one, don't you think?"

As if I didn't get a goodly share of my day's ration of fresh air every morning! Sunny and I were now accustoming Georgie and Charlotte to the water, along with Irene, and so both of us, often accompanied by Jane as well, were now at the beach each morning.

"Tomorrow then?" Lord Dayne asked. "Ten-thirty?" And so it was arranged.

Mr. Thurlby, not to be outdone, stated that he had come

down in his landau and thought perhaps Mama and Miss Sunny, along with the younger children, would enjoy a drive in the afternoon, to which Mama replied that she couldn't think of any more delightful way to spend the midday hours.

We prepared to take our leave, but when Lord Dayne suggested that he look for a sedan chair, Mama insisted she was strong enough to walk home. Such a beautiful night, she said, with the moonlight on the water . . . It would be a shame to be transported in a chair, and if the squire would lend her his arm? . . . Which, of course, he was more than willing to do. I found myself by Lord Dayne's side, while Sunny and Ben led our little procession. They were too young and impatient to match their pace to Mama's and were soon far ahead, leaving Lord Dayne and me to chaperon my parent—although even with Lord Dayne's handicap, we, too, found it difficult to match Mama's slow gait.

Mr. Thurlby and Mama fell so far behind that at last it was necessary that we pause. We stood together, admiring the ocean glittering and sparkling, listening to the low crash of waves on the shore. Even the bathing machines, which are really rather ugly, looked charming and picturesque when silvered by moonlight. There is something awesome about such a night, which causes one to wish to speak in low tones, even to refrain from any speech at all, and it wasn't until we resumed our progress that Dayne spoke. "Not at all like the night we met, is it, Miss Maudsley?"

Mozart, the moonlight, something in the tone of his voice, together they all spelled danger, a lure into deeper water, and that could not possibly be good for my peace of mind. I replied lightly, "I wonder if one can call a struggle in the water and a douse in the chops a *meeting.*"

"It has a certain *cachet.*"

"Yes, exactly the way I like to meet gentlemen. Balls and routs are so terribly ordinary, don't you think?"

"I don't believe, Miss Maudsley, that in whatever circumstance we might have met it could have been ordinary."

Chapter Six

As Mrs. Oliphant and I finished our consultation on the day's menus and I rose to go, she stopped me with one of her "ahems," which always preceded the announcement of a problem.

I reseated myself. "Yes, Mrs. Oliphant?"

"It's the little girl, Miss Lia."

"Charlotte?"

"Yes, miss."

"And what has Charlotte done?"

"Well, I don't say it's naughty, but—"

"Yes. What is it? What has she done?"

"Well, she's been putting milk out in a bowl for the brownies, or fairies, or whatever they may be . . . if you can credit it, Miss Lia. Every night she does it. She's right pert about it. First she asks me why *I'm* not putting milk out for the wee ones, and when I ask, 'What wee ones,' she says, 'Why, the house brownies, that's who. They don't do nice things for people who don't give them food,' she says. She'd have me leave crumbs on the floor, too, for her wee creatures. You can be sure, I told her, that the only wee creatures we'd get would be a pack of mice. Trouble enough with *them* without feeding them on purpose."

"I quite agree. I remember too well when the house was overrun with them the year we were renting to those high-nosed Johnsons."

"Yes. And you can't tell me that that woman who cooked for

them kept the kitchen as clean as she should have, or they wouldn't have had mice. I just told the pert little miss that I'll have none of any crumbs on the floor of my kitchen, brownies or no brownies. And I will say for her that she hasn't made any more fuss about that. But every night she sneaks down here and sets out a bowl of milk for them, and when I told her it was nothing but foolishness, she said that our cow wouldn't give milk anymore if we took it away from the brownies."

"Our cow? But didn't you tell her that we don't keep a cow. . . ."

"Well, of course I told her that. She wanted to know where the milk came from, and I told her we buy it from Mrs. Ryder. And would you credit it, Miss Lia? She and Miss Angela went to visit Mrs. Ryder at her cow house, and she comes back telling me that she told that good woman—who has the neatest dairy in Brighton, as you well know—that she should set out a pan of milk for the brownies. And that she'd set one out here and maybe they'd be so good as to look in on her, since we buy her milk!"

I couldn't help laughing. "And what happens to the milk she puts out?"

"Well, that's the trouble. Every morning it's gone."

"So we're feeding the neighborhood cats."

"That's what you and I may think, Miss Lia. That little miss may be your Papa's—although I, for one, will never believe it—but she was brought up in Scotland, and those people up there are known for stubbornness. I've nothing against a Scotsman, except the hardness of their heads, as Mr. Oliphant used to say. And mark my words, it won't be long before we'll have a hundred cats encroaching on us. I saw one of them, hanging around the garden under the tamarisk, and if she hasn't got babies somewhere . . . I flapped my apron good and tossed a stone at her, but I'll give you two to one, as Mr. Ben says, that she'll be back."

"Well, don't worry about it, Mrs. Oliphant. I'll speak to Charlotte. And to Mama also."

"Thank you, Miss Lia. I don't like to be bothering you, with all you have on your mind. . . ."

"No, you were right to speak to me. We've all noticed

Charlotte's . . . mmm . . . determination."

"Call it determination if you like. I call it stubborn. And forgive me for saying this—" Mrs. Oliphant hesitated, "but your Mama . . ."

"Quite all right, Mrs. Oliphant. I understand."

Mama and Charlotte had had an immediate mutual sympathy. In the little over two weeks since Charlotte had come to us, she had learned all about Mama's Communications with Adam and Star. It gratified Mama exceedingly that Charlotte would listen, eyes wide and lips slightly parted, while Mama told her about how these two of her children had died, and how amazed she had been on her first Communication with them, and all the particulars of her intercourse with the Beyond. Charlotte, in turn, poured into Mama's willing ears all her Scottish superstitions. "Really, dear?" Mama would say, opening her own eyes a little wider. "But how *terribly* interesting!"

Charlotte knew fairy tales by the score, some of them rather hair-raising affairs unlike the more gentle ones that Angela loved. The two girls had had their first disagreement over the nature of fairies, and Ben, after listening to one of Charlotte's discourses, had said he was confounded if he knew how people up there in Scotland managed to get through a day. "I'd be afraid to lift a finger," he told Charlotte, "for fear of a leveler from some bogey or other."

"You know what I think?" Angela had asked shyly. "I think that all the bogeys and brownies in England went to Scotland . . . maybe a hundred years ago?"

Chunk, our future scientist, was contemptuous. He looked up from the dead insect he was meticulously drawing for his naturalist's notebook. "Pooh! Charlotte believes any old thing she hears!"

"I do not!" she exclaimed, rounding on him. "I didn't believe *you* when you told me that the Aerie was haunted! I'm not one bit afraid to sleep up there. Am I, Angela?"

"No," Angela said, rather tentatively. "But you have your charm, so you needn't be afraid."

I thought it was time to make some inquiries. The Aerie is what Papa called the top floor of the villa, which had been unused since his death. "Chunk," I said, "have you been telling the girls frightening stories?"

"Hummph!" he sniffed, in another rather good imitation of me. The whole family was doing it. "Just listen to one of *her* stories. Tell 'em about the death bogle, Charlotte, you're so smart!"

"Please stop that bickering," Mama said. "It is so distasteful to others." Mama had, from the very beginning, treated Charlotte—and Georgie, too, on those rare occasions when he was brought into her presence—as one of the family. Her chidings were usually reserved for Chunk and Charlotte, who from the first moment they met had been at daggers drawn. Charlotte might have been intimidated by Ben, even by Mama and Sunny; and she treated me as though I were some sort of governess who demanded the utmost respect. But Chunk was beneath her gaze.

Chunk ignored Mama. "Go ahead, Lottie, tell 'em about the death bogle!"

"Don't call me Lottie!" Charlotte said, her eyes narrowing and her lower lip thrust out belligerently.

"A *thousand* pardons." Chunk's face was a perfect mask of contrition, while his voice dripped sarcasm on the rug.

"Who's this death bogle?" Ben asked. Ben still had a youthful interest in ghost stories.

Angela shivered. "Oh, it's *so* frightening, Ben. A cold, frightful chill wraps itself all about you, and a feeling of the most *dreadful* terror. . . ."

"And Charlotte would die of fright right there," Chunk said.

"I would not!" Charlotte declared. "I should run. As fast as ever I could, for if it touches you, you'll die before the year is over!"

"And what does this apparition look like?" Ben asked. "I presume there's an apparition?"

"It's like a pillar . . . a pillar of cloud, or fog, or mist . . . but it holds together like it was—was—"

"—more substantial than fog or mist?" I asked, rather interested in the bogle myself.

"Yes. And it sort of bounds after you."

"Like hopping around in a gunnysack?" Chunk asked.

"Well, I don't care whether you believe me or not," Charlotte said haughtily. "But if you ever see one, you'd just better run."

Mama, with the barest trace of a smile, had looked up from her needlepoint. "I'm sure, my dears, that any one of us would run as fast as we could should such an encounter ever take place. But, you know, ghosts and bogles and things of that sort are not known to favor Brighton. Perhaps it's the climate. So windy, and so lacking in fog and the sort of things ghosts like. I have always thought Brighton more the sort of place for fairies and for fairy frolicking. Don't you suppose that they, like us, have their favorite spots for merrymaking?"

Mama had then told us a delightful fairy story that her old nurse had often told her and which none of us had ever heard before—a story about a beautiful fairy who was left behind after a Midsummer Eve fairy revel and was found by a prince, who eventually made her forget her fairy companions and become his wife. I had wondered, listening to the story, if Charlotte's tales of brownies and bogles had stirred Mama's memory, or if it was that she had formerly just resigned fairyland to Papa.

I went directly from my conference with Mrs. Oliphant in search of Mama. I found her just finishing her breakfast. A piece of needlepoint that she had been working on the night before lay on a chair beside her. I picked it up and ran my fingers over the beautiful work. "How will we ever be able to use all these lovely things you make, Mama?"

I was immediately sorry I had asked such a question, for poor Mama actually blushed and—unless my imagination was too active—looked guilty. I supposed she felt that it was wrong to spend so much time on her needlework, which she loves doing, when there's so much other work to do in a large household. So I added, "Yesterday Sunny and I hung the curtains that you mended, and they look good as new. You must come up and see how we've arranged the Aerie for Angela and Charlotte."

"Yes, so I must. Perhaps later today."

Preliminaries over, I turned to the subject of my interview with Mrs. Oliphant. "Mama, I must tell you that we have a little difficulty involving Charlotte."

"Yes, dear? Such a well-behaved child, I shouldn't think . . ."

"Nothing serious, except that she insists on setting milk out for the house brownie."

"Really? Well, I can't see any great harm in it, dear. Surely it isn't enough milk that it makes a difference?"

"No. But it bothers Mrs. Oliphant. And it's attracting cats—or some other creatures, for Mrs. Oliphant says the bowl is always empty in the mornings."

"Could those other creatures be the house brownies?" Mama asked, with the air of innocence she sometimes likes to affect.

"Well, perhaps they're sharing with the cats. Mrs. Oliphant has already shooed away one cat. It was lurking in the corner of the garden under the tamarisks. She thinks it has kittens somewhere."

"Does it really do any harm to feed a mother cat, which needs all the nourishment it can get for its babies?"

I gave up on the spot. Mama could surely handle this inconsequential domestic contretemps. "I was going to ask you to speak to Charlotte, but if you don't disapprove of feeding cats and brownies, then I shan't object. Will you soothe Mrs. Oliphant, however?"

"Why, yes, of course, my dear. I shall be happy to discuss it with her. Now hadn't you better run along? Dayne will be here soon, and you haven't changed into your riding habit or done your hair. Perhaps you could ask Sunny to put it in a French braid, which will be much more secure in the wind. . . . And she does it so smartly. But do, please, refrain from going out with your hair in braids down your back. Really, my dear, if you knew what we had to put up with when I was young! Such complex dressing, the styles required! And powder! It was terribly trying."

"Yes, Mama," I said dutifully. "I'll ask Sunny to help me." So then I had to find Sunny, who was in the kitchen learning how to skin and bone a rabbit for a ragout. Ben had shot it that morning on the downs; it seemed his friend Dandy Rogers kept a pack of harriers. It was a welcome addition to our larder, but its preparation was an exercise in housewifery that I preferred not be undertaken in my presence and, if possible, that it be done without my knowledge.

Dayne

Breverton Dayne was seated in Lady Sarah Pellett's breakfast room with a coffee cup in his hand. He had just learned that his elderly relative intended to call on Lady Maudsley that afternoon. "And you, Breverton," she said, "can order my carriage for me again. Elmore's ain't far from your lodgings. Won't take but a minute. Save me the trouble of sending the footman."

"Lady Maudsley, I believe, has an engagement this afternoon."

"Well, tomorrow, then. But how is it you know so much about the Maudsley social engagements?"

"I accompanied the family to the concert on the Stein last night."

"I see," the lady said, favoring him with a penetrating stare. "Well, have another egg, Breverton. Or some of these oysters. You need building up."

"Yes, Aunt," he replied dutifully, helping himself to a plate of oysters.

He and his brothers had always had a fondness for their Aunt Sarah. On her occasional trips to England, she had taken them to circuses and to entertainments at Sadler's Wells and, when they were older, to the theatre. She had sent them exciting birthday presents from Italy, always carefully chosen to suit their advancing years; and she had welcomed them heartily when, with his mother and brothers, he visited the Continent and Italy after his father's death. He'd been twelve that year; Algernon had been sixteen and his younger brother, Walter, only seven. By the time they reached Naples, they had all three been bored with sightseeing and weary with attending their mother. Lady Sarah had had a way with boys, and now, once again exposed to her blunt and hearty spirit, he remembered why. The contrast between Lady Sarah and their bravely suffering mother, with her die-away airs, had been a draught of a clean, bracing sea breeze.

"Now, Breverton," Lady Sarah said, piling two slices of ham on her own plate, "what's this I hear about you arriving foxed at Mrs. Barrington's musical evening?"

Lady Sarah's butler, with considerable hemming and hawing, presented himself at that moment to ask her ladyship's indulgence. But could she step into the kitchen? A bit of trouble with a tradesman . . . the same one who had tried to sell them the tainted meat. . . . Dayne, attacking the oysters, reflected that it was just as well Lady Sarah had already undertaken a renewal of her friendship with Lady Maudsley without need of his suggestion, for she had a more penetrating eye than he'd remembered. And thanks to the progress that he and Chaff had made, neither did he need a character from her.

"Well," she said on her return, "what was I saying?"

"You were about to lecture me. But I assure you, Aunt, that I'm a model of respectability now. You know how it is with reformed sinners. And, anyway, Mrs. Barrington's musical evening was three months ago, when my leg was paining me damnably. It was the anesthesia of drink or of laudanum. . . ."

"Don't make excuses, Breverton. I don't like it."

"No, Aunt."

"Oh, well, I never believed you were as rakehelly as gossip made out. Ain't the type. No young man who gets command of a frigate at twenty-five is a wastrel."

His aunt was wrong; there were many worthless young men of twenty-five, who because of influence with a lord or an admiral, held commands they were unworthy of. But he only replied, "Thank you, Aunt."

"But, Algernon . . ." She looked down at her hands. "What ugly hands I have!" she remarked irrelevantly. Then she sighed. "That poor boy had a crack in his upper story, and no one will ever tell me different. The Dayne character don't run to dissipation." She suddenly laughed. "But don't tell me you're any pillar-post of properness and propriety, either."

"No. I've never cared for primosity."

"Primosity? Ain't fair to make up words."

"How about primly pompous?"

"So you remember our games, do you?" Lady Sarah looked

pleased.

"Yes, I remember them very well. You know, Aunt, you contributed many of the bright spots for us during those bad years when my mother—"

"Well, well . . . It's over now. She should have remarried long ago. Some women can't live without a man to lean on. Always thought she leaned too much on Algernon. But tell me, what's this *primosity,* and what's it mean?"

"A word Camelford made up. Means what it sounds like."

"Now that fellow, I hear, was downright loony. How is it you knew him?"

"I'd say his personality led him to excess in whatever he did, but he wasn't loony. He was a great friend of Algernon's, and I've met him at Chaff's. He was a patron of the Fancy, like Chaff."

"By the way, where is Chaffinch?"

"He had to visit some relatives in Edinburgh. Should be returning soon. And that reminds me that I should be on my way. Shall I order your carriage for tomorrow?"

"Yes, if you would. Tell them three o'clock. And that reminds me of something. Want you to play the pretty with the Maudsley girl. . . ."

"I've told you, Aunt, that we've called there, Chaff and I, a few times. Diverting family, but—" He shrugged, waiting for his aunt to play to his hand.

He couldn't ask for better luck than that she ask him to see more of the Maudsleys. Otherwise, he'd be making excuses to her for the intimacy, now that she'd picked out a bride for him. Lady Catherine deVandt, of all women! His aunt might understand the male sex but she was blind on one count, which was the kind of woman a man would want for a wife. On the other hand, she could probably pick a mistress for him that would suit him to a tee, old sinner that she was herself.

"Family's all out at the elbows," Lady Sarah was saying. "The oldest girl, Aurelia, makes no pretense about it. I remember her as a child. Defiant little thing, but she had a kind of sauciness that won your heart, even when you wanted to turn her over your knee. From what I could guess, she's taken over the family. And Tilly . . . Lady Maudsley . . . well, Tilly never was one to manage things. But, anyway, that's what I want to talk to you about. What Aurelia should be doing is finding herself a rich husband. . . ."

Lord Dayne frowned.

"No, no, not you. You'll marry for family interest, with Walter making his way in politics and your Uncle James already a power in the party. But I mean to tell her, straight out, without any backing and filling, that she isn't doing her brothers and sisters any good by becoming a mother to them, or doing any good for her mother, either. I've already told her she should marry."

"How do I fit into this scheme of yours, then, if I'm not destined to be the rich husband?"

"You'll lend her consequence. I'm giving a small ball on the eighth. If you notice her, you can be certain that it'll give her the start in society she needs. And I'll look out for the rich husband. Between the two of us, we'll get the family back on its feet." Lady Sarah leaned back in her chair with a self-satisfied nod. "I've already got my eye on Mr. John Trimmer. Crammed to the eyeballs with money; a two-year widower; on the lookout for a wife, and no heir but a sickly sixteen-year-old boy."

"But he must be on the shady side of fifty, at least!"

"What's that to say to anything?"

Lord Dayne shifted his tactics. "I don't know Miss Maudsley well, but I suspect that she's too proud for—"

"Fiddlesticks. Pride's a luxury no poor girl can indulge in. Just has to be brought to see her duty. Give me your promise, and I'll let you go."

Lady Sarah had played to his hand, but the wrong card.

He rose and, stooping to kiss her cheek, said, "Very well, Aunt, I promise."

"Help me up, jackanapes, and I'll see you out myself."

As they walked down the hall, Lady Sarah's hand tucked lightly into his arm, her cane in her other hand, she observed, "Your leg's much improved, I see. Can't tell you, my boy, how happy I am for you. You were right to defy the doctors. Regular butchers, the majority of 'em."

"Yes. Swimming is excellent exercise for strengthening the limbs. I'm swimming up to two miles every day now."

"Been to Mohammed's yet?"

"Mohammed's Indian Vapor Baths? Come now, Aunt."

"Don't give me that superior 'Come now, Aunt.' Who's to say that just because he learned his trade in India his treatments ain't effective? One of my oldest friends in Brighton was telling me just last night what benefit he's had from the baths and the rubbing afterward. I intend to try them myself. And it won't hurt you."

"Very true."

Well, he thought, as he descended the steps. He might have known. There was no association between duty and desire in Lady Sarah's concept of the world, and her life was an illustration of that very fact. She had married an elderly gentleman for duty, and when he died, she'd enjoyed her pleasures. She'd been prudent and discreet enough to seek those pleasures in Italy, rather than flaunting society, but she had not been proper. He increased his pace, not wanting to be late for his morning appointment with Miss Maudsley. He observed with satisfaction how much less he now depended on his stick. And then his thoughts turned to Aurelia Maudsley, a defiant little sauceboat who Lady Sarah had marked out for a sacrificial lamb.

Lia

Jane announced the prompt arrival of Lord Dayne with the observation "Lor', but that gentleman is *never* late!"

"Undoubtedly his naval service," I said. "I believe time is kept quite accurately on naval vessels."

Jane gazed at me with the air of bewilderment that so often clouds her features as well as her brain, but only said, "He asks will you join him outside. Or should I show him in?"

"Outside, thank you." Jane will henceforth certainly believe, unless Mrs. Oliphant sets her straight, that time is kept haphazardly on land in comparison to the sea. One must be very precise in speaking to Jane.

Lord Dayne handed his reins to the groom. "I'll toss Miss Maudsley up myself," he told the young man who was grinning cheekily at me. Young Edgar, who I knew very well, greeted me with a tip of his cap.

"Good morning, Edgar. And good morning to you also, my lord."

"Good morning, Miss Maudsley." Lord Dayne stepped back a pace. "That is a most fetching hat."

"Thank you. I like it myself." I wondered if he knew enough of women's fashions to know that it was three years out of style.

When he was certain that I was well seated, he mounted his own horse. "Young Edgar here says you were a neck or nothing rider in your . . . uh . . . more youthful days, Miss Maudsley, and on his advice I've brought you a more spirited horse than I would have chosen had the choosing been mine alone."

My spirited horse had up to that moment shown no signs of any character trait other than docility, but spirited horses sometimes have a tendency to erratic moods. I was also ever so slightly up in the boughs at what I considered a delicate warning that my horse needed a firm hand. "I'll not give him quarter until I know him better, and he me, I assure you."

"Very much in character, I must say," Lord Dayne pronounced, grinning broadly at me.

I am proud to tell that I did not sniff or say "Hummph." Charlotte was rapidly curing me of that habit. Instead, I smiled sweetly back at him and asked where he planned we ride.

"I was thinking that we might follow Chunk's example and explore Hollingbury Hill. I've never taken in that particular sight, which I'm assured is one I should see. Or have you visited it too many times?"

"No, seldom. In fact, I think I've only been there once, and then I was quite young. Ben and I hugely enjoyed rolling over and over down the ramparts, but I don't recall any archeological thrills such as Chunk apparently experiences."

"Excellent. Then it will be as new to you as to me. We can return by way of Preston for our lunch, and then across the Downs to your villa."

The weather was fair, although one of the bracing breezes for which Brighton is famous caught at my skirts and nearly sent my hat sailing. I buckled the strap more tightly under my chin, while Lord Dayne held my horse's reins. Then we rode north through Brighton and out on the Ditchling Road, chatting easily of this and that.

We had walked around Hollingbury Hill, examining the barrows and speculating about the Saxons who had harassed the Roman invaders and eventually conquered this southern shore. After declining Dayne's invitation to roll down the ramparts together, we sat down respectably to enjoy the view over the downs and the sea beyond, while Edgar lay dozing in the grass below and the horses grazed contentedly nearby.

The storm came up with a swiftness that nearly took us unawares. The wind was suddenly colder, and as I shivered with the unexpected chill, I thought of Charlotte's bogle. "If you see a column of fog bounding toward us, run," I told Lord Dayne.

"A column of fog?" he asked.

"Yes, Charlotte says it's a death bogle. Although, come to think of it, even though I feel the chill, I don't feel any overwhelming sense of terror, and that's supposed to be one of the symptoms . . . or warnings . . . or whatever. Do you feel an overwhelming sense of terror creeping over you, my lord?"

"Not at all," he said, smiling into my eyes.

"Hi! Your lordship! Miss Maudsley!" Edgar was calling from below. "Those clouds, they're coming up fast. . . ."

The darkness closed in on us almost between one minute and the next. There are few trees on the Downs. As Dr. Johnson is reported to have said, a man would have a hard time finding a tree on which to hang himself. But Edgar knew the Downs, and he shouted over the wind, "There's an old barn."

My horse, whose name I'd been told was Toad, was showing some of the spirit he was supposedly noted for as he pretended to be afraid of the storm. No horse named Toad was going to get away with any such nonsense. I kept a firm hand on the reins and spoke to him soothingly, as Lord Dayne brought his own horse close to ask if I could manage. I tossed my head and was off beside Edgar. It was a glorious run, but Toad was not as swift as Dayne's mount. I slid out of the saddle and into the lordly arms just as the first drops of rain spattered down.

"Beat you," he said as he released me.
"By a fraction," I countered.
"In there, Miss Maudsley," Edgar shouted to me. "We'll take the horses in the stable door. His lordship and me."
The door he indicated had sagged off all but the bottom hinge, and I had to scramble and squeeze to get in. It was dark in the passage, and smelled of old musty hay and manure, but it was not unpleasant. Edgar and Lord Dayne were speaking quietly to the horses, calming them after their exciting run. The rain was a deluge on the roof. "Miss," Edgar shouted above the drumming, "is there some straw over there? There used to be an old straw pile. . . ."
I looked around and sure enough, there it was, at the end of the passage. I gathered an armful, carried it to the manger, and dumped it in. "I'll bring you another," I said. "Then I'll come and help."
"No, don't need you," Lord Dayne answered as he and Edgar set about rubbing the horses down. "Just bring us more straw."
When they finished, Lord Dayne climbed over the manger and joined me on the straw pile. "You *can* ride, can't you?"
"Yes, I can."
"Did you ever hunt?"
"No. Papa did. But I . . . well, I feel sorry for the fox. And the chase . . . If I were a man, I'd be ashamed of myself! Running a poor dumb creature until its hooves are worn off and it can't run any longer . . ." And I burst into tears.
"Here, here. What's this?" Dayne asked in surprise. "Miss Maudsley . . . I beg of you. Don't cry. Whatever has caused this?"
Whatever had caused this, indeed? I knew what had started it, of course—the memory of that poor stag, stumbling into the sheltering copse, unable to run any longer, and waiting, its sides heaving, for the hounds to tear it . . . It was a black memory of my childhood—Papa, describing that royal stag hunt to Mama. It was as though I had been there myself and had seen the stag. . . . I had begun to scream and cry hysterically—to strike at Papa for participating in the hunt—even declaring that kings and princes and royal dukes should be punished just like poachers are punished. And Papa, once he had succeeded

in calming me, had severely scolded me, no doubt because of his own dismay at having participated in such a sport. But how could I know what had brought that long-forgotten memory back, with such vivid force, and what, of a number of other things, had started it? To be riding again . . . I covered my face with both hands. It was impossible to speak.

He took my hands in both of his and drew them away from my face. I turned my head away from his earnest gaze.

"Forgive me," he murmured as he gathered me into his arms. "I really can't let you cry like that. You must tell me what's wrong."

I shook my head. So he patted me tenderly while I wept on his shoulder, and then as I calmed, he drew away and searched for his handkerchief. I dried my eyes and blew my nose, then stuffed the crumpled linen ball into my own pocket.

"Are you better now? You needn't tell me, if you'd rather not, but sometimes—"

"I hate cruelty to animals," I said. And then I told him about the stag, with an occasional unladylike gulp, and he murmured soothing things and assured me that he had no love of the chase or of hunting of any kind, except for birds. He did enjoy a good morning's shooting, he had to confess. He led me on to reveal more about my childhood, and I found myself telling him about a rebellious little girl who defied her parents' orders and sometimes ran away into fields and woods for a day at a time. A little girl who had tantrums and stormy days, and who was as distant from me as though she'd been someone else.

"I don't know why I was so naughty," I said. "Charlotte says that sometimes fairies steal human babies and leave their own offspring in exchange. Perhaps I was some sort of changeling. . . ."

"Then someday the fairies will come for you."

Just then Edgar called, "Stopped raining, your lordship."

Lord Dayne got to his feet and reached his hand down to help me up. "I believe, Miss Maudsley, that you may have had too many bonbons than were good for you when you were a child."

"Too many sweets?" I asked, staring at him.

He bent over and retrieved my hat. "Too many pleasures,

too many gifts, too much excitement, too much of fairyland."

I set my hat on my head, tilting it so it would shade my reddened eyes. "Perhaps," I said thoughtfully as I buckled the strap. I never thought to wonder how he knew so much about my childhood.

As the clouds dispersed, we rode sedately toward Preston over the wet turf. We dined sedately at the tea room, while Edgar, two coins jingling in his pocket, went off to refresh himself at a less exalted table. Lord Dayne assured me that my eyes were as clear as two deep sea-green pools (my riding habit is green) and that I could remove my hat without concern. I hadn't a thought about the propriety of dining, sans chaperon, with a gentleman.

We knocked on the door of Preston House, where Anne of Cleves once lived, to beg permission to view her portrait, and then as we strolled about the fine gardens, we tried to remember which of Henry the Eighth's six wives she was. All we remembered well about her was that she was one of those who managed to keep her head. And then we rode sedately home, across the Downs to Xanadu, crossing Belle Vue field, where the Sea Fencibles practice repelling invaders with boarding pikes.

He helped me dismount, asked me to convey my regards to my family, saw me to my door, and then rode off with Edgar. That I had been in his arms twice that day might just as well not have happened. In fact, it would have been much better for my peace of mind if it hadn't.

Dayne

After returning from his ride on the downs with Lia Maudsley, Dayne was reluctant to go back to his rooms in North Street. Happening to encounter at Elmore's Stables two officers of the Tenth Hussars with whom he was acquainted, he contrived to waste away some time at a cock fight at the White Lion and in convivial conversation in the taproom, with the result that when he walked into his own parlor, he nearly fell over a valise that had been left directly in his path. "Damnation!" he exclaimed. "Who left this damn thing here for me to fall over?"

Chaffinch appeared in the doorway of his bedroom. "I say, Brev! Are you hurt?"

"No, but I'm considerably annoyed."

"My apologies. I just walked in the door minutes ago. No excuse, of course, for being so thoughtless . . ."

"No harm done. If I weren't half disguised, I'd have seen it." Dayne was not a man to nurse an annoyance. He threw himself into a chair and pulled off his gloves. "A successful trip? You were gone long enough."

"Had to spend longer in London than I'd thought. And I don't know that I'd call the trip successful. Interesting, however. A new facet of 'Papa's' fascinating life. I'm beginning to feel that I know the man. But let me get some of the dirt of the road off, and then I'll tell you about it at leisure. It's a lengthy story."

"I've been riding and need to do the ablutions myself. Then I ran into Roarke Staffen at the stable. 'Hail, fellow, well met'—and with the result that I'm a bit on the go."

Mr. Chaffinch picked up his valise. "I asked your man Tilt to order our supper up at seven-thirty. Have you eaten?"

"Not that I notice. Hungry as a bear, now you mention it."

"Well, do your ablutions and we'll talk after supper. By the way, Henny here yet?"

"Yes. I've got him comfortably settled in a boarding house near the stables."

Two hours later, after consuming—among other dishes—a superb beefsteak and a bowl of prime strawberries with cream, excellently served by Mr. Tilt, the two friends dismissed the manservant and settled themselves down to a bottle of port and a comfortable discussion of Chaffinch's discoveries in Scotland.

"Well," he began, "I found the friend the Maudsleys mentioned as Sir Whitney's fellow golf enthusiast—Mr. Jeremiah Stoutworthy. Both of them are known by any number of people at St. Andrews. I found several other of Sir Whitney's acquaintances in Edinburgh. Stoutworthy I ran to ground on my last day in the north—and very fortunate I was, for he'd only arrived the day before. . . . Would have missed him altogether if I hadn't dutifully visited an old uncle. If you remember, Miss Maudsley mentioned once that Stoutworthy was undertaking the construction of a golf course?"

"Yes. He was also a former diplomatist, if I recall."

"Right. I gave all the names we've learned from the Maudsleys, including Stoutworthy's, to the intelligence people at the Home Office, and also to the Foreign Office. Home Office reported no suspicious political activity by any of them. The Foreign Office was highly offended that we should question Stoutworthy . . . suggesting that one of *theirs* might be less than honorable! And, incidentally, the Home Office had quite a file on Sir Whitney. A flaming radical in his early days, and unusually outspoken. One reason he left diplomacy. Enthusiastic about the revolution in France and always harping on democratic reform in England. The Terror lowered his flame only minimally."

"Do you think that's why he was recruited? That he was sympathetic to the French cause?"

"Perhaps, and his financial affairs made him vulnerable. In any event, considering Stoutworthy's former profession and pure character, I thought I could be more or less candid in revealing my mission. Told him Sir Whitney had had some information on a spy ring that he'd died too soon to reveal, and I was following a scent. . . . And, of course, that my visit and whatever was discussed was confidential . . . a matter of national security."

The wind was rising, setting the windows to rattling. Papers on a small desk in an alcove stirred, and with a particularly strong gust, several blew to the floor. Dayne set his glass on the table beside his chair and rose to collect them. "Distasteful business, this political spying on our own citizens," he said as he put papers away in a drawer out of the way of the drafts.

"Well, there have been a few traitors. . . ."

Dayne opened the window in order to close the shutters. "A few. I'm sure you could amend that to a very few. But to suspect religious dissenters or people who just want some moderate reforms . . ."

"Don't mistake. Sir Whitney was no moderate. Although he

lived like a lord—beg pardon, Brev—he was radical in his politics. A leveler, a dissenter in religion . . ."

"Certainly managed to level his family! A complicated man, beyond doubt." Dayne latched the shutters securely, closed the window, and returned to his seat. "I tell you now, Chaff, no more hole-in-the-corner spy business for me after this is done. Give me straightforward intelligence work, spying out Bonaparte's preparations for invasion or the condition of the Spanish fleet. . . . So, what did you discover?"

"Took some preliminary shifting and feinting with Stoutworthy. Had to convince him that I was a legitimate servant of the government, but once convinced, he was perfectly open. Or so I judged. He didn't know anything about espionage; rather, it seems, he and Sir Whitney were two of a small group who smuggled babies out of France."

"Babies!"

"Real babies. During the Terror, primarily, but a fair number after that while the Vendée was still active. Up until Bonaparte became First Consul in 1800. His amnesty policy ended the need for the service."

Dayne poured himself a second cup of tea. "Well. So that explains Charlotte and Georgie! What a disappointment it will be for Lady Maudsley. I do believe she's been enjoying the novelty of two by-blow stepchildren. But how was it done? And who are they? Why were they placed with a woman of such obviously modest means? Why not with one of the émigrés?"

"It explains Charlotte. Not Georgie. Seems that in France the leader of the baby-smuggling group was an Irishman, who pretended to be there to urge an invasion of Ireland. Or so it was claimed—that he was only pretending, that is. Stoutworthy never knew his identity; it was a capital offense in France to communicate with foreigners during the Terror, so names were carefully guarded. But he did know the method. From France, via the usual cross-channel routes . . ."

"The Correspondence?"

"One presumes, although in the early days of the revolution communication across the Channel wasn't as well developed or as efficient as it is now. And from there, it depended on the child's destination. Mr. Stoutworthy kept the records of the children, the names of their parents or relatives in France. Under lock and key, I might add. You'll recall that relatives of émigrés could be imprisoned. Most of the children returned to their parents after the Peace of Amiens in '01. As for Charlotte, her parents are dead. She was born in prison during the Terror; her father was guillotined in November of 1793. Her mother died four months later. No need for the guillotine. Prison was enough; she died in childbirth."

"It's hard to believe that such barbarity ever came to pass." Dayne shook his head. "Who were they? And what was the charge?"

Chaffinch shrugged. "Not known. Only the family name is recorded—Bonhomme—and the name the mother gave the girl at birth. Lucrèce. It's to be presumed, however, according to Stoutworthy, that there were no relatives to claim the child. Doesn't mean they don't exist, but at the time of her birth there was no one, perhaps because they, too, were in danger of execution. And apparently none here in England among the émigrés. Sir Whitney assumed responsibility for her. He had a 'tendency to generosity,' as Stoutworthy described it. In any event, it was only with my visit that he learned that Sir Whitney hadn't provided for Charlotte in his will or that she wasn't with his family."

"And the money for her support? Good Sir Squanderall paid on time?"

"I'll tell you what little I know about the money later. Just listen to this, first! I found a fellow at the Foreign Office who made up some of the false documents for 'Lord Bagley.' Proud of himself that they got away with it so long. They were very judicious, of course. In any event, he never knew who 'Lord Bagley' was until toward the end of Sir Whitney's career. . . ." Chaffinch held up his hand as Dayne appeared about to interrupt. "Patience. I'm arriving at the point now. Toward the end, Sir Whitney conferred with the backroom fellows about the documents, and just before he died, he happened to mention that he was writing an account of his adventures as a double agent . . . said he thought it might sell well after the war!"

"But surely . . . But it would have been found among his papers when he died!"

"Ah. You underestimate Sir Whitney! He wrote in code! And who's to say it was among his papers? Perhaps it's in a bank box somewhere. There'll have to be a burglary of Price's office—that's Reresby Price, Sir Whitney's man of business. Top-notch man. Sir Whitney always wanted the best. And, incidentally, Price has been snooping around Edinburgh, too. I'm assuming for the moment that Miss Maudsley requested him to do so."

"Planning to write an exposé, was he! By God, I'm sorrier every day that I never knew Sir Whitney," Dayne exclaimed. "And doing it all with the idea of turning it to account sometime! Well, it must not have been among his personal papers, or the family— But, then, they might not have recognized what it was. . . ."

"Exactly. Well, in any event, Price made it devilish hard to learn anything from Mrs. Clendenning. Suspicious about so many people nosing around. I said I'd only stopped to tell her that the children were well, had arrived safely in Brighton, and been welcomed with open arms. Tried to engage her in some further conversation, but uphill work all the way."

"And the little boy . . . Georgie?"

"Nothing on Georgie. Probably the child of a woman named Goodman. No better than she should have been, I gather. Mrs. Clendenning quite obviously disliked her, although she thinks she's the children's mother. Landlady at the Goodmans' former—and quite elegant—lodgings thinks she was Sir Whitney's mistress. And I wonder if she was an associate of Sir Whitney's in a more deadly game."

Before Chaffinch could elaborate, he was interrupted by a pounding at the door. "Ho! Chaff! Brev! Are you there?"

Chaffinch, after a questioning glance at Dayne, went to the door.

A gentleman stood in the narrow hallway, grinning broadly. "So here's where you've been hiding, you sly foxes," he said, vigorously shaking Chaffinch's hand. Dayne rose to greet him and to offer his own hand for a vigorous pumping. "How are you, Brev? Saw Walter in London, and he told me where you were. That young brother of yours is going places. Not going to be an old reprobate like you."

Dayne wasn't certain that he liked being called an "old reprobate," but he returned the newcomer's cheerful grin. "What are you doing in Brighton, anyway? Thought you hated watering places."

"To be sure I do. I'm on my way to Millside. Decided Brighton wasn't too much out of my way. Have to be pushing on early tomorrow. I'm putting up at the Unicorn—practically next door. How about joining me there for a late supper? Frightful wind out. About tipped me over out there on the downs. What do you say? Join me?"

"We've had our supper, but we'll have a brandy while you enjoy yours," Chaffinch said.

They found their hats, Dayne picked up his stick, and donning light cloaks, they repaired to the Unicorn Inn, to the accompaniment of their friend's lighthearted chatter.

Chapter Seven

Our improvised nursery was a long room at the back of the house with three large, round porthole windows, which by rights should have been on the front of the house overlooking the ocean. It was the room that Angela had shared with Irene until Charlotte and Georgie came to us, but was now the province of our two babies and Jane. When I looked in on them, Jane was up to her elbows and our two infants nearly up to their necks in sudsy water. I had concluded, since our early days in Brighton, that Jane was a treasure beyond compare, despite what Ben calls deficiencies in her knowledge box. Both Georgie and Irene had loved her immediately. Of course, as I've said before, Irene will make up to anybody, but Georgie was a shy little thing and still wasn't ready to trust any of his new acquaintances except Jane and me. And I fear he came readily to me only because I had been the supplier of molasses cakes. Nothing much missing in his little knowledge box.

When Irene caught sight of me, she began to splash the water and babble at me in her incomprehensible language. Georgie, not to be outdone, also began to splash enthusiastically and to babble in his still nearly incomprehensible baby-talk Scots. Jane admonished both infants, who immediately began what appeared to be a dispute over a wooden duck, which Georgie was holding firmly in his grasp. Jane handed Irene a rubber ball, telling her that she would rather have the ball than a duck, to which – surprisingly – Irene agreed after only a moment of thought. Jane smiled up at me. "I tell you, Miss Lia, these two are a caution!" She began wiping water from the floor, where it had splashed beyond the rug under the tin bathtub. "Did you want anything, miss?"

"No, just to see how our babies are getting along."

"Oh, they're great friends. . . .

Irene, apparently to prove Jane's assertion, lunged at Georgie with every evidence of desiring to exchange kisses.

"No, no, naughty child," Jane exclaimed, setting Irene firmly back in her own end of the tub. "Mustn't stop watching them for one minute, Miss Lia. The naughty little darlings." Jane smiled benevolently at her charges.

Just then there was a commotion downstairs and we heard Chunk shouting, announcing to the household in general that a squadron of warships was in the roads, and to come and see. I heard Ben's decisive tread and then women's voices—Mama and Mrs. Oliphant making their way more sedately out to the front steps. Jane said to the infants, "Who minds about some old ships? We'll just stay right here in our bath, won't we, chickies?"

I abandoned Jane and the chickies and ran to the head of the stairs, but just as I put my foot on the first step downward, my eye caught the open door to our attic rooms. I recognized Sunny's voice, and the lighter ones were no doubt Angela and Charlotte, who now shared the attic. The two little girls had become close friends in the little time that Charlotte had been with us.

The large, roomy top floor of the house had been Papa's retreat—The Aerie, he'd called it—where "Papa Eagle sat ever alert," watching over the welfare of his brood. We were sometimes allowed to join him there, but never to play there alone. The door was always locked when Papa himself was not at home in his Aerie. Perhaps that's why, after he died, we had left his things just as they were and locked the door on them. The servants' rooms were behind the kitchen, so the attics weren't needed for that purpose. When we rented out the cottage, we continued to keep the attic door locked, telling our tenants that we had household goods stored there. I suppose it was cause for speculation on the part of our tenants, and their youngsters probably made up delicious stories about ghosts. In any event, for three years the attic had remained untouched, until Charlotte and Georgie came to us, and we needed Angela and Irene's room for a nursery. Papa had kept a telescope there, for watching the ships. . . .

Of course! I thought. The telescope.

Papa's telescope was not one of those spyglass things that ship captains use—the kind a person sets to one eye and squints through, then folds up and stows away. It was a more powerful instrument, all brass and lustrous polished wood, mounted on a tripod. I ran lightly up the steps. And there, as I expected, were the three girls, all by the seaside windows, Sunny peering through the telescope, and Angela and Charlotte with their noses to the glass.

"My turn for the telescope," I said gaily as I approached the group. "The privilege of age, my dears."

They all three turned to me with absolutely *stricken* stares, looking as guilty as cats caught at the cream pot. Now what? I asked myself as I reached the window. What was there to cause such consternation from simply viewing a squadron of the king's ships?

I looked questioningly at Sunny, but she seemed to be rendered momentarily speechless.

"What's going on here?" I asked, my suspicions fully aroused, although to what I couldn't think.

Sunny, suddenly finding her voice, said accusingly, "I caught these girls . . ."

"*You* looked, too!" Angela actually stamped her foot. "You *did!* And you looked a long time! Didn't she Charlotte?"

Charlotte, still too new to the family to engage in such arguments—except with Chunk—had her nose now firmly pressed to the window. "So many ships," she said. "Do they every one belong to the king?"

Sunny grabbed Angela and shook her. "I looked to see what you two deprived children were giggling about! And I'm going to tell Mama!"

I grabbed Sunny. Such behavior was quite unlike her, cranky as she sometimes is. "Stop it! Just what was it that these *depraved* children were doing?"

Sunny left off shaking Angela, but she also jerked herself away from me. "Look for yourself," she said, pointing dramatically at the telescope.

It was only then that I noticed the barrel of the instrument was pointing rather more downward toward the sands than outward toward the sea.

"Go ahead and tell Mama!" Angela said hotly. "I don't care. I'll tell her that you looked, too. And she'll punish you, too!"

Sunny responded with a "Hummph," and I put my eye to the telescope.

Suddenly, there was a bathing machine, seeming so close I felt I could touch it, and I was overcome by an unexpected wave of nostalgia. How many times had Ben and I—and sometimes Sunny—watched merchant ships or warships pass in the roads, or the yachts and the fishing fleet offshore? . . . Or sometimes, in the railed cupola that surmounted the roof and which we reached by climbing a narrow stairway, we looked at the stars, while Papa told us about the constellations and the planets, and the wonderful forty-foot telescope that the Herschels had built, and the comets that Miss Herschel had discovered. . . .

I realized I had been staring, unseeing, at the bathing machine. And just at that moment, a gentleman rose from the water to mount the steps to reenter it, and . . . Why, he was stark, staring naked!

"Goodness gracious!" I said. "What a prime article!"

There was a smothered giggle behind me. I swung the telescope to the right and then to the left, observing as I did so several men floundering about in the water, their bathing men in close attendance, and others, farther from shore, who were swimming. On the far leftward swing I could see the women's bathing area, where four women done up in flannel smocks were being dipped. And then on the swing back to the right I caught a glimpse of another gentleman, this one in his underdrawers, descending cautiously from a machine into the water, as a bathing man waited below, prepared to plunge him into the briny element.

I should explain, for those who are not familiar with Brighton, that the bathing machines here do not have hoods, like those at Margate and other sea bathing places, which shelter from public view the bathers as they descend into the water. I should also explain that one of the gentlemen's bathing areas lies nearly below our cottage—just to the east of the wharf I'd fallen from, in fact. Many gentlemen prefer to bathe completely unclothed, as in fact do some of the ladies also, although in the ladies' case, it is usually those of an older generation, such as Lady Sarah.

The newspaper had only the day before reported disapprovingly of a gentleman undressing himself completely right there on the sands, with his wife offering him assistance, when he leisurely strolled out of the water, by supplying him with towels. Some of our leading citizens were attempting to regulate bathing attire and to forbid bathing from the sands, as well as demanding hoods on the bathing machines, but all efforts at regulation had been unsuccessful thus far. So Charlotte and Angela had discovered, probably by accident, that they could use Papa's telescope to study anatomy.

I stood up and favored Sunny and the two little girls with my severest expression. "Well," I said, "I presume you have all settled your curiosity about what men look like – without clothes, that is." I had to admit, at least to myself, that I had gone a ways toward satisfying mine.

"Pooh!" Charlotte said. "They look like Georgie, except bigger, and they have – "

"Quite right," I said hastily. Charlotte is the product of a more rough and ready environment than either Angela or Sunny. Or myself, for that matter. Back there in Mam Clendenning's large and undoubtedly crowded household, I suppose Charlotte had had numerous occasions to bathe small boys and perhaps even to glimpse older specimens of the sex. I don't believe Scotsmen wear underdrawers beneath their kilts.

Angela and Sunny had managed to recover their guilty faces. "We didn't mean to look," Angela said. "But – "

I made a quick decision. "I don't see any reason why we should tell Mama, but I don't think we should spy on the gentlemen again."

"If we leave the telescope here, they'll do it again," Sunny interrupted.

"I don't think they would if they were forbidden to do it, would you, girls?"

"No, *I* wouldn't." Angela now looked angelic again. "And Charlotte wouldn't either, would you, Charlotte?"

"Of course not," Charlotte replied, her chin up and her

honor on the line.

"No, of course you wouldn't, either of you." I smiled at Sunny in order to include her among the adults. "But it would be such a terrible temptation! And, anyway, it would be hard for the rest of us to use the telescope, now that the Aerie is just yours alone. So I think we should move it downstairs. We'll put it in the front parlor."

"The perfect place!" Sunny said, grinning. The front parlor has a big square bay, with windows on all three sides perfect for viewing a wide sweep of the sea.

That reminded us all that we hadn't yet looked at the ships through Papa's telescope, so we all took our turn. Some signals were passing back and forth, for the flags were being run up and down, and a cutter was lowered from one of the larger ships with an officer who'd evidently decided to come ashore at Brighton. A yacht had hoisted sail and was accompanying the larger ships, maneuvering gracefully around and among them. Ships aren't terribly interesting to those who have little knowledge of them, and except for the fine sight they made, there was little to hold our attention. Sunny went off downstairs to put our proposal to Mama regarding the telescope, and Charlotte and Angela drifted off into a corner where they had established a "house" with Angela's dolls and some improvised furniture.

My eye lighted on Papa's writing desk, a tall affair with a drop leaf for writing. It was a rather battered object, but Papa had loved it for the many small drawers. He was a prime one for filing things—another of his futile attempts, I believe, to simplify and sort out his complex mind.

Mr. Price had gone through the desk after Papa's death, hoping to discover receipts and bills, along with other such clues to Papa's confused financial affairs. He had found very little. Papa's affairs were rarely committed to paper, at least in any orderly way, although, as we subsequently learned—to our sorrow—his creditors were not so careless.

Mr. Price had come down from the Aerie after his examination of Papa's papers, looking as disappointed as Mama had warned him he would be. "I found only these few more bills," he'd said. "Although the search was not entirely useless. The bill for your court dress was paid, Miss Maudsley, and we'll be able to tell that pushing Frenchwoman to run along and try to cheat someone else. It was a very substantial sum."

"Do have some tea," Mama said. "Old papers are so dusty and depressing! You must be terribly thirsty."

"Yes." Mr. Price gave Mama a strange look. "Thank you, I will have some tea."

After a few polite words with Mama, he had turned again to me. "I found several papers in cipher. I was wondering if they would be of any importance. . . ."

"No." I couldn't help laughing. "Papa loved puzzles. He made quite a study of cryptography, and he even taught Ben and me some ciphering and coding tricks. He used to write us funny notes in cipher, or what he called "words of advice for youth." Sometimes he'd tell us about a gift he'd bought for us. Or a surprise of some other kind."

"Well." Mr. Price set his teacup back on the tray. "It was only the merest hope. I left all those papers—the ones in cipher—and quite a number of others—letters primarily, some newspaper clippings, some poetry in a strange hand. . . . Odd stuff, the poetry, about a Xanadu . . . Like . . . uh . . . the name of this cottage."

"Oh, Mr. Coleridge's poem!" I exclaimed, actually clapping my hands. "I'm *so* happy you found it! Mr. Coleridge himself wrote it out for Papa. We looked everywhere for it, I believe, except in Papa's desk. . . ."

Mr. Price was now giving me a strange look. He had come to think, you see, that I was the practical one of the family, and to go into such raptures over a poem by one of the modern poets . . . and one who was not too highly regarded in the more conservative literary circles . . .

I laughed. "It's very personal, Mr. Price. And sentimental. Papa named our cottage Xanadu because of that poem, and he always thought Mr. Coleridge should publish it, finished or unfinished."

Clasping my hands dramatically before my breast, I recited the first lines.

"In Xanadu did Kubla Khan
A stately pleasure dome decree . . ."

And then Mama, smiling, although her eyes were bright with unshed tears, had recited the final lines.

"Weave a circle round him thrice,
And close your eyes with holy dread,
For he on honey-dew hath fed,
And drunk the milk of Paradise."

There were tears in my own eyes and my voice caught as I explained. "You see, Mr. Price, although it's only a scrap of paper, it has great sentimental value for us. If you'll excuse me, I'll retrieve it now."

"It's in the top middle drawer," Mr. Price said as he handed me the keys. He rose as I left the room, and I heard him say, "I'm sorry, Lady Maudsley, if I've upset you. . . ."

"No, no," Mama answered. "I was only reminded that Whitney was . . . so, so *romantic*. He made life. . . ."

And then I was out of hearing. Papa had, indeed, made life . . . Wherever he was, there was excitement and pleasure and gaiety. I found the poem, and up there in Papa's Aerie, as rain washed against the windows, I had wept and wept and wept. It was my final farewell to Papa and to our old life—our old life of make-believe, irresponsibility, and too many bonbons. I guess I'd realized, finally, that wonderful as Papa was, what he had given us was not the whole of life.

I wandered over to Papa's desk. The ring of keys still dangled from the keyhole of the drawer where I had found Papa's copy of Mr. Coleridge's poem. I began idly unlocking and pulling out drawers. Except for retrieving the poem, I had not looked at Papa's papers since that afternoon three years ago. "I should really clean this desk out," I remarked to the room in general. I pulled out a few more drawers. Almost every one was filled with papers. "Angela," I said, "would you run downstairs and bring me a basket? Or something to put Papa's papers in. If we empty these drawers, then you and Charlotte can use the desk."

It was just as Mr. Price had said. Most of the papers were newspaper clippings and old letters. In one drawer I found the several pages in cipher that had so momentarily raised Mr. Price's hopes, as well as other old letters and a few examples of what looked like Papa's own attempts at poetry. Mr. Price had clearly not returned all the papers to their proper drawers. I tossed everything indiscriminately in the basket that Angela brought me, thinking that I could attend to the sorting in the privacy of our small bookroom later—when I could find the time.

However, one of the old letters caught my eye. It was from Great Aunt Edula, from France, and the date was April 1789. I suppose everyone knows that the upheaval in France began in July of that year, but I wondered if Aunt Edula had observed the unrest or had any suspicion of what was soon to occur. I sat down to read. The letter turned out to be absolutely nothing—merely an account of her social engagements in Paris. Trust Great Aunt Edula not to see what was under her nose!

Just then a frightful crash downstairs brought me to my feet. I picked up the basket of papers and rushed out, Charlotte and Angela behind me, and clattered down two flights of stairs to the front parlor. The furniture was pushed back against the walls and the rug rolled up. Ben and Chunk were on their hands and knees, beside an overturned table, busily picking up large pieces of china, while Mama, Mrs. Oliphant, and Sunny fussed, lamented, or scolded, as their natures dictated.

"What on earth were you two *doing?*" I demanded.

"They were *boxing!*" Sunny said. "Can you imagine anyone other than two great idiotic boys being so *dense* as to be setting-to in the front parlor?"

Even Sunny, who as I've said is quite proper, has picked up the lingo of the Fancy.

"It's just an ugly old lamp that nobody liked," Chunk said defensively. "Mama put it back in that corner so nobody would see it."

"Nonetheless," I said, with deadly calm, "the lamp worked. And how—" my voice was rising, but I didn't care, "—how do you think we will be able to afford another one? Without that lamp, we won't be able to see to do anything in here. . . ."

"Lia, please lower your voice," Mama commanded in a voice just slightly more forceful than her usual gentle tones. "A lady does not shout."

I drew breath to tell Mama that if she had an ounce of sense, she would be taking some responsibility for keeping the family clothed and fed, but years of restraint—or of spoiling Mama, just as Papa had—deterred me. I closed my mouth again, and confining myself to a gusty sigh, I turned and left the room.

I very calmly went into the bookroom, where I left the basket of papers, plucked a book from the shelves without looking at the title, then sought my own chamber, where I locked the door securely and threw myself on the bed. But, aside from a few tears before I could help myself, I refused to cry. The book I'd blindly chosen was in Latin, so I threw it across the room. What use was a book in Latin?

Instead—and to cheer myself out of the dismals—I thought about my first ball in Brighton—in fact, my first real ball anywhere since Papa had died. We had received our formal invitations that morning. It might not be a glamorous affair—Lady Sarah's "small gathering of young people and old friends," as she had described it to Mama—but she had engaged one of the Castle Inn public rooms, so it couldn't be too small an occasion. And I had a very pretty dress to wear. Thanks to Mama's skill, I thought wearily. I was doubly thankful now that I hadn't thrown accusations at Mama. In her own way, she did her best to help.

I had just abandoned myself to some girlish daydreaming, when there was a tentative knock on the door.

"Lia, are you all right?" Chunk asked.

Then Ben said, "We'll buy a new lamp, Lia. Chunk and I have it all worked out. I know where I can sell the watch Papa gave me. . . ."

"You can't sell your watch!" I yelled. "Go away!"

"Yes, I can. You don't have anything to say about it! And, anyway, as soon as I'm twenty-one, I can wear Papa's own watch."

I didn't think that they intended that very minute to go out selling their possessions, so I didn't answer. The sacrifice would be Chunk's as well as Ben's, for Ben had promised him the cheaper watch as soon as he was allowed to wear Papa's much more expensive Brueguet.

"I don't care if I don't get a watch till I'm grown up," Chunk said, sounding very coaxing.

I sighed. "We'll talk about it tomorrow. Maybe we can think of something else."

All was quiet for a short time, and then there was soft scratching on the door.

"Lia?" Sunny this time.

"Are you all right?" Angela was with her.

"Mama has something to tell you."

It really is next to impossible in this household to have the sulks.

I sighed again. "I'm perfectly all right. I just want to be alone for a while."

"Lia," Mama said, "I have a little money that I've been saving."

"What?" I asked, sitting up. Where would Mama have gotten any money? Mr. Price sent all drafts to me for the rent on High Oak, or any of the other dribbles that came in.

"Mr. Price sold a piece of jewelry for me—oh, a long time ago, and for much more than I expected. Remember, dear, we needed a warm coat for Ben and some other things. . . ."

I did remember. It had been a particularly ugly piece, the last of a small store of jewels that Mama had kept, saying at the time that it was like having money in a secret bank account, which we would keep for special expenditures or when some emergency required more money than we had in the bank account that Mr. Price supervised. I didn't remember, however, that there had been any money left from that sale. But as I've said, Mama can be rather sly sometimes.

"I thought we spent all that money," I said suspiciously.

"I really can't talk about it through a door and when I can't see you," Mama replied. "Please open the door and I'll explain."

She could talk to Adam and Star perfectly well without seeing them, but I didn't bother to argue. I sighed again, got off the bed, and opened the door.

I hadn't known that Mrs. Oliphant was among those standing around in the hallway. They all walked in and they all sat on the bed, leaving a place for me between Mama and Angela—all except for Mrs. Oliphant, that is. She looked at me searchingly and, evidently seeing no signs of extreme distress, remarked that she must get on with our dinner now that it was clear I was perfectly all right.

"Well," Mama continued comfortably, putting her arm around me. "There's certainly enough for a new lamp. And a prettier one, too. We must never tell Ben and Chunk, for of course it won't do to have them practicing their fisticuffs in the house, but I'm rather glad they broke that really terribly ugly lamp. And wasn't it lucky there was no oil in it!"

Angela confided that Charlotte was in the kitchen making some tarts for me, with Mrs. Oliphant's assistance, and that Jane had asked her to tell me that she *thought* Irene *might* have just said a word in English.

"What word was it that Jane thought Irene *might* have said?" I asked.

"Oh!" Angela clapped a hand over her mouth. "I forgot to ask."

Well, as I said, it's almost impossible to have sulks in this house. We all hurried to the nursery, where Irene had a lot to say, but if any of it was English, we couldn't identify it.

Since the distance to the Castle Inn was at least three quarters of a mile from the villa, the good Lady Sarah sent her carriage for "her old friend, Tilly," and for Ben and Sunny and me.

If it had been just Sunny and me, who she considered lacking in enterprise for not having captured the rich gentlemen who would make our lives all right again, she would no doubt have made us walk to her ball. Sir Benjamin, on the other hand, was a young gentleman who shouldn't marry until his thirties. "Good for a young buck to sow a few wild oats, drink, and carouse a bit," she'd pronounced authoritatively. "Settles 'em down."

Sunny and I had felt just a touch annoyed after watching Lady Sarah petting and praising Ben the last time she'd visited Mama, and then giving us another scold and a lecture on the opportunity that her "small affair at the Castle" was to provide us. On the other hand, we couldn't imagine that any heiress in her right mind would be prepared to marry Ben in his current state of callow enthusiasms, so I suppose Lady Sarah was only being realistic, in her way, by singling me out as the family's salvation.

The assembly room was already well filled when we arrived. A liberal scattering of red coats made Sunny's eyes snap, and mine at least were pleased to observe that Lord Dayne and Mr. Chaffinch were present.

Dayne turned just as we were released from Lady Sarah's greeting, and his face lit up in open admiration on seeing me, and . . . perhaps surprise? I do look well with my braids coiled over my ears. In any event, at that moment there was only one person in the room, as far as I was concerned, and I had to give myself a sharp reminder that haughty naval gentlemen who are sixth barons are not about to make the fortunes of poor but proud daughters of deceased baronets. Dayne made his way across the room to greet us, and then Mama was surrounded by old admirers and friends, while Sunny and Ben drifted off with Mr. Chaffinch.

He bowed over my hand. "How nice to see you, Miss Maudsley. You are looking remarkably well."

"Thank you," I said, as calmly as possible. He was dressed in the severe stark white against stark black that was affected by some of the fashionables, and it suited him really quite well.

"May I see your card?" he asked.

"My—my dance card?"

"Yes. I can't think why I should need any other."

"But—but your—your injury. I would have thought—"

"—that it's difficult for me to dance? Quite true, and very awkward for a partner, besides. Although I do hope that by the time of another ball, I shall be able to take a sedate turn or two down the floor. However, although I'm not quite limber enough in my . . . er . . . nether limbs to do so yet, I should nevertheless like to engage a dance. Unless you object to sitting down during a dance rather than standing up."

"I always object to sitting down at a dance, but perhaps this once . . ."

"Then I shall engage you for . . . let me see . . . ah, this one, just before supper. It would never do for future partners to see you sitting down for the first dance. They might presume that you don't care to dance at all."

"Very true, my lord, but if you engage me for the dance before supper, you will be required to lead me in to supper as well."

"Why, so I shall. I hadn't thought of that! Will you object?"

"Oh, I think not. Perhaps Ben and Mr. Chaffinch will join us and we can discuss the latest mill. And the new one coming up. And perhaps debate whether Humphries or Mendoza showed more science in their set-to in '89. Or whether Tom Belcher will equal his brother Jem in pugilistic skill. Or perhaps you would rather discuss spies."

He looked up sharply from my card. "Spies?"

"Well, the last time we met, spies—or Bonaparte's intentions, at least—seemed to have been the only topic of conversation, other than the mills." Mr. Chaffinch had come to call, accompanied by Lord Dayne, soon after his return from Scotland. A mill of some import was in the immediate offing—the one in which Tom Belcher would be put to the test—and also in the offing was the collapse of the Addington government and the return of Pitt, which had led to a discussion of the abortive peace with Napoleon Bonaparte in 1801 and speculation whether Bonaparte had used the interim to strengthen his spy network as well as his military machine in preparation for invasion. These were not, to my mind, fit topics for a ballroom.

"My dear Miss Maudsley, I had no idea I had been so lacking in gallantry. May I compliment you on your gown?"

"You may." I wondered if my cheeks were flushing, for he had just barely flicked his gaze—it might have even been a mere blink—at my rather well-exposed bosom.

"Then I do compliment you. The color becomes you. And I do believe that it puts roses in your cheeks."

"Indeed, it is not due to the color of my gown at all. I spent half an hour pinching my cheeks and biting my lips before we departed the house—and all the way here in Lady Sarah's carriage, besides. Such a well-sprung vehicle."

He pretended ignorance of female tricks. "And why such self-punishment?"

"To ride in a first-rate equipage?"

"No, my dear young lady. No, I was referring to such foolishness as pinching and biting one's cheeks and lips, and wondering why a sensible woman like you would engage in it."

"Why, to put roses in my cheeks and turn my lips to . . . uh . . ."

I trailed off on that remark, for the romantic novel writers frequently suggested that lips like cherries were meant to be kissed.

He handed back my card. "Lips like cherries?" he asked, gazing intently at my now tightly clamped specimens. He bowed. "But I must not monopolize you. A gentleman in a red coat is very obviously desiring to speak to you."

I turned to discover a Captain of the Tenth Dragoons smiling down at me, and I came close to launching myself into his arms—much as Irene lunges at Georgie—simply from the sheer pleasure of seeing an old friend from my childhood days. "Jerry Richmondson!" I exclaimed. "I haven't seen you since—since . . . why, I believe it was the last Christmas we were at High Oak, before Papa —"

He bowed over my hand and then gave me a searching look. "No. I called on you after Sir Whitney died. . . ."

"Of course. Forgive me."

"Nothing to forgive. It was so very sudden, and there were so many people who wished to pay their respects to Sir Whitney's memory and to his family. I felt as though I'd lost a favorite uncle. He was a wonderful man."

I smiled mistily at him. "Are you often at Ashways? Or do your military duties keep you away from your old home?" Ashways and High Oak lie in the same valley and march together. Jerry—Jerald—was one year my senior. We had played together as children and had flirted with each other at numerous county parties in later years.

"No," he replied to my question. "Although I've just returned from a visit there, I go to Ashways infrequently these days and try not to stay too long. I don't feel so welcome now that Max has married. I'll be looking about for a property of my own when this war is over." Jerry signed my card for the first dance, after assuring himself I had not previously promised it, and then asked, "I've already spoken to your mother and to Ben. I knew Ben right away, but can that possibly be Sunny standing over there with that great tall gentleman and those officers?"

I have never mentioned, I suppose, that Sunny is very pretty and perhaps on her way to becoming a beautiful woman. She does tend to attract admirers, although her sharp tongue is too much for the weaker among them. To be realistic, Sunny may be a better candidate for saving the family than I am.

"Yes, that's Sunny," I said.

"Quite grown up, by God. The last time I saw her she was all eyes and teeth."

"No longer, as I suppose you can observe."

"I must say hello. Will you re-introduce me? She quite likely has forgotten me."

"Quite likely. You were not one to notice infants." Whether Sunny was still an infant I suppose depended on one's reckoning. Lady Sarah thought her old enough for balls and would even have her married, while I still thought of her as barely out of childhood.

Both Sunny and I filled our dance cards, and could consider ourselves a success. I can't say that any rich gentleman seemed struck with the notion that it was his duty to rescue us from poverty, but the gentlemen who did distinguish us were amiable, inclined to ask permission to call, and admiring enough to satisfy our vanity. I discovered that although I'd lost forever my former giddiness, I had not lost my proficiency at flirting, and I was amused to discover Lord Dayne frowning as he caught my eye from across the room.

When he came to claim my hand, he suggested that we make an attempt to go down one dance together, so that no one would think I was a wallflower, but I assured him that my dance card was filled, and that I had no fears of being left to bloom unnoticed against the wall. We chatted merrily through the dance and at supper, without one reference to mills (even when Mr. Chaffinch joined us), or spies, or even politics.

"I'm seeing a new Miss Maudsley tonight," Dayne said as we returned to the dancing and waited for my next partner to claim me. "Or perhaps not a new Miss Maudsley, but another."

"No, I'm one and the same. You only see me in new surroundings."

"Will you save a dance for me at the next ball?"

"I'm afraid there won't be another. It must be clear to you that we have not the wherewithal to—"

He turned to me suddenly and took my hand in both of his. "No, Miss Maudsley, don't say it. Forget for one night the too many responsibilities that rest on your shoulders."

That gave me something to think about before I went to sleep.

Dayne

"Sometimes I think I'd like to get my hands on Sir Whitney Maudsley." Breverton Dayne strode restlessly up and down the room, limping now, after a long day and an evening spent almost entirely on his feet.

"He was a first-rate spy. . . ."

"Double agent . . ."

"Yes, of course. I must be tired indeed if I must be corrected by an amateur."

"A first-rate agent, perhaps, but a ne'er-do-well who frittered away a fortune and left a family in poverty!"

"They speak with great affection of their father."

"More fools, they."

"Come now, Brev, sit down. It's late, and I'm exhausted. Why is it that dancing and doing the pretty can make me as tired as a coalheaver after a long day's work?"

Dayne's expression relaxed. "Because you don't like doing the pretty." He shed his coat, threw it over the back of a chair, and limped across the room to stand before the cold fireplace.

"Our two Miss Maudsleys were quite the centers of attention tonight." Chaffinch cast a surreptitious glance at his friend from under his brows.

"Yes," Dayne answered shortly, his own brow lowering.

"Careful, Brev. We're on delicate ground here."

"And what does that mean?"

Chaffinch decided that it was not the moment to warn his friend. In the world of espionage, intimacy was always dangerous, and there were signs that Brev was becoming rather too involved with Miss Maudsley. Or worse, that Miss Maudsley was succumbing to whatever it was that put the ladies into a twitter over him. He decided to compromise. "I don't believe your aunt was well pleased that you sat through an entire dance and then supper with Miss Maudsley. . . ."

"Oh, hang my aunt. I was only obeying her instructions to notice the girl in order to assist her in the capture of a rich husband. My aunt apparently has taken on the Maudsley family as a project." Dayne pulled off his neckcloth and flung it in the general direction of his bedroom door. "As for me, she has some scheme or other for marrying me off in such a way that the family interest will be furthered . . . even though family interest was the death of my brother. If Algernon hadn't been forced into marriage with that pie-faced, pudding-headed Claudette—just because her father is influential in Whig circles . . . But he was given responsibility so young, and I admit I wasn't much help to him—mad for the Navy and for cutting the swell. He needed a wife who'd be a friend and an advisor, like Miss Gossit, whom he wanted to marry. But my uncles wouldn't have that. He went to those low-life places in St. Giles to get away . . . to relax. . . . And got himself killed. Well, my uncles aren't going to do it to me! Even if they have enlisted Aunt Sarah to do her best. Her best! Do you know who she has in mind for me?"

"No, can't say I do."

"Lady Catherine deVandt!"

"deVandt?"

"Yes, an insipid woman who is either sickly or given to vapid airs, and certainly much too given to nasty gossip. No thank you. I'd prefer the meanest bordello in Seven Dials to facing her in bed."

"She's not bad-looking. In fact, some might call her a beauty."

"If I ever marry, I'll want spirit more than beauty. Some toughness . . . capable . . . The kind of woman who could face danger or difficulty without collapsing with the vapors. I'm going back to sea, Chaff, whether or no. Made up my mind. Walter can attend to the estate and to family interest. He's made for it. I'm not. Nor for Catherine deVandt! Impossible!" Dayne ended his oration by flinging himself into a chair, from which he stared darkly at his friend.

Chaffinch confined himself to a ready agreement that "the deVandt" didn't seem to be promising stuff. That his friend had been describing Lia Maudsley, whether he knew it or not, he thought best to keep to himself. But what that very determined young woman would have to say if she ever found out her friendship had been sought for reasons having nothing to do with her own charms. . . .

"Well," he said, changing the subject. "I had a chat with one of Sir Whitney's old cronies tonight. Managed to add two or three names to the list of people he knew or saw occasionally, but except for one of them, I can say without hesitation that there is no cause for suspecting them."

Dayne stretched his legs out before him. "Wind's come up again," he remarked. He massaged his forehead for a moment before he replied. "Gave me a headache thinking about the deVandt woman. But I thought, Chaff, that you'd told me that in your business you could never say anything 'without hesitation.' "

"Nature of the game, it's true." Chaffinch ruminated. Finally, he shook his head. "If we could just locate the Goodman woman. Clear up what was going on up there in Edinburgh. Why did Sir Whitney entrust her with the secret of Charlotte's parentage . . ."

"We don't know that the Goodman woman knew Charlotte's parentage. All we know is that both the children have been known as Goodman since they came to Mrs. Clendenning. I've argued before, Chaff, that either he thought she would be willing to go through with it because the child was French and so was she—"

"The woman who bought her hat shop said she wasn't from Edinburgh. Spoke of coming from the south . . . not that she was French."

"—or he didn't tell her at all what Charlotte's parentage was. He had a fertile brain, to say the least. We've heard from his family about his ability to make up fantastic stories and fairy tales. Now, let's see. . . . There's a baby to place, which must not be identified as French. Although Sir Whitney's friends are unaware of Miss Goodman's existence, others believe that she's his mistress and will say so, as both you and, no doubt, this man Price discovered."

"Go on."

"Sir Whitney had established a reason for seeing the Goodman woman regularly, and he thinks she can be useful to him in his other activity for the same reason—as his mistress. A child may not be incontestable evidence of a liaison, but is certainly suggestive of one. He tells Miss Goodman that a friend's daughter has been indiscreet; the child needs a home. . . . Will she agree to acknowledging the child as hers, the product of her liaison with him?"

"Possible . . . Goodman's landlady says Sir Whitney engaged the rooms for her, and as nearly as she can remember, it would have been about the time Charlotte was taken to Mrs. Clendenning. . . ." Chaffinch paused. "It was too long ago. People don't remember." He shook his head. "Well, whatever she had to do with Charlotte and with Sir Whitney, it's important we locate her. The Home Office seems confident she can be traced . . . and the Runners are good men. The Home Office goes to Bow Street for work of this kind."

"And I suppose the Home Office's informants and spies in Ireland have been alerted?"

"So I understand." Chaffinch rubbed a hand over his eyes and yawned deeply. He leaned back in his chair, his eyes closed. "Sir Whitney learned or suspected who the top agents were. How? Through the Goodman woman? Or was it someone else known to him?"

"Someone who would have known just how desperate his financial situation was and that he might be susceptible to taking money to spy on his own country . . ."

"And someone who knew his politics, someone his family also would have known"—Chaffinch opened his eyes—"as I've maintained."

"I think he'd try very hard to keep such a dangerous game at a distance from his family. He was a devoted family man, so everyone says. I vote for Miss Goodman. *Cherchez la femme,* as you suggested."

"Nonetheless, we couldn't overlook the possibility that someone close to him was a spy—perhaps the one who recruited him

. . . perhaps someone more important, whom he only later identified. That he managed to gain the confidence of important members of the ring suggests as much."

Dayne suddenly laughed, his fulsome, delightful laugh. "I think I'll lay my wager on that 'odious little man who was always at the door asking for Papa.' We owe that information to Miss Maudsley's iron determination to be honest about the family's financial affairs. Refreshing, I must say. But what better occupation for discovering tottering financial states than a writ server?"

Chaffinch heaved himself from his chair for a leisurely stretch and another yawn. "Exactly. But it was someone else who used the information about Sir Whitney's vulnerability. 'That odious little man' just did the leg work, and as soon as we find him, we'll have a long talk with him. I've got one of my own men looking for him, but I'm afraid it was all too long ago. He's probably dead by now. You get a 'feeling' in this work, Brev. And although some trails are cold, I'm convinced that the French spy network never ceased to function, even during the peace."

"I understand intuition, Chaff. I've relied on it myself in more than one engagement. And I agree that Boney wouldn't have permitted an excellent spy system to get out of trim during the peace, knowing that he might be at war with England again soon. But I'm beginning to think it unlikely we'll learn anything here."

"No. Part of the answer's here. And with the Goodman woman, wherever she is. Call it what you like. I'm certain."

"Well, a question on a new tack. When do we burgle Price's office?"

"Eager to begin your life of crime?"

"Making up for a misspent youth. I've never stolen anything."

"We'll both go to London . . . do some more investigating there. Get our burglary out of the way . . . Toward the end of the week. Agreed?"

Chapter Eight

The most exciting event of the next week was a letter from Mr. Price, in answer to my inquiry regarding Charlotte and Georgie. I opened it eagerly, and after quickly glancing through the contents, I gathered Ben and Sunny, and closeted in the kitchen with Mrs. Oliphant, we read the letter. The reader may wonder that we included our housekeeper . . . may even wonder why we chose the kitchen for reading and discussion of Mr. Price's discoveries. The reasons are simple: First, Mrs. Oliphant had been with us since we were children and might as well have been one of the family; and second, Mama never set her foot in the kitchen. She often remarked that as long as the good Lord continued to provide her with a cook, she would consider herself a fortunate woman.

Mr. Price's letter began,

"My dear Miss Maudsley: I received your letter late in the afternoon on the eleventh of last month. I spent the evening of that day and a good portion of the night reflecting on the implications of the information you conveyed regarding a Mrs. Clendenning and two children named Charlotte and George, presumed by the same Mrs. Clendenning to be the children of your father and a woman who bore the surname Goodman, since that is the surname by which the two children are known."

Mrs. Oliphant interrupted to exclaim, "If that isn't just like that Mr. Price! Why, anyone would think that you'd asked him to do no more than investigate which was the cheapest of two different warehouses where you expected to buy a few yards of muslin!"

"Yes," I agreed. "I've seldom seen Mr. Price disturbed. Disapproving . . . but seldom disturbed."

"Go on with the letter," Ben urged.

"I add parenthetically," Mr. Price wrote, "that I was delighted to learn how calmly and cheerfully Lady Maudsley sustained the knowledge of Sir Whitney's supposed delinquencies. I advisedly use 'supposed,' for women were never among your father's weaknesses."

"Well!" Mrs. Oliphant interrupted again. "It's just as I said! Sir Whitney was not a philanderer, whatever else he might have been. Now some of his set, I make no bones about it, were regular Turks, but your Papa was not. Devoted to Lady Maudsley, he was."

Sunny hugged Mrs. Oliphant. "You and Mr. Price have such faith in Papa!"

"There, now, child." Mrs. Oliphant gave Sunny a quick, motherly kiss. "I'm not saying he didn't have his faults, for he did. But I'm morally certain that wasn't one of them. Now let's all be still and find out what else Mr. Price has to say. He's a sensible man, and you couldn't have done better, Miss Lia, than to ask his help." Mrs. Oliphant and Mr. Price were acquaintances of long standing, for Mr. Price had regularly traveled to Brighton to conduct business with Papa.

The letter continued:

"The unexplained cash withdrawals from your father's accounts may have been in some cases for payments to Mrs. Clendenning, for certain of them do coincide with receipts as reported by that lady. On the other hand, she received a regular quarterly stipend for the children's care for two years after your father's death."

We all exclaimed at that news, for Mrs. Clendenning's letter had led us to assume that the money had stopped shortly after Papa's death. Mrs. Oliphant reminded us that she, at least, had work to do, and that we would never learn anything if we didn't all hush up. I returned to the letter and began to read again.

"The day after receiving your letter, I set out by the stage to Edinburgh, where I rented a conveyance to carry me about the countryside. An accounting is attached, for conveyance and *per diem,* the charges to be added to my next statement. I have not charged for the stage, since I took the opportunity to visit old friends from my schooldays in Edinburgh."

"Well, I never!" Mrs. Oliphant exclaimed.

"Oh, dear!" I said. "I didn't expect him to go to Scotland!" I flipped to the end of the letter and there attached was the bill—an amount that nearly made my hair stand on end. "Six pounds, twenty shillings, five pence!" I read in horror.

"Well," Ben said philosophically, "bread and milk and porridge for the next week."

I took a deep breath and tried for equal philosophical detachment. "Well, we can think about the cost later." I turned my attention once again to the letter.

"I easily located the woman, Mrs. Clendenning, in whose care the children had been placed, and discovered the following—not, however, without many assurances of my sincere interest in the welfare of the children. Of modest means Mrs. Clendenning and her spouse may be, and humble their abode, but they are people of some education, even though a clearly limited one. Their affection for the children cannot be questioned, nor that they gave them the best care they could within their scarce means.

"The fruit of my inquiries was as follows:

"1. Your father himself brought Charlotte, as an infant in arms, to Mrs. Clendenning, asserting that the baby was his and naming a Miss Goodman as the mother. Your father arranged to provide for the support of the child with a quarterly stipend to be paid to Miss Goodman, who resided permanently in Edinburgh. It was Miss Goodman herself, however, who brought George, a newborn infant, to Mrs. Clendenning. She promised an increase in the quarterly stipend, but it had in fact decreased in amount about the time of your father's death and was never again raised. After that it was paid through a bank in Edinburgh directly to Mrs. Clendenning. It finally ceased a year ago. The drafts were drawn on a bank in London, which I am currently investigating.

"Although Miss Goodman seldom visited Charlotte, except very occasionally on quarter days, she did show some emotion at her parting with the infant George. She charged Mrs. Clendenning to care for both of the children well and stated that she would return for them when her situation permitted."

"Well, I *ask* you!" Mrs. Oliphant exclaimed. "Just like that! She would leave her babies with a stranger, never visit them once, and then coolly take them away after they've learned to love their new home and the good people who've cared for them so many years! And as though their father's family had no right to determine who would have the care of them!"

Sunny, equally incensed, echoed Mrs. Oliphant. "And then to stop sending Mrs. Clendenning money so she was forced to send them to us! And now we've learned to love them, too!"

Although I—and even Ben—joined in the denunciations of Miss Goodman, repetition would only serve to emphasize how quickly Charlotte and little Georgie had made their way into our hearts. And so I will spare the reader further expressions of our indignity and continue on with Mr. Price's letter.

"2. As to Miss Goodman: Miss Goodman owned a hat shop in Edinburgh. She lived in her last residence for six years, where I spoke with her landlady, a Mrs. Falconer, who states that her hats were stylish and expensive. Mrs. Falconer is an incorrigible snoop, I strongly suspect, which (although one may decry such a character trait in general) was exactly to my purpose. She knew your father's name, described him perfectly, had often seen him in the company of Miss Goodman, and believed her to be his mistress. Mrs. Falconer seems to have accepted Miss Goodman's situation in life, provided that decorum was preserved. Beginning in approximately January of the year 1800, an Irishman also lodged with her. Miss Goodman was discovered to be with child some time after the advent of the Irishman, and it is the opinion of Mrs. Falconer that he and not your father was responsible. Miss Goodman sold her shop and departed with him and the baby soon after your father's death without leaving a forwarding address, which is proof sufficient for Mrs. Falconer. I believe we can be assured that the youngest child, George, is that baby.

"Although I could find nothing equally certain regarding the older child, Charlotte, I believe we may at least entertain the possibility that she also is an out-of-wedlock child of Miss Goodman's and that your father chose to support the infant.

We are all aware of his generosity. I am convinced that whatever reasons he may have had for a connection with Miss Goodman, she was not his mistress.

"I asked Mrs. Falconer if Miss Goodman was a native of Edinburgh, and she replied that she thought perhaps she came from Cornwall, from her very slight accent—'for they do speak a strange language down there,' she said, and which, if you will permit me to interject, I thought somewhat amusing considering that Mrs. Falconer grew to young girlhood, so she says, speaking Welsh and to my ear has an accent herself. But, of course, I speak the king's English.

"Incidentally, your father continued to visit Miss Goodman during the epoch of the Irishman. When pressed, Mrs. Falconer added that your father seldom let more than three months go by without visiting the woman.

"3. One curious piece of information gleaned from Mrs. Clendenning I pass on in regard to Charlotte. When your father brought the child to her, she was wrapped in a blanket, which although somewhat soiled was of very fine wool and bore the initial 'B,' surrounded by a complex design of flowers intertwined with symbols. Mrs. Clendenning did not discover the initial until she washed the blanket, and she was understandably curious that a child named Charlotte Goodman, purportedly fathered by a Maudsley, should arrive in a blanket marked with a 'B.' Although she questioned Miss Goodman—she never saw your father again—she received no satisfactory answer. The blanket was much loved by Charlotte as a child and eventually fell to pieces. One must wonder why a sensible woman would permit a child to destroy a fine and no doubt costly article; but, then, there is no accounting for occasional lapses of judgment even among the most sensible, which I take Mrs. Clendenning to be."

That information, the reader can well imagine, set us all to speculating about the mysterious blanket. "I know!" Sunny exclaimed. "Charlotte's mother was the daughter of a noble and vastly wealthy family. She—she was seduced by some terribly dissolute rake, who then heartlessly abandoned her, and her father applied to Papa for assistance. . . ." Sunny was rapidly inventing a plot that my readers will no doubt recognize as bearing some resemblance to a romantic novel.

"Then why would Papa pay the blunt?" asked Ben, who never read romantic novels.

"Don't be such a simpleton! The poor girl's father paid it to Papa, and Papa paid it to Mrs. Clendenning."

"No," I said, with the facts of the letter in mind. "He paid it to Papa, and Papa paid it to Miss Goodman, and Miss Goodman paid it to Mrs. Clendenning."

Mrs. Oliphant, accustomed from years of experience to such discussions, said, "Well, but who paid it after your papa died?"

We all frowned.

"Is there more?" Mrs. Oliphant asked.

"Yes, Mr. Price has a fourth and fifth point yet. Are you all ready to hear them?"

They all assured me that they were on tenterhooks, and so I picked up the letter again.

"4. I spoke also to friends of your father regarding his character and activities in Edinburgh. You will agree that the circumstances of my inquiry and the reputation of Sir Whitney and his family required that the investigation be conducted with the *utmost delicacy.* I therefore explained my inquiries by stating that a Miss Goodman was making some claims upon your family that I considered to be a hoax. None of your father's friends had ever heard of her nor known your father to be in the company of such a woman. He resided when in Scotland with one or another of his friends, of which he had many. I did not have an opportunity to speak with a Mr. Stoutworthy, with whom Sir Whitney had sustained a long friendship, for the gentleman happened to be visiting his estates near York. I am confident that his knowledge of your father's activities in Scotland would coincide with other of his friends; however, to leave no stone unturned, as the saying goes, I am writing to him regarding Miss Goodman.

"5. You ask how Mrs. Clendenning found you. I can answer that easily. Although she was in possession of my name, she had not my direction. However, believing Sir Whitney to be Miss Charlotte's father, and later Master George's also, she followed his activities closely in the society pages and knew his different residences. She was particularly diligent after his death in following his family, for she always feared she would one day be required for financial reasons to send the children to you. She discovered your recent removal to Xanadu in the Brighton News in the *Morning Post.* Mrs. Clendenning is a woman of ability.

"Finally, I will require some little more time to conduct my investigations into who paid Miss Goodman (and later, Mrs. Clendenning) for the children's care and how it was paid. Should my suspicions prove justified, I will take the liberty of visiting you in Brighton."

With that mysterious statement, Mr. Price brought his letter to a close.

"Coming to collect his bill personally . . . that's what he's thinking." Ben, who had been balancing his chair on two legs—which he had been told countless times not to do—brought it back to the floor with a crash. He held out his hand. "Give me the letter, Lia." He unfolded it again, and after studying it for a minute, he said, with an expression of disgust, "We don't know any more than we did before! Papa *might* have paid Mrs. Clendenning, Mr. Price says, but he doesn't think Charlotte is Papa's, although *maybe* her mother's this Miss Goodman, who Mr. Price doesn't think was Papa's mistress. But he *does* think that Georgie was Miss Goodman's and suspects that she saw a chance to fob Georgie off as Papa's, like the two of them did Charlotte. . . . And we all know that it was easy enough to bounce Papa out of his money. . . . We're as much in the dark as ever—except that Papa did know some woman named Miss Goodman, who might have been a fancy piece, and he saw her often. . . ."

"Benjamin Rousseau Maudsley, I'll not have you using such terms around your sisters," Mrs. Oliphant broke in sternly, "nor speaking so disrespectfully of your good papa."

"I'm sorry, Mrs. O.," Ben said, without a sign of contrition. "Forgot myself. But if I were you, Lia, I wouldn't pay his bill! Humbuggery, if you ask me!"

On rereading the letter, the rest of us could find nothing with which to contradict Ben's assertions, except that some doubt had been cast on Mrs. Clendenning's belief that the children were Papa's, most particularly because of the continuance of the stipend for their care for two years after his death. Nonetheless, as Ben maintained, it was all a bit smoky, to say the least.

We took the letter to Mama, who after reading it agreed with Ben, and so for the time being Georgie and Charlotte remained our half brother and sister. As a matter of fact, we were all becoming so accustomed to the idea that, as Sunny confessed later, she would have been almost disappointed if Mr. Price had told us, as incontestable fact, that Charlotte and Georgie were *not* Papa's.

One positive benefit of Lady Sarah's ball was the increase in the number of our callers. Our front parlor was now often lively with officers, most of them Sunny's admirers, although there were one or two of my own. We even found time to walk out occasionally with one or another of them; we walked on the Downs, promenaded on the Stein, played loo in the libraries, and on another occasion made one lengthy excursion on the backs of donkeys to Rottingdean. We were chaperoned on these outings by an officer's wife, a lady whom Mama pronounced to be not only eminently respectable, but also of a good—although somewhat countrified—family. On other occasions, our chaperons were Ben and his sporting friend, Dandy Rogers. Thus a number of sunny days passed pleasantly, although to be truthful, I missed Lord Dayne and Mr. Chaffinch, both of whom had gone to London and were not expected to return for several days.

Jerry Richmondson of the Tenth Dragoons, an old friend from our palmy days, when we spent a part of each year at High Oak, was often among the company and conspicuously dangling after Sunny. I had never seen any harm in Jerry, but I had never seen any substance, either, and I began to worry that he was paying her a more serious court than was desirable. I spoke to Ben about it, and as so often happened, he was entertaining the same concerns, remarking unkindly that he'd always thought Jerry a finicking fop. But as usual when I worry about Sunny, Mama said she was a sensible girl, who was enjoying so much the attentions of several young men that she would not be lured by one so much her senior. Well, it's not so unusual for a girl of sixteen . . . No. Seventeen!

Both Sunny and Angela celebrate their birthdays in June, and we had made quite a party of it. Lord Dayne and Mr. Chaffinch, before leaving for London, presented small remembrances to both of them, but the most special gift of all was a pair of Indian shoes that Dayne presented to Angela. "They're called moccasins and are very easy on the feet," he told her; and in a confidential stage whisper, "I have a pair that I wear for house slippers, and I don't know what I'd do without them." Then, perhaps suspecting she would think they were only meant for boys, he added, "These are for little Indian princesses, and they were so pretty that I just had to buy them, even though I didn't know a little girl to give them to." Angela was thrilled and delighted with her gift, and she asked me later if she could have a book about Indians when we had enough money. She even began writing a story about a little Indian princess.

Our neighbors, the Marquis and Marchioness of Downshire, returned to Belle Vue House, and although we were only speaking acquaintances, it did lend a certain *ton* to the West Cliffs when they were in residence. There was still anxiety about a possible French invasion, but it wasn't the panic of the previous year, which had left Brighton almost deserted except for the natives. The town was filling up with company as the opening of the season approached, hastened by a grand coming-of-age ball at the Castle Inn on Midsummer Night, at which the prince would honor the memory of one of the bosom friends of his rakehell days by honoring the son with his presence.

Lady Sarah Pellett had her own opinions of the visitors to Brighton. "Half the scoundrels and blackguards in England, and most of the Cyprian Corps," she remarked one evening as she bowed politely to a duchess in a passing carriage.

Lady Sarah prevailed on Mama several times to ride out with her in the early evenings, and sometimes even Sunny and I were persuaded. She favored "the vehicle promenade," as she termed it, on the Level, where she—and Mama, too—often encountered old acquaintances. Invitations began to arrive for Mama, which often included Ben and Sunny and me, but Mama always refused, replying that she was living quite retired since her dear Whitney had Passed On. And perhaps at least some of the Fashionables accepted that we were eccentric rather than just poor—perhaps like Lady Newdegate, who lived retired, enjoying the bracing climate and the beauty of the sea, and openly avoiding society.

Lady Sarah and Mama would return to the villa, where over a cup of tea or a glass of wine and some of Mrs. Oliphant's delicately made sandwiches, they would discuss the people they had met that evening or those Lady Sarah had recently read about in the newspaper. Mama never spoke ill of any of them, but she did listen and smile at the sharp commentary at which Lady Sarah excelled.

Lady Jersey had just appeared as the centerpiece of a gossipy news item—as she frequently did—which reminded them of the prince's affair with her, and of her cruelties to the Princess Caroline when she came as his bride to England. "Remarkably reminiscent of the arrival of Anne of Cleves in England," said Lady Sarah, "for if you remember, Tilly, Anne was met at Rochester by one of those pushing Howards and most cruelly treated. Wanted to maneuver the young Catherine Howard in front of old Henry the Eighth. And succeeded in losing the poor girl's head for her, while Anne got the rents from several manors, the king's friendship, and comfortable retirement. Of course, Anne had some sense, which I fear our Caroline doesn't."

"I'm afraid I never was very good at history," Mama replied. "And there were so many Catherines among Henry's wives! One day I really must devote some time to history. But I do remember how scandalously Lady Jersey behaved to poor Caroline." Mama paused to offer Lady Sarah more sandwiches. "Whitney and I came upon the princess once, when we were out driving, during those sad days when she was increasing and Lady Jersey was ruling the prince. She was sitting alone, in the shade of a small grove with a very few of her attendants nearby, and sewing. We spoke to her. She replied very civilly, and we spent much of the rest of the afternoon with her.

I've never liked the prince since. How he could have permitted the queen to appoint his mistress – whom everyone knew to be vicious and nasty-tongued – as lady-in-waiting to his new wife has always puzzled me greatly! Well, Brighton's forgiven him, of course, but at least we never accepted Lady Jersey." As the reader will note, Lady Jersey was one of those whom Mama did speak ill of.

Lady Sarah nodded. "I, for one, am glad to see that Mrs. Fitzherbert's back in favor again. Keeps the prince from kicking up too many of his disgraceful rigs."

"I met Mrs. Fitzherbert on the Stein one evening. She was here seeing about the house she's having built. Your nephew invited us to attend a concert. . . . He's quite charming, you know, and with his friend Mr. Chaffinch has been most kind. It's helped so much to keep Ben from pining. Young men aren't meant for retired living."

"He could be worse. Breverton, I mean. For a while there we thought he might follow Algernon. But he ain't touched in the head like Algernon was."

"Oh?" Mama asked in surprise. "Algernon Dayne had mental difficulties?"

"So I've always thought." Lady Sarah helped herself to yet another sandwich. "Now, Aurelia, you can just pour me a bit more of that wine. Who's your wine merchant, by the way? Gets you better stuff than mine does for me." Without waiting for my answer, she turned again to Mama. "But tell me about Mrs. Fitzherbert. Was she looking well?"

"Oh, yes, very. But getting quite plump, you know." Mama took great pride in her own slender figure.

"And the prince is getting plain fat. Well, the two of them are quite like an old married couple, I suppose. Growing into flesh together – and no doubt much more comfortable without the ardor of their first years. Of course, the prince is still the sensualist. She's never going to cure him of that. I remember . . ."

"Sunny," Mama said, "would you run upstairs and get my sewing basket? You don't mind, do you Sarah, that I take up my needlepoint?"

By the time Sunny returned, the scandalous story had been told (although not so terribly scandalous, I repeated it to

Sunny later), and Mama and Lady Sarah were discussing the political rumors. Mama remarked that it appeared Pitt would be back in power again soon, and although she really had no taste for politics, she had thought the Addington ministry sadly incompetent. Lady Sarah had heard it rumored that the king was going mad again and that there was talk of a regency, as there always was when the king had one of his lunacy spells. That reminded her again of the prince, which reminded her of the approaching grand ball.

"Meant to tell you, Tilly, my nephew and I will be dining with the prince on Midsummer Night and afterward the ball at the Castle for some young duke or other. I'd like to request cards for Aurelia."

I was so surprised that I was just about leveled, as Ben would say, but Mama replied as though such opportunities came our way every day. "Well, as you know, Sarah, we are living very retired. . . ."

I almost fainted with anxiety, but Lady Sarah just snorted at that remark. "If what I hear is true, your gels ain't so retired. Hear they've been walking out with some officers. . . . I wouldn't permit that, Tilly. Ain't no money to be had in the Army—second sons and ne'er-do-wells, the lot of 'em. Oh, occasionally, I'll admit, there's a well-juiced gentleman. . . . Some in the prince's own regiment who're well breeched, but more important for you, some who've got the lucre."

"I was just going to say," Mama gently interrupted, "that although we are living quite retired, I've been happy to let the children entertain their friends here of an afternoon and to indulge in simple pleasures such as walks along the shore and on the Downs. However, I do require that they not indulge in fast society or elaborate affairs."

"Now, Tilly, if you're going to tell me that you're so silly as not to permit Aurelia . . ."

Mama laughed, her light, gracious, rippling laugh. "But of course I will permit her to attend both events! Can you think me so foolish as to refuse such a kind invitation?"

I had the dismal thought that Lady Sarah could think Mama so foolish because, it must be admitted, Mama can be. On the other hand, Mama can also be, as I have noted before, quite sly. She could be certain that the prince would never expect a return invitation from the Maudsleys or, for that matter, would the young duke whose twenty-first birthday would be honored. So I could be permitted to enjoy the prince's dinner and the duke's ball without fear of incurring any obligations. Mama carefully avoided obligations, except to Lady Sarah, whom she considered such an old friend that her kindnesses to us needed no return other than a proper civility.

When Lady Sarah left and I'd finally escaped Sunny's raptures over my good fortune by retiring to the bookroom, saying that I had a letter to write, I could begin to wonder if Lady Sarah had bullied Lord Dayne into escorting me to the ball, the same way she bullied everyone into complying with her wishes.

Then Ben came in, having just heard the news and wishing to also rhapsodize, in his fashion, by telling me what a prime—nay, first-rate—show it would be and how many weighty swells I could expect to encounter, and what quantities of champagne I could swig at the prince's and the young duke's expense.

"Have you been out with your boxing friends?" I asked suspiciously, for Ben's conversation always took on a heavy larding of lingo whenever he had. I must say that I was grateful to Mr. Chaffinch for speaking a straight tongue, with very few regressions into boxing cant. But now Ben had met some less weighty and considerably younger enthusiasts of the ring, who had none of Mr. Chaffinch's restraint, and who took pride in airing their knowledge of the fighting history of every pugilist of note since Broughton and Fig.

"Yes, but I left early." Ben began cracking his knuckles, one after the other in succession, first the right hand and then the left.

Ben cracks his knuckles when upset or under some kind of stress. "What's wrong?" I asked.

"Nothing. Dandy and I ran into . . . doesn't matter . . . just some of the fellows who like to box, but they were on their way to the theatre and supper afterward, and then billiards—which they never play but to gamble. Well, you know, Lia, I can't afford that kind of thing. Just the theatre's more than I can afford. Dandy's a right one—knows my situation, perfect gentleman about it. Never wants to do anything I can't stand the shot for. Clear as a piece of glass that he wanted to go with them, but he wouldn't say so. So I begged off. Said I'd promised you the evening. But sometimes I feel . . . oh, I don't know. Humiliated, I guess."

"We'll think of something," I said comfortingly. "Maybe at the duke's ball I'll meet the rich old man who'll rescue us from our many misfortunes."

"You're bamming me, I hope. Rather be in the workhouse than see either you or Sunny married to some old codger. . . ."

Ben was obviously exaggerating, for I don't think he'd really go so far as the workhouse, but I smiled affectionately at him anyway. "Oh, there are rich gentlemen, I'm sure, who aren't such old codgers at all and who'd be quite acceptable partners in matrimony. I've already had one such looking my way. Lady Sarah introduced us, and with such a great disdain for diplomacy that she all but said right out that since he needed a wife and I needed a rich husband, we were made for each other. He dances very respectably, seems to have all his teeth, and asked if he could call when he returns to Brighton to pass a few weeks during the season."

"Well, hang on a while longer. Great Aunt Edula may come to our rescue yet."

Great Aunt Edula lives permanently in Bath, now that Bonaparte has made France uncomfortable for English people. Her custom, whatever her residence, has been to simply *descend* on all her relatives every other year, including us, "to renew family ties." Although this was her year for renewing ties, when she heard of our plan to have a summer holiday in Brighton, she wrote Mama to say that if we undertook such a remove from Lewes we would be deprived of her company, since she can't abide seaside watering places. We couldn't say we were sorry, even though she has been the most generous of our relatives in easing our financial embarrassments, for she is not an easy visitor. We have also been promised some hope of modest financial gain when Great Aunt Edula Goes, but she is just not the sort – as she warned Papa long ago – who Goes Before Her Time. Although three score and ten is adjudged a generous life span, Great Aunt Edula fully expects to be with us until she is four score and ten, if not more. And we fully expect her to fulfill her own prediction.

So Ben and I played our old game of building castles in the air, which relieved our spirits, if not our anxieties. And that night I lay awake for what seemed to be hours, trying not to toss about and wake Sunny, while I desperately tried to think of some way in which we might recoup our fortunes. Charlotte and Georgie strained our resources unbearably, and I could now think I had been foolish to ask Mr. Price to investigate, as I considered his bill for services. What did it matter whether they were Papa's or not? Or what those unexplained sums had been spent for? We had always supposed they went for gambling and for his usual extravagances. Why not continue to suppose so?

Ben was born to be a country squire, even as a boy he'd said that he wanted to be a farmer. But High Oak was gone, except for the home farm, and I couldn't believe he wanted to be a lawyer, although he declared it was a profession he would like. And then there was Chunk, with his scientific mind. . . . Could I open a shop? A school? I thought I'd do rather well as a headmistress. And I was sure I could learn quickly how to manage a shop. . . . And what would it matter if I forfeited my status as a gentlewoman by going into trade? Pride would not put food on the table or support a family. . . .

I would write to Mr. Price to inform him that henceforth I could not afford his services and would he please forward to me all relevant papers. It was a duty I would rather have not done, for we owed what income we had managed to salvage to Mr. Price and his assistance in sorting out Papa's affairs. But he was so expensive! Papa had always insisted on the best, and having Mr. Price to manage his affairs was as essential as buying his coats at Weston's.

It was an uneasy night, as I slipped from bouts of worry and wakefulness into uneasy dreams, only to wake and worry again.

Sunny and I took Irene and Georgie and Charlotte into the water every morning, and on more than one occasion, after gaining the West Cliff, we met some young man from among our new acquaintances who found himself at leisure and therefore free to escort us back to Xanadu. On the morning following my uneasy night, however, it was Mr. Pocock, the coal merchant from whom we have purchased our coal since before Papa died, who fell in step beside me. Sunny walked on with the lieutenant who had "just happened" to be strolling on the Cliff as we climbed the West Street gap, chaperoned quite adequately by Charlotte and Irene. I stayed for a moment to talk to Mr. Pocock.

He was waxing enthusiastic about an esplanade, from Cannon Place near the West Battery to Preston Street, and wanted to tell me every detail of his plan. "Now it's true that the West Cliff's not developing as fast as the East Cliff," he said. "But we've got West Lodge and Cliff House and there are plenty of lodging houses out here in the west end of town. How's it sound to you, Miss Lia? A fine esplanade overlooking the sea, with benches for people to rest on?"

"I think it's a wonderful idea," I said, setting Georgie on his feet. He's a lightly made child, not as heavy as Irene, for all he's older, but my arms had grown weary and I was relieved to put him down. And unlike Irene, he was not constantly pulling on my hand, or desiring me to look at something, or trying to run off. Mr. Pocock and I chatted a while longer about Brighton's future, and then I hoisted Georgie up again and set out slowly toward Xanadu. As I lifted him up, he twined his arms around my neck, planted a wet kiss just above my collar and then snuggled into my shoulder and fell asleep. At that moment I didn't mind at all that he was my little half brother. Like Sunny, I was becoming so attached to the children that I almost didn't care who their father had been, even if it should prove to have been my own. I hugged him more tightly, remembering that somewhere there was a Miss Goodman who had a claim on him, too, and who had told Mrs. Clendenning that she would someday return for him and for Charlotte.

But I had had an idea: Why not build? The meeting with Mr. Pocock seemed almost to be an answer to a prayer, although I admit I'd done no praying on the subject of our flagging fortunes. Nonetheless, it did seem that it was fortuitous I'd met Mr. Pocock the very morning after several futile hours considering the subject of money. Others were beginning to build crescents and squares along West Cliff, even as far away as Bedford House, almost at the extreme end of the parish. We had the land; if I could find a partner with the capital . . . It would mean sacrificing Xanadu, which would break our hearts, but recouping a fortune is no doubt worth a little heart-break.

The minute I reached home and had given the babies their chocolate, I plopped sleepy little Georgie into his bed (the water always sends him to sleep), then shut myself in the bookroom to write to Mr. Price. I'd ask him to do just this one last thing. I was in the middle of that task, chewing on my pencil as I pondered how best to present my case to Mr. Price, when Angela came to me, asking for Mrs. Oliphant's basket. "What basket?" I asked vaguely, my mind on the glorious possibilities I foresaw as we restored our fortunes from the collection of ground rents.

"The basket you asked me to bring to you in the Aerie." Angela giggled. "To put Papa's papers in. You remember, the day the ships were passing?"

"Oh, yes," I said with a distracted frown. "It's over there in the corner. Then would you see if Ben is home, please? Maybe he'll go to the post office for me."

I wrote on. The day had turned grey and cloudy as we were returning home from bathing, and rain had now begun to fall. The bookroom is small, but almost the entire eastern side of the room is a large, rounded bow window, looking out on our walled garden, so it's bright for reading and working, especially in the morning, and makes one feel that the room is larger than it is. Doors on each side of the bow window open onto a narrow veranda that follows the curve of the bow. At one end a short flight of steps give onto the terrace and at the other end a longer flight leads down into the garden and the gate opening onto the Shoreham Road. I stepped out on the veranda to watch the rain from its shelter and, after a moment, sat down on the curved bench that also follows the bow of the windows. I love rainy days, particularly after so many days of sunshine, and I had just fallen into a pleasant daydream of riches when Angela opened the door behind me.

"I'm sorry, Lia," she said in a small, apologetic voice. "I forgot all about finding Ben. Are you mad at me?"

"No, dear child, not at all. I'd forgotten all about it myself."

Angela went to the veranda railing and put her hand out into the rain. "When I remembered, I went to look for him. He went away somewhere. Mama didn't remember where."

"Where's Charlotte?" I asked.

"Oh, she's in the kitchen helping Mrs. Oliphant. She likes to work in the kitchen. Like Sunny does. But I hate it." She wiped her hand on her skirt and then, still not looking at me, she ran a finger along the veranda railing.

I reached out and pulled her down beside me and put my arm around her.

She rested her head against my shoulder. "Am I bad?" she asked.

"No, of course not. I don't like the kitchen, either, and neither does Mama. But Mama sews beautifully and makes pretty clothes for us all. And you sew beautifully, too. And you can write wonderful stories, too! I very much admired your story about the little girl stolen by gypsies, and I think I may admire even more the one about the Indian princess."

"What do you like to do, Lia?" Angela asked, moving away from me to look into my face.

I thought for a moment. "I like taking care of you all," I said, hugging her against my shoulder again.

I hope my readers have not taken me too seriously if in past pages I have seemed to complain too much of my lot. I don't really like being poor, but I do like being the head of the family and making decisions. Sometimes Sunny, when she opposes one of those decisions, particularly one that goes against her wishes, shouts at me and tells me I'm a despot, but I don't mind. Sunny likes to exaggerate.

I decided right then that I would mail my letter to Mr. Price myself. "Want to go with me to the post office?" I asked Angela. She sat up brightly, "Oh, yes. But will Mama let us go out in the rain?"

"I think so, if we ask her nicely."

Sunny discovered us putting on our oiled slickers and our pattens, and decided she, too, would love a walk in the rain.

And then Angela thought Charlotte might want to go, too, and maybe even Chunk. But Chunk can always find something to do on a rainy day with his archeological collections and natural history notebooks, so half an hour later, only four of us set off for the new post office in Prince's Place.

Brighton's streets and lanes are laid with brick, but they have become terribly uneven and thus on rainy days are quickly spotted with puddles. Our shoes were soon wet, despite our pattens, and in a moment of complete abandon (perhaps I was buoyed by my morning's optimism about our future as landlords), I permitted the entire party, including myself, to forget about wet shoes and just slop through puddles. Only Charlotte tried to step around them, but even she had capitulated to the sheer joy of such imprudent heedlessness by the time we reached Black Lion Street. We were just crossing Brighton Place, in a state of high hilarity, merry as grigs, when out of the Druid's Head Inn stepped Lord Dayne and Mr. Chaffinch.

"Ah, the Maudsley girls!" Dayne exclaimed. "What brings you out in such force in this dirty weather?"

"But it does bring a sparkle to their eyes and roses to their cheeks," Chaffinch said, smiling down at Angela and Charlotte before turning his admiring gaze on Sunny's countenance and mine. Mr. Chaffinch has the most amazing ability to make the most fatuous statements, but we all laughed and giggled like veritable cockleheads, which led him to add that it seemed to have put us in merry good humor as well.

The two gentlemen accompanied us to the post office, and then invited us to take some refreshment at the Old Ship coffee room, which overlooks the ocean—grey and turbulent, with whitecaps frothing the surface—and where we encountered two of our new acquaintances from the scarlet coat contingent. It was patently not much to our hosts' liking, but they were constrained to be polite, while making it clear that they and they alone were escorting the Maudsley girls and needed no assistance.

The upshot was that they walked to Xanadu with us, and as we battled the wind, now setting in strongly from seaward, it seemed only one more excuse for exuberant hilarity. We entered through the garden gate in order to shed our wet gear on the veranda, but the gentlemen would come no farther, professing themselves too wet and disheveled to make a polite appearance before our mama. However, they sent regards; and then I found myself recklessly inviting them to dinner, although in truth, I had no idea what our scant larder could provide that would be adequate for a company meal. But we had made no effort to suggest that we were other than of limited means, and I could be certain that even though the meal would be simple, we could at least expect it to be carefully prepared and well served. Papa was most particular about his food, with a very elegant taste. Except for our long since departed French cook, only Mrs. Oliphant had ever received his unstinting approbation. And Mama, of course, could preside like a queen over a bowl of porridge.

Chapter Nine

After dinner—which did Mrs. Oliphant proud, as I anticipated it would—we retired to the front parlor, which at Xanadu serves as drawing room.

The first object that caught our guests' eye was Papa's telescope, which we had assembled in the rectangular bow window facing the sea.

"What's this?" Chaffinch asked, striding over to the windows. "A telescope, by God!"

Lord Dayne crossed the room and ran his hand over the lustrous wood. "What a beautiful instrument! Your father's?"

"Yes," I answered as I joined them. "Papa liked to watch the ships in the roads and the fishing fleet going to sea in the evening."

Ben, coming up beside us, said, "Papa liked to study the stars, too. He used to give money to the Herschels—you know, the ones who've put up the large telescope near Windsor." He, too, touched the instrument admiringly before looking up again at our guests. "Have you ever visited the Herschels and seen their telescope? It's grand!"

"No," Mr. Chaffinch said. "I've seen it from the Bath Road but never visited it."

"I have." Lord Dayne was now bent over, examining the telescope more closely. "A sailor must know well the constellations and stars. Some of us develop a more serious interest."

Jane had already closed the curtains, although it was not yet quite dark. "There's still some daylight," I said. "Perhaps we can see the fishing fleet going out. . . ." I drew the heavy curtain back. Immediately, the room was flooded with rosy light.

We all exclaimed, "What a beautiful sunset!" Mama said,

rising to come to stand beside us.

It was not a sunset of the kind that usually brings forth exclamations of delight, but rather the sky was suffused with a red overcast that turned the whole world to rose, tinting the ocean and the square sails of the fishing boats, and even our faces as we stood at the windows admiring the scene.

"Red sky at night, sailors' delight; Red sky at morning, sailors take warning," Lord Dayne recited. "If the old saying is true—and I've observed that it often is—we'll have clear weather tomorrow."

No one spoke as we watched the sky quickly fade from rose into grey dusk. Only a ghost of red, now sparked with gold, lingered along the horizon.

"Close the curtains, dear," Mama instructed me as she returned to her seat. She picked up her needlepoint, apologizing prettily to the gentlemen for continuing with her work.

"The making of such an elegant and beautiful piece can only be the height of elegance itself," Dayne said with a flourish almost equal to Chaffinch's best efforts.

"Sir Whitney," Mama pronounced as she put her needle to the piece, "had a truly lofty mind. So singular! Chunk will follow in his footsteps, I believe. He had such an admiration for men of science—Sir Whitney, that is."

"The beauty of his telescope would tell one that." Mr. Chaffinch, who was still standing by the windows, gave the instrument one last caress. "Was this where he used to watch the ships, Lady Maudsley?"

"Oh, no. In his Aerie."

"That's what Papa called our attic rooms," I explained. "He had his desk there, and the telescope, and that's where he retired when he'd had enough of the numerous progeny."

"How naughty of you, Aurelia. Your papa took great delight in your games."

"I'm sure he did, Lady Maudsley, but I suspect that papas—and perhaps mamas, too?—need their Aeries," Lord Dayne said, "unless the children are constantly confined to their nurseries, which has never seemed to me the happiest of circumstances. At least it did not seem so to my brothers and me."

This statement led Mama into a discussion of our dear papa's childrearing notions, which were theoretically based on the educational principles of Rousseau, to which Lord Dayne and Mr. Chaffinch attended most earnestly, while the rest of us quietly fidgeted.

Sunny had brought out the anagrams, a game we had found to be generally entertaining on previous occasions when an odd number of people of various ages were to be accommodated, as it only required that the players know how to spell. As soon as Mama had finished her eulogy of our dear papa, we seated ourselves around the table to play until tea was served.

Ben or I were the winners in the several games we played, and even Sunny outdistanced Mr. Chaffinch and Lord Dayne. In fact, our superiority was so marked that we were embarrassed, although the gentlemen took it in good part. Chaffinch commented, as Sunny gathered up the letters, "Well, Brev, we've clearly been brought to a stand. It looks like the championship must be fought between Ben and Miss Maudsley, for I acknowledge myself fairly beaten."

"I acknowledge the amazing skill of the entire family," Lord Dayne said. "Perhaps next time we should play with Chunk and the little girls, and leave their elders to each other. I suspect that with only a little more practice, Miss Sunny might challenge Ben and her older sister to effect."

Sunny gave Dayne a brilliant smile, but refrained from preening herself, or simpering, or some other gauche characteristic of the barely seventeen. "I was only thirteen when Papa died," she explained, "and so I hadn't done as much ciphering as Ben and Lia."

"Yes," I added reflectively, "I suppose ciphering does account for our skill at anagrams. I hadn't thought of that."

Dayne looked perplexed. "Doing sums assists one to spell? Although I can hardly credit it—if it's indeed true—then I own that I should return to my schoolbooks, for I've always been a poor speller."

"But what is so amusing in that?" Chaffinch asked, as we all laughed—even Mama—at Dayne's remark. "Although I admit English is an abominable language, I should think Brev deserves censure rather than such disguised praise as you're according him with your laughter."

"Oh, no, it's not that we think it admirable Lord Dayne is a poor speller," I hastily assured him, "although you're most certainly correct in describing English as an abominable language, at least the orthography. But we laughed because by ciphering, we don't mean the doing of mathematical sums. We mean ciphering like—like codes. Although, of course, strictly speaking, ciphers aren't the same as codes, you know."

Both gentlemen stared. No other word for it. They were simply thunderstruck.

Lord Dayne was the first to recover his countenance. "Of course! How dull-witted of me! Of course Miss Sunny would have learned her sums before the age of thirteen."

Chaffinch, after a startled blink or two, rallied with, "I remember playing with ciphers when I was a boy. Friend of mine and I used to pass notes in the most simple cipher: Each letter of the alphabet was assigned a number, and we thought ourselves very clever because we began numbering with the letter *X*, rather than with *A*. But we lost interest rather soon, as I imagine most youngsters do, when they discover they've no mysteries or secrets to conceal."

"Well, Papa had secrets," Ben said. "He informed us of gifts in notes written in cipher, and if we didn't decipher them, we didn't get the gift!"

"Papa loved puzzles," I added. "Devising ciphers and deciphering are like puzzles. In fact . . ."

A knock at the door was quickly followed by Jane, wearing an expression of great distress and wanting me to "come upstairs for a minute." She thought Irene seemed feverish. Jane takes wonderful care of our infants but she's a worrying sort, and although I found Irene fretful, I didn't think her feverish. I could feel a sharp point of a tooth coming through, which always puts her in a fret. I instructed Jane to rub her gums with the preparation the apothecary had given us for a previous teething episode, then to give her a dram of poppy syrup and her teething coral and, if she still fretted, to rock her until she fell asleep. Mrs. Oliphant doesn't approve of indulging Irene and Georgie by rocking them so much, but I don't think it does any harm.

Mrs. Oliphant was just bringing the tea things when I returned to the parlor, and in the bustle of making and serving the tea, I forgot to mention to Dayne and Chaffinch that Ben had devised one of our favorite ciphers when he was twelve, and that we called it Ben's Cipher in his honor. It was not the most difficult of the ciphers Papa used in his notes to us, but it had a simplicity that he liked. Poor Papa! Always searching for simplicity. It made me remember that I hadn't sorted Papa's papers yet, and I reminded myself to ask Angela where they were. I really did need to get that task out of the way. I'd been so engrossed in my letter to Mr. Price that morning—and my dreams of a future Maudsley (or Xanadu) Crescent—that I hadn't been paying much attention to anything else, and so I'd forgotten to take the papers from the basket before Angela returned it to Mrs. Oliphant.

Mr. Chaffinch and Ben drew each other aside to discuss their favorite topic after the tea was served, and Dayne came to sit beside me, while Mama worked on a beautiful needlepoint tapestry and Sunny played softly on her French guitar.

"I was just asking your mother, Miss Maudsley, if she would permit you to accompany me to the banquet at the Pavilion on Midsummer Night and to the ball at the Castle Inn afterward. . . ."

It was beyond my capacity to appear other than simply delighted by the invitation. "I—I believe Lady Sarah has already spoken to Mama. It would give me great pleasure, and I thank you, my lord."

"Yes, your Mama told me she had already given her consent to Aunt Sarah. I look forward to the pleasure of your company, as does my aunt."

"Will I be able to see the Chinese decorations?" I asked, just like an eager child invited to her first grown-up party but not really caring.

"I'll make certain that you do. And there are to be fireworks, I understand. Although I don't imagine that fireworks will be so wonderful to you after you see the Chinese decorations."

"Oh, but I love fireworks."

"You know," he said, "so do I."

Mrs. Oliphant interrupted this interesting conversation to inform us that a Mr. Richard Thurlby, apologizing for the lateness of the hour, begged leave to present his compliments. Now what, I wondered, could bring the squire back to Brighton so soon?

Mama greeted him graciously, her hand extended to be elegantly bowed over. "How delightful to have you in Brighton again!" she exclaimed. "I have remembered with such pleasure our afternoon ride in your landau, and so have the children." (Sunny, who had refused to join the landau party, had later reported to me that "the children" had included Charlotte, Mama's "dear little stepdaughter," as well as Angela, her "own dear daughter.") Mama gently withdrew her hand, which Mr. Thurlby seemed inclined to retain. "You have met Lord Dayne," she stated, and after the acknowledgment by both gentlemen that it was indeed true, she introduced Mr. Chaffinch. "And what brings you to us again so soon?" Mama asked.

"Another matter of military necessity, my dear Lady Maudsley, which I confess I do not find unduly taxing, for it provides the excuse to see you and your charming family once again. You are very much missed, you know, in our modest society at home."

Sunny rolled her eyes at me, behind the squire's back, and lifted a corner of her lip in a way that was most assuredly vulgar, but that also exactly expressed my own reaction to the squire's brand of poppy syrup. I replied by casting my own eyes upward, and then, catching Lord Dayne's amused glance, turned away quickly in order not to giggle like a sixteen-year-old fledgling.

Before the gentlemen took their leave, Ben and I received an invitation from Dayne to ride on the Downs, perhaps to Lord Pelham's estate on the Lewes Road, which is noted for its fine park. "That is," Dayne added, "if the old verse is correct, that a red sky at night foretells good weather."

"Oh, I say," Ben declared, "I'd like to ride with you and with Lia, but I've just agreed to spar with Chaff tomorrow. He's rented a room, you see, for sparring. . . ."

"Another day will do," Chaffinch said quickly. "In fact, I look for you often, Ben, and without a formal invitation. It's not a Gentleman Jackson's parlor or a Fives Court, but I'll make it available even when I'm called to London, as I frequently am.

I'm sure you'll be able to get practice aplenty with the other young gentlemen interested in the art of self-defense."

But Ben wasn't interested in sparring with other young gentlemen; he wanted to spar with Mr. Chaffinch, that notable patron of the ring. Lord Dayne, no doubt divining as much, stepped in to say, "No need for you to break your engagement, Ben. I'm sure young Edgar at the stables will be happy to accompany us again."

Richard Thurlby, Esq., meanwhile, was arranging to call on Mama the following day, as soon as he could be free of his military duties.

Dayne

Richard Thurlby, noting that neither Mr. Stuart Chaffinch nor Baron Breverton Dayne had called for a conveyance, and having seen no sign of horses or grooms, inquired politely, as he stood beside his landau taking his leave of them, "May I carry you gentlemen anywhere? Be most happy to do so."

"No thank you," Dayne replied. "I have made it my policy never to ride when I can walk."

Chaffinch thought Dayne's answer unduly brusque, and added, with a friendly smile, "I can highly recommend it, sir. Although in the beginning I'd not have said so, I find it's an amazingly invigorating activity."

"Very well." Mr. Thurlby hesitated a moment. "I—I have some business tomorrow morning pertaining to the militia, but I'd like to call on you if I may in the afternoon, if it would be convenient. You're in North Street, I believe?"

"I've engaged to ride with Miss Maudsley tomorrow," Dayne said, "and I believe Chaff also has an engagement. Perhaps . . ."

Mr. Thurlby's lips compressed slightly. "Perhaps I should say that this will not be a social call?"

Both men stared at him before Chaffinch recovered sufficiently to say, "We're both free in the evening, if that would be convenient for you."

"Lady Maudsley has kindly asked me to dine," Mr. Thurlby

said, not without a certain satisfaction. "May I suggest the following morning?" The Chaffinch fellow was amiable enough, he thought, but Dayne—who, after all, was only a baron because his older brother had been a disgraceful rakehell and been murdered because of it—was a little too high and mighty to be entirely pleasing. He also was discovered too frequently in the lap of the Maudsley family, which would require that he deliver a serious warning to Lady Maudsley. Mr. Thurlby never did anything by halves and never shirked a duty. Some time past he had taken Lady Maudsley and her family under his wing (although not necessarily with their permission) and it was incumbent on him to see that no harm came to any of them. He would not have any ramshackle lord playing fast and loose with one of Lady Maudsley's daughters. . . . Even if certain people in high places did think well of Dayne, he personally had a very indifferent opinion of him.

Both Chaffinch and Dayne were agreeable to Mr. Thurlby's suggestion, and they watched him drive away with amazement. "Now what is that all about?" Chaffinch wondered.

"Just about the last person one would expect to have business with us. Well, if I was astonished when I thought he wanted to make a social call, I'm even more so now!"

They strode rapidly along toward their lodgings. Noting his friend's nearly even stride, Chaffinch remarked, "I'd never have believed it, Brev, but I think you've done it."

"Done what?"

"You're hardly limping at all. But I wouldn't want you recovering too soon, or we'll no longer have an excuse to skulk around Brighton."

"So it's more vapor baths at Mohammed's, is it? I was hoping I could hang my stick up soon, among the other canes and crutches, spine-stretchers and head-strainers shed by the sufferers who preceded me."

Chaffinch laughed. Lady Sarah Pellett had, by her customary methods of determined persistence, persuaded Dayne to try Mohammed's vapor bath treatment, for which the Indian claimed cures for everything from gout to dropsy, as well as an improvement in general health. Dayne in turn had lured Chaffinch into accompanying him to the baths, where he had been wrapped in canvas, stewed in a steam bath that bore the scents of strange-smelling herbs, and then thumped and rubbed to a jelly by disembodied hands inserted through holes in his wrappings. The two friends had staggered from the establishment, feeling as weak as two starved kittens, and had made all possible haste to the nearest taproom, where they recruited their strength over several glasses of strong ale.

The thought of strong ale and the near proximity of the George Inn suggested to Chaffinch that a glass of ale would not be unwelcome. There they encountered some of their officer acquaintances who were getting up a game of hazard in their quarters, and the rest of the evening and a good portion of the night was whiled away with the dice. It was therefore not until their breakfast the following morning that they found an opportunity to discuss the revelations of the evening before.

"This business of the ciphers is the first real break we've had," Chaffinch remarked as he lifted the cover from a steaming dish of bacon and eggs. "May be just what we're after. Here, help yourself first, Brev. Know how you hate a well-cooked egg."

Lord Dayne scooped two eggs off the tray, the yolks quivering in what Chaffinch considered a most disgusting display, and added a modest quantity of bacon. Chaffinch replaced the cover, to allow his own eggs to steam for a few minutes more. He helped himself to a bowl of oatmeal porridge, one of his Scots habits that Dayne considered abominable. "Well, now," he said, adding sugar and cream to his porridge, "what do you make of this cipher business?"

"A long shot."

"We can't afford to pass it up, nonetheless. Lady Maudsley did say that she thought there might have been some papers in cipher that somebody found after Sir Whitney died. . . ."

"I thought you said she thought Miss Maudsley threw them away."

"She wasn't certain, and I saw no way to persist in my questioning. It's our last chance for the papers—if Sir Whitney did indeed write it all down. One thing we do know: He could lie convincingly. So, now we're certain there was nothing in Price's office. . . ."

"Disappointing. One does like one's crimes to pay."

Chaffinch laughed. "You're a little too nice, Brev. At least for burgling. Well, if we'd missed anything among the papers in Price's office, the Foreign Office cryptography fellows would have found it. They're good men. No incriminating messages masquerading as receipts for works of art."

"But certainly revealing how his family came to their present pass."

"Yes. And the burglary did turn up something, don't forget. We now know at least some of Sir Whitney's sources of income. We know the French paid him for his services, and the Foreign Office can begin to look into those sources. However, to return to the issue at hand, you and I are on the trail of a piece of paper or a manuscript, and—like it or not—it's time for a burglary of the Maudsley villa."

"Why don't we just ask to see any papers in cipher?" Dayne asked. "Much simpler." He reflected a moment. "Interesting that Lia Maudsley was so knowledgeable. Only one woman in a thousand would be able to distinguish the difference between code and cipher—and not many more men, either, I'd wager. Could she help us? If there actually are important papers in cipher, she could more quickly decipher them than the clerks at the Foreign Office. She knows the cipher Sir Whitney used."

"She knows the one he used with his children. But beside the point at the moment. What's important to decide is, do we want the family to know what we've been about? The Foreign Office doesn't want them brought into it. . . . That has to be considered."

Although the exact reasons were not entirely clear in his mind, Dayne was reluctant that the Maudsley family—and especially Miss Maudsley—know what they were after in Brighton. "Well, I've said before that this hole-in-the-corner business isn't to my liking. Nonetheless, since no ciphered papers turned up in Price's office, I suppose it's breaking and entering here." He sipped his coffee thoughtfully. "Could Sir Whitney's note to the Foreign Office have contained a hidden message?"

"No. Our cryptographers say not. The note said only that he had important information of a confidential nature regarding his employer and asked the foreign minister to call on him at his house in London. We know that a French spy ring was paying Sir Whitney, so we presume that the 'employer' referred to was the head of the ring. And since Grenville, as foreign minister at the time, was his 'employer' on our side, he would hardly be referring to him." Chaffinch scooped the last of his porridge from his bowl, swallowing it with evident relish. He set his dish aside and applied his napkin to his lips. "Actually, what strikes me as the most curious feature was the notation in the margin of the note that a copy was made for the Admiralty, especially since you were unable to turn it up in your search. . . ."

"Well," Dayne said, "it either wasn't delivered, or it's been lost in the mountains of paper they have over there. I suppose if the Foreign Office could misplace Sir Whitney's original memorandum for three years, the Navy could do equally as well."

Chaffinch helped himself to four eggs, the yolks of which no longer quivered, and a quantity of bacon. "Unless it was destroyed. The 'most secret' files usually are."

Dayne, of a more lean and sinewy physical structure than his large, heavily muscled friend, watched in fascination as Chaffinch began his generous second course. He reached for an orange and began to peel it. The sharp scent of citrus filled the room. "You know," he said reflectively, "I'm beginning to wonder if we shouldn't perhaps look for a spy in the Admiralty. . . ."

"What? A traitor in the Admiralty! Come now, Brev, you're not serious!"

"Never more so. The Admiralty has a better record keeping system than the Foreign Office. I went through reams of paper there last week, in both likely and unlikely places, and discovered nothing. I admit that the copy of Sir Whitney's memorandum might have been destroyed. It's also possible that I could have missed it, that it may have been filed so incorrectly it'll never be found, but that in itself is suspicious. But what bothers me is that as far as anyone knows, no one at the Admiralty ever consulted the Foreign Office about it."

"Not so strange. Sir Whitney died before the day appointed, so the note became a dead letter. And it was just before the Battle of Copenhagen, if you'll recall, and Boney was already proposing peace; Pitt's ministry was all at sixes and sevens over it. . . . I'm not making any case for efficiency at the Foreign Office, you understand. Or at the Admiralty, either. Quite the contrary. Only saying that in the turmoil and rush of events, with peace a likely prospect, Sir Whitney's note may not have seemed so important. Or they may have even thought it was all a product of his fertile imagination. And it was unlikely, in the ordinary way, that he'd ever have come face to face with anyone more important than his recruiter and probably go-between. Not likely to be someone important, although possible. My money is still on his supposed mistress, Miss Goodman."

"Did the Foreign Office know about Miss Goodman, if she was in fact his contact? The Admiralty didn't know anything; they just made up an occasional false document and sent it off to 'Lord Bagley' at the Foreign Office to be passed on to the French. And there's still the possibility his contact was right here in Brighton."

"Never heard of a Miss Goodman at the Foreign Office." Chaffinch set aside his plate and helped himself to some herring and a piece of buttered toast. "By the by, are we going to tell the Maudsley family what we've learned about Charlotte and what we suspect about little Georgie?"

"If Price was also snooping around, he's probably discovered the truth by now. Or at least as much as we know. And how are we to tell them without revealing our own hand?"

"True enough. Pour me some of that coffee, will you, Brev?" He suddenly looked around. "I say, where's Tilt this morning?"

Dayne poured the coffee, added more to his own cup, and passed the cream and sugar to his friend. He preferred his own coffee without adulteration. "Out on an errand. I told him we could serve ourselves."

Chaffinch, slowly stirring his coffee, let his gaze wander to the window and the blue sky visible above the rooftops on the opposite side of the street. "Well." He put his spoon down with a decisive clink. "It's time for the burglary. Price's offices posed no problem. But the Maudsley villa is another matter. We should propose some kind of excursion . . . get them all out of the house."

"Do you realize that 'all of them' includes two infants, a

housemaid, a housekeeper? . . ."

"Well, if you put your mind to it, I'm sure you'll think of something. Isn't your talent for tactical maneuver one of the reasons that you're known as one of His Majesty's most daring and resourceful frigate captains?"

Dayne ignored the gentle jesting. "You're certain Lady Maudsley said that she thought they still have some of Sir Whitney's papers?"

"Yes. Perhaps you didn't hear, for I believe Mrs. Oliphant was just bringing in the tea things and there was a bit of a bustle. It was while Miss Maudsley was out of the room in answer to some distress call or other."

"Oh, yes, teething, she said. . . ." Dayne set down his empty coffee cup and stood up. "Speaking of Miss Maudsley, I have an engagement to ride with that young lady, and if I remember, you have an engagement with her brother."

"Yes, but not until I've digested some of my breakfast. We're meeting at eleven. I'll stroll over to one of the libraries in the meantime and take a look at the newspapers. And after my sparring engagement with Ben, I'll look in on Henny. See how our housebreaking expert is doing. Shame he never turned his crafty brain to a more conventional profession."

At the door to his room, Lord Dayne turned. "And tomorrow Mr. Thurlby, with his mysterious business . . . Very curious."

"Espionage and counterespionage require patience, my friend. Put it all out of your mind and enjoy your day with Miss Maudsley. However, you should use the opportunity to suggest an excursion. . . ."

"By God, Chaff, do you ever think of anything else but your work?"

"Not often. Do you think of much else than your work when in command of your ship?

"Not often."

"Well, there you are. I'd suggest Sunday. The sooner the better. We don't want evidence going up the chimney before we get to it."

"One more reason why—reluctantly—I think we should tell the family . . ."

"Well, let me think about it. Now go on . . . But a Sunday excursion nonetheless. Agreed?"

"I suppose. Roarke Staffen's offered his yacht anytime I want it. . . ."

Chaffinch groaned, and Dayne smiled. Served the fellow right.

Lia

Lord Dayne paid his respects to Mama before we set off for our gallop on the Downs, for he and Mr. Chaffinch had got it into their heads that we should all go sailing. Lord Dayne claimed that he and Mr. Chaffinch had enjoyed our hospitality so many times, without reciprocating, and had had the marvelous idea over their breakfasts for an all-day excursion on the sea, for all our family.

"Friend of mine, Roarke Staffen, Colonel in the Tenth Royal Hussars . . . uh . . . perhaps you've met?"

"No, I don't think so."

"He was fond of society, before he joined the Hussars. Still is, for that matter. I thought perhaps you might have met. . . ."

"No," I said. "Or if so, it was too long ago and too brief a meeting to be memorable." One thing I did know about this Colonel Staffen, however, was that he was probably rich. The Tenth Hussars was the prince's own regiment, and it was filled with sprigs of nobility and fortune. They brought with them, to their military assignments, their blood horses, their smart curricles, and their bits of muslin to entertain their leisure hours.

"In any event," Dayne was saying, "Staffen's brought his yacht around to Brighton. Ran into him last night, and he asked if I'd like to get up a party. . . ."

"And you thought of us!" Mama exclaimed. "How terribly considerate! Dear Whitney was always so devoted to the sea. It was a sorrowful day when our yacht was sold . . . but he did feel that it was too dangerous for children."

"I'm sure Sir Whitney had his reasons, ma'am, but I can't think that a boat would be so dangerous on a calm day—especially for *your* children, who swim so well. I wouldn't be surprised if even little Irene could manage, should she fall overboard, for Miss Maudsley tells me that she's swimming as though the sea were her natural element." He smiled at me. "In China, they say, whole families live on boats, just as some of our canal boatmen in England, and the babies are as accustomed to living on water as the adults. We'll put the infants on tethers, just as the Chinese and the canal families do."

"The infants?" I asked.

"Why, yes. As I said, we're proposing a family excursion. The fresh air will be good for Irene and little Georgie."

"In that case, we'd have to take Jane."

"Of course. And Mrs. Oliphant, too."

Mama protested that, indeed, we couldn't think of putting the colonel to so much trouble. . . . Babies and children everywhere underfoot, and widows in their mature years, when he would surely much rather be entertaining just the young people . . . Was Colonel Staffen's mother perhaps one of the Gloucestershire Roarkes? She'd been acquainted with a gentleman of that name before she was married. . . .

Dayne didn't know if the colonel's Christian name had been his mother's maiden name, but he good-naturedly spent some time aiding Mama in her attempt to trace, through cousins and marriages, some possible connection. She finally determined that only a conversation with Colonel Staffen himself could help her answer the questions of ancestry and birth she was posing.

"You'll have ample opportunity Sunday," Dayne told her, "for we're planning to leave in the morning and return with the sunset."

"Sunday?" I asked.

"When you and I, Miss Maudsley, are recovered from the festivities at the Pavilion and the Castle."

Mama's eyebrows were ever so slightly raised. "We attend church on Sunday."

"Oh, I assure you, Lady Maudsley, so do Chaff and I. Often. We were thinking that following the services?"

Mama had insisted, as soon as we were settled in Brighton, that we again purchase a pew in the Dissenters' church in

Meeting House Lane, and no arguments about our struggling circumstances availed. Papa and Mama had not taken to evangelical religion during what people were calling The Great Revival, but they had abandoned the Church of England for the Independents, or the Congregationals, as they were sometimes called. It was thought shocking among some of their friends, but Papa was never one to care about such things, nor was Mama, for that matter, and I suspect they rather enjoyed kicking over the Established Church.

Dayne thought that an afternoon would make a nice excursion, but Mama said she wouldn't think of accepting an invitation and then insisting on a change of time . . . that we could miss church just this once. . . .

Dayne expressed himself delighted, saying that we were not to worry about anything . . . that he and Mr. Chaffinch would make all the arrangements and provide the lunch. . . .

Mama and I demurred enough to be polite, but Dayne simply overbore us and carried us away with his enthusiasm. I couldn't help a niggling and annoying suspicion—although I couldn't say why or what exactly I was suspicious of. Lightheaded young officers might propose such an affair, but not Lord Dayne and Mr. Chaffinch. Later that day, when I mentioned these vague suspicions to Mama, she just laughed. "Really, Lia, you've forgotten how to be young!" Clearly Mama hadn't, for she was as excited at the prospect of a pleasure cruise as any of us.

In any event, the coming Sunday was agreed upon, and Dayne and I could depart for a gallop on the Downs, for the seafarer's verse had proved accurate and the day was fine.

We rode to Signal Hill, so-called for the great semaphore by which messages were relayed from Dover to Portsmouth and Plymouth. The hill had once been a Roman fortification and was difficult of access, with deep entrenchments on two sides and a steep slope up from the sea, but the magnificent view made the climb worthwhile. We lingered there for over an hour, enjoying landscape and seascape, while Dayne explained to me the system of signaling by semaphore, on land and at sea.

As they had been for days, the local people were collecting

furze for bonfires and setting barrels filled with tar on the hilltops in preparation for Midsummer Eve, when the sun reaches its northern zenith and the fairies dance on the Downs. Bonfires, the antiquarians say, are a part of our Midsummer celebrations because of the ancient pagan superstition that such fires imitated the sun and were, in some mysterious way, an assurance that it would return again after the long dark nights toward which, after midsummer, the year declines. But the pagans are gone, and the fires are now only an aspect of the general revelry, which hasn't an ounce of concern about the sun in it. Now we think of love and lovers on Midsummer Eve, because the Christians who conquered the early pagans discovered that the sun reached its northern zenith close to St. John's birthday, and so, since St. John is the patron saint of lovers, Midsummer Eve became a day for lovers.

There had been talk about preventing Midsummer Eve bonfires, because they might be mistaken for an announcement of invasion, putting the whole south coast in arms, but it hadn't come to anything. Everyone in England knows about Midsummer Eve fires. And as Lord Dayne had observed, invaders from across the Channel would need a calm sea and a moon, the latter of which they would not enjoy on Midsummer Eve. Unless it was true that Bonaparte's engineers had invented flying machines wafted by balloons and hot air, we were safe. "And Miss Maudsley puts no stock in such foolishness, do you, Miss Maudsley?" Dayne asked, smiling at me.

I had reached the point where Lord Dayne's very utterance of my name could cause a flutter somewhere in the vicinity of my heart. I would say to myself that I must not be taken in by a man who was only in Brighton to regain his health and vigor, and who—with his amiable friend—came to us so frequently only because Brighton was so thin of other company. But I couldn't accuse them of any other questionable motives than those, and it would be unfair to say that they didn't enjoy their visits. I believed that they had become truly attached to our infants and to the children. They were a good influence on Ben and even on Sunny, who by their presence was improving her company manners and acquiring some polish. It was their influence on me, and most specifically Baron Breverton Dayne's influence on me, that was at the root of my distress.

For distressed I was. Despite all my resolutions, despite all my responsibilities, and despite the disproportion in our fortunes and prospects, I was in love with the man. Hopelessly. Well, perhaps not hopelessly. I am not the sort who dies or fades away of heartbreak, but it would require a most determined effort not to sink for a time into melancholy when he went away.

After we parted at the door of Xanadu, at the end of the long afternoon, I determined that once the prince's banquet and the young duke's coming-of-age ball were over, I would refuse to ever be alone with the man again, for it was when we were alone that I was in the greatest danger. It was when we were alone that he made love to me, as he had all that day on the Downs. He hadn't kissed me, but there are many ways of making love to a lady. He hadn't even touched me, except to toss me into the saddle (which isn't very romantic, as the reader knows) and to help me dismount. And that, I admit, can be a little more romantic.

His hands were around my waist, my own hands on his shoulders, and there we stood, unable to part, while young Edgar, our (mostly theoretical) chaperon, hastily turned away to gaze at the sky and whistle some nonchalant tune.

Although I may have been only one of Dayne's flirts, I'd known since Lady Sarah's ball that he wanted me; and—may all the duennas and pattern cards of propriety in the world forgive me—I wanted him. If it hadn't been for Edgar . . . Or for that despicable animal, Toad . . . My spirited horse was not one to nonchalantly whistle and look the other way while his temporary mistress stood by his side being made love to. He began to impatiently sidle and prance about, until Lord Dayne released me, with a low laugh that told me a good deal about his emotional state. "I believe the animal's jealous!" he said as he casually stepped away from me. I turned to Toad, and while my heart slowed and my breath returned and my wobbly knees solidified, I gave the odious beast my undivided attention.

Chapter Ten

It was the morning of Midsummer Eve, and Lord Dayne and Mr. Chaffinch awaited the appointed arrival of Richard Thurlby. The peace of the morning was sullied by the bumping of barrels being rolled down North Street toward the Level, where they would be filled with tar. Vendors cried their wares, and the noise of vehicles of several sorts bouncing along the uneven roadway added to the hubbub. Dayne sat at a writing desk in the corner, composing an overdue letter to his mother, while Chaffinch read a book, one leg leisurely crossed over the other. Both were oblivious to the noise from the street, but when the knock came that announced their visitor, they both looked up eagerly.

Richard Thurlby, Esq., not appearing at all as though he were anticipating any pleasure from the coming interview, entered the room and bowed punctiliously. "Lord Dayne. Mr. Chaffinch."

"Won't you sit down, sir?" Chaffinch asked. "Shall I ring for some coffee? Or perhaps you'd prefer tea?"

"Thank you, nothing." Mr. Thurlby seated himself but did not relax in his chair. His feet planted firmly on the floor, he kept his walking stick upright between his neatly clad legs, with his two hands resting on the silver knob. "I will not be long in conveying the information I have been asked to bring you," he stated dryly.

Both Dayne and Chaffinch put on polite waiting expressions, only slightly edged with curiosity.

"I have been asked by a gentleman in the Admiralty, who had

apparently contacted another gentleman, a military gentleman who has been rather well-known to me for some time, to furnish you with a name."

All alert interest now, but his face impassive, Chaffinch repeated, "A name, sir?"

"Yes. A name. I understand that you have made some attempts—inept, I might add—to contact certain seagoing people here in Brighton. Your efforts have not been looked upon with favor."

"You mean the smugglers, I presume?" Dayne asked, irritated by Mr. Thurlby's manner.

"I would not so lightly use that word, my lord."

Dayne was surprised by the response. "No?" he asked curiously.

"No. Smuggling is an illegal activity, punishable by death. You are seeking, I understand, the names of seagoing persons who might in the past, and who may be engaged presently, in contacts with France."

Chaffinch held up his hand. "Before we proceed further, sir, may I have some indication of your . . . uh . . . position?"

"Of course. I have a letter from the Foreign Minister. And another from the Secretary of the Admiralty, Mr. Napean." Mr. Thurlby presented the two letters, permitting both Chaffinch and Dayne time to glance through their contents, before stating that he was also aware that they were investigating the case of a "certain note," delivered to the Foreign Office in the year 1801.

Chaffinch assented that such was true, and he urged their visitor to proceed.

"You will understand," Mr. Thurlby stated, "that the nature of a certain intercourse between the coast of England and the coast of France is of a highly confidential nature, and that only the influence of a certain well-known gentleman in the Foreign Office has persuaded certain other people to arrange an interview for you."

Chaffinch shifted irritably in his chair. "I am very surprised, sir, that an accredited servant of His Majesty's government, engaged in a secret investigation, should be denied any information that would lead to the discovery he hopes to make."

"The correspondence between England and certain people in France is of such importance that it must be guarded with great care. Nor was it clear, I believe, in just what way your investigation would benefit by contact with the . . . with . . . uh . . . certain people. I myself do not know the gentleman whose name I will give you, but if you ask for him of the captain of the fishing boat *Mermaid,* he will arrange for a meeting."

Chaffinch, exasperated by the repeated references to a "certain this," and "certain that," asked coldly, "Am I permitted to wonder what your own role may be?"

"I'm sorry, you may not." Mr. Thurlby hesitated. He had an interest in the investigation of Sir Whitney Maudsley's affairs, aside from the role he performed as a patriotic duty. However, that interest was personal, and he had learned discretion, from long years of association with a certain clandestine and wholly illegal activity. . . . However, his *opinion* of the whole business, he felt, on consideration, might be aired freely. "I will, however, take the liberty to say," he pronounced in his measured tones, "that I would not like to see the Maudsley family grieved for any reason. I was not acquainted with Sir Whitney Maudsley, but his family are close acquaintances and I feel a certain responsibility. . . ."

Chaffinch, who by an effort of will kept his fingers quiet rather than tapping irritably on his chair arm, replied, "I can assure you, sir, and Dayne will confirm it, that we have been most delicate in our relationship with the Maudsleys. However . . ." He was about to make a statement to the effect that one way to learn the habits of a dead man was to speak with his family, particularly a family as talkative and open as the Maudsleys, but Dayne forestalled him.

"As Chaffinch says, we have been most discreet in our relationship with the Maudsleys. We do not wish them to be in any danger, and as for Sir Whitney's activities, should it be necessary that they learn of his activities, they will have reason only for pride."

Mr. Thurlby appeared mollified but not entirely satisfied with this reassurance—he hadn't much to say for either of the young men, whatever their reputations in intelligence and counterespionage circles—but he took his leave of them with a politely correct farewell after pronouncing, in a low voice, the name of the man for whom they were to inquire from the captain of the *Mermaid*.

The two friends waited several minutes without speaking, until they heard the street door close behind Mr. Thurlby. Then Dayne went to their own door and cautiously opened it. The stairs were empty, and the door was tightly closed on the apartment across the landing. "Gone," he said as he quietly closed the door again.

"Damn Hawkesville! Most incompetent foreign minister we've had since—since—I can't think of anyone more incompetent," Chaffinch fumed through clenched teeth. "The whole Foreign Office is a bunch of interfering dullards! Who are they to decide what information I need in my investigation? Hawkesville's so insouciant that even were a spy to walk up to him and declare himself, he'd fumble it!"

"Calm yourself, my friend. Emotion is no part of the espionage business; I've heard you say so—many times."

Chaffinch stomped to the window, where he stood with his back to Dayne, breathing deeply. "I'm trying," he muttered, "but I just caught sight of Thurlby rounding the corner, and I'm getting into a state again."

"If it's any help, in the Navy we also put up with chains of command and decisions made too far from the fighting to be realistic. My sympathies."

Chaffinch returned to his chair, sitting down so emphatically that, sturdy as the chair was, it resulted in a loud crack.

"Well, looks like that chair's just become Thurlby's victim," Dayne observed.

With a growl, Chaffinch ejected himself from the chair, sitting down more circumspectly on the one that Mr. Thurlby had recently vacated. Then, catching Dayne's grin, he said, "Oh, be off with you. Try Mohammed's Vapor Baths again. A good stewing is what you deserve."

"Better for you . . . You'll emerge too weak for bad humor."

Chaffinch laughed. "Well, I suppose I'd better go make my confession to our estimable landlady and discover what my fit of pique has cost me."

"And I suppose I'd better be wandering down to the beach.

As the naval person, I presume that I'm the one to whisper the sacred name. I'll just poke around a bit today, like I have before, spot the *Mermaid,* and consider how to strike up a conversation with her master or how to find him. Although now I think about it, I resent the implication that my previous attempts have been inept."

"Fine. And then?"

"Then I'll drop by Aunt Sarah Pellett's to arrange for tomorrow night at the Pavilion. And you?"

"Some paperwork to finish up. I'm leaving with Ben early tomorrow morning to take in the Tom Belcher fight with Jack Warr. By the way, your man Tilt clearly wants to go. Any objections?"

"None whatsoever. He can do some errands for me."

"Want us to lay a little wager on Belcher?"

"I'll give you a few pounds to lay for me as you judge." Dayne picked up his hat and stick, but at the door turned to ask, "Will you be calling on the Maudsleys with me this afternoon?"

"Might as well. I need to make a few final arrangements with young Ben. Also a few final arrangements with Henny for the burglary of the Maudsley house on Sunday, but that can be taken care of in short order."

Lord Dayne strolled leisurely among the fishing boats pulled up on the beach. A few fishermen who were still working at their cleaning or repairing chores greeted him as he passed. He stopped occasionally to discuss some technical detail of boats or sea or sailing, or even of fishing, for in the two months he had been in Brighton he had often talked with the fishermen and on one occasion had gone out for a night with the fleet. He'd learned nothing for his efforts that would aid Chaff's investigations and nothing about smuggling, but a good deal about fish and fishing.

He found the *Mermaid* close under the East Street Cliff, and by good luck her master was still working about her. After a decent preliminary interval – during which he learned that the *Mermaid* was a newly built vessel of only a year's service, that the master was the nephew of one of the older Brighton fishermen, and that he had served for ten years in the Royal Navy before his release and the acquisition of his boat—Dayne mentioned the name he had been given by Mr. Richard Thurlby.

The *Mermaid's* master looked up sharply. "Well, and who might you be, sir, that you're seeking to know him?"

Dayne suddenly realized that Mr. Richard Thurlby had failed to provide them with any means of identifying themselves, to either smugglers or fishermen, as trustworthy agents of the intelligence service, and reflected that the service was perhaps a bit untidy in its operations. He hesitated. "I believe that the person who was asked to give us his name by the Admiralty felt that the very fact we knew the name would be sufficient." He paused again. "I believe I may also reveal to you that I and my colleague are intelligence officers, although you will understand that it must not be known."

"I know who you are. I was in one of Riou's frigates at Copenhagen also."

Dayne exclaimed in pleased surprise, and a lengthy veterans' discussion of that splendid sea battle followed, at the end of which the master of the fishing boat *Mermaid* and the former captain of the frigate *Eleanor* were well on their way to becoming friends. After an hour, Dayne rose. "I've an appointment with my aunt, I'm afraid, and must be on my way."

"Will you be going back to sea, Captain?" asked the *Mermaid's* master as he also rose.

"As sure as I'm standing here."

"Well, good luck to you, sir. I'll be letting you know when and where the gentleman will see you. How shall I contact you?"

"I'll come again in two days. I often come down to talk to the fishermen."

"Yes, I've seen you. Speak well of you." A sudden smile lit the man's dark features. "Not above yourself, they say."

"I value the compliment," Dayne said sincerely as they shook hands.

As he climbed the low, crumbly cliff that would give him access to the Stein, his thoughts turned—most unprofessionally—from ships and battles, from spies and counterintelligence, to Lia Maudsley, a golden afternoon on the Downs, and the prospect of seeing her again.

* * *

Lia

We were all in the garden except Ben that afternoon of Midsummer Eve and the day after the long afternoon on the Downs with Lord Dayne, when I'd at last admitted myself to be hopelessly in love.

Charlotte and Angela had cut some branches from the tamarisks to hang over our door with a bunch of daisies, as the old country Midsummer Eve custom required. I permitted them to buy a small quantity of lead to melt, in order to divine their future by the shape that a drop of it assumed when plunged in a molten state into cold water. According to Charlotte, this particular divination was only undertaken with any success on Midsummer Eve.

Lord Dayne and Mr. Chaffinch came to call on us that afternoon. Such was their intimacy with our family that, while the rest of us continued with our own tasks or amusements, they played on the floor with Irene and Georgie. Then they began tossing the infants up in the air in the way men will do. The babies loved it, of course. As soon as they were set back on their feet, they were pulling at the gentlemen's trousers and demanding, in their incomprehensible languages, to be taken up and tossed some more. Irene drooled, requiring that she be wiped up regularly, and I had some fears that Georgie might express his excitement in a more disastrous way, but he seemed to have become too much a man for such an infantile weakness. It would soon be time to promote him to pantaloons.

As the infants showed signs of getting into an overexcited state, Sunny and I brought out some rugs and the dining room chairs, and constructed a pen for them by laying the chairs on their sides, a device that up to the moment, at least, had been successful. Neither Irene nor Georgie had yet shown any inclination to escape this makeshift confinement, as long as it followed a good romp.

To lure them away from the enchanting tosses, I fetched some of their most favorite toys and scattered them about the pen. Then what should Georgie do, at sight of his favorite toy, but escape *into* the pen by pushing one of the chairs aside! And then the little rascal, his toy grasped firmly in his chubby little hand, actually puffed out his chest and swaggered around inside, casting coy looks at all of us that clearly told us we should consider him a very intelligent boy. I scooped him up for a session of kisses, which he disdained, preferring to continue his strutting.

Irene, meanwhile, was telling her very special friend, Lord Dayne, all about it (so it could be assumed), but when he put her down in the pen, she immediately set up a frightful fuss, holding up her arms to him and jiggling up and down, demanding to be picked up again. He remonstrated that playtime was finished and that it was now pen time, but she would have none of it. And then, evidently frustrated beyond endurance, she began to cry and, with tears streaming down her face, uttered her first word in English. "Up!" Dayne, laughing heartily, swung her up in his arms for a hug, and we all clustered round the two with congratulations and exclamations of our favor. But congratulations were not what Irene wanted. She wanted—and she actually *said* it—she wanted *down*. So Dayne set her on her feet, and she toddled over to the pen and entered it through the breach that Georgie had made. Then she turned to us with a satisfied smile and tried to push it shut.

Georgie, who is one of the most tranquil of children, was by this time asleep in one corner, where Irene joined him. When her efforts to wake him failed, she settled by his side with her toys and within another several minutes was asleep herself. It had been a most outstanding day for the infants. Sunny found a shawl to throw over them and we left them there asleep, our two little cherubs.

Mama and I returned to our sewing, and Sunny picked up her guitar. Angela and Charlotte and Chunk had been playing bilbocatch, which had evidently stirred in the breasts of the two gentlemen memories of their youth, for they now turned to this new diversion. After an expert performance by Chaffinch, Chunk bore him away to look at a new Roman coin he had discovered on the Downs, and Dayne took possession of the cup and ball to demonstrate for the two little girls his own exceptional skill.

Angela shyly confided, as Dayne returned the cup and ball to her, "We're going to melt some lead tonight, and it will tell us about our future, Charlotte says."

"Are you really? And what do you want to know about your future?"

"Oh, will I live in a castle or in a cottage. . . . Or whether the man I'm to marry will be tall or fat."

"And can it tell you if there is some special person, some special boy, who loves you?"

Angela smiled at his naivete. "We do that with daisies. Or you can do it with other flowers, too. You pull the petals off. We all tried it with the daisies. There are so many of them, you see."

"So many boys?"

Angela laughed. "No, *daisies.* That's why we all tried it."

"All of you?"

"Yes, Charlotte and I, and Sunny and Lia."

"And how is this done? Do you think it would work for me?"

Angela looked inquiringly at Charlotte, the acknowledged expert in such things, who gave the question a moment of thought. Then she said, consideringly, "I think it would."

"Do you want to try it?" Angela asked eagerly. "We still have lots of daisies."

So Lord Dayne and the two little girls went into the garden to gather daisies. "What do I do?" he asked as he sat down again with his handful of flowers.

"Well, *we* say, first, 'He loves me, he loves me not.' But you must say 'she' instead of 'he.' And then, if she loves you, you take another flower and you say, 'A little, a lot, passionately, not at all.' And then, if you want to find out when you'll marry, you take another flower and say, 'This year, next year, sometime, never.' "

"And the last part with the daisies? Is it necessary that she love me before I do the last part?"

"Oh, no. That part just tells you when you'll marry," Charlotte explained.

"And you don't even have to *think* about anyone for the first parts," Angela added, "because maybe someone loves you secretly, you see. Someone you don't even know about! Don't even *suspect.*"

Dayne laid the flowers out on his knee. "Very well. Now, let me see." He examined them and selected one. "Now, it's 'she loves me, she loves me not,' right?" He looked up at the girls. "What if she doesn't love me? I think I would be terribly unhappy."

The girls looked at each other. Both knew it was a game but they didn't want to spoil it, and Dayne, seeing their dilemma, hastily added, "Well, one must be brave." He diligently plucked the petals, making a great show of it, to arrive at the gratifying discovery that "she" loved him.

"Well," he sighed. "That is a relief. Now I must find out how she loves me." He took a deep breath, as if preparing himself for a trial by fire. "She loves me a little," he said as he plucked the first petal. "Now what's next?"

"She loves me a lot, she loves me passionately, she loves me not at all," Angela instructed.

He appeared to ponder, a frown puckering his brow. "But, you know, I've discovered that she loves me, so why should I add that last? The part about she loves me not at all."

The two girls looked at each other again. It had clearly never occurred to them that there was an inconsistency in their game.

"No," he said before they could reply, "it won't be useful to include that part at all." He began to pluck more petals, intoning 'a little, a lot, passionately,' until he reached the last petal with 'passionately.' "

"I'm even more relieved," he said. "Now that I know the lady's sentiments, I will henceforth be more bold."

"You didn't pull any petal for 'a lot,' " Charlotte said. Charlotte was sometimes too sharp-eyed for polite society.

Lord Dayne looked shocked. "I didn't? You mean that she only loves me a lot? Not passionately? You mean I have not yet won her heart completely?" He smote his forehead.

The girls giggled.

"Well," he said, "one must be philosophical. Tell me, what did the daisies tell you girls? And your sisters?"

"They said Sunny will marry sometime, and Lia next year."

"Hmmmm . . . very interesting."

The girls continued cataloging the results, but the game had been played several hours before and other things had taxed their minds since, so they were soon confusedly arguing about the outcome. Lord Dayne looked across at me for the first time since the game began, but I bent my head over my sewing to avoid his eyes. "Well, Miss Maudsley, the girls seem to be confused. How did he love you?"

"Not at all," I said promptly, without raising my eyes.

"No," Charlotte said. "That's not right. He loved you *passionately.* Yes, he did, 'cause I didn't know what *passionately* meant and you told me."

"And what did she tell you *passionately* means?" he asked.

I felt him still observing me and determinedly kept my eyes on my sewing. I desperately hoped that although I felt very hot, it did not mean I was blushing.

"She said that it means more than a lot—a lot, a lot, a lot," Angela told him, spinning around to more adequately demonstrate excess.

"Well, she's more lucky than I," he sighed. "*She* only loves me a lot, but *he* loves Miss Maudsley passionately."

Charlotte, bound to confession, said, "It was me, the one that he doesn't love at all."

Lord Dayne smiled at her. "Well, more fool he. There'll be another boy. In fact, I'd say there will be many another. But the important one will be a strong young man, I think, who prefers salt to sugar. Yes, I'm sure he'll prefer salt."

Charlotte looked perplexed, but Dayne gave her no chance to question him. He ran his hand over Angela's hair. "And your young man?" He looked at her speculatively. "What do you think, Chaff?" he asked as his friend walked back onto the terrace trailed by Chunk. "What sort of young man will be the important one for our *chiquita* Angelita?"

Chaffinch rubbed his chin. "He'll be a studious young man but not too studious, because he will also like walking and Mr. Wordsworth's poems."

"And he'll like strawberries better than apples," Lord Dayne added.

"Oh, indeed so."

Chunk, who by virtue of being a boy was required to be uninterested in romance, said, "Hey, Angela, you want to go down to the beach?" Then he added, as though in afterthought, "You can come, too, Charlotte, if you want to."

"Oh, let's do, Charlotte!" Angela exclaimed enthusiastically. "We can look for some more pretty pebbles."

"We'll have to change our clothes," said practical Charlotte.

Neither girl was fooled by the nature of Chunk's invitation. They knew that Chunk secretly thought Charlotte as good a companion as Angela—perhaps better.

I looked up from the towel I was hemming. Even though Mama is our needlewoman, the others of us had to do our share of the routine mending and sewing. A large household requires such a lot of stitching to maintain! I'd often thought how wonderful it would be to have a machine that could sew, like the new ones that weave cloth. I might even enjoy the task then. "Remember that Charlotte doesn't yet know how to swim well," I admonished. "As Lord Dayne has pointed out, the sea's rough today."

There were places along the beach between Belle Vue and Hove—beyond the wharf and the public bathing areas—where our family swam and where we were unmolested by the bathing machine attendants, who took an unfavorable view of those who dispensed with their services and bathed directly from the sands. But only those of us who knew how to swim well, and never one of us alone. There were also places where it was not safe for a beginner like Charlotte to even be wading at the edge of the water. Chunk was a strong swimmer, but should Charlotte panic . . . I was reminded of my own struggle in the water with Dayne, who had found it necessary to give me a douse in the chops before he could rescue me. The image of Dayne unclothed flashed across my brain, the way a picture will flash across the vision as one leafs rapidly through the pages of a book. And then I looked up and his eyes were on me, and I knew he was remembering, too.

I looked away quickly. "Do you understand, Charlotte?"

Charlotte was an accomplished and competent ten-year-old, and her quick and skillful hands had already lightened chores for all of us. As the reader will understand, we could not maintain such a large household with the services of only one maid and a housekeeper. Each of us, except for Mama and, of course, the two infants, had our daily tasks to perform. But to return to Charlotte, she had a somewhat exaggerated view of her own competence, which had already once or twice led her into difficulty.

The three youngsters assured me that they wouldn't even *touch* the water, then they departed, already arguing about just which particular part of the beach they would visit.

Sunny had been quietly picking at her guitar, trying to master the latest popular song. She put it down as the children left. "It would be fun to go out tonight. We could dance around the bonfires. . . ."

Mama looked up from her needlepoint. "Such festivals are for the common people, not for us."

"I don't see why. We went with Papa when we were little. We even made our own bonfire once. I remember."

"So do I," I said. "It was one of the most exciting nights I can ever remember."

"Can't we go, Mama? It's not like we were just people for whom Brighton is a health resort. It's almost our home. And it truly was Papa's. We know the local people, lots of them, and they know us. Do say we can go! They wouldn't let anything happen to us. And Ben and Dandy Rogers will go with us, I know they will, because we talked about it this morning."

Chaffinch spoke up. "Don't really see any harm in it, Lady Maudsley, if Brev and I accompany them. And Ben, of course. How about it, Brev? You game?"

"Always game. Can't think of anything I'd rather do. It's been years since I leaped through the flames on Midsummer Eve."

Dayne

Lord Dayne excused himself from his friend, found a towel, and took himself down to the beach for a solitary swim. The sun was just below the horizon, and a dusky afterlight lingered on the water and over the town. The bathing machines had all been pulled up on the beach, the horses led away for their evening feed, and the bathing men and women gone to their homes. The fishing fleet was out. Beyond the bobbing yachts, disappearing from sight, their sails could be faintly seen. When it was full dark, he disrobed. By arrangement with Mr. Scruggs, he left his clothes and towel at the firecage. He waded out until the water reached his waist, then dove through an incoming wave and began to swim.

He was a strong swimmer, but he set himself a leisurely pace—westward until he reached the lights that marked Belle Vue, and then eastward as far as the firecage at the foot of West Street, now filled with a bright-burning fire. When he felt himself tiring, he rolled over on his back and floated for the space of a few minutes, then resumed his rhythmic stroke and kick. And all the while, as his muscles automatically carried him westward and then eastward and then back again, his mind was occupied with Miss Lia Maudsley and what he was forced to recognize was his own passion.

How had he progressed from that day three weeks ago when in the shelter of an old barn he had held her dispassionately in his arms while she wept on his shoulder, to that single minute when it had required every effort of self-control to prevent himself from kissing her under the very nose of the young groom who was acting as her chaperon? . . . From kissing her and carrying her off to some secluded grove, if truth were admitted? Would she have gone with him? She would certainly have wanted to; he had felt her tremble under his hands. But she would have resisted. . . . She had a family to look after, and she would have remembered in time the consequences of throwing bonnets over windmills. Although, in that family, they would no doubt close ranks behind her and defiantly tell the world that the little fatherless child was "a dear little grandchild" or "sweet little niece (nephew)."

She wasn't as pretty as her younger sister, and her figure, although neat enough, couldn't compare with some of the incomparables with whom he'd dallied in his past. He'd always thought that beauty and pulchritude were his weaknesses. . . . When had he gone to the villa to see her rather than to pursue his assignment? After she confessed she had read and enjoyed Caesar's *Conquest of Gaul* . . . even if it was translated? What had drawn him to her? Courage, for one thing. The courage to admit her poverty. Her determination. Her independence. And how fiercely she cared for her family.

He realized, with surprise, that he loved them, too. His own family, except for Lady Sarah Pellett, had been . . . barren. His father had been a cool, distant patriarch—pleasant to his children, firm in his discipline, but preferring that they be kept out of his sight. And after he died, Algernon going to ruin, Walter becoming a small, humorless version of his father, and his mother forever languishing on a sofa with a headache. He couldn't make excuses for himself; he hadn't been any help to Algernon, or to his mother, or to Walter. He had been at sea since he was fifteen, and when ashore he'd been more interested in revelries with his friends and, as he grew older, in dissipation. The very last thing he'd wanted was to spend time with his family.

That first morning in the Maudsley breakfast parlor, when he'd taken little Irene on his lap and seen the surprise, and then something like admiration in Lia's eyes . . . He'd fallen in love with the family, so unlike his own, that very morning, he believed. Was it her family and not Lia herself? And then he remembered his hands around her slim waist, and that he'd hardly had a thought since except of returning to her; that even while he'd conducted his business with the master of the *Mermaid*, the thought of her and the anxiety to be with her again had been there, lying in wait. He admitted that he was in love.

What to do about it was another matter. He began the last lap of his swim, which would bring him back to the firecage and the foot of West Street. He was going back to sea and to battle. Could he ask any woman to marry him under those circumstances? Should Algernon be alive somewhere—which despite all that was rational he still hoped for—he would once again be simply a second son, with a very substantial income but far from rich. For himself it didn't matter; it was what he'd always expected, and the Navy was his career, but for a wife? . . . For Lia, who deserved all the pleasures she'd been so long denied, and with a family to provide for . . . as his Aunt Sarah had so often pointed out to him?

He absentmindedly greeted Mr. Scruggs as he retrieved his clothing and pondered his own rash, ill-considered, and uncharacteristic conduct. He'd made love to her this very afternoon, in front of the whole family, with all that nonsense about "she loves me, she loves me not," and had quite openly declared himself while teasing her to respond. She hadn't; she'd avoided his eyes and refused to play his game. But she'd trembled under his hands. Or had she trembled in fright? But Lia, afraid? No. Still, he wasn't a green boy. He knew full well that a woman could yearn for love without being in love with the man who offered it.

He walked slowly up West Street toward his lodgings. "A bit of a vinegar," Chaff had called her. Was she holding him off because she didn't love him—for surely she must at least suspect that he loved her—or was it that he hadn't won her yet? Or was it because she thought she couldn't leave her family? Was he moving too fast? He'd only known her for a little over two months. But he'd been enough in the world to feel confident that he'd not fallen prey to an infatuation; she wasn't the sort of woman men became infatuated with. There was nothing of the coquette about her. But she could flirt well enough. He remembered his displeasure over that activity at his aunt's ball. . . . Flirting with every man in the place, except himself. Did that mean she loved him, or that she didn't like him at all? But had she had sufficient experience to know in such a short time her own heart? Was she holding him off in order to be sure of her own feelings for him? Should he declare himself—that is, if he should decide it would be right to marry her—or should he allow more time for courtship?

He brought his thoughts up short. He couldn't believe that he was pondering such juvenile questions.

And then he fell into a lover's reverie, which carried him at last to his own door without remembering one step that had brought him there.

Chapter Eleven

Perhaps because it was Midsummer Eve, when fairies dance in sylvan glens, Adam and Star chose to sally out from the Beyond to visit Mama.. When Dayne and Chaffinch departed that afternoon, Mama went to her room to rest. Her eyes were tired, and of course it was no wonder! She devoted almost every minute to her fancy work and, since Dayne's invitation to the Pavilion, to finishing a new ball gown for me. In two days she had only laid it aside when the gentlemen came to call, for she thought it inappropriate to be working on the gown that Dayne would later admire when I presented myself to his discerning eye. She furthermore still refused to wear eyeglasses when she was sewing; although she insisted that eyeglasses would only weaken her eyes more, we all knew it was vanity.

In any event, she went to lie down, with a handkerchief soaked in rosewater across her eyes, and while she was lying quietly thus, Adam and Star came to her. It wasn't the first time since we had been in Brighton that they had visited Mama, which was certainly as it should be, considering that it was at their urging we were in Brighton, and that they had claimed to be capable of enjoying the seashore themselves, even in their otherworldly state. On this visit to Mama, rather than chatting about ordinary things as they usually did, they told her she should not permit me to go upon the Downs. No strictures on Sunny and Ben, or Charlotte and Angela and Chunk, only on me! And no explanations. Not only did I have to promise that I wouldn't go on the Downs that night, but Dayne and Chaffinch and Ben all had to make the same promise. And when Ben's friend Dandy Rogers joined us, just as we were preparing to leave, he had to promise, too.

So we went about the town, where bonfires were burning and tar barrels blazing in the open spaces, the flames on the Stein sometimes reaching higher than the roofs of the houses. Wandering by a slow progress toward Race Hill, where the largest bonfires of all were constructed, all of us agreed the hill was so close to Brighton—not more than two miles from the center of town—that it couldn't be properly considered the Downs but more a part of the town itself. As Sunny had predicted, we met many of the local people who knew us, people we saw often in our marketing and shopping and the regular conduct of our everyday affairs. We drifted with much hilarity and camaraderie, toward the hill and the bonfires with a crowd of these local people, some of them carrying torches, our arms linked and our voices raised in popular songs.

We met others from the visiting gentry who were known to one or another of the gentlemen, but we chose to stay with our local friends, even though "young gentlemen of distinction" might refer to them—as one of the young coxcombs did describe them in an aside to Ben—as the "vulgar spawn of trading quizzes." I have never liked that attitude toward honest and respectable people who, lacking large estates or invested wealth, must make a living for themselves and their families as best they can. I liked it even less after my own family found itself reduced in circumstances, especially now that I was considering how to increase our income as a crescent builder, and failing that by opening a shop or starting a school, or some other activity that would endanger what little rank I still could claim as a gently born sister of an impoverished young baronet.

The bonfire on Race Hill was in fact two bonfires built close together, to make it easier for the young and daring of the male sex to leap through the flames. Our wine merchant's son broke the circle of dancers weaving hand in hand around the fires, to admit us to the revelry. Every now and then one of the dancers broke off to perform a leap through the flames, to the clapping and cheers and encouragement of the rest. This usually inspired other young men to dare the flames, and finally our own party, led by Ben and Dandy Rogers, and followed first by Chaffinch and then by Dayne, also flung themselves through the blaze. I longed to cry out for Dayne to stop, that his leg was still too weak; but men must prove themselves men, just as boys must prove themselves boys, and Dayne, as he'd told me the day before on the Downs, must prove himself capable of returning to a command. He cleared the flames as handily as the others, and Sunny and I welcomed all four back to the circle as heroes.

It was by then nearly midnight, and we began to meet revelers who had been partaking of too many libations to Bacchus, as Papa used to say, which meant that it was time for gently bred females to be in their homes. The gentlemen treated those of the local people who returned with us to ale and wine at the King and Queen Inn on the Lewes road, where we separated, our party to return to Xanadu and hot rum punch, and they to continue the frolicking or not, as parents and guardians, or their own circumspection, permitted.

Not one untoward incident occurred. No one showed us the least disrespect, which Mama had feared; and I encountered nothing threatening or remarkable that might account for Adam and Star's warning. I concluded that it was just one of those tricks that Mama was not above using to achieve her goals, which in this case was that we not wander farther afield than she considered safe or appropriate. My mind was too full of Lord Dayne to give even a passing thought to the man with the strange eyes whom I discovered more than once watching me from a distance—from across the circle around the bonfire, from a box at the King and Queen, and once on the Stein as we paused to speak to some acquaintances.

Ben was up early the next morning to meet Chaffinch at

his lodgings, whence they would set out for London. The Belcher-Warr fight (unless the constables got wind of it) would take place at Tothill Fields that afternoon. As I understood Ben's enthusiastic description of the outing, they planned to stay that night in town at the Dayne townhouse, but not before downing a few at Limmers Hotel or perhaps at the Jolly Brewer, both boozing kens patronized by the Fancy. The latter establishment is owned by Jem Belcher, the former boxing champion of England, who as my readers surely know retired from the ring after the loss of an eye playing racquetball. Chaffinch and Ben were hoping that his younger brother Tom would show the makings of becoming as great a boxer as Jem in the coming set-to. I'd managed to provide Ben with enough money to defray his expenses, with which he had to be content, for even though he assured me, with the greatest sincerity, that Belcher was a sure thing, the funds for laying bets were beyond our power.

The kittens came later that same morning. The reader will recall that Charlotte insisted on a nightly ration of milk for the house brownies, which was gratefully consumed each night by a poor, thin female cat whom Mrs. Oliphant believed to be the mother of kittens. Sunny and I were in the breakfast parlor with Charlotte and Angela and the infants, taking our cup of chocolate after our morning bathe. I happened to look up from tying Irene's bib more securely, just in time to see the cat trotting across the terrace with one of her babies in her mouth. She was out of my sight before I reached the open French doors, but it was clear that wherever her kittens had been, they were now somewhere in the territory of Xanadu.

Angela wanted to immediately go hunting for them, but Sunny counseled caution. "She may be afraid, if we come upon her suddenly, and then she'll move the kittens again. Let's leave her today to get settled nicely, and tomorrow we'll hunt for them."

I seconded Sunny. Neither of us gave a thought to shooing the cat away. "Later, you can put down some scraps, and then you can sit very quietly beside the bowl to see if she'll come out. If she won't, then we'll do the same thing tomorrow, and then the next day, until she feels more at home. She may not have any experience with people, you know."

Mrs. Oliphant, who had just brought in some hot buttered toast, said, "Well, if it isn't just like I said! If Miss Charlotte *would* put milk out, we could be sure we'd soon have all the cats in the kingdom on our doorstep."

"Only one, Mrs. Oliphant, with her kittens." I smiled at Charlotte.

"And how many kittens do you suppose she has?" Mrs. Oliphant demanded. "I've known a mother cat to have as many as ten. . . ."

"She surely couldn't have fed ten," I soothed her. "Not as thin as she is."

"Probably no more than three at the most," Sunny volunteered, also smiling at Charlotte.

Charlotte had not yet lost all her shy deference, or what I guessed was a fear that we might send her away, which sometimes made her seem wistful and pathetic; but she wasn't made of bread pudding, either. Her chin came up, as it always did when on her mettle, and she said, "The house brownies sent her to catch mice."

"Mice!" Mrs. Oliphant all but screamed. "There are no mice in my kitchen!"

"No, I know there aren't, Mrs. Oliphant," Charlotte agreed in a small, tentative voice. "But maybe some are trying to come in from the fields, and the house brownies know it."

"Well, I never!" Mrs. Oliphant said, her hands on her hips as she stared at Charlotte. "You'll have your house brownies, and nobody's ever going to tell you different, are they?"

"Mam always put out milk for them," Charlotte said, retreating to the bosom of higher authority.

Georgie brought the discussion to an end by beginning to wail. He loved me almost as much as he did Jane, but he was attached by a firmer bond to Charlotte, and he caught her moods and fears in a way that was simply uncanny.

I hurried to pick him up, which set Irene to yelling, "Up,

up, up, up, up!" so that Sunny had to bestir herself to appease her baby sister by handing her a piece of toast.

Mrs. Oliphant, who was truly fond of Charlotte, her most willing kitchen helper, said, "There, now, child. Lady Maudsley has permitted us to feed the cat, knowing full well that she'd more than like move her kittens here, and if you want to say you're giving the milk to the brownies, or it was the brownies that brought her here, I am not going to say more. So tell Georgie to be quiet and eat his toast." She surveyed the table. "You'd best all help yourselves, or it'll be cold before you know it. And that's fresh butter today, too."

Mama came in just then, still in her wrapper and with her hair rather untidily tucked up under her cap. She looked nearsighted, harassed, tired, and cranky. "Aurelia, I need a piece of ribbon to finish your ball dress for tonight. I must have made a mistake when I measured. . . . If you could run right away to Mrs. Yewdall's shop in Great East Street. I need another yard . . . or perhaps you'd better bring me two yards." She dropped some silver on the table in front of me. "Fortunately, I found these in the bottom of my notions box yesterday. . . ." She sat down with a sigh. "Is that chocolate? I believe I'll have some. And buttered toast, too? How wonderful! Will you bring me a cup, Mrs. Oliphant, please?"

"Well, I should think you *would* like some chocolate and toast! No breakfast, and staying up 'til all hours!"

"Oh, Mama," I said, "have you been staying up late again? The gown you started for me in Lewes would have done."

"Indeed it would not! So I want to hear no more about it . . . from *anyone,*" she said, giving Mrs. Oliphant an exceedingly severe stare. "And as far as you're concerned, Aurelia, I want you to buy the ribbon for me, and I don't want any advice. Sunny, you go with her. Jane will have to undertake some of your chores when she finishes with the babies. What time did Ben leave?"

Every now and then Mama gets into one of her commanding moods, when she sweeps everything before her. She was obviously in one of those moods now, so Sunny and I, after hurriedly drinking our chocolate and finishing our toast, smoothed our hair and tidied ourselves for our errand. We found Mama back in her dressing room, still in her wrapper, with my dress over her knees. She looked up when we entered, but only handed us a small piece of blue ribbon and said, "Two yards," then returned to her work. However, as we turned to leave, she looked up again. "And, Aurelia, I want you to rest today. You were out too late last night and had too little sleep, and your eyes haven't their wonted luster. When you return, we'll try the dress again, and then you are to wash your hair and Sunny will prepare an oatmeal pack for your face. You will lie perfectly quiet for two hours this afternoon, with a soothing lotion on your eyes. Mrs. Oliphant will prepare it for you. She has a very effective remedy for tired eyes."

I was a trifle annoyed with Mama. I would not under ordinary circumstances use an oatmeal pack, nor would I rest, but I certainly intended to bathe and wash my hair, and I didn't like being told that I should do so, as though I were ten years old. No matter. Mama concluded by telling me that I would bathe before lying down to rest, and that I would purchase a perfumed soap at a notions shop near Mrs. Yewdall's exclusive dressmaking establishment in Great East Street and a face cream to follow the oatmeal pack.

So Sunny and I, like good girls, set off. We purchased the soap and face cream, then proceeded to Mrs. Yewdall's. On showing the piece of ribbon, the very smart young woman who attended the shop said, "Oh, miss, I'm sorry, but there isn't an inch of it left!"

Sunny and I looked at each other in dismay. We hadn't thought to ask Mama what we should do in such an event.

"May I show you something else? We have a wide selection of ribbon. . . . Perhaps we can find something of a slightly different shade. Is the dress blue as well, Miss Maudsley? Different shades of one color are very fashionable. . . ."

I was fussing over the ribbon samples, at a complete loss what to do and contemplating a walk back to Xanadu for instructions, when Sunny said, "Doesn't Mrs. Yewdall have a second shop? I thought Mama said that she was opening a shop in St. James Street. Would she have some of this ribbon there? Or perhaps Mrs. Yewdall herself could advise us. Is she at the other shop?"

I wondered if crossing a line between sixteen and seventeen could mark such a great leap in maturity and good sense. While I dithered, Sunny had been thinking.

The very elegant young salesperson exclaimed, "But, yes. Mrs. Yewdall would be able to advise you. I believe she helped Lady Maudsley plan your ball gown, Miss Maudsley, although they neither of them expected that it would so soon be needed. The prince came down yesterday, you know."

"Yes," I said, more irritated by the moment. "We heard the bells ringing and presumed they were for the prince's arrival, not a victory over Bonaparte." Who was this person, who knew so much of our private affairs and who could make such simply stupid observations?

Sunny slipped her arm through mine. "We'll just walk over to St. James Street and see Mrs. Yewdall. But if she can't help us, I do think that the slightly darker blue would do very well. And thank you for your help. Come on, Lia."

So I came on as requested and was led out into the street, then into Stein Lane, fuming. When everyone else gets bossy, I get irritated.

To reach St. James Street and the row of fashionable shops that now served the houses along the Marine Drive to the east of Brighton, we had to promenade around the Stein. And who should we encounter but Lord Dayne, with Lady Sarah Pellett leaning on his arm. Both had their sticks in their free hands, of which they both were making some use, and all in all it struck me as a very funny sight. I did not, of course, laugh. I also felt somewhat like a bride—that I shouldn't be seen by my escort of the evening, any more than a bride should be seen by the groom before she comes down the aisle in all her finery.

Although I'd drawn my braids up on top of my head and neatly tucked in the wet ends, I hadn't bothered to take them out, dry my hair, and rebraid it, so my crowning glory looked slightly frowsy from my early morning dip in the sea.

My dress had even less to recommend it, for while clean, it was old and of the cheapest material, and not very flattering to my figure. Sunny and I had no more business on that fashionable promenade ground than we had on a fishing boat—perhaps less. And I realized, with sudden force, that when Lord Dayne was not with us, he was no doubt consorting with the rich and fashionable, doing rich and fashionable things, leading an entirely different sort of life entirely—being, in a word, rich and fashionable himself.

Lady Sarah Pellett, never one to stand on ceremony, hailed us immediately, with a harsh comment on dressing properly for promenading. "What if Mr. Trimmer or another of the gentlemen I have in my eye for you should come by? Gels on the lookout for rich husbands should know better than to come out in public looking like kitchen maids."

Lord Dayne, clearly suffering from embarrassment, said, "I think Miss Maudsley and Miss Sunny look charming. In any event, if clothes don't make the man, surely they don't make the woman, either."

"Don't matter what you think, Breverton. You ain't one of the ones I have in mind. And you're a fool besides, if you believe that old saw."

Sunny seemed to be awestruck by this attack, and in defense retreated into the vacant expression she assumes now and then. I said, with as much good humor as I could rally, "I'm sorry, Lady Sarah, that you meet us in such a state, but we do not have an abundance of fashionable morning dresses, nor maids to help us with numerous changes of costume during the day. I assure you that we had no intention of coming near the Stein when we set out this morning on an errand for Mama that she considered something of an emergency."

"An emergency, is it? And what might that emergency be?"

"I'm sorry, Lady Sarah, but I don't feel at liberty to divulge the nature of our errand." I had no intention of telling the woman that our emergency was two yards of blue ribbon.

Lady Sarah Pellett was never inclined to take no for an answer, and she immediately began to importune me to reveal our errand. When she discovered that I was not to be moved, she turned her attack on Sunny.

Lord Dayne, who was growing visibly more uneasy at his aunt's want of manners, intervened before Sunny was forced to the wall. "Come, Aunt. We must accede to Miss Maudsley's wishes and leave her to complete her errand. And as for you, ma'am, I believe I'll recommend you to the government as an interrogator of prisoners. Upon my word, you do show an uncommon talent for it."

"Don't waste your witless witticisms on me, Dayne," Lady Sarah responded.

Sunny and I, stunned by this vicious remark, were even more stunned when Dayne threw back his head and laughed—that fulsome, joyous laugh the very sound of which was enough to restore its auditors to humor. "Oh vain vanity! Verily vanquished!" he said, when he had had his laugh out. Sunny and I would have been witless ourselves if we hadn't recognized the game that Dayne and his aunt played, and after we made our escape, I muttered to Sunny, "And he has trouble with spelling!"

"And anagrams!" Sunny added.

One person's humor hadn't been restored, and that was mine. I was feeling more sullen and crankier by the moment, a state of mind that was not improved by the approach of a plump lady, on the arm of another, who immediately hailed us. "Oh, *d* dash *m-n,* it's Mrs. *F* dash *t,*" Sunny murmured, clutching my arm. I reassembled my sullen expression into the semblance of placid pleasantry appropriate to well-bred young people strolling the Stein. (Lady Sarah's game is catching, as the reader may notice.) Mrs. Fitzherbert has many admirers and a reputation for charm, and the charm was evident as she greeted us, remembering our names and appearing oblivious to our poor attire. After introducing us to her companion, she asked after our health and our mama's. "I have just sent a note to your mother this morning," she said, "asking her to call on me. You may second my entreaties by carrying the message to her verbally. I've promised to send my carriage for her. I do so long to talk over old times."

Sunny and I thanked her and promised to urge Mama to call as quickly as she possibly could.

Mrs. Fitzherbert bestowed on us another measure of her charm before moving on. "Your father was such a wonderful man and always a good friend to me. I miss him yet—and your mother, who also stood my friend in trying times."

Sunny and I, after taking leave of her, hurried on, concerned that Mama would begin to wonder what had happened to us. We managed to avoid meeting anyone else we knew, arriving within a few minutes at the door of Mrs. Yewdall's new shop in St. James Street. It was not a dressmaking shop like the one in Great East Street, but a small, elegant establishment selling expensive notions, lovely silk flowers, decorative china, articles and beautiful wall hangings, among other exquisite items. The minute we entered the shop, one of the wall hangings caught both my eye and Sunny's.

"Why," Sunny exclaimed, "that tapestry is just like the one Mama was making!"

"I believe you're right. But I thought Mama had designed the pattern herself."

We were denied any further speculation or a closer examination of the tapestry, by the entrance of Mrs. Yewdall from the back of the shop.

"Ah, the Miss Maudsleys," she said. "Good morning. May I help you with something?"

"Uh . . . yes," I said, tearing my eyes from the beautiful needlepoint tapestry. I presented the sample of ribbon Mama had given us and explained our difficulty.

"I believe I do have rather a quantity of this ribbon left. I removed it from stock to resell to a warehouse that disposes of items that haven't sold. With luck, I'll recover the cost. The particular shade has not been successful this season, although used properly it can be most striking. However, there are very few who have your mother's taste and creativity with color. If you'll excuse me, I'll check."

Now that I'd begun to think about a shop myself, my ears

pricked up at this frank description of the commercial lay, and I decided that the next time Mrs. Yewdall called on Mama I would grasp the opportunity to question her more specifically on the business. Sunny was meanwhile taking advantage of Mrs. Yewdall's absence to examine the tapestry more closely. "It's exactly like Mama's," she whispered. "Or very nearly the same."

I moved closer to examine it myself. "Yes," I concluded. "If it's not exactly the same, it's certainly very like it." Neither Sunny nor I had ever paid close attention to Mama's fancy-work, having little interest in the skill ourselves.

"I wonder what it costs?"

Very expensive shops do not mark prices, so we held a low-voiced debate on the wisdom of asking. We were saved the trouble by Mrs. Yewdall, who glided back into the shop as quietly as if she moved on well-oiled wheels, carrying what looked like several yards of the ribbon we needed. Discovering us standing before the tapestry, she remarked, "It's lovely, isn't it? I am asking twenty pounds for it."

"Twenty pounds?" Sunny and I exclaimed in unison.

Mrs. Yewdall gave us a cool and rather superior smile. "I have already sold one for fifteen pounds, not as large as this. I believe the traffic will bear more. It is exquisite work, requiring many hours of labor and the most expensive materials. It is furthermore a unique and striking blend of color and pattern. . . ."

Sunny and I were not in the market for any such object. We had more than a sufficiency at home and therefore certainly no need for what Ben would call a pitch. We murmured a few more sentences having to do with its beauty. Sunny added that our mama made similar articles, to which Mrs. Yewdall replied that she was aware of the fact. I changed the subject to ask about the ribbon.

Mrs. Yewdall cut and wrapped the required two yards, and we emerged on the street to debate the most anonymous route to Xanadu. We decided to follow Manchester Street to the Marine Parade, and then down onto the sands. We would have to make our way through the beached fishing boats and past the fish market, which would be just closing but where we were not likely to meet anyone we knew except local people, who would not take our attire amiss or think it remarkable. Then past the women's bathing machines and a few invalids waiting their turn for a machine, who might think us sensibly dressed for a stroll on the sands.

My temper was a little restored, but my general emotional condition was not. Anger and annoyance were gradually becoming disillusion and despair. Lady Sarah's word game was diverting, but the game she was playing with me was not. She had made it clear that Dayne was not destined to wed a Maudsley, and the implication was that she would oppose it vigorously if applied to for approval. It was easy to see Dayne was fond of Lady Sarah, and it was also clear that she had assigned him the role of escort in pursuit of her game of finding me a rich husband, whether I wanted one or not. But if a gentleman weren't rich, I couldn't marry, no matter how he might strike my fancy, for I still had my family to care for. Now here was Dayne, who struck my fancy and was rich besides, but whose own family would never permit a liaison with the impoverished daughter of a deceased baronet.

All my afternoon was spent fretting.

Mrs. Oliphant brought me cheese and a simple salad at five o'clock, which I consumed alone in my room. Although terribly vulgar to say so, this provision was made so that my stomach wouldn't growl while waiting for the prince's dinner at seven. Mama explained that guests of the prince assembled at the time requested in their invitations, and that they were usually permitted a half hour of conversation before dinner was announced. The social part of an evening at the Pavilion was always after dinner.

With Mama, Sunny, Angela, Charlotte, Jane, Irene, and Mrs. Oliphant all twittering around me, I didn't need a dresser or a lady's maid. I had the advice of every other female in the household but Irene, who for all we know had something to say like the rest, except she wasn't saying it in

English. (So far Irene's progress was stalled at *up* and *down.*)

Sunny did my hair beautifully, in a tightly braided crown on the top of my head that was as different in style from my usual circle of braids as the difference between night and day. She crimped with the irons the wisps of hair at my neck and temples that refused to stay where they belonged, which—providing they stayed curled—would save me from my more normal look of slight *deshabille.*

Mama helped me dress. But just as she was ready to slip my gown over my head, she hesitated, then lay it carefully back on the bed. "Just a moment," she said and hurried out, to return within minutes carrying a lacquered box. She opened it, and there within lay Mama's secrets. "A bit of artificiality won't be amiss," she said, and to the amazement of us all, she proceeded to delicately darken my lashes and to apply a faint brush of color to my cheeks.

"But, Mama, you never approved of painting. . . ."

"Not when you were a girl—of course not. But you're older now, and that first freshness, the appeal of youth, is gone. You may now be permitted a touch of enhancement."

"Well, for tonight, if you think it proper, but I think in general I shall have to depend on the appeal of character. . . ."

"Keep your lips closed, please," was Mama's only reply.

She lifted my gown from the bed and commanded me to raise my arms. The soft material fell over my head with a cool rustle of silk. Mama had designed a gown of great beauty, although the style was not different from any other dresses of that season. Her achievement was in the perfection of the cut, which showed my figure to its very best advantage, and in the combination of shades of blue, my best color. A soft light blue skirt and tunic, worn over a dark blue underskirt, fell softly away from the high bodice, which ended just under my bosom. Ribbon, in an odd shade of dusky blue, was threaded in an intricate design through the hem of the tunic. The same ribbon also edged the low neck of the bodice, to come together in a curving V between my breasts, where it was caught together in a rosette from which it fell gracefully in two streamers nearly to the hem of the tunic.

Mama buttoned the back and then turned me about, making little adjustments here and there that made not the slightest difference in the world, since the fit of the dress was perfection itself.

Sunny handed me the jewelry we had chosen together earlier that afternoon: drop earrings of pearl and turquoise—one of the few pieces of my jewelry that hadn't been sold—and a cluster of three small pearls on a thin gold chain, which fell just within the cleft of my breasts. It was jewelry suited for a girl younger than I, but Sunny pronounced the effect "delicious," an opinion with which I concurred, although I would have added "tantalizing" as well.

Sunny, meanwhile, was studying me with a look that suggested she was not *quite* satisfied with the total effect. We had decided against any hair ornament—even a ribbon—in order to emphasize the soft austerity of my dress and my simple jewelry. Sunny picked up my flowers, a cluster of lavender and purplish sweet peas that Lord Dayne had sent, no doubt on the advice of Lady Sarah. "Perhaps these flowers . . ." she said speculatively. And before I could stop her, she had begun to pick the nosegay apart.

"Hold still," she commanded, and proceeded to arrange the sweet peas in a circlet around my braided crown. The effect was perfectly stunning, and it occurred to me that Sunny, who is really very clever with her fingers, even if she doesn't like needlework, might also have Mama's creativity with color and her eye for style.

As I turned from the mirror, Mrs. Oliphant said, with barely disguised pride in her oldest chick, "You've done her hair just as it should be, Miss Sunny. Such a lovely long neck the child has, and such a well-shaped head. And you've shown Miss Lia's fine figure to wonderful advantage, Lady Maudsley. She'll be the toast of the ball."

Mama had been watching from where she sat on the bed. "Turn around, Lia." I did so, admiring the graceful swing of my skirt. "Yes, I believe it is well-done. There will be many beautiful dresses tonight and many women with pretensions to beauty, but you may hold your head up among them, Aurelia. You won't outshine all others, but none will outshine you, either." She wiped away a tear and rose to kiss me. "How I wish your dear papa were here to see you, my dear. But I described your dress to Adam and Star last night, and perhaps they will describe it to your papa. They wish you a wonderful ball. Not a bit of jealousy!"

All my other attendants, with great care not to disturb my finery, also kissed me and wished me a wonderful time—also without a shred of jealousy (and with more cause), but with a few tears. We were all—except for Charlotte, of course—remembering the past, when Sunny and little Angela had sat admiringly by, watching me being dressed and anticipating the time when they, too, would be clad in a pretty gown, shod in satin slippers, and sent off to dance a night away. Papa—and Mama, too, if she hadn't been supervising my dressing—would come in and kiss me, and he would tell me what a beautiful girl I was. . . .

I carefully thrust those thoughts aside, then nearly did burst into tears when I emerged and discovered Chunk, sitting on the stairs waiting for me, almost as if he knew that even a twenty-four-year-old woman, on setting out for a grand ball, needs an approving male relative to tell her how beautiful she is, even if that relative is only a big, loud, dirty twelve-year-old boy.

By this time, Lord Dayne had been waiting below for all of ten minutes to escort me to the carriage where Lady Sarah waited. He was wearing formal evening attire, including knee breeches, and for the first time since we'd met, I could surreptitiously assess the condition of his injured leg—that is, aside from the improvement of his limp, which was now hardly noticeable. The few glances I managed to sneak at his leg through the evening told me that it was once again well muscled and filled out to normal size—unless, of course, he had resorted to padding. But I rather thought not. He might have been vain enough to prefer to swim in the dark, but he was not the kind of man who would resort to padding.

The expression in his eyes, when I entered the front parlor where he waited, turned my heart again to jelly in my breast.

He raised my gloved hand to his lips, kissed it, and murmured softly, without taking his eyes from mine, "How beautiful you are."

I replied, idiotically, "And how handsome you are." There is something about a man all done up in formal attire, and especially in the somber black and the crisp white that the fashionables now favored. . . . I thought, quite irrelevantly, how odd it was that while women dressed to display, men dressed to hide. And yet I'd never been more conscious than at that moment, as I gazed into Lord Dayne's eyes, of the man beneath the fine fabric of his beautifully tailored coat and neatly fitting breeches, more conscious even than in the first days of our acquaintance when the memory of his near nakedness had been at the front of my mind.

Mama entered the room then, carrying a lovely shawl, and after a few polite words of greeting, Dayne took it from her and put it around my shoulders. "You may not need this at the Pavilion, but it's cool outside, as it always is in Brighton in the evening." I kissed Mama, placed my hand on his arm, and floated away to fairyland.

Lady Sarah, waiting impatiently in the carriage, stated that I and my mother both needed to learn promptitude, but that at least I was more presentable than I had been earlier in the day.

Dayne remonstrated. "No, Aunt Sarah, you will not be permitted such a cold assessment of this glorious creature I've brought to you. Tell Miss Maudsley, please, that her dress is beautiful, and I'll tell her that she is beautiful." He took my hand and again raised it to his lips. "You're beautiful, Miss Maudsley," he said.

I hardly heard Lady Sarah saying, "Well, well. No need for your antics, Breverton. As you say, the dress is beautiful. Now behave yourself. And you're looking very well tonight, Aurelia. Your mother has always had excellent taste."

Carriages, along with a few sedan chairs, were already arriving at the Pavilion as our own drew up to the gate, so that we were required to wait for several minutes. Lord Dayne conversed easily of generalities, but Lady Sarah speculated on the number of people who would be sitting down to dine with the prince.

"I understood the prince's party was to be quite select, but so many carriages! I can't abide large dinner parties. And you must watch me, Dayne, to remind me that I must sit as chaperone for several hours, and that if I eat too much I shall surely fall asleep. You may watch me, too, Aurelia. Just raise your eyebrows when you catch my eye. . . . The prince's cook lays a fine table, and I will be the first to admit that I easily fall into the sin of gluttony."

At last the knot of carriages in the street in front of the gate began to move, and we were within the grounds. The Pavilion was ablaze with light. Lord Dayne, with Lady Sarah on one arm and me on the other, his stick nowhere in evidence, said softly in my ear, "And now, the land of enchantment. The marvels of Cathay await Miss Lia Maudsley."

Chapter Twelve

The prince, everyone knows, loves his food—he is, as Lady Sarah observed before alighting from the carriage, "very regular in his sensual habits." Although he had set dinner back from six, the usual hour, to seven, it was not to be expected that he would permit his guests to linger long before it was announced. The knot of carriages at the Pavilion gate had not been due to a great crowd of guests—for we numbered only twenty in all, including Mrs. Fitzherbert and the prince himself—but to the requirements of punctuality.

"So for pity's sake, Dayne, if you must make a point of showing Aurelia the prince's frightful *chinoiserie,* do try not to appear as though you're a pair of country gawkers hurrying through a waxworks museum."

We were greeted most graciously by Mrs. Fitzherbert and the prince. He was indeed running to considerable flesh, but his reputed charm was not diminished. "So this is Whit Maudsley's daughter! And such a beauty! Your father'd be proud of you if he could see you tonight. Wonderful man, damn me if he wasn't. But I have it in mind we've met before, Miss Maudsley."

I conceded that we had, on the occasion of my coming out ball, which he had honored by his attendance. I didn't bother to mention that it had been for only fifteen minutes, but that on other occasions he had seen rather more of me. I had once been invited to Carleton House in Mama's stead, when she was recovering from one of her rare bouts of illness, and another time I was invited, with both Mama and Papa, to assist in the entertainment of a very young lady whose father merited the prince's attention due to his outstanding scholarly accomplishments. (Papa, who knew a little bit about everything and could talk to anyone about anything, was a welcome guest at such events.) The prince had also been oftentimes present at Brighton balls in those days before Papa died, when we could afford assemblies and balls—or Papa let us think we could—and had even danced with me on one memorable occasion.

"Well, now, Miss Maudsley," the prince continued, "you must give my compliments to Tilly. I'm told that she's living retired since Whit's death. But time heals."

"Yes . . ." I replied vaguely. If he was aware of our pecuniary embarrassment, he certainly showed no sign of it.

"Miss Maudsley is most anxious to see your Chinese rooms, sir," Dayne said, as other guests arrived to claim the prince's attention.

"I hope they give you pleasure, Miss Maudsley," he told me with a pleased smile. "And now, Lady Sarah, let Sir Philip here find you a chair. Won't do to tire ourselves before a grand ball."

Dismissed, we wandered away. We strolled casually about, pausing occasionally for a moment of conversation with one or another of the guests. Dayne adroitly moved us from group to group with only the briefest exchanges of pleasantries, and although I would have liked to study my surroundings with much more thoroughness than time and civility allowed, I had time enough to be bedazzled. Dayne asked me later what most pleased or repelled me, and I could only reply that nothing repelled and all pleased.

The wonderful Chinese wallpapers in the saloon, of which I had heard so much, were framed in decorative gilt as though they were paintings rather than mere wallpaper. The charming pattern was a representation of a scene over a garden wall, on which brilliantly colored pheasants strolled among the peonies and chrysanthemums blooming in their decorative pots. In the gardens behind, colorful birds perched in delicately leafed and flowering trees. Insects and butterflies flitted among them, and on the branches hung bird cages and baskets of flowers.

"Do you suppose," Dayne asked, "that the insects in China are really that beautiful?"

Having a budding naturalist in the family, I could say with assurance that since England has some beautiful insects, I could suppose that China must also.

A display of weapons in a large cabinet, and then a model of a junk, detained Lord Dayne, while I drifted on to the gilt and lacquer cabinets that held examples of the prince's collection of Chinese porcelain. Another cabinet held pagodas carved in ivory, and another was filled with curious masks. Lady Estelle, Countess of Nederton, to whom I'd been introduced by Dayne, spoke from behind me "Most interesting, isn't it, my dear? I've always been fascinated by things Chinese and would have a pagoda in my garden if my lord would permit it." With a satirical moue, she bowed her head in the direction of the earl, who was conversing with Lord Dayne. "Our two sailors are no doubt discussing the seaworthiness, or the rigging, or some other nautical aspect of that junk. But there is so much to see, that unless we're very careful, the best will be missed. Shall we leave them to their discussion and explore the Chinese passage by ourselves?"

She slipped her arm through mine and led me away, tossing a negligent excuse over her shoulder to Dayne. She had no circumspection at all, being perfectly content that we should both gawk like country cousins at the strange enchantment of the Chinese corridor. It was small and almost as though one were enclosed in a large, illuminated box—or, as some people have described it, like being inside a Chinese lantern. Glass wall and ceiling panels were decorated in that unique Chinese way, which combines squarish geometric figures with flowing and curving designs. The lighting of the corridor came through this glass from without, producing a splendid otherworldly effect. From the ceiling hung numerous Chinese lamps, with red tassels hanging from every corner and angle. Life size models of mandarins, clothed in real robes and hats and holding real fishing poles, stood in niches along the walls, which were separated by wallpapered panels portraying graceful clumps of bamboo. Unlike the saloon, where all was gilt, the corridor was rich with reds and greens.

"Now, what do you think?" the lady asked. "Are you of those critics who consider it one of the most monstrous things ever conceived? Or one of those who love it, despite themselves?"

I told her that I thought it romantic, beautiful, wonderful, and barbaric.

It was just as well that Lady Estelle had drawn me away from Dayne, or I might not have had leisure to admire the corridor, for we were very shortly claimed by our dinner partners. The band, composed of French horns, clarinets, and other loud instruments, was already assembled and playing some vigorous air as we entered the dining room. "Maddening," Lady Sarah had described the band. "Don't know why I accept these invitations!"

I was not a stranger to well-laden tables or to French cuisine, but I had become accustomed to simple menus and plain food since Papa's death. There was nothing simple or modest about the prince's table, however. There were so many courses and so many dishes with each course that I couldn't describe it if I would. Therefore, "not to detain the reader with minute circumstances," as Henry Fielding says, I will brush hastily over the sumptuous feast. There were pâtés, croustades, aspics; all kinds of meats and fish and poultry in a bewildering number of sauces; vegetables with herbs and butter and delicate sauces I didn't recognize. I could only sample a few dishes from the great array: a watercress soup, a small piece of turbot in lobster sauce, a bit of ham in Madeira sauce, some partridge in aspic with herbs, and asparagus with a hollandaise sauce. Besides all this, there were cheeses and biscuits and breads, which I sampled not at all. And then the desserts! Soufflés, tarts, charlottes, cakes, and ices . . . I contented myself with an apricot cake.

Lady Sarah was far down the table from me, and I kept my eye on her as she'd asked. However, after a nod in my direction shortly after we were seated, she would not recognize me again; I don't believe that in truth she wanted either me or Dayne to remind her of the sin of gluttony. And in any event, Dayne, also on the other side of the table, would have found it impossible, without craning his neck in a most vulgar way. He smiled at me from time to time, while my dinner partner, a young gentleman who was still green around the edges, persevered in telling me everything he knew about horses once he discovered me not entirely ignorant of equine matters.

The band performed almost without pause, and whenever I turned away from my dinner partner to converse with the viscount who sat on my other side, he would point at his ear and say in a loud voice, "Can't hear a thing with all that damned tootling." During one rather longer pause between songs, he confided to me that he had had an accident as a youth that had left him deafened in one ear. "Try to avoid these affairs, but not always possible. Don't take it amiss that I can't converse properly with you. Old Q, you know, now he's near stone-deaf. Never invites more than one guest to dinner. . . . Said if he did, they'd talk to each other and not to him, but if he has only one guest, the fellow's got no choice. And goes without saying, he don't have any damned French horns raising a row over his shoulder."

"Who is old Q?"

"Duke of Queensbury, great friend of the Duke of Cumberland, Prinny's uncle."

"Oh, yes, of course. My father knew him. An *aficionado* of the racetrack, I believe?" The reader will notice that some Spanish had crept into my vocabulary since Dayne and Chaffinch entered our lives.

The gentleman gave me a close look. "Didn't catch your name earlier." He pointed to his ear again.

"Aurelia Maudsley. My father was Sir Whitney Maudsley."

"Whit Maudsley! Well, what do you know? Whit Maudsley's daughter! How's Tilly? Is she well? Terrible about Whit. Nobody he couldn't get along with. Or get around." He accompanied this last remark with a wink, undoubtedly referring to Papa's relations with tradesmen. Then he shook his head. "Too young to go off like that. Cut me up. Best of friends. Didn't get to the funeral. I was down with the gout when he died. Always regretted it."

The band struck up again, and pointing to his ear, the viscount turned his attention to his jugged lark.

We were at the table until after ten o'clock, when finally the last wine was drunk and the ladies could withdraw to renew forces before setting out for the ball. We met a half hour later in the saloon. Although some of the younger male guests chose to walk to the Castle Ballroom, which was no great distance away, females—old or young—were not permitted such freedom. So we awaited Lady Sarah's carriage and were soon entangled once again, this time among the carriages and sedan chairs arriving for the ball. Ridiculous, I thought to myself, and it occurred to me to wonder if I might not have become too accustomed to certain freedoms to ever again return to the restrictions of high society.

The rooms at the Castle Ballrooms were lavishly filled with orange and lemon trees, the ceilings had laurel hanging from them and were decorated with flowers, and illuminated lamps cast a fairy light on the trees and flowers. Lady Estelle, who with her husband had entered directly behind us, whispered, "To steal a line from Fanny Burney, 'It must have cost our young lord at least two thousand pounds to prove to the world that he's arrived at twenty-one years.' "

Lady Sarah grimly smiled her approval of the sentiment. Lady Estelle, although many years younger, was a woman after her own heart. "Always have said lavish coming-of-age affairs were nonsense! A good country celebration, with a roasted ox or two, and all the farm laborers and local people eating and drinking and dancing, and the young lord or squire and his folks mingling with them . . . that's what I call a proper coming-of-age!"

Lady Estelle agreed. "However," she added, "perhaps because the young man has been a duke since the age of nine, it does justify a certain elevation of the event. I should point out, Lady Sarah, that our young lord is giving a quite lavish celebration tomorrow for his upper servants and their friends. And I'm sure the country people weren't slighted. . . . The young man appears so free with his money."

Lady Sarah was clearly not certain whether Lady Estelle spoke in jest, was simply ingenuous, or was possessed with an unbridled tongue, but I was not permitted to hear more of their exchange, for Dayne drew me aside to present me to a smiling officer, with fine *mustachios,* who had been making his way toward us.

"Miss Maudsley, may I present Colonel Roarke Staffen, who will be hosting us on his yacht next Sunday? He has most happily agreed to stand in my place for the first dance tonight. I thought it best, due to my recent injury, to wait for the dance before supper, which I hope to enjoy with you. I understand that waltzing will commence at one, and I will most certainly wish the favor of the last waltz before supper, as well as a quadrille or another waltz after supper."

Although the German waltz had not yet been accepted in London, standards were not so starchy in Brighton, which took its tone from the prince rather than from his straitlaced parents.

Colonel Staffen bowed. "Been anxious to make your acquaintance, Miss Maudsley, ever since Brev proposed to me the honor of the first dance with you—with your kind acceptance, of course. He's told me what a charming young lady I would be partnering, but he failed to tell me that you are beautiful as well."

Lady Sarah stated that she couldn't think my mother would approve of waltzing. However, there is no comfort in being nearly on the shelf unless one can make one's own decisions, and I was not willing to allow a nominal chaperone to decide my conduct. I had been dying to prove my waltzing skill on a real dance floor. It was a skill I had acquired in a *quid pro quo* arrangement with Ben. Ben had more than once coaxed me into walking through boxing maneuvers, as he followed the directions in a little book entitled *The Manly Art of Self-Defense.* In return, I had exacted instruction in the waltz, at which his Cambridge companion, Dandy Rogers, was adept due to his earlier years of education in Leipzig. I might not have been much in the world for the past three years, but I had not been buried in New South Wales, either.

The first tune was struck up at eleven o'clock, as soon as the prince made his appearance. Colonel Staffen, it was readily apparent, was one of those younger sons who although destined for military careers, are rigorously trained in all the accomplishments considered necessary for the graces of a gentleman—including the arts of polite conversation and dancing. When he solicited one of the waltzes, I was happy to accept. For the other dances, except when Dayne claimed my hand, Lady Sarah was prepared to keep me amply furnished with partners. Fortunately, our old friend Jerry Richmondson was present, and thanks to his acquaintances and those of Colonel Staffen, I was saved from most of Lady Sarah's rich prospects.

There are dances and dances, and there are those that undoubtedly we all remember, when we were too often among the desolate flowers along the wall, and the young man of our dreams, unaware of our existence, attached himself, with the most supine and disgusting idiocy, to an unworthy, shallow-minded, beautiful flibbertigibbet. But there are other dances, which every girl also remembers—the magic ones at which partners vie for her hand and some particular young man, in a state of enchantment, shows himself all but ready to cast himself, enslaved, at her feet. I was too old for juvenile transports, but the young duke's ball was of the latter delightful category. Although through Lady Sarah's efforts I found myself occasionally beside a bold widower or an urbane old beau, I went down many more dances with admiring officers in scarlet coats. (And don't we all, in the end, find something alluring about a scarlet coat?) I danced also with young gentlemen I'd not seen since I was a rich and flighty girl in the London social whirl, one of whom confided that his life had been a desert since I had forsaken London. Another, whom I'd known since my come-out, stated that my no-longer-lamented former suitor, the third baron, had been a blockhead and a dupe.

"Married money in the end, but got no bargain. Woman's a regular virago. Dances to her tune. Like a trained bear, if you want to know."

Unworthily, I was more pleased by that blunt statement than by all the gallantries of handsome officers, for the reader will remember that despite the expectations the third baron had raised, he had slipped quietly away after he discovered that I had no fortune to offer along with my hand. I caught Dayne's eye just then, where he was standing with two naval gentlemen, and was suddenly so overpoweringly grateful to the third baron for not pressing his suit that I forgave him on the instant. Girls should not be permitted to marry until they are women of twenty-four and old enough to recognize true worth when they meet it.

"Who's that?" my partner asked, noting our exchange of glances.

"Breverton Dayne," I said.

"Oh, yes. Dayne. A sixth baron. Related to that crowd of Whigs, the Calcotts. One brother an MP, and an older one who came to a bad end. What was his name?"

"Algernon, I believe."

The dance separated us, but when we once again came together, my partner said, with a slight frown, "This Breverton . . . If I remember, something of a cutup in his own right. Navy finally sobered him up, I hear. My uncle's an admiral; heard him mention Dayne. Frigate, right?"

"You are still the most impossible gossip!" I reprimanded him. "Is there anyone or anything you don't know?"

"Don't know a thing about my coachman's affairs," he said, "but I can tell by looking that Dayne's mixed up in yours."

"Impertinent fellow!" I admonished. But old friends may be granted a certain license, and I smiled at him.

The moralists are wrong to criticize the German waltz, in the more ordinary scheme of things. Colonel Staffen performed the dance with more grace and proficiency than Lord Dayne—I believe he had been posted to Hanover with the Duke of Clarence—but my pulses were not stirred, except for the exertion of performing such an energetic dance. Nor did my pulses race while in the arms of my gossipy friend, who eyed me narrowly and observed that I hadn't been living as retired as he had thought.

Dayne came to claim me for the waltz before supper, and I admit that the moralists who criticize the dance might have the right to do so in the case of two people who are longing for each other's embraces.

"Well, Aurelia Maudsley," he said, and I went into his arms

in a way that I suspect was nothing short of shameful—on his part as well as mine. And if there was anyone else in that room during that dance, I'm sure I didn't know it.

The supper rooms were thrown open at two o'clock. The tables presented a magnificent display, which wasn't surprising, since according to the papers, all kinds of cooks and decorators had been imported from London to exercise their talents. There were transparencies at one end of the room, behind the head table where the young duke presided. Speeches and toasts and band music accompanied our repast, and I thought of the viscount, with whom I had engaged for a country dance while we were still at table at the Pavilion. "Can't converse, but my bad ear don't keep me from stepping out pretty lively," he'd said. He had proved to be no boaster in the matter of stepping lively, and I'd nearly felt gratitude to the urbane but creaky old beau sent to me by Lady Sarah for the next dance.

The fireworks on the Stein followed the supper. Many of the guests chose to stay within, partaking further of the young duke's bounteous feast, but many more of us went out to watch the rockets and starbursts and pinwheels, and the set pieces—a waterfall, the flag, and the finale, the duke's arms in every color known to the art. It was three-thirty when we returned to the dancing, which would continue until the sun rose, but such dissipation was not to be mine. I had danced only one dance when Dayne came to tell me that Lady Sarah was not feeling well and that with apologies to us both she desired to leave. There was nothing for it but to comply.

Any annoyance I might have felt at having my evening cut short immediately disappeared in the face of Lady Sarah's discomfort. I was seriously concerned when I saw how pale and drawn she was, but she waved my solicitations aside. "Just liverish. Knew I shouldn't have had that almond cheesecake at supper."

We could have walked to Lady Sarah's house in the Pavilion Parade—and back—by the time her carriage arrived. I supported her as best I could while we waited, for of course there are never sufficient seats at such events, until Dayne returned with a chair he had appropriated from the card room. When we were at last in the carriage, Dayne ordered the coachman to Xanadu, but Lady Sarah, laying a hand on his arm, protested. "No, Breverton. I'll go home first. Too full of wind to bear all the bumping and jogging. And I'm too blasted liverish to be civil. And don't either of you tell me that I paid no attention to your warnings to restrain myself. I will not again put my feet under the prince's table. The agony is not worth it."

I was tempted to laugh at Lady Sarah's frank description of her ailment, and I would never, as Dayne did, have protested that we had given no warnings—that she had avoided any opportunity for us to do so and that, in any event, she was old enough to know better. Dayne, however, evidently felt it was his duty as one of her family to remonstrate.

Lady Sarah leaned back against the squabs and closed her eyes. "Shut up, Breverton, and leave me to suffer my remorse in peace." And to my amazement, the grand old woman fetched forth a rich belch. "There," she said, complacent. "Few more of those, and I may sleep. But I need the draughts my good Carrie knows how to fix for me."

A few minutes passed in silence while I considered that my chaperone was deserting me, which thought seemed to transfer itself to Lady Sarah, for she sat up suddenly and said, "And I expect you, Breverton, to behave yourself like a gentleman. I'm leaving Aurelia in your care, and you know what honor requires of you."

Dayne gave his aunt a hard look. "Of course I know what honor requires of me. You need have no fear for Miss Maudsley's honor or her reputation. I find your implication, Aunt, insulting."

"Well." Lady Sarah smiled as she once again leaned back and closed her eyes. "You have only yourself to thank."

We continued in silence until we reached Lady Sarah's door, where Dayne helped her alight. Her Neapolitan footman, all solicitation, was immediately at her side. I offered her my thanks, most sincerely, for the wonderful evening she had given me and kissed her cheek. She took my face between her hands and kissed my forehead. I felt like a faithful

Russian servant at receipt of my old-age pensioning off. Whatever Lady Sarah's interpretation of her gesture, she did not immediately release me but said, "And I trust, young lady, that you will permit no more impertinencies from this young man." She released me then and taking her footman's arm, spoke to Dayne. "Now leave me. Giovanni can attend me very well. I will expect you to call tomorrow morning to see how I do. Good night. *Avanti,* Giovanni."

It had been wrong of Dayne, of course, when he greeted me, to stare boldly into my eyes rather than bowing his head over my hand, and then to take the liberty of kissing my hand—even gloved as it was. It implied more than had ever been openly stated between us; and it was therefore equally wrong of me to accept it, for acceptance made me culpable of a moral looseness. But I had accepted it, because there was that in his eyes that told me there was nothing of disrespect or discourtesy in the gesture, but that he was making love to me . . . and at the same time challenging me to respond. However, with Lady Sarah's reprimand still fresh in my ears, I resolved to be a model of propriety for the short time remaining to us of the evening.

Dayne had apparently taken the same resolution, for he kept carefully to his own corner of the carriage. The scolding had thrown a restraint over us that prevented conversation, and the ride to Xanadu passed almost entirely in silence.

I could not, however, part from him without thanking him for giving me such an enchanting evening, but when I tried to do so, he took my hand—very properly—and asked me to please hush. "The pleasure was so much my own," he said, on a most tender note.

Well, one can't stand by a carriage all evening, with a coachman and groom looking on (or not looking on, according to their delicacy). Lord Dayne instructed the coachman to turn the coach around, for which he was required to drive on for some distance in order to find sufficient room in the roadway. "Meanwhile, I'll see Miss Maudsley to her door." Then he added, no doubt remembering his aunt, "And don't be all night doing it." I remarked that I was to enter by the garden gate. One of the bookroom doors would be open, so that I could enter the house without disturbing anyone.

"Your mother left a door unlocked? That really wasn't very wise, especially now the season's begun. There'll be all kind of scoundrels around. And on the night of a ball such as this, there are always those ready to take advantage of such an event, when servants are careless and the master and mistress of a house are not likely to be at home."

"Oh, I'm sure nothing untoward has happened. Certainly everyone's asleep now." The house was quiet and completely dark. If a candle or lamp had been left for me it had long since burned out.

Dayne took the key to the gate from me, and unlocked it. As he opened it, I said, "You see, my lord, Ben even oiled the hinges so I could come in without disturbing anyone."

He stepped into the garden behind me. "I don't like this. How can I be sure you're safe within doors when I have to leave you at a garden gate?"

"That is a puzzle. But really, Lord Dayne, you needn't concern yourself. . . ."

"Don't you think you could call me Brev?"

I pondered a moment. "No, I don't think so. Brev is too short."

"Too short?"

"Yes, too . . . uh . . . too brev-iated!"

"You're impossible!" he said with a groan, and before I could find anything to say to that, I was clasped in his arms and being kissed, with a passion that brought my arms up and around his neck. "This is what you deserve," he murmured, and kissed me again, most improperly.

Recovering myself momentarily, I pushed him away, but not so far away that I couldn't grasp his lapels and hide my face on his chest while he cradled my head against its manly expanse. "Your Aunt Sarah will not like this," I murmured. "You promised her. . . ."

"Utterly impossible," he said, as he put a hand under my chin and lifted my face for a long, tender, declarative kiss. Then our arms were around each other more tightly, while he murmured my name between ever more demanding kisses and I whispered absolutely idiotic endearments. Once

again there was no one in the entire world but Lia Maudsley and her lover.

And then suddenly my arms were empty.

My readers have no doubt read the phrase, "Her lover was snatched from her arms. . . ." The usage is ordinarily metaphorical: The lover is snatched by death, or by a call to arms (the military kind), or by some supernatural event, like fairies reclaiming their own. Seldom, however, is a lover ever *literally* snatched from a woman's arms.

The assailant had hit him on the head and, as his hold around me loosened, had grasped one of his arms and flung him aside. At almost the same moment, a firm hand was clamped across my mouth while an arm across my chest held me immobile. Lord Dayne was struggling groggily to his feet, at which the assailant kicked him. He fell over, doubled up, groaning and writhing. The man stood over him, his attitude telling me that he was prepared to kick again.

I tore loose from my own captor in a blinding rage, but I was caught from behind before I had taken two steps.

"Whoa, my pretty. We've no need to harm your friend. We just want a little information, and when we get it, we'll let him go. If you keep quiet, I'll take my hand from your mouth. But one peep from you, and my friend will kick him again. How about it, pretty one?"

I nodded, and he let me go. I moved away in a crabbed semicircle—I was determined to see the man—and discovered that of all that was outlandish, he wore a domino and a mask, as though he were on his way to a masquerade ball. The hood of the cloak was thrown back, and his teeth flashed beneath the mask in an insolent smile. "Just a little information, pretty one. But one scream, and . . ." His hands had been on his hips as he watched me, but as he spoke, he lifted his arms and spread his fingers in a gesture suggesting a shrug of resignation.

"Information?" I asked, trying to see Dayne from the corner of my eye. He was breathing in hoarse, rasping breaths. I took a step backward.

And then it came to me. I'd done this before. With the ease of practice, my weight came forward on my left foot, and my knee flexed like a spring as with my following step my right arm swung upward. I hit the man a crack just below the ear, which sent him staggering. Dayne croaked hoarsely—some instruction, no doubt—and yanked the foot of his own assailant, who was momentarily distracted by my pugilistic efforts and the results, from under him. And then, while I was hopping about in pain, my hand feeling as though I'd broken every bone in it, a terrible scream rent the air.

The man who had attacked me was in much less pain than I and obviously coolheaded, for he leaped to the assistance of his companion, who was now in mortal combat with Dayne. They had somehow struggled to their feet and were reeling about together in a wrestling grip. Dayne received another kick, this time from my assailant, which gave his opponent the opportunity to bounce a leveler off his nob. Even that did not stop my heroic lover who fought on, but he was outnumbered, and a blow to his breadbox put him out of the game long enough for the two men to escape, presumably over the garden wall at the back of the property, for Lady Sarah's coachman and the groom were already entering by the garden gate. (We discovered later that the intruders had broken the lock to the back gate, and that they both entered and escaped by that route.)

The coachman, the groom, and I all ran to Dayne, who was gasping for breath. "Just . . . wind . . . knocked out . . . this time," he told the coachman, who was the first to reach him. I fell on my knees beside him, weeping so desperately that my tears spilled onto his face. "Don't . . . cry . . . my darling," he said, and his eyes closed. "Not . . . hurt much."

Then Sunny was there, with her arms around me, still holding the candlestick with which she'd armed herself to enter the fray, and Mama was instructing the coachman and the groom to help Dayne into the house. Chunk carried his cricket bat, the search for which, we later learned, had delayed his arrival until too late to become a hero. (He would henceforth keep it under his bed.) Angela and Charlotte, shivering in their nightgowns and their arms around each other, stared in fright at Dayne, until ordered back to bed by

Mama. It was Jane, however, awakened by the sound of the carriage, who had gone to a window "to see Miss Lia come home" and who had saved the day with her screams. She had kept it up during the entire melee, although I'd heard only that first rending shriek. She wasn't present, however, to assist Mama and Mrs. Oliphant tend to Dayne—while the groom galloped off on one of the horses to find a doctor—because her screams had awakened the infants, who had promptly added their shrieks to hers. They had also awakened our neighbors at Belle Vue, for one of the servants came to ask if anything was amiss and stayed to hear the whole story, which made it doubly certain it would be all over town the following day that robbers had attempted Xanadu and Lord Dayne had been injured in its defense.

Dr. Thorn, from West Street, came immediately. One of Dayne's eyes was already swollen shut and turning blue, and he had a headache from the two cracks on his head, but he was not permanently injured. "He'll be badly bruised about the midsection tomorrow," the doctor told Mama, "but nothing's broken and I'm quite sure there are no internal injuries. I'd say he was lucky. The attacker was aiming at breaking his ribs with some of those kicks, or I miss my guess. Looks to me like his lordship met up with one of those toughs I've heard about, who're more skilled with their feet than their fists. Now, let's take a look at Miss Lia's hand."

After some painful probing and, at the doctor's insistence, some flexing of my fingers, he determined that no bones were broken but that my hand was severely bruised.

Finally, he looked in again on Dayne. When he came out of the room and closed the door, about which we were all hovering, he said, "There's no sign of concussion, so I've given him a draught of laudanum and he should sleep until well into the morning. I'll return at noon, and we'll see if he can be moved. I'd suggest someone sit with him until he wakes." The doctor closed his bag with a snap. "And Miss Lia, he wishes to speak to you before the laudanum takes effect."

I entered the room quietly and nearly burst into tears again, but he held out his hand to me. "Lia," he whispered.

"Keep the doors locked. There may be danger. . . . They wanted something. . . ."

"Of course," I said soothingly. I put my free hand on his head to determine whether there was fever, but it was cool. He was drifting rapidly off, still clinging to my hand and mumbling indistinctly. Mrs. Oliphant looked in and, seeing him quiet, entered. "I'll sit with him, Miss Lia. I've helped Dr. Thorn more than once with a patient, and in worse condition than Lord Dayne."

I put my finger to my lips and whispered, "Wait. He's almost asleep."

"Mumble, mumble, mumble, locked," Lord Dayne said. "Mumble, mumble."

A few more minutes and I felt his grip on my hand loosen, and then after another short wait I carefully pulled it away. He moved his head restlessly on the pillow. "He'll soon be completely asleep," Mrs. Oliphant whispered. "Now you run along and get that dress off. It's stained and your mother wants to attend to it. And then you get in your bed. Doctor left a small draught of laudanum for you, too. That hand will be painful."

Angela and Charlotte had been sent back to their beds, but Chunk was waiting for me, eager to find out about the fight. It was clear that my pugilistic accomplishments had attained for me a prestige and importance that I had never quite merited before. Mama granted him five minutes with me, but insisted that he *must* get back to bed immediately thereafter and that I should accord him no more than a synopsis of the events. "The whole story can wait until tomorrow, Chunk. Lia's tired, and her hand hurts. You may talk to her until I return with a warm posset to help her sleep. I know you don't want to keep her from her rest."

Chunk listened admiringly to my description of how I planted a facer on the robber, then stated that Bam Sitwell's sister would have fainted. (Bam is Chunk's best friend in Lewes.) "She's just an old scared-cat . . . always fainting . . . Just like that stupid Camilla . . ."

Chunk stopped in mid sentence, grimaced, and clamped his teeth tight together.

"Why, you *scamp!*" I grabbed him for a hug, but he pulled away.

"You won't tell, will you, Lia? Not even Mama? And not *Charlotte!*"

"No, of course I won't. But how've you managed to sneak the book away from Sunny and Angela?"

"Oh, they're always leaving it around where they can't find it," he said negligently. "Girls are so silly."

Not to keep the reader in the dark any longer—if there's a reader alive who hasn't read Fanny Burney's *Camilla* or at least heard of it—this very popular book, despite some sharp observations, and many lively and even amusing scenes, goes on most tiresomely for five volumes and nine hundred pages, describing the tribulations of a young girl named Camilla and those of her relations. Camilla and her relations, in the course of the five volumes, shed enough tears, it has been estimated, to float a good-sized boat. They are always collapsing on each others bosoms or falling senseless on the ground, until one wonders how they survive uninjured.

Although we couldn't afford subscription money for the assemblies at the Castle and Old Ship ballrooms, I did manage the subscription fee for one of the libraries, for both Mama and I enjoy reading, and have always encouraged the younger ones in this worthwhile activity. Ben has never been known to sit down with a book if he can help it and Sunny's only interest is novels, but Angela and Chunk are both great readers. Chunk, especially, is one of those youngsters who will read anything that comes to hand—and it seems that *Camilla* had come to hand.

I was pointing out to him that Camilla was physically courageous, even if she didn't have a strong mind, when Mama returned with my posset. "Now, Chunk, off to bed. Mrs. Oliphant has made a nice pallet for you in the Aerie. . . ."

Chunk's jaw set in a stubborn line. "I won't sleep up there with Charlotte."

"Mrs. Oliphant wouldn't have even thought of putting you with Angela and Charlotte," Mama replied soothingly. "You are in the little tiny room at the back, which they don't use because we keep it for storing things. We must let Lord

Dayne have your room tonight. I'm sure you do understand that."

"Lord Dayne can have my room and I don't care, but I don't want to sleep up there in the girls' room."

Mama sighed. "Please, Chunk, just tonight. It's so very late. . . ."

I added my pleas. "Yes, Chunk, just tonight. And it's only for so few hours. It's already almost morning. Tomorrow night, if Lord Dayne is still here, we'll find another place for you and for Ben, because he'll be back then, you know. . . ."

Chunk at last agreed but he grumbled as he left us, and Mrs. Oliphant found him later that morning, when she opened the curtains, sound asleep on the sofa in the front parlor, wrapped up in Sunny's old shawl.

Chapter Thirteen

I slept soundly, under the influence of the laudanum, until the sun was well above the horizon, then I slept fitfully for two hours more. But by nine o'clock I was up and dressed and in the breakfast parlor, where Mama was sitting, frowning over a note from Lady Sarah.

Presuming that Lady Sarah's coachman would already have informed her of the robbery attempt, Mama had sent a message to assure her that Lord Dayne, although badly bruised, was otherwise uninjured and under the care of our own noted physician, Dr. Thorn of West Street. She added that Mr. Chaffinch was expected from London late in the afternoon, at which time it could be decided if Dayne was well enough to be moved. Since I hadn't mentioned Lady Sarah's own indisposition during the confused events of the night before, Mama had included no more than routine good wishes for Lady Sarah's own health.

Mama handed me the note and observed that she should perhaps have been more precise about Lord Dayne's injuries, for surely his aunt would have wanted him immediately under her own care had she known the full truth. Instead, Lady Sarah had replied testily that she was not well and that she would like an explanation at once from "that young man" as to just how he managed to come in the way of robbers. Lady Sarah had, however, most obligingly sent her Neapolitan import, Giovanni, to us, since she was aware we had no male servant to assist with the more delicate aspects of her nephew's care. She caustically added that Mama should have hired a male servant when we first came to Brighton.

Mrs. Oliphant came bustling in in response to Mama's ring and, on my mama's orders, brought me milk-toast and a coddled egg and weak tea, the Maudsley family formula for an invalid breakfast, which Papa had always inelegantly referred to as invalid slop.

"I'm not sick, Mama. I just hurt my hand. I need fortifying. Do you think I could have just a small slice of that cold tongue?"

"No," Mama said.

Sunny came in to join us, carrying a pitcher of frothy chocolate and a plate of buttered toast, which she and Mama consumed with relish while I ate my slop left-handed (no mean feat) and, piece by piece, recounted the details of the fight in the garden, then the particulars of dinner at the Pavilion and the ball at the Castle. Both Mama and Sunny were more interested in the latter—so interested, in fact, that I managed to refill my teacup with chocolate and drink it before they noticed.

It must have been nearly two hours later, after we had retired to the terrace, when Giovanni appeared, escorted by Mrs. Oliphant. "He says," she informed us, "that Lord Dayne is awake. . . ."

"Ees allrright," Giovanni interrupted. "Eat good. Verry good. Now he want to see . . . to see . . . signorina." He suddenly beamed at me. "Brave young lady."

Mrs. Oliphant, as though she were some kind of interpreter, said, "Lord Dayne's had his breakfast and wants to speak to Miss Lia."

"Alone," stated Giovanni. "He beg pardon, *peró*—"

Mrs. Oliphant, putting an end to her interpreter role and assuming her more usual interfering character, sternly informed Giovanni that she had told him Lady Maudsley would not permit anything so improper.

I stood up. "I'm sorry, but I'm going to see him alone if that's what he wants. It would be the most gross ingratitude to refuse his request. He received those wounds defending me and defending our property. . . ."

"Yes, dear," Mama said tranquilly. "Of course. I'm sure

Mrs. Oliphant will see the rightness of that sentiment, just as I do. However, Lia, I suggest you confine your interview to ten minutes, for consideration also requires that we not tire your rescuer. I'm sure you also see the rightness of that."

Giovanni opened the door to Ben and Chunk's bedroom, where Lord Dayne lay propped up on several pillows. He was wearing Ben's dressing gown, and he had been shaved and his hair neatly combed. Both eyes were black and blue, but only the right was swollen completely shut. The room smelled of camphorated spirits.

Dayne reached out his hand as Giovanni quietly closed the door behind me, and said, "Come here, my brave girl."

I was as much in the grip of the tender passion as ever I had been, but I had also suffered a return of circumspection. I could only give him my left hand, for my right arm was in a sling (to protect my hand, Dr. Thorn said), and after a moment I gently pulled it from his grasp in order to bring a chair closer to the bedside.

"No, no," he commanded. "Turn the chair to properly face me, for you must give me your hand again." So I sat down and gave him my left hand to be kissed, and then, as he held it tightly, he searched my face intently with his one slit of an eye and asked, "Are you all right? Is your poor hand terribly painful?"

"No. Dr. Thorn says it's only bruised and will be well again long before your bruises are gone."

"You must take some lessons from Chaff, I think, if you're going to act the *bravo* whenever your lovers are attacked. Or I guess," he said, frowning, "that would be *brava.* I must ask Giovanni. Italian and Spanish have many similarities, you know."

"Do they?"

"You didn't scream once," he said, caressing my fingers with his thumb.

"I guess I'm just not the kind. . . ."

"Giovanni is already in love with you. I told him how you fought. He says that if he were a younger man . . ."

"It was Jane's screams that brought your rescuers," I reminded him.

"He says that women of spirit . . ."

"Don't be improper." I frowned severely and attempted to pull my hand away from his.

"A kiss would do me no end of good," he said, tightening his grip on my hand and drawing me toward him. But it was the hypnotic power he exercised over me, even with that one squint of an eye, that was responsible for what I did next. I leaned over and tenderly kissed him. Or at least that's how it began. One would think that an injured man would have preferred the gentle touch, but no such thing here, for that kiss ended—how shall I say it?—in an intensity of longing that left me absolutely addlepated.

"Oh, Lia. My God," he said.

I sat back in my chair, dazed. "I must go," I mumbled. "Mama required that I stay no longer than ten minutes," I added, gaining command of myself with each word as I, like Charlotte, took refuge in a higher authority.

He let my hand go and drew a long breath. "Much as I regret wasting even one of those precious minutes, we must talk of other matters. Did you see the man who attacked you? I had the impression he was wearing a cape and a mask."

"Yes, as though for a masquerade ball. It was incongruous."

"Anything you remember that might identify him?"

"I remember his height. . . . Not terribly tall, or I couldn't have hit him so squarely. I think he was slight. And he had very white teeth. They flashed in the dark."

Dayne nodded. "Hmmm. . . . The man who attacked me wasn't wearing a mask. I suspect he was a hired tough. . . ."

"Did he have strange eyes?"

"Strange eyes?"

"I was thinking this morning, I remember a man with strange eyes, whom I caught several times watching me. . . ."

"At the ball?"

"No. No, the night before. On Midsummer Eve."

"Place your hand on my forehead, Miss Maudsley. I believe I'm feverish."

I sniffed. Stress was causing me to revert to conquered habits. "Did you see his eyes? Were they strange?"

"Strange how?"
"I don't know. Almond-shaped, but slanting down at the corners. A hard, mean expression . . . Watchful. Wary. I don't know. Just strange."
He sighed. "Not much to go on, if indeed Strange Eyes had anything to do with last night's affair. I hardly saw my own attacker. He might have had glass eyes shaped like rolling pins for all I know. But I want you to be on your guard. I'm speaking very seriously now. Doors locked at all times . . ."
"He had a cultivated accent and kept calling me 'my pretty' and 'pretty one.' "
"Who? The man with strange eyes?"
"No, the man with the mask."
"Hand on my forehead, please. I do believe I am acquiring a fever."
I obliged him. "No fever." I smoothed his hair back from his forehead, and I again noted an increase in the rate of my heartbeat.
He peered at me owlishly from his one good eye. "Did he say anything else?"
"He told me not to scream or that odious man would hurt you. And . . . and . . . oh, yes! He said he just wanted information."
"Information?"
"Yes. At first I thought they wanted to know where we keep the jewels and the money. But I've thought about it, and I'm very sure that all he said was that he wanted information and that maybe it was you who had the information he wanted. Are you in possession of naval secrets that Bonaparte's agents might want?"
"My dear Lia! Beg pardon—Miss Maudsley! You can't be serious! I thought you had no faith at all in spies."
I looked away and out the window, where towering white clouds hung on the horizon, like a range of fairy-tale mountains whipped out of snowy meringue. "Well, I've thought the rumors of spies to be very much exaggerated, but I was not born yesterday. I presume that it is very much in the interest of countries at war to know as much about each other as pos-

sible." I paused a moment. "*Could* you be in any such danger?"

I looked back at him then, and from his one good eye beamed a shaft of such tenderness that it penetrated to my very soul. I barely kept myself from an encore to my previous performance, but—although as usual belatedly—circumspection was now in control. What if Giovanni should come walking in!

"To all her other excellencies, judgment," he said. "But we must keep ourselves to serious matters for the moment. Anything else?"

"No. Then I hit him."

He whooped and, with a lunge, managed to catch my hand and pull me half out of my chair and half onto the bed.

"Let me go!" I demanded, pulling away. But I needn't have spoken, for I was precipitately released.

"Damnation," he groaned. "I forgot my poor bruised ribs."

A knock at the door sent my hand to my hair, to ascertain whether my braids were firmly in place around my head. "That was just terribly improper," I scolded.

"Guilty and doubly guilty. And I suffered for it. The impulse of the moment. I apologize. I'm dying. I must have my fevered brow soothed. . . . Your fault, anyway."

I left my chair and opened the door to Giovanni. "I believe," I said, "that Lord Dayne requires you to soothe his fevered brow."

"*Prego?*" Giovanni asked.

"He'll explain what he needs." I turned at the door. "I'm afraid he's becoming violent, so take care." And with a smile at my lover, I left him.

Dayne

"Well, Brev!" Stuart Chaffinch said as he was shown into the bedroom at Xanadu, where his friend lay on his pillows reading a magazine. He set a tray on the table by the bed. "Lady Maudsley sends red wine, to build your strength. I'm having a cup of strong tea after the dust of the road."

The two men shook hands, and Chaffinch sat down on the chair that stood at the bedside. "Are you all right?"

"Except for a mass of bruises. I've recovered from worse."

"May I hear your version of what happened?" he asked as he handed Dayne the wine. "Your eyes look terrible."

"In a minute. Who won the match?"

"Belcher. Showed to good advantage. Warr is a good enough article, but not in Belcher's class. I think we may have a rising star, although I'm not as optimistic as some. Including young Ben. But I picked up a tidy sum on bets and your man Tilt did very well. He's returning on the evening stage, incidentally. Your brother Walter is sending down some fruit and other foodstuffs from your country estate. Are you in need of assistance?"

"Aunt Sarah has kindly sent her Neapolitan to nurse me."

"So. Well, my young companion popped his watch, against my expostulations and lecturings, to get money to place a bet on Belcher, so he came home the richer also. I'm sorry for it, in a way. It would have been a better lesson if he'd lost. But he's begged me so many times not to breathe a word to Miss Maudsley, and I believe he's too clearly aware of how gambling contributed to his father's ruin to fall prey to the same vices. Well, now that I've given my homily for the day, tell me what happened last night."

"Miss Maudsley and I were attacked, in the garden here, about four in the morning."

Chaffinch reached for his teacup. "No one among the Maudsleys seems to have thought to wonder, but how did they manage to take you so unawares? That's the most mysterious part of the whole business."

"I was kissing Miss Maudsley, if you must know."

"Ah."

"You should have seen her, Chaff! Threw herself into the fight without a thought to her own safety, to her pretty dress, or whether her hair would be mussed. No screaming. No fainting away. My attacker wasn't a fair fighter. . . . Much given to kicks in the most telling spots. A master in using his feet, and shod in heavy boots to make every kick more telling . . ."

Chaffinch decided to forgo any comment on his friend's love affairs. "Kicking, was it? The specialty of a certain class of tough. I've seen contests between them. . . . Barbaric."

"I confess that I'm not prepared for that mode of fighting. But dauntless Miss Maudsley planted a facer on her own attacker, and just about that time the maid Jane set up a screech to raise the dead. She was doing a little peeking, I suspect, hoping she'd see just what she probably saw. But she's slow, and it apparently took her a little time to realize that the two extra people on the scene were behaving even less properly than her mistress and her escort."

"Has it occurred to you that it might have been of more service to you if Miss Maudsley had screamed?"

"She's suggested the same. But they told her they'd do me serious harm if she screamed. So she didn't. It may have been Lia they wanted, you know."

"Miss Maudsley?" Chaffinch asked in surprise.

"Yes. They told her that all they wanted was information, without specifying from whom. She thinks they may have wanted information from me, for of course she has no idea that she could have any other information than where the family valuables are kept. It hasn't occurred to her yet that kicking a fellow to a jelly isn't likely to leave him in any shape to convey information."

Chaffinch poured himself another cup of tea and, indicating the decanter, with a lift of his eyebrows asked if Dayne required more wine. Dayne shook his head and Chaffinch settled back in his chair. "So someone thinks that Miss Maudsley knows something of her father's affairs. . . ."

"I've been thinking. If it was my search for the copy of Sir Whitney's memorandum at the Admiralty that alerted them, it points to our man. Or at least one of them. And in the Admiralty."

"That would mean that someone knows that we're counter-espionage agents, or at least that we're on the scent of something. . . ."

"You're an agent. I'm just a simple representative of the Admiralty, waiting to get back to a more straightforward war."

"So we can at least suppose with some certainty that the attackers were French agents or their hirelings."

"The one who attacked Miss Maudsley—probably. He had a cultivated voice and kept calling her 'my pretty.'" Dayne grinned. "She particularly remembered that. I think the other was a hired thug, and that he'll be found in a ditch or floating in the Thames one day soon."

Chaffinch shook his head and frowned. It did seem likely that the attacker had wanted information from Miss Maudsley rather than from Dayne, but it was not certain. And in whichever event, the attack suggested that French agents were aware that Sir Whitney Maudsley might have had information that would expose them. Furthermore, his friend's usefulness was now diminished by the entanglement with Miss Maudsley, whom he would be tempted to protect even at the cost of failing in his assignment.

Dayne had been following a similar line of reasoning. "I think we should ask outright for the ciphered papers, and no matter what they tell us—which more than likely will be nothing—inform the family that there may be French agents who think they have information."

"But why Miss Maudsley? Lady Maudsley would be the logical one. I'm suddenly tending toward the notion it was you they wanted. Let's give some more thought to this. . . . Their intent may have been to discover any damaging information and suppress it, or it may have been to suppress you because they think you have information."

"Possibly. But we've other, immediate worries. There's the mysterious gentleman whose name Thurlby gave us. I was supposed to wander among the fishing boats this morning and learn the place of rendezvous . . . although the news of the supposed robbery is no doubt all over town and that I was injured. . . ."

"Yes. And another chore. The runners may have something on Miss Goodman for us by now. I managed to get away from Ben for a short while in order to call at Bow Street. The runner I saw in London suggested I talk to Townsend. He's here with the prince. So I'll have to go around to the Albany to see him."

"I'll be laid up tomorrow, but the doctor attending me says I can be on my feet the next day. I'm going to Aunt Sarah's. . . . I was only waiting for you to return. The Maudsleys don't have room for me and for Giovanni. If you'll go by and ask her to send her carriage, I'll be obliged. . . . You can collect me from there the day after tomorrow. She sent a rather stiff note this afternoon ordering me to come as soon as the doctor permits, although earlier she'd only been concerned to know how I could have allowed myself to be robbed."

"I'll send Henny around to keep an eye on things here. Shall I send an express to London, asking for some bravos of our own?"

"You'd better. And you take care of yourself, Chaff."

Chaffinch nodded. "No need to remind me."

"Miss Maudsley says that a man with strange eyes was watching her on Midsummer Eve. Almond-shaped, slanting down at the corners. With an evil expression. If she'd seen the Pavilion before she saw this man, I'd say it was the *chinoiserie* influence. . . ."

"Not Miss Maudsley's style to be fanciful . . ."

"No, that's one charming characteristic I'll have to forgo. . . ."

"Which means? A declaration in form?"

"I suppose I'll come to it, but I tremble. . . ."

When his friend had taken leave, Dayne closed his eyes and tried to relax against his pillows. He'd gone too far to draw back now. It seemed that despite his continual private resolutions, whenever he was near Miss Aurelia Maudsley he forgot resolution and started making love to her. His Aunt Sarah was right that she should marry a rich man, and under Sarah's sponsoring she probably could. But there was too much fire there to settle for a match devoid of love. Of course, he was rich, he thought with a smile, and fit both bills. But he was also devoted to the Royal Navy. She returned his sentiments, of that he was certain, although the little sauceboat would pretend she didn't. . . . Until he kissed her . . . or she kissed him. And so, man of the world, daring commander, former dissolute, Breverton Dayne, sixth baron, lay on his pillows thinking about a mere kiss as though he were a fifteen-year-old boy.

Lia

Ben was giving us an account of his day in London while Mr. Chaffinch was visiting Dayne. He'd been introduced to Jem Belcher and seen his famous fighting dog. "What a pair of grinders!" he told us admiringly. "Lord Camelford—he was killed in a duel, you know—was a great patron of the Fancy. He gave it to Jem. Said two champions belonged together." And whether we cared to hear it or not, he gave us a round by round account of the Tom Belcher-Jack Warr fight. Since the set-to had gone nineteen rounds and thirty-three minutes, the account was not brief. I don't mean to imply that Ben hadn't been concerned about the attempted robbery or that he wasn't proud of my own pugilistic debut, but on the other hand, I hadn't even lasted the required half minute to complete a round.

Ben had taken a very professional look at my injured hand. "You wouldn't have hurt your hand, Lia, if you'd struck correctly. I'll show you tomorrow—or as soon as it's well."

"No, thank you. I don't intend ever to enter the ring again. And, anyway, I suspect that rather than a fist like Dutch Sam's, mine is made of glass."

Dutch Sam is a Jewish fighter, noted for his fists of iron. He's highly respected among the fighting fraternity, but he's too small to be able to aspire to the championship. That's what Ben and Mr. Chaffinch say, in any event.

Only Chunk and I remained attentive as Ben reached the fourteenth round. Or the fifteenth. Even Ben wasn't sure. "Warr could hardly see by now, he'd been taking so many hits to the head, but he perked up in the fifteenth—or maybe this was the fourteenth. . . . Got in some good body blows. Put one to the chest that sent Belcher to the ropes. . . . Warr's got bottom, can't deny that, and I was beginning to regret I'd . . . uh . . . I'd been so strong on Belcher. . . ."

I was on to him immediately. "You were betting! Where did you get the money? If you borrowed from Mr. Chaffinch, I'll—I'll—"

"No, I didn't borrow from Chaff. What do you take me for?"

"Well, you got the money someplace, and—Why, I know. You pawned your watch! That's as bad as borrowing from your friends."

"Come down out of the boughs. It isn't as bad as borrowing from friends. The fellow could have sold the watch if I hadn't redeemed it. It was just business to him—nothing of honor about it."

"Don't talk to me about honor. You promised that watch to Chunk. What if Belcher'd lost? What about the honor of a promise?"

Chunk, who's a young man of honor himself, broke in to announce that he had given his permission to his brother to pawn the watch before Ben left for London. "I got a share of the winnings, too. Now I can buy Captain Cook's book on his explorations."

It occurred to me that instructing children in good judgment is so terribly difficult in a world of chance events, and I was just on the verge of delivering a little lecture when Mama took the opportunity to ask Ben and me not to engage in arguments in the parlor, and to tell us that our voices had been raised in an ungentlemanly and unladylike way. How is it, I thought, that Mama can so often seize on the irrelevant when she takes it into her head to reprimand one of us?

Mr. Chaffinch came walking in as Ben—and poor Mr. Warr—were ending the nineteenth and final round. "His eyes were completely closed, but he'd have gone on fighting if his friends had let him. . . . As it was, he had to be carried off. But everybody was congratulating him for a good fight and calling him a chip off the old block." (Warr's father, the reader may remember, was also a pugilist of some standing.)

"Yes, young man has bottom," Chaffinch agreed. "And so do you, Miss Maudsley. Brev can't praise you enough. Nor that fellow Giovanni, either. He says if he were a younger man . . ."

"Yes, I've heard Giovanni's sentiments already."

Ben gave a shout of laughter. "So Lady Sarah's Neapolitan's got a kindness for you, has he, Lia?"

"Ben," Mama said firmly, "I have asked you once to keep your voice down, and such loud laughter is exceedingly ill-bred."

I glanced over at Mama with some concern. It wasn't like her to scold in front of a guest or to curb high spirits (as opposed to arguments). The attempted robbery must have affected her nerves more than I'd realized, I thought.

Ben offered her an apology for his loud laughter but was in no way repentant about teasing me, and I knew I should hear in the future more than was supportable about my new Italian beau.

Dayne

Lady Sarah Pellett, followed by a maidservant carrying a tray and trailed by Giovanni, entered her sunny parlor where Dayne, reclining on a sofa, was reading a novel by Smollett that he had found on a side table. The rearrangement of the furniture and the setting out of numerous plates and dishes led him to surmise that Lady Sarah intended to join him for his lunch. He closed the book. "That looks like a pretty monstracious lunch for a sick man, Aunt."

"Reading *Humphrey Clinker,* are you?"

"Rereading. Found it here on the table. A favorite of yours?"

"Like Smollett better than Fielding, no matter what people say to the contrary. Mrs. Slipslop can't hold a candle to Tabitha Bramble and Mrs. Win Jenkins when it comes to butcherating the lank witch."

"Very good, Aunt!" Dayne laughed.

The luncheon proceeded amiably to a discussion of whether, as Lady Sarah maintained, Fielding had stolen the character of Humphrey Clinker for his innocent and chaste hero, Joseph Andrews, and then moved on to other comparisons between the two authors, Lady Sarah defending Smollett and Dayne defending Fielding.

When an hour later Giovanni had removed the last dish, poured coffee and offered Dayne a cheroot, which he declined, Lady Sarah leaned back in her chair and sighed.

"Still not recovered, Aunt?" Dayne asked.

"Oh, I'm recovered. I'll be repentant for a month or two, eat as commonsensibly as I did today, but eventually I'll forget the misery I suffered yesterday and I'll indulge myself again. One day it'll carry me off. I just hope it carries me off while I'm enjoying my food, not while I'm suffering the consequences. I could go happy to my Maker with a bite of almond cheesecake in my mouth."

They both sipped their coffee silently, each engaged in private thoughts, until Lady Sarah suddenly said, "Hate to take you to task, Breverton, when you've just been through an ordeal. . . . Kicking people in the ribs, indeed! What is the world coming to, anyway? Just read the other day that the Tourays' house was robbed in Grosvenor Square. . . . Well, but what I have to say is serious enough that I'm not going to beat around the bush. Ain't my style. Your behavior with Aurelia Maudsley was disgraceful, and that she permitted it was even more disgraceful. And if I hadn't been so sick, I would have given you both a good scold. . . . Why, if you'd kissed the girl right there on the ballroom floor, it couldn't have been more obvious. . . ."

"One moment, Aunt. My relationship with Miss Maudsley is my own affair. . . ."

"I'm not talking just to hear myself talk, Breverton. Don't be a fool. It's obvious you'd like to bed the girl—too bad you can't. Quickest cure in the world for infatuation . . ."

"I am not infatuated."

"I suppose you think you're in love! After two months!"

Suddenly, Dayne smiled. "Wild horses couldn't force me to marry Catherine deVandt."

"Catherine deVandt? We're talking about Aurelia Maudsley."

"No, we're talking about your idea about whom I should marry, and that happens to be Lady Catherine deVandt. Great as my affection is for you, Aunt Sarah, I'll choose my own wife."

"You're a fool if you're thinking about Aurelia. Family's poor, no influence . . ."

"Sir Whitney was a respected diplomatist."

"He was a spendthrift and a fool."

"But Lia is neither."

Lady Sarah regarded him consideringly. "Tilly's shrewder than I thought. Should have known she'd turn Aurelia out like an angel. All along she's had her own ideas about getting the girl married. I can just imagine what went through her head when you came calling—title, money, just what the doctor ordered! And to think I was fool enough to fall for that innocent stupidity she likes to put on. . . . And Aurelia, simpering and—"

Dayne, forgetting that a similar suspicion had long ago once crossed his mind, frowned. "Aunt Sarah, I have more affection and . . . and love . . . yes, love for you than for my own mother. But I can't listen to you say such things. I'm a guest in your house, and I won't fight with you. . . . Why, Aunt Sarah . . . what?"

Lady Sarah was crying. Dayne had the terrible feeling that he was watching a great and venerable oak, staunch as the timeless hills, slowly topple to the ground. He made a painful move to rise, with a vague notion of administering comforting pats.

"No, damn you, Breverton. Stay where you are." Lady Sarah removed a handkerchief from her sleeve and wiped her eyes. She sniffed. "Moment of sentimentality, nothing more. And . . . oh, well, might as well admit I'm wrong. If Tilly saw you looking calf's eyes at Aurelia, which you've no doubt been doing, she'd encourage it, in her scatter-headed way, but she wouldn't *scheme.* I'm the old schemer, and like most schemers, I got what I deserved."

Dayne sank back on his cushions. The venerable oak still stood.

"Lia's brave and honest and loyal," he said. "And you like her. Why should you object to my marrying her?"

"She's also impertinent, saucy, disrespectful, prideful, and she can do nothing for you or for our family. . . ."

"Just a minute, Aunt Sarah. Let's speak plainly with each other. Algernon married for family interest, and he's dead. . . ."

"Melancholy, touched in the head . . ."

"No. He was unhappy. He listened to my uncles and married a woman who could 'do something for him,' and all she did was drive him to drink. Literally. My mother and father . . . neither of them happy, but family interest was served. And you, Aunt Sarah. What if my Great Uncle Rob hadn't had the good grace to die at sixty? What if he'd lived until he was ninety? You'd have had to wait until you were sixty yourself to escape to Italy with Uncle Rob's pot of gold—not when you were . . . how old were you, Aunt, when he died? Twenty-five? Thirty-five?"

"I was thirty," Lady Sarah replied with dignity. "I gave Robert the best years of my life."

Dayne hooted. "Oh, what a whopper! Oh, my ribs! No more! No more, please, dear Aunt!"

Lady Sarah, after a struggle, laughed, unable to maintain a straight face herself.

The door opened, and Chaffinch walked in. "May I come in?" he asked. "I knocked, I assure you, but you couldn't hear me above all the racket you were making. How are you, Lady Sarah?" He bent over her hand. "Laughter's good medicine, they say."

"Do they indeed? Then why is Breverton in such agony?"

Dayne, on the sofa, gasped. "Aunt's been telling whoppers."

"Has she?" Chaffinch sat down. "I'm not surprised."

"Well," Lady Sarah said, "not only must I bear with an impudent nephew, but with an impudent visitor, too. Well, Chaffinch, and what have you to say to this disgraceful event?"

"Shocking. The increase in crime . . ."

"Don't be dense. I'm talking about my nephew and the Maudsley girl."

Chaffinch turned a questioning eye on Dayne. "You've told her?" The unwisdom of such a confidence was manifestly clear from the tone of his voice.

"Ha! Didn't need to. Whole world knows his blood's on the boil for the girl. Might as well have worn a sign on his back."

Dayne laid a despairing hand across his forehead. "Preserve me, Lord. Protect me from interfering aunts. . . ."

"I've given you my opinion, Breverton. And I've conceded that the fault is as much yours as the Maudsleys. . . ."

A laugh escaped Lady Sarah's much beset nephew, despite his annoyance. "She's exonerated the Maudsleys, Chaff, of charges of scheming to ensnare me, and confessed to the crime of scheming herself. Now go away, Aunt Sarah, or I'll have a relapse and you'll be required to nurse me for a week at least."

Lady Sarah rose with an air of affront but could not help the faint smile that pulled at the corners of her lips. She was very fond of this particular nephew. "If you're determined, I won't stand in your way. But don't expect me to approve a foolish marriage. I shall never approve it. Just wish I weren't so fond of her silly mother. Won't be able to bring myself to cut her, after condescending to her so generously these past weeks. But that daughter of hers is an ungrateful wretch, after all I tried to do for her. *She* needn't expect civility."

"I do hope, Aunt, that you will not be uncivil to Lia. Lady Maudsley would surely consider it an insult. I hesitate to confess that I haven't yet declared myself, for I fully intend to do so, but I can't be certain that Lia will accept me. Her sense of responsibility to her family is excessively strong. . . . You should admire her character, Aunt. So if you have any regard for me at all, I beg that you continue as though nothing has happened to change your opinion of her or her family. Need I say that incivility to her will be tantamount to incivility to me?"

"An empty threat, Breverton. I'm always uncivil to you. Chaffinch, you'll excuse me. I see that you're all impatience to discuss some kind of business with my nephew, but as you're a sensible man, I suggest you try to talk some sense into him."

Lady Sarah sailed out of the room, and Chaffinch turned inquiringly to his friend. "She's opposed to a liaison with Miss Maudsley?"

"I'd think that would be more than clear to a good intelligence officer. I am very annoyed, Chaff, with my aunt."

Chaffinch murmured soothingly to the effect that elderly aunts could be a trial.

"Her back's up because she had other plans for Lia, as well as for me. Aunt Sarah likes to manage, as you know, and we've confounded her schemes . . . as she almost admitted in a moment of uncharacteristic weakness."

"Well, she's out if she thinks I'll try to discourage you. I have the greatest admiration for Miss Maudsley and for her family. You couldn't have done better, Brev. I say that sincerely."

"Tell that to my aunt."

"Willingly. I'll also tell her that Miss Maudsley will make an admirable sailor's wife. . . . But I warn you, Brev, she'll be hard to handle. You'll have to keep her on a loose leash."

"I won't keep her on any leash at all. Why should I try to change what attracted me in the first place?"

"Words of wisdom, but not always easy to honor. Well, in any event, I've just come from there. Thought I'd look in to see how they were getting on after the attack. Miss Maudsley's hand is still paining her, but their doctor insists no bones are broken. Something he calls *trauma.* Very modern fellow. They all, including Miss Maudsley, send you their best. Henny's keeping an eye on the place at night. The way the land rises behind the property makes it easy to maintain a lookout. We'll have a couple bravos down from London by Sunday morning. Let's see, what else? . . . Oh, I stopped by the Albany and was lucky enough to catch Townsend—Prinny's off to London today. They're afraid the old king's slipping into one of his spells again."

"So you saw Townsend? What did he say?"

"Bow Street's top runner was more concerned about attending to the prince's safety than any little problem with spies and was in a bit of a dash, so—"

They were interrupted by Giovanni, who had come to collect the remains of Dayne's lunch.

"I say, Dayne, could this good fellow bring me some of that coffee? Smelled delicious when I came in."

"It's Lady Sarah's Italian brew we were drinking. Shall I ask for the same, or something more properly English?"

"Italian, hmmm? I take it you mean it's strong enough to support a horse. I'll try Italian."

Giovanni, who understood more English than he spoke, stated that the grand (meaning big) signor had excellent wisdom, and would he like his coffee (a slight indication of disapproval) with milk? Giovanni had strict notions about the proper kind of coffee to be served at different hours of the day, and milk in an afternoon coffee was not to be supported . . . except by the English. . . . But what else could be expected from a people who preferred tea?

"I'll take it without milk." Chaffinch smiled.

"Ees allrrright," Giovanni stated approvingly. "I make new."

"Well," Dayne asked, after waiting for Giovanni to bow his way out, "and what did Townsend say?"

"Nothing yet on the Goodman woman, except they believe she's in Ireland. Not surprising, since she ran off with an Irishman. However, they expect results soon. A rather disappointing interview. He did promise to send a runner down to inform us should there be any new development."

"And did you see the master of the *Mermaid?* Have you discovered who we're to meet and where? Is the mysterious gentleman a smuggler?"

"Yes, I saw him. As for the mysterious gentleman, I have no idea if he's one of the trading Gentlemen, but either both of us or I alone—depending on how soon you're up and about—will meet him. I've elaborate instructions, which I won't bother to go into now, but you should expect to be engaged all of Monday afternoon and until rather late into the night."

"I'll be up and about. Tomorrow I intend for you to transport me back to our lodgings. Fond as I am of Aunt Sarah, I think it'll be better if I make my stay here short."

"Just as well. Your own man's nose is out of joint because some Italian is taking care of you."

"I wouldn't have missed my hours with Giovanni for the world, but it was remiss of me not to think of sending for Tilt. But if I had, you'd have had no one to serve you. . . ."

"Thoughtful of you. And one last thing. The outing and the burglary. Think we should go ahead with it. If you remember, Lady Maudsley said if they still had any of Sir Whitney's papers, they would be in his old desk. Miss Maudsley once said that Sir Whitney's retiring place was on the top floor, so we know where to tell Henny to begin looking." Chaffinch looked thoughtful. "You know, I think Henny's like one of those water witches; only he divines where the loot will be with his nose. He claims his mother had a small slip in her youth with a gypsy and he's the result."

A knock on the door heralded Giovanni with the coffee, which Chaffinch declared to be "downright bracing." Giovanni retired much pleased, with repetitions of his judgment that the grand signor had excellent wisdom.

When the door closed, Dayne said, "Sunday's four days from now. I'll be full of stiff meat by then."

Chaffinch raised his eyebrows at this piece of boxing cant, before sipping his coffee cautiously. "The Maudsley youngsters were so obviously disappointed. . . . They thought that your injuries would mean we wouldn't go. Made it easy to insist that you insisted we not cancel our planned excursion. Will Lady Sarah join us?"

"I don't plan to invite her. I can't keep her from continuing to call on Lady Maudsley—and, indeed, would not want to—but on the other hand, I don't want to give her more opportunity than necessary to be uncivil to Lia. I have hope of bringing her around."

"It's agreed, then. I'll not cancel the arrangements."

"Right. But I still think we should tell Lia that they may have important papers. I cautioned her not to let the children roam so freely. And to be careful herself. If it was Lia from whom they wanted information, they might try kidnapping. But what I told her before I left the villa was that our attackers might try to get at me through them . . . that maybe they did think I knew something . . . had me confused with someone else. An inept attempt, no doubt, to warn her, without being specific. In any event, I mumbled along on those lines and explained to her that the position in which they found us, and no doubt what they overheard, would suggest that I'm vulnerable. I'm sorry about it, Chaff. Didn't mean to get entangled. Last thing in the world I expected or wanted."

Chaffinch shrugged. "Such things happen. But did the lady believe you?"

"Probably not. I think we should tell her the whole story. We needn't tell the rest of the family, but she should know. We have an obligation to think of their safety."

"I've given it serious thought, Brev. But I just can't like the family knowing. If they should by any chance learn names, they might somehow hinder or upset a capture. We aren't even certain that we want to arrest anyone; we may want to find a means to use the French agents for our own purposes. We may be required to act secretly. . . ."

"You mean assassination. I don't like it. . . ."

"Come now, Brev. You're in the business of killing."

"Yes, but in a fair fight . . ."

"What do you think would have happened to Sir Whitney if it had been discovered that he'd learned the names of important members of the spy ring? Can we be certain he died a natural death? I assure you that we can't. He died most conveniently, from the point of view of the French. Do you think our agents' lives are safe in France? A spy has to think of himself—or herself—as a combat soldier."

"Well, my assignment was to aid and assist you, Chaff, so I have to consent to your decisions."

"And I was instructed to consult with you on all actions. . . ."

"Nonetheless, the responsibility for final decisions is yours. I recognize that this is a Foreign Office operation, but—"

"There's another thing. Their greatest safety, I still believe, is in ignorance. Have you considered that their man of business—this fellow Price—whom they all trust and are fond of, might be our quarry? He certainly was in a position to know—although Sir Whitney was putting a good face on things—just how shaky his financial affairs were. And perhaps even to engage in a little blackmail. We put that notion aside when we discovered that Charlotte wasn't Sir Whitney's by-blow, but it's still a possibility. And wouldn't it be better that they not find it out?" With some sign of agitation, he poured himself another cup of coffee. He, too, had become fond of the Maudsleys, and was torn between his judgment as an intelligence officer, his dislike of deceit, and his own concern for their safety.

"Well, let's go over it all again, and all the possibilities." Dayne had known Chaffinch for many years and recognized his agitation.

"Won't hurt. Although we've been over it to the point of exhaustion. But call that factotum to take this coffee away. If I don't stop drinking it, I'll be as up in the world as if I'd been tippling your Aunt Sarah's best brandy."

Chapter Fourteen

We had been heartened to hear, in a note from Mr. Chaffinch, that Dayne sustained the drive to Lady Sarah's without serious discomfort. The next day Chaffinch called in person to discover how we were recovering from the dramatic events and to settle plans for our Sunday yachting excursion. The youngsters, along with Sunny and Ben, had found it difficult to hide their disappointment when they thought Dayne's injuries would prevent the outing, especially with the barometer telling us that continued fair weather lay ahead. Mama, who had always loved yachting, was equally disappointed, but much too disciplined and well-bred to show it. The reader will recall that our own yacht was one of the first sacrifices to Papa's extravagance.

We had some concern about leaving the house unguarded after the attack in the garden—undoubtedly foolish, since almost everything worth stealing had been sold long ago. However, Chaffinch reassured us. "Dayne's man Tilt will guard the house, and we've hired a fellow to also keep watch. Name's Henny. Very reliable. You needn't have the least worry." Mama couldn't praise his thoughtfulness enough.

When the gentlemen greeted us at the West Street Groyne that bright Sunday morning, Dayne appeared to be as hale and hearty as Mr. Chaffinch, except for yellowing bruises around his eyes. In response to our inquiries, he assured us that although his bruises were still tender, he suffered no pain with movement. We all expressed our joy in his rapid recovery and Mama said, "And it was *so* unnecessary! I've always understood that thieves prefer silver and jewels and of course we really have nothing of that sort and very little money at hand, either. Of course," she added quickly, "they weren't to know that and I'm sure I don't mean to sound ungrateful. . . ."

"No, I should never think you ungrateful, kind Lady Maudsley. It's I who haven't thanked you enough for the care you gave me. . . ."

While Mama and Lord Dayne were vying with each other for the prettiest speech, Chaffinch was explaining to Ben and Chunk that their technical questions would have to await Dayne's pleasure. "Have to confess, I'm not much of a hand at sailing," he said.

We were rowed out to the yacht from the West Street Groyne. It was one of those rare, almost cloudless mornings. Above us the sky was a great overturned bowl of delicate blue glass, pale and limpid at the horizon, brighter and bluer in the depths of the bowl, where a few scattered wispy clouds floated.

I immediately picked out Colonel Staffen's yacht—the *Sea Nymph*—from among the others, for Chaffinch had pointed her out to us the afternoon before, and all of us, even Mama, had studied her through the telescope. "A beauty, isn't she?" asked Dayne.

Our own greeting had been a model of circumspection, but the tenderness in his glance spoke his admiration and regard. I did not yet dare call it love, perhaps from some murmur of superstition. One must remember that at some remote date all our ancestors were heathens, painting themselves blue, dancing around bonfires and consulting magicians and auguries. Although, of course, there's that old saying, "There's many a slip, 'twixt the cup and the lip," which isn't superstition at all but an observation on life. But I was not of a mind to consider the future that lovely Sunday morning.

The breeze was fresh. "Excellent sailing weather," Dayne observed and Mama, her eyes sparkling with a zest we hadn't seen in years, replied, "Oh, yes! But not so excellent that our newcomers to the sea will be uncomfortable." She was voicing a secret concern of my own, that we would soon have half the party below decks being sick.

"We'll be anchored most of the time," Dayne said reassuringly. "Another time, perhaps, for a more exciting sail."

Mama, who as I've remarked walks at such an agonizingly slow pace that one would think her an ancient of ninety rather than a mere forty-two, was as nimble as a girl in the transfer from the boat to the yacht and once on deck was all eagerness to see and all delight in what she saw. The infants, firmly tethered to our indispensable Jane and to Mrs. Oliphant, were happily toddling around the deck, while Ben and Chunk, led by Dayne, were discussing all the technical aspects of a small sailing vessel. Once Mama was installed in a deck chair, looking charming and girlish in her broad-brimmed hat, Colonel Staffen escorted Sunny and me on a less technical tour. Angela, together with Charlotte, leaned on the railing and picked out the more prominent landmarks of Brighton, including our own villa.

When we were under weigh, and as I leaned on the stern rail gazing down at our wake, I took off my wide hat, wishing I could throw it overboard and be done with it. And how wonderful it would be to unbraid my hair to blow free in the wind. Dayne was obviously in his element and Chaffinch obviously was not in his. He had gone to sit by Mama, while Dayne and the colonel discussed ships and sailing. Charlotte, frightened at first, was soon treading the decks with Chunk as handily as any of us, but Angela had retreated to a deck chair beside Mama and Chaffinch, content to watch the others.

After Dayne was at last satisfied that he had seen everything and had thoroughly discussed the weather, the sailing conditions and the best set of the sails, he joined me at the rail. "Do you enjoy sailing, Miss Maudsley?"

"Yes, very much. I suppose I'm the only one of us who remembers Papa's yacht well—except Mama, of course. I was eleven when he sold it and still remember how disappointed I was and how angry that he should say it was unsafe for children. But Ben was only six and Sunny three, so they hardly remember at all."

"What was her name?"

"The *Belle Femme*. I never liked the name, I guess, because I had a governess then who was supposed to be teaching me French. . . ."

"Supposed to be?"

"Well, neither Papa nor Mama ever insisted that we learn anything, except to read and write and do our sums, and I didn't have much taste for learning anything in those days, so—"

"So you rebelled against learning French?"

"No. I just didn't learn much. But I did know that *belle femme* meant 'beautiful woman' in English. I didn't think it was an appropriate name for a yacht. Papa said that words in foreign languages are just sounds, especially if they're not pronounced correctly, but I couldn't believe that. I knew what *belle femme* meant, just as he did. He spoke excellent French."

"And, saucy and disobedient child that you were, you defied your good parent and argued with him."

I looked up sharply at him. He was smiling down at me with that tender look that was simply melting my every defense, although all he said was, "And how did your worthy papa defend himself?"

"There's a lane near High Oak—High Oak was our country house—called Grere's Meadow Lane. Long ago it led to a piece of land owned by a man named Grere, but we always pronounced it Greresmeadow, as though it were one long word and never thought that it actually meant something. Papa argued that the name of our yacht was just like Greresmeadow Lane—Bellefemme, without any real meaning. He didn't believe it, of course, but playing with words fascinated him, and he encouraged us to play with them too. Remember he liked making up ciphers? But you and Lady Sarah play word games."

"Yes, we both like playing, punning and pontificating with pretty . . . uh . . . phrases."

"Phrases?"

"Well, it *begins* with the right letter." His brow wrinkled. "Doesn't it?"

It took me a few seconds, for the game was new, but Papa's training had been excellent. "Forgive me, but frankly, you forfeit, for you fake—for it *sounds* like *f*."

"I surrender, sweet. I am so seriously sunk under your spell that words fail me." I glanced up, expecting a teasing smile, but his expression was . . . ardent. My own smile faded and my unsteady heart began to beat more heavily. It was an odd choice of words with which to make a declaration of affection, but such it was and it, too, completely overpowered my brain—and perhaps his—for any more games. His next words made no sense at all. "I must point out something to you," he said. Then he stepped behind me and, turning me to look toward the shore, pointed off in the general direction of the cliffs, while his right hand covered mine on the rail. Without the least intention in the world to do so, I leaned back into the curve of his arm. "Do you see it now?" he asked conversationally. And then he whispered, "Lia . . ."

"What are you looking at?" Chunk asked from behind us.

I jerked my hand away from under Dayne's. "We . . . we were just . . . j . . . just looking at . . . looking at . . ." I actually stuttered.

Dayne said, with the aplomb of the accomplished plotter (I've already observed that the game is catching), "I was pointing out something to your sister. If you'll go down to the cabin, you'll find a spyglass . . ."

"Oh, yes! I saw it. May I bring it up?"

"Yes, run along and do that."

We watched Chunk run eagerly off, then watched Colonel Staffen, with Sunny on his arm, stroll toward us. Sunny had changed her mind about the romantic age of men, raising it from approximately twenty to approximately thirty. "What were you spying out back there?" the colonel asked.

"Well," Dayne remarked with a sigh, "there are better eyes for spying out interesting sights than mine, it seems. I've sent Chunk for the spyglass."

Dayne and I had no opportunity to be alone again that long day, but I had abandoned myself to happiness. Afloat on a vast sea, detached as it were from the steadiness of dry land, I could abandon common sense and live—like the romances—in the moment.

We ate our alfresco luncheon on shore. We disembarked at the private wharf of an estate, whose owner—a friend of Colonel Staffen—and his young wife came down to greet us and to offer us the hospitality of their home. The luncheon had been chosen with great care and with attention to possibly queasy appetites: plain cold chicken delicately flavored with herbs, slices of roasted beef lightly peppered and salted, fresh nectarines and apricots and pears. And with it all, crisp-crusted bread spread with sweet butter and ice-cold sparkling water and champagne. Afterward, we wandered through the beautiful groves and plantations that sloped down to the sea from the pleasant manor house.

We returned to Brighton with the sunset. The summer twilight had just faded to darkness when we at last reached the gate to Xanadu's small dooryard. We were tired—that delicious fatigue that a day on the sea stimulates—a little sunburned and our hair stiffened with salt spray. We stood around in the dooryard arguing over who should have the first washes, while Mrs. Oliphant unlocked the door. She pushed it open and uttered a scream.

"What is it? What happened?" We all crowded close behind her and then into the house, jostling each other as Mrs. Oliphant cried, *"Thieves!* We've been robbed! They came back! And that Mr. Chaffinch promised us he had a man guarding the house! The liar! Liar!"

"Pants on fire!" Chunk yelled, at which Mrs. Oliphant took a hearty swipe at him with her free hand. He ducked easily, since she was carrying Irene on her other arm. Such an uncharacteristic action attested to her high state of agitation.

"It just popped out, honest!" Chunk retreated toward the still open front door as both Sunny and I descended on him with the same intent as Mrs. Oliphant.

Ben, who had been bringing up the rear, pushed past us to take Mama and Mrs. Oliphant by the arm. "Come out of the house . . . they may still be here!"

Jane, carrying Georgie, started to scream, which set the child to screaming, which set Irene to howling. Sunny and I abandoned pursuit of Chunk, Sunny to pull Charlotte and Angela from the steps back into the yard and I to take Georgie from Jane—none too gently, I fear. "Stop that screaming or I shall slap you. Hard!" I hissed at her through clenched teeth. I soothed and cuddled Georgie and as he quieted, sobbing on my shoulder, Irene stopped her racket also.

I realized suddenly that Ben had disappeared into the house, at which I thrust Georgie into Charlotte's arms, prepared to follow him. Charlotte had been hovering nearby, anxious to take her little brother, for although she was willing enough to give over his care to the rest of us, in moments of stress the two children sought each other.

Mama, with one arm around Angela and a hand on Mrs. Oliphant's arm as though to restrain her from entering the house behind Ben, cried sharply, "No, Lia!" as she realized that I was about to follow him, but I was already through the door. I ran across the small entrance hall, shouting, "Ben! Ben! Where are you?" with an edge of fear in my own voice.

"Lia! Here! In the scullery!"

He was on his knees beside a man whose bonds he was cutting with Mrs. Oliphant's favorite kitchen knife. Another man, whom I recognized from our introduction earlier that day as Mr. Tilt, Lord Dayne's manservant, was sitting up, rubbing one wrist across the other and wiggling his feet back and forth. When he saw me, he said, "I'm dreadfully sorry, Miss Maudsley. Took me by surprise."

The other man, who I assumed was the guard Mr. Chaffinch had sent, said venomously, "The bastards! Beg pardon, miss," then uttered a spate of curses that well nigh singed my ears.

"*Mr.* Henny!" Lord Dayne's man said loudly. "There is a lady present. Apologize at once."

" 'Pologize, miss," Mr. Henny muttered, "but I'm orful mad. Bashed me on the nob, they did." He began rubbing his own wrists. "And the gennelmens are going to be even more terrible mad!"

"It's all right," I said. "But if you'll excuse me, I'd better tell Mama that Ben's not been bashed on the nob."

"Lor, where's the offices? I'm just about dead with holdin' it," I heard Mr. Henny say as I ran back through the kitchen toward the front door. The man hadn't a lick of delicacy.

Concern had overcome caution among the rest of the family and they were already crowding into the hallway.

"Ben?" Mama asked immediately, her eyes frightened.

"He's all right. It seems our two guards were overcome by

superior forces. Ben found them tied up in the scullery."

There were many exclamations of concern and wonder at this, as everyone rushed for the scullery, then had to be shooed away and sent about essential business. The babies needed soothing and feeding and to be put to bed; Lord Dayne and Mr. Chaffinch had to be notified; the two guards had to be given food and drink (they'd been tied up for six hours); and we had to assess the extent of the robbery.

The house was a shambles. The robbers had pulled all the drawers out of all the desks and chests, including the one we kept in the foyer for pattens and rain cloaks, and had scattered the contents. Sunny, who is not neat, was actually embarrassed, not only because the robbers had seen her intimate garments—a matter that bothered all the females among us—but because they had found her wardrobe such a mess.

"As if it matters what some horrible thieves might think!" Mrs. Oliphant finally exclaimed in exasperation.

After a cursory inspection, we discovered that the thieves had taken such money as they could find, a matter of a few pounds, but had overlooked our largest cache—the money we kept in an old sugar bowl in the kitchen. They took what little jewelry we had, including my turquoises and pearls, and a silver-plated cake dish from the dining room. We had long ago sold most of our jewelry and all of our real silver pieces. Later we discovered that the robbers had also taken some trinkets of minor value. Mrs. Oliphant lost her watch, but she seemed almost more incensed by the theft of a joint of mutton and a pan of gingerbread from the kitchen, which she had intended for our supper.

Ben had gone for Dayne and Chaffinch who arrived, posthaste, in Chaffinch's racing phaeton. They looked both angry and chagrined. They insisted on paying for all we'd lost, since their guards had been so remiss, at which Mr. Henny said, "Sneaked up and bashed me on the nob almost afore I knowed it and what was I to do about that? Come to, and there I was trussed up like a hog. First I've been bested ever. And that ain't no slum. And I'm right sorry, miss."

Chaffinch, looking like murder, ordered the man from the room, at which we all protested. After all, he'd been injured in the line of duty. But there was really little more for either Mr. Henny or Mr. Tilt to report, and so they were turned over to Mrs. Oliphant, who had already begun slicing bread and cheese for them.

"I insist," Dayne told Mama, "that we pay for the damages. It was so entirely our fault. Tilt has been with me for seven years—I'd trust my life with him—and we were assured that Henny was one of the most reliable . . ."

Chaffinch broke in. "I must second Brev on this. The fault is entirely ours, and you must permit us to pay for the damages."

"We really can't accept," Mama said firmly. "Poor Mr. Tilt and Mr. Henny did the best they could, I'm sure, against men who obviously make thievery and violence their business. Surely no one would expect that with someone guarding the house, the robbers would have dared. . . . Now, I'll hear no more about it."

Dayne sighed. "At least you must allow us to entertain you at dinner. . . ."

"Oh," Mama said, smiling sweetly. "We couldn't possibly. It's been such a long day. . . ."

"We all need baths and clean clothes," I interrupted. My tongue's censor had gone awry again.

"Of course," Dayne said smoothly as Mama raised her eyebrows at my lack of delicacy. "We'll just send out for something. Tilt can order us something at the Old Ship. . . ."

"Let me talk to Mrs. Oliphant," I said and went off to the kitchen, where our two guards were finishing off their plates of bread and cheese with glasses of Mrs. Oliphant's home-brewed ale.

"I'm just slicing up some more bread for the children, Miss Lia, and I'll take it up to them. They can have bread and milk tonight. After all they ate this afternoon, that's all they need for their suppers. . . ."

"Yes, of course. And what have we for the rest of us?"

"There's plenty of bread. Good thing I baked on Saturday, even though I did think for a minute that seeing as we were to be gone all day Sunday . . . But then Monday's wash day and even though the big wash isn't until the week after, I just thought to myself, 'No, Bridey Oliphant, you'd better do it today.' And then Miss Charlotte was so helpful. . . ."

"Bridey, is it?" asked Mr. Tilt. "Is that for Bridget? My wife's name was Bridget, God bless her soul." He cast his eyes heavenward, making it abundantly clear that Mrs. Tilt had Gone Before.

"Yes, Mr. Tilt, Bridget it is. But never in my life has anyone called me anything but Bridey, except my mother, when she was displeased. . . ."

"Excuse me, Mrs. Oliphant, but should we send out for more cheese or other provisions? We should all take a little nourishment before we sleep and I haven't a taste for bread and milk."

"Well, there's bread and butter aplenty and some of those sausages that old Mr. Maiben makes and there's milk and eggs. And Mr. Tilt's fired up the stove real nice, so I can make up some of my quire-of-paper pancakes in no time and with some honey or some of that pear sauce Miss Sunny made up from the two basketsful the squire sent down from the country last week . . . So many more than we could use, the squire's always been so generous . . . But if Mr. Ben's of a mind to go, a mite more of cheese . . ."

Having two men in her kitchen with whom she'd had no previous acquaintance was making Mrs. Oliphant unusually talkative, so I had to interrupt her again to suggest that her pancakes, for which she was rightly noted, would be excellent with some of Mr. Maiben's sausages and Sunny's pear sauce. Dayne and Chaffinch, on hearing that plan, insisted on sending off for the cheese—a wedge of Stilton and a fine cheddar—and for wine and ale.

The children were permitted to join us. Neither Mama nor I nor Mrs. Oliphant could bear to consign them to bread and milk after such an exciting day. Mr. Tilt helped Mrs. Oliphant in the kitchen, and they even succeeded in putting Henny to work washing up. (Henny had "never lifted a finger in a kitchen before," and hadn't never thought he would, he told me when I discovered him in the scullery washing dishes.) Although we shouldn't have been in spirits at all, it was a merry meal and we put aside consideration of our losses and enjoyed the moment. I was beginning to think that living in the moment was a philosophy adequate for life, until I realized that it was a philosophy dangerously close to Papa's.

Dayne

Although the night was clear, the moon was past the full and new risen. Mr. Stuart Chaffinch was driving at a pace that under the circumstances was little short of reckless. He had maintained his good humor admirably until he and Dayne had taken leave of the Maudsleys, but once on the road, his irritability burst violently forth, clearly expressed in reckless driving. Henny, clinging as best he could beside the groom, had the poor taste to groan loudly when the vehicle struck a rock that sent a jolt through it from axle to silver moldings.

"Quiet!" Chaffinch roared. "Or you'll be groaning loud enough to be heard in the next county when I'm through with you!"

" 'Tweren't my fault, your honor. If—"

"I said QUIET!"

Mr. Tilt decided to take a hand. "I do think you ought to listen to him, sir. It was—"

Dayne intervened. "Time enough to tell it all when we get back to our rooms." He refrained from commenting on the speed at which they were proceeding, merely tightening his grip as they neared the West Street corner, which Chaffinch was approaching with barely diminished speed. Although he took the corner nicely, as a member of the Four-in-Hand Club should have done, Dayne thought it perhaps a bit too nice as they swung into West Street on one wheel.

Chaffinch brought the phaeton to a sharp stop in front of their lodgings. "Open the door, Tilt and get a candle lit, while I see to my horses."

The groom, who admired Mr. Chaffinch's skill with the whip to the point of veneration, jumped down, alert and cheerful, to run to the horses' heads. "I can manage them, Mr. Chaff," he said, to which Chaffinch responded with a growl. His groom took it for an affirmative and, whistling cheerfully, led the team off to the stables behind the house.

They quietly mounted the steps; even in a vile humor Chaffinch had a thought for sleeping fellow lodgers. While Tilt went about lighting the lamps and Dayne directed Henny to sit down and keep quiet until spoken to, Chaffinch made for the dresser and the various decanters of spirits and wines. Chaffinch favored Scots whiskey over French brandy in difficult moments and he poured himself a healthy measure.

He held out the bottle. "Dayne?"

Dayne shook his head.

Henny would never learn tact. "I could use some a that. . . ." he suggested, rubbing his head.

"You've had enough for today. Tilt, sit over there."

Henny looked injured. "I ain't had a drop. Don't even like it, 'cept now and then. Tilt'll tell you. Ain't it so, Tilt?"

Mr. Tilt nodded his head. "I don't believe that Mr. Henny was drinking, sir. He seems most responsible. . . ."

"Very well." Chaffinch gave both men a hard look and, throwing back his head, tossed off his whiskey.

"Now," he said, setting his glass on the table. "Let's hear it."

Henny was more than ready with his story. "You know I've always done my best by you, Mr. Chaff and you've always been satisfied with my work afore. If those two new coves you got from Lunnen had been payin' attention to their duty, it wouldn't a happened. I can't fight four men at once."

Dayne reflected, as he quietly listened, that he hadn't liked the looks of the hired bravos himself. They had seemed to him to have no more merit than two bruisers hired out of Seven Dials, rather than the trained and responsible guards Chaff had requested. Chaff hadn't liked their looks any more than he had, and he had impressed on them firmly that any dereliction of duty would mean no payment.

"So where were the two guards from London?" Dayne asked.

"Well, those two housemaids from over at Belle Vue, they comes sashayin' and gigglin' along and they starts flirtin' and makin' eyes—oh, I knows 'em, I've seen 'em afore, but I don't have nothin' to do with such silly wenches. . . . But when they saw those other two coves, they saw new material and new material more to their fancy than a sober gennelman like me. . . ."

Dayne coughed.

"Something in your throat, Brev?" Chaffinch glowered.

"No, no . . . Go on, Henny."

"Well, those two coves had no more idea of payin' attention to what they was doin' than of jumpin' over the moon, once they saw those two wenches, sashayin' along smackin' their lips and winkin' their eyes . . . They just up 'n left, like two he-dogs followin'—" He stopped, rolling his eyes at Mr. Tilt, who he had already learned was a Methodist and a churchgoer. "Well, you know what I mean. So I was all by myself when these four thievers jumped me."

"Four," Tilt repeated, to emphasize the odds against which Henny had been pitted.

"Had you searched the house yet?"

"No. I was just comin' down to do it. . . . Mr. Tilt, here, is sittin' on the front step readin' his book. . . ."

"A religious work," interjected Mr. Tilt.

"He knows I'm supposed to be comin' in the back, but I thought it might be a good idea to warn him, so I'm just ponderin' whether to make me entry and then give him a hist from a winder, or whether to go round and tell him my intentions first. . . ."

"And they jumped you," Chaffinch stated.

"They did, four of 'em and afore I could yell to warn Tilt. So they bashed me on the nob and then they went around and bashed Tilt, too."

"Very painful," Tilt added. "Then we woke up in the scullery."

"I woke up quicker 'n Mr. Tilt. I reckon he ain't as used to it as I am, or his head's softer, with all that religion. I could hear 'em cussin' and swearin' 'cause they couldn't find what they was lookin' for. And they thought it was some good joke to take that Mrs. Oliphant's leg a' mutton and especially her pan of gingerbread. Oh, they was a rum crowd, alright."

Dayne leaned forward. "So they didn't get what they were looking for? Do you have any idea what it was they wanted?"

"Some papers, near's I can guess. So I figured they was lookin' for the same stuff I was supposed to be lookin' for."

"Only one of the men could read. Mr. Henny heard him instructing the others to show him any papers they found. They didn't expect Mr. Henny to recover his senses so quickly, I presume."

"Yes," Henny said, with some pride. "My head's good and hard, sure enough. They was lookin' for papers, all right. And they groused around after they finished, sayin' the job was out a' their line and poor pay for it, besides."

"Are you sure they didn't find them?" Chaffinch poured himself another tot of whiskey but left it sitting on the table beside his chair without drinking it.

"They made out like they'd found somethin' important when they looked in and saw we was come to, but it wasn't true."

Tilt nodded. "I was just regaining my senses."

Chaffinch also nodded. "Now, tell me what they looked like."

"Couldn't see. They was all wearin' masks. While we was mixin' it up, afore they hit me on the nob, I couldn't tell nothin'. And it was over right quick, like I've said. But the two that come in just before they was leavin' . . . one was a sort of medium sized fellow. He didn't say nothin' and in fact, he was shuttin' the other one up. The second one was shorter and kinda heavyset. Big, powerful arms. He said enough that I figured he come from up around York. You know how they talk up there, kinda . . . well, kinda funny."

Tilt nodded again. "That's right, except the taller one had red hair. I could see some of it sticking out from below his cap."

"Did either of them have strange eyes?" Dayne asked.

"Strange eyes?" Henny looked astonished. "Can't see no eyes when they got masks on."

"Of course not," Dayne said. "Wasn't thinking."

Irrepressible Henny said, "Can I have some a' that whiskey now? My head's poundin' fit to kill and it didn't do me no good washin' them dishes, neither."

Dayne, unable to contain himself any longer, laughed. "Come, Chaff, take pity on these poor souls. They've had a difficult day. And when you think about it, the work's been done for us. I'm sorry Tilt and Henny were knocked on the head and had to spend so much time tied up there in the scullery, but as far as any papers at the Maudsley villa, it comes out to the same thing as if Henny had done the burglary himself."

"Well!" Henny exclaimed. "I hope I'd a done a better job of it. Wouldn't a known I'd even been in the house, if I'd a done it. I'm a perfessional, but them four was just low-down thieves. They din't know nothin' about proper burglarin'."

"And what happened to the extra guards we hired?" Dayne asked. "Did they come back?"

"Oh, they come back. They come sneakin' in, one of 'em sayin' to the other they'd better make tracks, 'cause there'd be what-all t' pay. Then one of'em looked in the scullery and when he saw us, he begun to laugh. If I'd a been loose, I would a killed him. Then the other one looked in and he said somethin' like, 'Let's get outta here.' And that was the last we seen of 'em."

Chaffinch, at last relenting, poured a glass of whiskey for Henny. "Well, Tilt," he said as he handed the glass to Henny, "will you have some of the same cure?"

"I don't drink, sir. It's against both my principles and my religion, begging your pardon."

Chaff looked at Dayne in pure wonder. "It is a mystery to me, Brev, how this man of yours can have the reputation he does, as one of the most formidable and daring fighters in the King's Navy."

"I'll have a tot, too, Chaff," Dayne said. "But as for Tilt, he proves that the bravest can also be the gentlest and most abstemious."

Tilt poured a glass of water for himself. They drank solemnly, then Chaffinch said, "Well, go along now, both of you. Watch your backs. I'll expect you, Henny, to be on the watch again tomorrow. Dayne and I have nothing more to do for the moment but think over our next move."

After Tilt and Henny were gone, Dayne pulled an ottoman close to his chair and put his leg up. He stretched, sighed, then leaned back in the chair, his hands behind his head and his eyes closed.

"Leg bothering?" Chaffinch asked. "Ribs?"

"A little of both. I'm all right." He opened his eyes, stretched again and straightened in his chair.

"So, what do you think?"

"I'd say there are no papers, so that slim hope's gone. And I suspect that our appointment tomorrow night with the smuggler—or whatever the mysterious gentleman is—will lead to nothing. After all, Sir Whitney delivered his false documents to a go-between here in England; he didn't send them directly to a contact in France. Or at least that's what the Foreign Office told us."

Chaffinch stood up to pace the room, his hands in his pockets. Finally, he sat down again. "But we're here, among other reasons, on the chance that he delivered from Brighton. Or that his French employer was here. How about it? Are you too tired to go over it all again?"

"No. In fact, I've been thinking. Ever since we learned that Charlotte was brought as a baby from France, we've assumed that Sir Whitney's activities here had to do exclusively with French children sent out of France for safety. Although there were reasons that parents or relatives might want a child's whereabouts in England kept secret, it was nothing our own government would object to. However, any cross-channel commerce provides an opportunity for spies—going both ways. Let's start from the beginning once again and see if there's anything we could have missed. Whoever the French agents are, they apparently know we're getting close to them."

"And also, perhaps, smart enough or watchful enough to take advantage of our carefully laid plot to get the Maudsleys out of the house. May have been a coincidence, but—"

"Six of one and half a dozen of the other."

"So we watch our own backs. Well, we've alerted both the Admiralty and the Foreign Office to what we've discovered so far. Let's proceed with our review, and then I'll get a dispatch ready for the Foreign Office on this latest occurrence."

Mr. Tilt knocked on Dayne's bedroom door shortly after seven o'clock the next morning.

"Yes?" Dayne answered sleepily.

"An express for you, my lord. I believe it's from your brother."

"All right. I'm getting up. Leave it on the table and bring me some coffee."

Grumbling, Dayne rose, found his dressing gown and

opened the door. He picked up the letter.

When Tilt returned, he found his master frowning down at the missive in his hand. "Now what?" Dayne asked the room in general.

"Something amiss, sir?"

"Can't say. Walter's asking me to come to London with all haste. An important family matter to discuss with me."

"Will I be going with you, sir?"

"No. You stay here and tend to Chaff. Walter's in residence in London, and his valet—or some one of the servants there—can tend to my needs. I don't expect to be long. My brother tends to manufacture emergencies where none exist."

Chaff appeared at the doorway, yawning. He smoothed his sleep-rumpled hair with both hands, blinked, and squinted his eyes against the light that flooded into the spacious parlor. "Thought I heard voices. Feeling better, Tilt?"

"Oh, yes, sir. I didn't have a headache. My head's harder than Mr. Henny thinks."

Chaffinch sat down. "Is that coffee? No, no, Tilt. I'll pour it myself. How about some breakfast? I'm famished."

"Right away, sir. Anything you need before I go, my lord? Sir?"

"No. See to breakfast, please. I'm starved, too." Dayne handed his letter to Chaffinch. "What do you think?" he asked after Chaffinch had read it. "Walter's always been one to make more of a fuss about things than is strictly necessary and I don't like to leave you to meet our mysterious gentleman alone."

"And you hate to be left out of any action." Chaff handed the letter back to his friend.

"Correct. I am read like a book. Now, tell me to send an express to Walter that I'm unable to leave today but will repair in all haste tomorrow to London. Be there by noon." He folded the letter and laid it aside. "Thank you, Chaff. I understand your sentiments. I'll write the express out as soon as I've breakfasted."

Chaffinch laughed. "You can check in on Bow Street. . . . See if they've learned anything about the Goodman woman. I'd better stay here. Since we now know that the French believe Sir Whitney was on to them—or on to something—I'm a little uneasy about their next move. They may still think there's something to be learned from the Maudsleys."

Lady Sarah Pellett received a note from Dayne at her breakfast table. She was thinking as she read it that Breverton's brother Walter had an unusual talent for disturbing people to no purpose. He had sent for Breverton to come to London on an important matter of family business but had said nothing about what the business might be, and so her nephew would go rushing off early the next day on what might well be a matter of no consequence.

But, then, why should it concern her, anyway? After all, she was a Calcott. It was her sister Clara who married into the Dayne family, a sacrifice to the Calcott political ambitions, which in their youth—hers and Clara's—were being furthered by marriages designed to increase the family wealth and influence and, with those two commodities, the family political power. Lady Sarah understood the pleasures of power quite as well as she understood the pleasures of money. Clara had brought Dayne money and influence into the Calcott family by her marriage to the former Lord Dayne, the fifth baron, but in turn the Calcotts had infected the Daynes with their political ambition. Her sister Clara, lying on her sofa all day with her headaches and soft complaints, had relentlessly pushed her husband and her oldest son, Algernon, into politics. Algernon had been, in Lady Sarah's opinion, too weak for politics, but young Walter was showing every sign of fulfilling his mother's ambition.

Lady Sarah had, in counsel with her Calcott relatives, been at first unwilling to urge Breverton, her favorite nephew, into a political marriage. She had protested at the time that, unlike his brother Walter, he would not be led in such a matter. But their interest was in cementing an alliance with the powerful deVandts and since there were no eligible Calcotts available and Walter had already dutifully made a political marriage, it remained to Breverton to add another nodule to the complex and intertwined aristocratic family connections on which Whig power rested.

Her quarrel with Breverton had been worrying her more than she liked, and that it also suggested a rift with her good friend Tilly Maudsley, added to her uneasiness. Lady Sarah, whose character was frank and forthright, did not like the position she had gotten herself into. She would have liked to go directly to Tilly and tell her straight out how foolish it would be to permit Aurelia to marry Breverton. But Tilly—at the very bottom—was stronger-minded than she seemed, as Lady Sarah had discovered very early in their acquaintance. Tilly was naturally compliant and good-natured and not being overburdened with firm opinions, her determination was seldom called upon. So one tended to forget. . . . And of course she'd been brought up to be silly, which Sir Whitney, much as Lady Sarah had liked that ebullient and charming gentleman, had encouraged past all reason. Landed them in a pretty mess of pottage, too. If it hadn't been for young Aurelia . . . On that thought, Lady Sarah balked.

Lady Sarah was quite certain that if she should suggest to Tilly it would be unsuitable for Aurelia to marry Breverton, she would be shown the door. But she wouldn't be able to keep the knowledge of Breverton's foolishness from showing and she probably would be uncivil to Aurelia, which would certainly alter her nephew's affection for her. Perhaps, Lady Sarah considered, she should leave Brighton. But her lease ran through the season. . . . She supposed she could sublet but it was such a bother and she'd been feeling so much better since she'd come to Brighton. Mohammed's vapor baths steamed away the evils of overindulgence and she enjoyed the sea. Much to her surprise, she was actually learning to swim—and at her age, too! Her dipper, Elsie, was proud of her, just as she was of herself, if the truth were known.

Nor was Lady Sarah quite as averse to a marriage between her nephew and Aurelia Maudsley as she had at first thought. She hadn't much use for the deVandt woman, whom her relatives had in mind for him, and she couldn't help liking Aurelia. And for all that she was convinced Algernon's mind had not been strong, she couldn't set aside, hard as she tried, the notion that an unhappy marriage had contributed to his dissipation and finally to his death.

In her day, people married for good, solid reasons—to get children within the protection of a legitimate family; to further family interest; to acquire a partner in one's endeavors. . . . Women married for protection—or to get away from chaperons. Men married for heirs. All sorts of practical reasons. But the younger generation . . . always talking about love . . . A soft and tender light shone in Lady Sarah's eye as the memory of a certain Italian gentleman invaded her thoughts, and a balconied bedroom above a blue sea . . .

She pulled herself ruthlessly away from such memories. She had some common sense thinking to do. She could go to London for just a week or two. . . . One never knew what might happen in the course of two weeks. She picked up Breverton's note and read it over again. What had that addlepate Walter thought so important that he'd sent for Breverton to go galloping off? But did it matter why? It should be sufficient for her own excuses. She had any number of social engagements she'd have to cancel. . . . And Breverton could go up to London with her in her carriage. . . .

Lady Sarah rang the bell and on the appearance of her butler, she demanded writing paper and a pen and that Giovanni be sent to her.

Chapter Fifteen

I wondered, as I lay awake the night after the robbery, what could have led thieves to presume we had anything so valuable that it merited two attempts on our house. I recreated once again in my mind the attack in the garden on the night of the grand ball. I visualized the scene and tried to live through it again. Had the man in the domino said only that he wanted information? I was certain that he had, but now there was an uneasy notion penetrating my thoughts that he had wanted information from me, not—as I first thought—from Breverton. I was distracted for a moment, trying out in my mind my lover's Christian name, and then, after satisfying myself that Sunny was asleep, I tried it on my tongue.

This silly and girlish activity kept me occupied for a short space, but soon I was puzzling again over the curious events of the past week. What information could I have? Did we own something of value of which we were unaware? A fabulous diamond, such as those that the nabobs brought back from India, secreted in a common household object? A secret drawer in Papa's desk? Or was the secret drawer in the small desk in the bookroom? Or had the man in the domino really meant information? Did I *know* something of importance?

It was much easier to suppose that Papa had somehow managed to hide some article of immense value from a creditor—although how would the man in the domino have learned of it?—than to believe I had any information of any importance to anyone. And the robbery surely suggested that our attackers in the garden had wanted information about a material object.

Had they found it? They had certainly turned the house upside down in their attempts. They had been actually destructive wherever money might have been hidden. . . . Had Papa somehow managed to hide a large sum of money somewhere in the villa?

I eventually went to sleep, but the thought was still in the back of my mind as the following day we went about putting our things in order once again.

The straightening up that the shambles of the robbery made necessary soon became a full-scale housecleaning, so Sunny and I, wearing dustcaps, were both in the back of a storeroom when Jane brought me the note from Dayne . . . that is, from Breverton. I climbed out over boxes and piles of clothing and furniture, which will give the reader some idea of the state of our storeroom, sat down on a rickety chair, took the note, and opened it with fluttering heart. He wished to tell me that he'd been called to London on a matter of family business and that he hoped to return to Brighton within a very few days. Although it was nothing more than a brief and businesslike message, the fact that he had sent the note to me rather than to Mama, I was gratified to believe, was a statement of his intentions.

I concluded that I needed a cup of tea, so I called Sunny to see if she wanted to join me, and we both went down to the kitchen. Sunny was all curiosity why Dayne would send a note to me rather than to Mama. Despite her new maturity, she was still so innocent in the ways of the world that she actually said, when we stopped in Mama's dressing room to inform her of the note's contents, "I can't imagine why he sent the message to Lia instead of to you, Mama. Is that quite proper?"

Mama, without fluttering an eyelash and with only the barest hint of amusement, said, "Indeed it is not. I can't think what he could have been thinking of! Perhaps the incidents in the garden . . ." She permitted the sentence to remain unfinished, leaving Sunny to recall one sort of incident and I another.

Mrs. Yewdall, the dressmaker, was with Mama in her dressing room. They had both been examining the most recent of Mama's beautiful needlepoint tapestries when we entered. I believe that the first faint glimmer of suspicion flickered in some back part of my brain at that moment, but subsequent events closed the shutter on it for a time. Or perhaps my brain was too loaded with other suspicions to properly entertain another.

We continued on to the kitchen, Sunny scolding again about Mama's intimacy with a shopkeeper.

"Careful, Sunny," I warned. "I may have to take up shopkeeping myself if one of us doesn't find a rich husband. Will you give up my acquaintance, then?"

"Oh, Lia, you *wouldn't!*" she exclaimed, characteristically missing the point altogether. I was saved a perfectly irrelevant lecture by our arrival in the kitchen—irrelevant, because I was firmly determined, by hook or by crook, to build a Maudsley Crescent.

The kitchen drawers and cupboards hadn't been searched as thoroughly as the other rooms. I guess the robbers didn't think that anything of value was ever kept in a kitchen. Which just goes to show how much they knew about housekeeping. Wherever there's a responsible housekeeper, there's money in the kitchen—in a sugar bowl or a small cash box. Or perhaps they were just looking for a cash box and didn't think about checking the sugar bowl that Mrs. Oliphant kept so conspicuously displayed on the kitchen dresser. What robber thinks to look in an old sugar bowl on a shelf underneath a row of somewhat battered teacups?

As we entered the kitchen, Mrs. Oliphant started flapping her apron. "You go along now," she said in a stern voice. "Coming in here and sitting on the chairs! Scat now!" As the reader has no doubt guessed, Mrs. Oliphant was speaking to the mother cat who had moved her kittens to Xanadu. It had been only a little over a week since she came, and already she had a name, Mrs. Black—or sometimes Mrs. Black Cat, due to the similarity of her character to that of a lady of our acquaintance in Lewes. Not to put too fine a point on it, both Mrs. Blacks are rather pushy. Mrs. Black Cat had made no objection to Angela and Charlotte playing with her kittens (indeed, at first the kittens objected more than their mother), and she had soon established her right to visit the kitchen and even to sleep on a chair.

And Mrs. Oliphant, try as she might to pretend otherwise, had taken an indulgent liking to the whole Black Cat family.

Although the robbers hadn't so thoroughly turned out the kitchen—or her own bedroom in the wing that opened from it—Mrs. Oliphant was giving her domain a thorough cleaning also, and the second thing she did when we walked in was to say, "Oh, Miss Lia, I was just coming to call you."

"Oh, dear, have you discovered something else missing?"

"No, nothing like that. But there are all these papers. I forgot all about them, I'm ashamed to tell you."

"What are they?" I asked.

"Why, your Papa's papers. Remember you wanted a basket—the day the ships were passing, it was—and you sent Miss Angela down to ask me for one? And then you just left it in the bookroom, and there it sat until one day when I needed it. I was going to market, but I'd thought to stop by with some of Miss Sunny's pear preserves for poor old Widow Newnham. I'd just gone out the door with them, when my old market basket broke right through at the bottom. . . . It was just a miracle that I managed to save the preserves. But in any event, Miss Angela and Miss Charlotte were in the kitchen, and I sent Miss Angela for the basket I'd loaned you, but she brought it back with all the papers still in it. She's a sweet girl, Miss Lia, but she doesn't always pay real good attention. So I just dumped the papers in this drawer—it's too deep, and in such an inconvenient spot, anyway. I don't know why this cupboard was built like it is, but you have to fold the doors all the way back just to open it. And then, too, it sticks—green wood, or I miss my guess. Always was a cheap sort of thing, and your papa was always going to replace it, but then he never did."

Sunny was already pulling at the drawer. There was a newspaper rolled up in the front of it which was caught somehow, and making it even more difficult to open. "Oh, just drag that old paper out. There was an article I wanted to read in it, but I didn't have time, so I stuck it in there. Forgot all about that, too."

"Don't bother about it, Sunny," I told her. "We can get the papers later. I don't think there's anything important in them. Fact is, I'd forgotten all about them. We were just going to have some tea, Mrs. Oliphant. I'll put the kettle on."

"I'll throw another stick of wood on. It's right chilly for the first of July. I'm glad of a little more warmth out here."

Sunny was still working on the drawer. Papa used to call her his "Fix-it Child." If it had been Ben trying to open the drawer, he would have yanked the whole cupboard down on top of him; and if it had been me, the drawer would never have been opened. But Sunny wouldn't be content until she had it open, had determined why it was sticking, and had fixed it if she could.

Mrs. Oliphant and I sat at the kitchen table while the water came to a boil, discussing again the events of the night before. "That Mr. Tilt is a real gentleman," she said, "but that Mr. Henny! No better than he should be, or I miss my guess. If he hadn't been an associate of that nice Mr. Tilt, and an acquaintance of Mr. Chaffinch and Lord Dayne, I would have thought that it was him who was the burglar."

"Rather difficult to tie one's self up," I said.

"Oh, I didn't mean that he did the burgling, just that he makes me think of what a burglar might be like."

"And I don't think he's exactly an *associate* of Mr. Tilt. Tilt is Lord Dayne's servant, and he just asked him to help guard the house. I think they hired Mr. Henny."

"Well, if I ran an agency, I wouldn't recommend him to anyone, except for burgling." Mrs. Oliphant nodded her head emphatically. The teakettle was starting to sing, and she stood up to collect the tea things. "He might also do for cutting a throat," she added.

"Just because he speaks so ungrammatically . . ."

"There!" Sunny exclaimed in triumph. She pulled the drawer all the way out and brought it to the table. "These are all Papa's papers from his desk in the Aerie?" she asked. "Here's your newspaper, Mrs. Oliphant."

"Well, maybe I will read that article after all."

"Yes, all Papa's papers from his old desk," I said, stirring around in them. "I'll just carry the whole drawer into the bookroom, and I'll start going through them tonight. Mama will probably want to look at them. We might as well decipher these, too." I held up a sheet of paper, filled on both sides with cipher.

Sunny took it from me. "Which cipher do you think it is?"

"We'll try the different ones. . . . But there were only three that Papa used much, so it shouldn't be hard to discover which one."

"Your Papa . . ." Mrs. Oliphant said, shaking her head.

It was two days more before I got to Papa's papers. I set aside most of them for Mama to look at and throw away or keep, as she chose. The newspaper clippings were mostly theatre reviews, notices of race events, or advertisements for products Papa had taken an interest in. His jottings consisted of fragmentary observations such as "moonlight shafting across the deep tonight," or "a majesty among the heavens thrusts through the clouds in glory . . ." Ben thought he meant by the latter the moon; I thought he meant Venus. Sunny, crankily, didn't think he meant anything. We kept some journal pages—Papa was a fitful journal keeper, and usually on loose sheets of paper—because they recounted incidents from the children's baby years. Mama read the letters, but when she finished, she threw most of them away.

Meanwhile, we began working on the pages in cipher. We had only determined which cipher Papa had used, and that it was a very long letter—one of his advice-to-youth letters, apparently—when other events intervened.

Dayne

Dayne received the note from Lady Sarah just as he finished dressing. He sent Giovanni back with the message that he had intended to call on her later that day, but if she found it more convenient to see him that morning, he would call shortly.

When he arrived at her house in the Pavilion Parade, it was to learn that Lady Sarah had gone for her vapor bath but would be back within the hour. It was fifteen minutes after the hour when she at last returned, and Dayne, after cooling his heels for over thirty minutes and pacing around the drawing room for another fifteen, was annoyed indeed when he at last sighted her alighting from a sedan chair. He was in the entryway the minute her butler opened the door, ready to level a few choice words at her pertaining to punctuality.

She forestalled him. "Don't get into a state, Breverton," she said immediately upon seeing him. "Take that thunderous look off your face. I'm in no mood for a scolding."

"You may not be in the mood for a scolding, but that's no difference to me. I'm very much in the mood to give you one."

"Don't be impertinent. It's not my fault that there wasn't a chair to be found when I left the baths, or that a gentleman was brought in to see Mohammed in the most severe agony with an arthritic attack. I could hardly tell the fellow to lie there and suffer because my nephew—perfectly hale and hearty—would be pacing the floor waiting for me. Now could I? By the way, how are your ribs?"

"My ribs are fine. My bruises give me some trouble when I swell with indignation. Like right now."

Lady Sarah patted his arm. "Now go into the breakfast parlor and wait for me. I'll be right there. You might as well take some lunch with me. Good food is an excellent antidote for frayed nerves."

"No, I might as well not. I have a number of errands to do. . . ."

But Lady Sarah was already on her way up the stairs.

Another twenty minutes of pacing around the table in the breakfast parlor, which was already laid for a luncheon for two, and Lady Sarah at last appeared. She rang the bell, then said, "Kindly remember your manners, Breverton. I wish to sit down."

So Dayne held her chair and then, somehow, he was seated, too, eating fresh peas and a delicious timbal of macaroni, while still protesting that he hadn't a minute to spare.

Lady Sarah spooned herself more peas. "I'm going up to London tomorrow. Walter can very well take me into his confidence, too. Not that I expect anything earthshaking to come of it, but I'm not of a mind to sit around and wonder. Never knew a fellow to make such a hullabaloo about nothing as that brother of yours does. He's probably notified everybody down to the shirttail cousins. You may accompany me in my carriage."

"Thank you very much, Aunt, but I've made arrangements to leave at five o'clock tomorrow morning. I'll breakfast on the road and be in London by noon. You won't arrive until nightfall—assuming you get an early enough start. Ten to one you'll end up sleeping on the road."

"You young men! Dashing about . . . always in a hurry! Don't know the meaning of leisure. And stop wolfing your food down like some clod-hopping peasant."

The upshot was that what with one thing and another, Dayne had only time to write a brief note to Lia Maudsley before he set out with Chaffinch for their rendezvous with Richard Thurlby's mysterious gentleman. As he folded the note, in which he informed Lia that he'd been called to London, to return in three days (or so he hoped), he considered whether to add a sentence stating that he loved her. After a moment's consideration, as he tapped his fingers thoughtfully, he decided it was a sentiment that should first be stated—if possible—in person. And in any event, if he ended with a statement of his love and admiration, should he not begin with a similar statement, saluting her as "my darling" rather than as "my dear Miss Maudsley?" Of such dilemmas and decisions is life made. He sealed the note and, handing it to Tilt, asked him to see that it was delivered immediately. Then, as Chaffinch had already done, he armed himself with a small but efficient pistol and announced to his waiting friend that he was ready.

They went to their rendezvous on horseback, Chaffinch mounted on a large, placid beast—the only animal in the stables judged to be up to both his weight and his competence—complaining that he never yet had met a horse with adequate springs, his present mount not excluded. They had taken some pains to give no clue to their destination by riding north to Preston and then cutting across the Downs to the cavalry barracks on the Lewes road, where they stopped for an hour with some of their acquaintances among the officers before riding on, now certain that they were not being followed.

They made a wrong turn off the Lewes road due to a missing signpost and were only prevented from losing more than the hour they'd already lost by an encounter with an itinerant peddler who, on being questioned, looked shocked and said, "Kingstone? It's back that way. But never mind, you won't be too far off if you take the Cross Cut—little lane leading off to the right."

They found the little lane and without further mishap arrived in Kingstone. Their destination was a farmhouse between that village and the next village of Iford. They rode up at dusk. Two cavorting and barking dogs caused their horses to shy and jitter about, much to the discomfort of Chaffinch and the annoyance of Dayne. There was a light in what was evidently the kitchen wing of the house, and within minutes the door opened and a dark form emerged, holding a lantern.

"The two gentlemen from Brighton?" the form called.

"Don't know whether I like being called a gentleman or not, in these parts," Chaffinch murmured before answering.

The man spoke sharply to the dogs, both of whom immediately sat down, tails wagging, to await developments.

"You'll leave your horses," the man said without further preamble. "Someone here will take them down to Southease, where you'll pick them up again. They'll be baited and rested. As for us, we've a bit of a walk ahead of us, as I'm hoping you were told."

"Yes," Dayne said. "Shall we introduce ourselves?"

"No need. Just call me Jack. Plenty of Jacks around here." He laughed good-naturedly, but offered his hand to be shaken. "Pleased to meet you both. Now I see you afoot, no need to identify yourselves. One gentleman well over six feet who's built like a wrestler, and a slim fellow—now just walk around me—yes, slim fellow with a bit of a limp, just under six feet, looking like he's been in a sharp set-to. So let's be off." A low whistle brought a silent young man who led the horses away and set the dogs to cavorting again.

They walked for over a mile before they reached the River Ouse, where they were handed on to a surly fellow, who grunted a greeting and indicated they were to enter the boat. The boat moved rapidly downstream with the current, and within what seemed a short time, it was pulled to shore and they were told to disembark. The boatman whistled, low and penetrating, and then shoved off to drift farther downstream. Within a few minutes a man moved out of the shadow of a large tree. After a moment of hesitation, he greeted them with a polite bow. "At your service, gentlemen. You're exactly as described. I hope, Mr. Chaffinch, that your work doesn't customarily require anonymity. With that bulk, you'd be hard put to remain inconspicuous."

"Do I know you, sir?" Chaffinch asked.

"No, and I'm sorry to tell you that I can't give you my name. However, I can tell you that Mr. Richard Thurlby was authorized to send me to you on a small French matter you are investigating. A memorandum was uncovered at the Foreign Office, dated 1801, written by an old friend of mine, Sir Whitney Maudsley. Does that satisfy you?"

Chaffinch acknowledged himself satisfied.

"There's a comfortable inn not far from here, where I want you to be seen. It has a reputation, for the . . . er . . . female company, as well as for the excellence of the liquors. Very respectable, and on occasion patronized by young sparks from Brighton and Lewes and Tunbridge Wells, not to mention certain of the local gentry. We'll meet in a back room, and I'll be on my way; you will then both take a cup with two very pleasant ladies—or, if you like, you may avail yourselves of their services. When you're ready to depart, just give the signal and a young man we'll call Jack—no, not the first Jack . . ." He laughed. "A small joke among ourselves. In any event, Jack will have horses for you. He'll show you the road to Southease. Your own horses, fresh and well-rested, will be waiting, about a quarter of a mile short of the village, with another of our Jacks to direct you to Telescombe. From there, it's an easy road to Rottingdean and back to Brighton."

Chaffinch, itching with professional curiosity, observed, "A rather large number of people! We've always felt that the fewer the number of people . . ."

"Oh, yes, to be sure. You were guided here by certain of the Gentlemen. They were told that you were both completely reliable, and it was hinted that you wanted to buy wines or invest in the Trade. They don't know your names or whom you're meeting. The fellow who brought you down river, you no doubt observed, did not see me. And no one at the inn will see me. Shall we go? Incidentally, why don't you call me John? A more elegant pseudonym than Jack. I plead with you to excuse the mask."

A short walk brought them to the back of an inn. They quietly entered a rear gate, the hinges of which were well oiled. The man who called himself John took a key from his pocket, and they passed through a narrow doorway, the hinges equally protected against incriminating screeches and squeaks, to enter a long hallway. Another key opened a room on their right, with a neat bed, a chair, and a washstand furnished with washbowl, pitcher, and chamberpot. A lighted candle cast a flickering light. There was a faint, lingering odor of perfume. They were in one of the rooms where the pleasant ladies entertained.

Chaffinch, after a quick but thorough inspection, sat down on the bed. Dayne chose the chair.

Their host leaned against the door. "I say, bad eye you've got there," he commented to Dayne before beginning his story. As he warmed to it he paced, with a contained nervous energy, around the small space.

"I knew Whit when we were boys. Drifted apart when he went to Cambridge. . . . he chose one life, I another. Nonetheless, we continued to think along the same lines and on rare occasions saw one another. We both had our fling with radicalism, read Rousseau, and if anybody'd asked either of *us* to devise policy, we'd never have lost our American colonies. We'd have granted them their own representatives in parliament and been done with it. When the revolution broke out in France, we thought the millennium had come. And then the Terror began. Whit, with his excellent French and his connections with the refugees, first heard about the people who for one reason or another couldn't leave France themselves but wanted their children sent to England. A few of them were actually revolutionaries, but wary enough to want their children safe—just in case. With a civil war—and royalists, revolutionaries, constitutionalists, and every shade of opinion between—everybody with sense was looking to their necks."

A knock on the door alerted all three men. John called, "Who is it?"

"Me," a female voice answered.

John opened the door, and a fresh-faced girl entered. Dayne guessed her age at seventeen.

John put his arm around her and kissed her temple. "Well, my little duck?"

"Riding officers out front. I told them I had a customer waiting. They can count rooms and girls as well as the next ones."

"Well, little dear, sit on the bed by that very large gentleman. No, no worry," he added, as both Chaffinch and Dayne gave signs of uneasiness. "She's as reliable as King George himself. More so, perhaps. She never loses her wits. And this establishment is so respectable that we can entertain the excise officers without a single flutter of the heart. No contraband has ever been stored here, no purchases or exchanges made, no questionable wines served, except occasionally and with a wink—the officers would surely suspect us if we didn't serve a contraband brandy now and again. But it's only information that changes hands here, and the closest search will never turn up information."

"Very sensible," Chaff said approvingly. "I presume the walls are admirably thick?"

"Admirably. A building built to withstand the ages. Well, to continue, Whit came to me. I arranged for the children to be brought over from France, and Whit took it from there. Beyond making the arrangements, I had no connection with it. And on the other side, Whit only suspected, as far as I know, that I had anything to do with the Correspondence, which as you gentlemen know concerns the sending and receipt of messages between France and England."

Chaffinch interrupted to ask, "Did Sir Whitney ever pass any messages through you or receive any?"

"I've asked around—quietly—if there were any dealings of that sort with Whit, and as far as this area and around Brighton, it seems not. However, in . . . I think it was late in 1800, we met. Routine business, old friends, and he further wanted to know if I could tell him how to invest in the Trade. . . . His financial affairs were giving him a good deal of concern. He'd heard that some of the London merchant banks had financed cargoes of contraband. I told him what I could. No names, of course. He seemed preoccupied, which I set down to his financial difficulties. But just as we were ready to part he—on the spur of the moment, I believe—warned me that if I had anything to do with the Correspondence with France, he believed there was a French agent in the Admiralty."

"What?" Dayne asked, startled.

"Gave me some strange story about how he knew—Whit always was good at stories. I couldn't believe it myself; but I reported it, and we kept a careful eye out for a time, I assure you. Especially as Whit died not so long thereafter." The man who called himself John paused. "I've wondered, since. Was Whit's death a—a natural death?"

Chaffinch responded with a grunt. "We asked the same question. His physician swears it was an apoplexy."

"And the Admiralty?" Dayne asked. "Did they uncover anyone?"

"If so, we were never told. You understand that messages to and from the Admiralty pass through a 'receiver'; it's as anonymous as delivering a letter to the post. We discovered nothing here. And that, gentlemen, is all I can tell you. As I say, I've asked around, pretty thoroughly, and there's nothing more."

Chaffinch stood up. "We thank you, sir. You will know how to contact us if you should come across something of interest?"

"I'll get word to Richard Thurlby. He'll contact you." He turned to the girl. "Now, sweetheart, run back and make sure the riding officers have gone."

The return to Brighton was exactly as the man called John had explained. They had taken their cup of wine but had not availed themselves of the other services the inn offered. Their own horses were waiting at Southease as promised, and they proceeded at a leisurely pace to Telescombe and Rottingdeane and thence to Brighton. The road was in good repair, but the waning moon shed a feeble light. Chaffinch remarked that he never could be easy on a horse on a dark night.

"You're never easy on a horse at any time."

"Never been sure why. Haven't any fear of the beasts."

"Not surprising. You're as big as they are."

"Well, just never have liked riding. Driving . . . now, that's a different matter. So," he said, shifting uncomfortably in his saddle, "Sir Whitney suspected there was a spy in the Admiralty. Confirms our suspicions. I can hardly credit it."

"And he has to be the one I suspect destroyed the copy of Sir Whitney's memorandum sent over from the Foreign Office. And whom I inadvertently warned, snooping around too openly."

"Means he's still there," Chaffinch observed: "Or was, two weeks ago. Two weeks ago we were in town, right?"

"Something like that. Too much happening too fast."

"Well, it's another job for you to do in London. Sir Whitney's warning, which our mysterious gentleman passed on to the Admiralty, would have gone to the secretary. Right?"

"That would have been Napean. I suppose he can tell me who in the Admiralty investigated our mysterious friend John's report."

"It's been three years."

"Yes. A long time."

"And we haven't heard anything from our warning that there might be a viper in the Admiralty's bosom at this very moment. Don't like that at all."

"I'll look into that, too. Try to get them moving."

Chaffinch was morosely pursuing other thoughts. "Can't like having to depend on Thurlby. Took an instant dislike to him. Should have been sent to the freebooters earlier. Blunderers at the Foreign Office . . . Hawkesworth as bad as Thurlby. Can't abide him."

Walter Dayne stood behind his desk, playing irritably with a pen. When his brother walked in with a cheerful greeting, he scowled. He put the pen down and leaned across the desk to shake hands.

"How are you, Breverton? From the looks of those eyes, I'd say you've been in a new scrape."

"I'm fine, Walt. Tell you about the scrape later. First I'm anxious to hear what this urgent business is." Even as he spoke, Dayne felt a twinge of annoyance—at himself, and at Walter.

They were twenty-five and thirty, and they were still playing the old silly games. Walter knew his brother disliked being called Breverton (their Aunt Sarah always excepted), and Brev knew that Walter objected strongly to any shortening of his not very distinguished name. Among the several minor resentments Walter carried through life was that he had not been christened with a fine three-syllable name like his two elder brothers.

Walter came out from behind his desk and indicated the sofa that stood in an alcove. "Sit down, Brev. I ordered tea brought up as soon as you came. I supposed that you wouldn't delay longer than to wash up, in light of the urgency of my letter."

Well, Dayne thought as he sat down, the first round's over, at least. "So, what is this urgent business, Walter? Sorry I couldn't get away yesterday."

Walter pulled a chair closer to the sofa. "I believe we'll be more comfortable here." Before seating himself, however, he walked back to his desk and picked up a folded newspaper. "I'm sorry you were delayed, for although this concerns us both, it will be of more concern to you than to me." He unfolded the newspaper, taking from inside the fold a wrinkled and dirty piece of letter paper, which he handed to Dayne. "It's from Algernon."

A flicker of annoyance crossed Dayne's face. "Algernon? It can't be. He's been gone for over five years! Don't tell me you've been taken in by someone's very poor idea of a joke!"

The tea was brought in, and both men remained silent until the servant retired. Walter poured, then handed a cup to Dayne. "No sugar—right, Brev? Now, read the letter. Then tell me what you think."

Walter's calm response was Dayne's first hint that it was not a joke. He took a sip of tea, then looked at the paper. The first line was unmistakably in their brother's beautifully clear hand. *"To my brothers, Breverton and Walter Dayne."* He stared at it, shocked, for a moment simply uncomprehending, as though he had suddenly lost the faculty of reading English.

"It sounds like a last will and testament," he said, in a voice that shook with the emotions that had surged over him.

"Not quite," Walter said dryly. "And if it helps, I was as

shaken as you are when I first read it."

Dayne took a deep breath. It didn't help. His hand was unsteady. He raced through the words, looking up once at Walter, who gave a slight shrug, and then read the note through again, more slowly. He felt dazed. "He ran away."

"Yes. Unbelievably and unforgivably."

The note had been brief. Algernon stated, simply, that he had been unable to face a future of what seemed to him complete futility. *"I think now that I may have been sick with a melancholy that rendered me incapable of judgment, incapable of thinking of others, or even, in a certain sense, of thinking of myself. But so it was, and the best I can do now is to make up for whatever those who loved me or depended on me may have suffered, and to assume responsibility for what I have done."*

Any thought of returning, he continued, became impossible when Parliament passed the law in 1798 making travel in France a capital crime for English citizens. He had lived on in France on the money that his friend, Lord Camelford, transferred to him through the Rothschild's continental banks, and by turning his hand for drawing to account by working as a street artist. When in 1799 the recruiters for the army of the revolutionary Directorate came too close, he escaped to Dresden.

Camelford had not only aided him with funds, but had helped him initially in his escape from England. Camelford had a liking for intrigue. Through all the years since his "departure" in 1798, only Camelford had known he was alive, and he had been sworn to carry the secret to his grave—a promise that had proved tragically literal. *"I read of Camelford's death in a duel, which caused me great suffering and initiated a period of profound shock from which I have only just emerged."*

The shock had brought him to his senses and to the reality of his situation. He no longer had a certain source of support, a fact he had to consider, but of more importance was the realization that he had run away from his responsibilities, an act for which he alone must suffer the remorse. However, he wanted to do what he could to rectify his misdeeds. He was in Antwerp, carrying false papers *". . . or perhaps I might say, carrying the papers of my new identity."*

He had two choices, and his brothers had two choices. He could remain as dead, emigrating to America, perhaps, although he did not feel that such a new and raw land would be friendly to the aspirations of a cultured artist. He would demand only a legacy, transferred to him in Antwerp, sufficiently generous to live on comfortably for the remainder of his life. Or he would come home, abdicate his title, clear his name of any charge of disloyalty, and hand over all responsibility for the family estates and interests to his brothers. By running away, he considered himself to have lost all right to the privileges of wealth and rank. In any event, his painting had become the most important thing in his life, and whatever the decision, he wanted only enough money to live comfortably, keep his wife Claudette from bothering him, and to buy his paints and canvases.

The note ended with directions for contacting him through an advertisement in the Antwerp journal that had enclosed his letter.

Dayne at last folded the note, very carefully, and returned it, somewhat formally, to Walter. He felt such an overpowering mixture of rage and joy that it required relief in physical action. As he paced the room with agitated strides, trying to regain a measure of calm, Walter sat quietly by, waiting for the storm of his brother's emotion to pass. He had experienced the same confusion of feelings when he had read Algernon's letter.

As Dayne strode back and forth across the fine Turkish carpet, he was trying to bring some order to his mind. He had never, somehow, quite believed that Algernon was dead, and he'd never entirely given up the hope that he would someday return. But on the other hand, that Algernon had made them all suffer not just the pain of thinking him dead, but what was worse, the pain of not knowing . . . their mother imagining the most terrible of deaths in some low and pestilential corner of London . . . And what this would mean to Lia . . .

When Walter judged that his brother was calmer, he suggested, "Come and sit down and have some more tea, Brev. Or perhaps a brandy?"

Dayne sat down, feeling remarkably weary. "Tea." He picked up his cup, surprised to find it empty. He did not remember having taken one sip as he read that shocking communication from a brother returned from the dead.

Walter handed him the refilled cup. "Our dear sister-in-law Claudette will have hysterics when she learns this. It should be a performance worthy of a Siddons. I'm rather looking forward to it."

"She's certainly enjoyed playing the sorrowing widow. But we should at least be fair enough to recognize that she couldn't remarry until Algernon was declared legally dead." As little as he had cared for Algernon's wife, Dayne felt an almost unreasonable anger rising again in his breast at this reminder of another of those responsibilities Algernon had fled. He reminded himself that their Aunt Sarah had always insisted that Algernon was not entirely in control of his mental faculties.

"Don't waste sympathy on Claudette," Walter said, divining his thoughts. "She'll demand a huge sum to live apart from him. Consider. She marries a baron, and he disappears. She's been cheated of giving birth to another baron. If Algernon returns, she'll demand her conjugal rights. And the title for her son, should she have one. Or a very large sum of money. Algernon's a fool. I think he's still sick."

"Aunt Sarah's always said as much."

"Well, they say there's some good in everything. One good thing in Algernon's 'death' was that one saw so little of Claudette. She pretends to a delicate constitution, but she's strong as a horse. And she has one interest in life, and that's Claudette. I see her as little as possible. My wife takes care of that duty. Says Claudette thinks she's got her hooks in an earl. If she's cheated out of an earl, she's not—as I've said—going to leave Algernon alone. Among all the other legalities, he'll have to go through divorce proceedings. I don't see any other solution."

"Claudette could bring proceedings on grounds of desertion."

"*If* she's certain of the earl. How long since you've seen her, Brev? You've no idea. Selfish is the woman's middle name."

"We're going to have to take some time to think this over and decide what's best. I confess, at the moment my mind's blank . . . numb. Have you taken anyone else into your confidence?

I've put Aunt Sarah in a tizzy, I'm afraid, by telling her the content of your letter. Fact is, she's on the road right now, prepared to take a hand. We're to call on her tomorrow, with full details of whatever foolishness you've dreamed up."

Walter laughed. It was a full, rich laugh, and in that moment it was easy to recognize the two men as brothers. "Of course she'd find it hard to stay away. Aunt Sarah's one of the world's great busybodies. And also one of the most managing women I've ever met. If she were a man, she'd be the Calcotts' outstanding parliamentarian and a power in the government." Walter, like Dayne, was fond of their Aunt Sarah. He knew that Breverton was her favorite, but she had a fondness for him, too, and she understood his passion for political power. "But no, I haven't told anyone else. Who would I tell? Our Calcott uncles? Our mother?"

"Eventually . . ."

"No. Not eventually. Not if Algernon 'remains as dead,' as he so nicely puts it."

Dayne shook his head. "I couldn't go through life pretending that Algernon's dead. Whatever solution we decide is best, I must reject that one. I'm not made for deceit, as I've recently discovered. And I don't think you are either, Walter."

The corners of Walter's mouth drew down in a sardonic grimace. "One legacy our stern father left us, if nothing else . . . or at least to you and to me." He leaned back in his chair. "But forget Algernon for a moment. Tell me how you got those black eyes."

Chapter Sixteen

The first event that kept us from deciphering Papa's letter was a visit from Mr. Price, his former man of affairs. My first eager question, after greeting him and settling him in a comfortable chair with a cup of tea, was, "Have you found a builder or an investor with capital?"

My most urgent thoughts—setting aside lovers and robbers—had been fixed on my dream of building a Maudsley Crescent. Our losses had not been great in the robbery but were sufficient enough that I was reminded once again just how slim our resources were.

"I regret very much to say, Miss Maudsley, that capitalists are hesitant to go into partnership with a woman, and particularly since, as you know, the cliffs to the east of Brighton offer better prospects for expansion. . . ."

I regarded him with a suspicious eye. "Did you even approach anyone? Or is that just an opinion?" I was preparing to launch a blast at good Mr. Price.

"Indeed not! I approached several gentlemen of means and four different builders."

I spent some time huffing around the room. It just made me exasperated, this notion that women have no heads for business, when all over England there are prosperous shops owned and managed by women. And didn't these "capitalists" ever go into the market to bargain with a market lady or to a fair to haggle with a farmer's wife? I was determined to get the money somehow, and I would not have Mr. Price giving up so supinely! I was declaiming along those lines as I paced about, looking quite wild, I should imagine, while Mr. Price attempted to interrupt. He began with a few polite "ahems," as though he were clearing his throat in a discreet bid to be heard by someone immediately in front of him at a polite assembly. He progressed to some mild variations on "I beg you," such as "have the goodness to" and "permit me," until at last, his patience exhausted, he raised his voice and said, "Miss Maudsley, there are other matters." And he repeated, in an even louder voice, "*Important* other matters."

"Oh?" I said sarcastically. "Has some other of Papa's partners failed? Some *man* with no head for business and whom we never in our lives heard of? How much is it the creditors are demanding this time? Tell me quickly!" I dropped into a chair and covered my eyes dramatically with one hand. "Don't spare me—even to one shilling!" (The reader will recall that we had been required to pay debts of dissolved partnerships in which careless and ever-optimistic Papa had had a propensity for investing. He had never accepted Mr. Price's advice to invest in joint stock companies, where only the business is responsible for debt and not the individual partners. Papa had told Mr. Price that he thought the personal bonds of shared debt as well as shared income were more conducive to good management!)

Mr. Price was obviously unable to decide whether I was serious, for he hesitated a moment before saying, in a rather prim voice, "I believe, if you will attend to what I have to say without this unseemly levity, that you will discover I do not exaggerate."

It was just what was needed to penetrate my indignation. Mr. Price, who was ordinarily all diplomacy and tact, had never spoken to me so sharply. I straightened myself in the chair, folded my hands in my lap, and regarded him attentively. "Do forgive me, Mr. Price. I was distressed."

Mr. Price hesitated again. "I have so much information of so much importance to convey to you that I hardly know where to begin."

"Begin wherever you think best. I have no pressing engagements."

"You will recall," he began, "that I discovered when I

traveled to Scotland at your request that the woman who previously cared for the children, Mrs. Clendenning, was paid by a bank in London, Jarvis Brothers & Company."

"Yes."

"Now, it seems that Jarvis Brothers is a correspondent for a number of continental and American banks."

"Is that unusual?"

"No, not in itself. Do you understand what a merchant bank is?"

"Yes. A bank that engages in facilitating foreign trade by various means, such as bills of exchange and issuing letters of credit. . . . But I'm only repeating what you've taught me, Mr. Price."

"And a correspondent?"

I was more puzzled than ever. "The bank acts as agent for a banking house in another country or for a foreign merchant. . . ."

Mr. Price looked like the cat that had just swallowed the canary, although where that old saying comes from I can't recall. If the cat that swallowed the canary was like Mrs. Black Cat, it would look as guilty as Mrs. Black did when caught with a half-eaten mutton chop.

In any event, Mr. Price, far from looking guilty, looked smug. "Jarvis Brothers is one of the most reputable and wealthy merchant banks in England; it has correspondents, or acts as correspondent for banks and merchants all over the world. And that means that it can do business with France, or with countries at war with France, through a neutral intermediary. Parenthetically, I have it on good authority—although I cannot, of course, reveal my source—that Jarvis Brothers and other well-known merchant banks have financed cargoes destined for the contraband trade through their relationship with banks in neutral countries."

(When Mr. Price says "contraband," he means what we here in Brighton call right-out smuggling.)

Mr. Price flashed me a triumphant glance. "Although I am only speculating, such a bank could also make payments such as those to Miss Goodman and—"

"Miss Goodman?" My heart took a plunge, which for once

had nothing to do with Breverton Dayne. I immediately saw Charlotte and Georgie snatched from our arms by a hard-faced female, no better than she should be. . . .

"I intended to say, payments to Miss Goodman *and* Mrs. Clendenning. For you will recall that until Miss Goodman's departure with the Irishman, payments for the children's support were remitted to her."

"Yes," I said, "I remember. Certainly."

"The bank was acting as agent, and I believe I have an idea for whom it was acting. And that brings me to a letter I have received from a gentleman named Stoutworthy, whom I mentioned in my letter to you a month ago. The information is given in the strictest confidence, you understand."

"Yes, yes, I understand."

I could hardly believe what Mr. Price then told me! That capable little Charlotte, as thoroughly a Scot as a bekilted Highland clansman, was in fact French simply stretched to the limit the imagination. "Her name?" I whispered, my throat dry. Could I have believed only three months before, when I had so staunchly refused to accept that Charlotte was Papa's by-blow, that I would now be wishing with all my heart she *were* papa's?

"Mr. Stoutworthy chose to withhold her name, but he felt that Lady Maudsley deserved to know that Charlotte was not the issue of Sir Whitney."

"Georgie?" I croaked.

"I'm afraid I have no further information. . . . But if Master Georgie were one of the French children, Mr. Stoutworthy would undoubtedly have so informed us. . . . Why, Miss Maudsley! Are you not well? Let me call for a glass of water."

Mr. Price informed me later that I had paled and that he feared I would faint. I do not faint—it simply is not in my constitution—but I was grateful for a glass of water. "It was just the relief," I explained after downing the water. "We can still hope that Georgie is Papa's."

I had no fear that Mr. Price would faint, but I did think he looked ever so slightly stunned and might also need a glass of water.

"Just more tea, thank you," he replied to my offer. He removed his glasses and polished them. "Perhaps you would prefer that we continue later. I am completely at your disposal until noon tomorrow, when I'll return by stage to London. I thought I might rather like to experience sea bathing—that is, when I'm free, for of course my first purpose in Brighton is to consult with you."

"No, let's get it all over at once. You'll love sea bathing. I believe our doctors consider early morning bathing the most salubrious, but we enjoy the sea at any time."

"Very well, but I warn you that I have what may be equally startling information, and also regarding Sir Whitney's affairs. Do you remember I mentioned one of Sir Whitney's investments that paid excellently but failed soon after his death? When we were settling his affairs?"

"Yes."

"My explanation was, in a way, a manner of speaking. The business, according to your father, was a woolen exporting business. He told me that he arranged for the sales, presented the bills of exchange for payment at Jarvis Brothers, and collected a commission for his services. The latter he occasionally put in my hands. The income was quite high. But he asked me never to reveal that he was the active agent for the company." There was the faintest trace of contempt in Mr. Price's voice. "Your father did not want it known that he had anything to do with trade. 'It wouldn't do, Price, wouldn't do,' he'd say. 'An old family like mine,' he'd say, 'landowners for centuries, gentility thicker in our veins than blood . . . Disgrace for my family if they knew. Never hold my head up at the club.' "

I nodded. Mr. Price's quoting of Papa was accurate. Papa was democratical in his acquaintance and in his politics—after all, he was a disciple of Rousseau—and he could charm anyone, from the lowest to the highest. But he had that pride of blood and that contempt of meanness and of haggling trade (*investment* in trade was different) that marked his class. And which had also impoverished him, and us. And, although I'm ashamed to admit it, probably numerous tradesmen and artisans as well.

"After his death," Mr. Price continued, "I expected a representative of the company to call, to ask for Sir Whitney's records of sales and receipts and the names of his customers . . . in order to—to end the relationship neatly, I suppose I was thinking. After all, I thought, the company might not know that he did not always entrust his man of business with his papers and transactions. I hoped that I might find something among the papers in your possession, but I did not. Then when no representative of the company called on me, it seemed just as well to leave it alone. Perhaps, I thought, he had dealt with the company more directly than I had supposed. And so I left it—until the business of the children."

"The children?"

"Master George and Miss Charlotte. The drafts for their care, you will remember, were bank drafts. . . ."

Suddenly, it clicked in my head as it had clicked in Mr. Price's. Or perhaps I should say that there were two clicks. "Whoever was paying for the children's care was paying Papa! Through Jarvis's. Which may have been acting as correspondent . . ."

"We can't be certain, of course, that there is a connection. However, I've been unable to trace any connection between Sir Whitney and any of the wool-trading merchants in the kingdom. Perhaps I missed a small exporting house, or your father handled the wool sales for a general exporter, but I don't think it likely. I don't believe such a business ever existed. Your father was receiving money from a clandestine source. Which suggests some very grave possibilities."

All sorts of ideas whirled in my head. Papa was one of the Gentlemen; the money came from smuggling goods into France. We were robbed because someone believed that he'd hidden his profits in our house. . . . It was the Gentlemen who were behind the robbery. . . . With it Papa established a fund for the children. He felt responsible for Charlotte. . . . Could Charlotte be ours after all? I did some quick arithmetic. . . . When was he with our embassy in France? No, much longer than ten years ago . . . Had he made other trips to France, unknown to us, perhaps with the smugglers, and Charlotte was his own child? Or had he only pretended she was a baby spirited out of France, and she was the child of Miss Goodman? And why had the money gone to Miss Goodman? And who *was* Miss Goodman?

Mr. Price was watching me very quietly, with a most sober face. "The money Sir Whitney received, in payment for some service he never revealed, and the money for the children's care were, I believe, in both cases, from a foreign source. Perhaps we will not inquire too closely into the wool business. . . . Your father's reputation, you understand . . . Your father knew Miss Goodman well. I don't want to distress you, Miss Maudsley. . . ."

So the figure of Miss Goodman was looming over us once again. "If only we knew where she's gone! We can't hope that she's disappeared forever. . . . She told Mrs. Clendenning she'd return for the children when she was able to do so."

Mr. Price was silent for a moment. "We could make inquiries through Bow Street. The runners are often successful in tracing missing persons. I remember . . ."

While Mr. Price recounted his story of the successful recovery of a missing heiress, I was remembering that Lady Sarah had told us neither the Bow Street runners nor a private investigation had discovered any trace of Breverton's brother, Algernon—not the best recommendation for Bow Street competence. But, in any event, we could never pay for the services of a runner, as I informed Mr. Price when he finished his rather long-winded story.

"Miss Maudsley, I have always billed you, as I did your father, exactly what I ask of my other clients for my services. I have never let my regard for my clients, or their financial position, influence me. Indeed, if I did so, I would charge some clients too little and others too much, which would be unfair to all. However, in this case, I believe that I have been involved as a principal. I handled monies received by Sir Whitney from a mysterious source. Furthermore . . ." Mr. Price paused, prepared to deliver his shocker. He even lowered his voice to a conspiratorial whisper. "Furthermore, my office was burgled!"

"Burgled!" I exclaimed, in a voice considerably louder than a whisper. "But—but, so were we. . . ."

"Twice!" Mr. Price nodded his head portentously. An expression of great offense crossed his face. "The first time, papers were removed that pertained to your business and your father's! I wouldn't have known, had I not been actively investigating that wool business. And you will imagine my surprise when I subsequently discovered that the papers had been returned, just as neat as you please and as if they had never been touched! I could hardly believe my senses! And then, a week later, the whole office was rifled. Turned upside down! It took a week for my clerks to sort everything out. You can imagine that I had something to say to Bow Street on the matter, and to several other people as well! That we have no adequate law enforcement is a disgraceful matter, indeed! That one should think the Charlies . . . uh . . . simple watchmen would have the courage or the skill . . ." Mr. Price caught himself in mid-oration. "Someone, Miss Maudsley, is up to no good, and when I received your express, asking for a transfer of funds and that you had been burgled also, well . . ."

Mr. Price had left his chair and was nervously pacing about and scowling, an activity in which I had very quickly joined him. My mind was racing. If it was smugglers behind our burglary, as I'd begun to believe, and they were looking for a cache of money, why would they steal *papers* from Mr. Price's office? And then return them? And then return again to search so destructively. It just didn't make sense. "If we could find Miss Goodman . . ." I said, a little wildly. "Someone is after the children!"

"Perhaps."

It was clear from Mr. Price's hesitation that he was not of the same mind.

"But what then?"

"I believe Miss Goodman is only the—the link, so to speak. It may be a coincidence, you understand, but I believe I could see my way to—to . . . well, I—I might finance a cursory investigation. She may be able to tell us, or Bow Street may make her tell us . . . I have certain friends among the runners." Mr. Price's eyes shifted away from mine. "Certain favors . . ." he mumbled. "Owe me . . . Advised once or twice . . . Understand, I'm sure. No need to spell it out."

I understood, not having been born yesterday. I also knew that this concession to our poverty was against all his instincts. I threw my arms around him and kissed his cheek, a demonstration of emotion that seriously embarrassed such a proper gentleman of affairs.

So Mr. Price departed, leaving us with much to think about. The first decision, as Mr. Price pointed out, was what to tell Mama. Clearly, she needed to know about Charlotte. And if we told her the rest, perhaps she'd know something that would throw light on the whole affair. But should we worry her? And was it possible that Mama could know anything about a wool business? Ben and Sunny and I went for a long walk by the ocean that night—it seemed natural now to include Sunny in our councils—and we were all of the opinion that, except for Charlotte's French parentage, we would wait to tall Mama the rest.

Later, when we told Mama about Charlotte, Mama said she had thought in the very beginning that the girl had a French look; her little face was so *piquant!* As for Charlotte herself, we thought it better to wait until we learned the result of Mr. Price's inquiries about Miss Goodman through Bow Street.

The other event that intervened was pure frivolity. The prince was now in residence for the Season, and with him Mrs. Fitzherbert. Mama received an invitation from that gracious lady to attend a cricket match on the prince's cricket ground, an invitation in which Sunny and Ben and I were included, as well as Colonel Staffen and some other officers from the prince's regiment. As I've remarked, the officers of the prince's own regiment tended to be rich young gentlemen, often of the prince's own circle and much inclined to social pursuits.

There was a flurry of preparation. Sunny and I were pressed into retrimming hats and hemming and stitching to make ready proper gowns for the occasion. Mama claimed that the fine muslins of which our dresses were made had been acquired from a water-damaged batch that Mrs. Yewdall had purchased for her dressmaking establishment from smugglers, and that she had sold them to Mama for "next to nothing" several days before the robbery. My suspicion of Mama was growing, but there were so many suspicions rattling around in my head just then that I wasn't thinking clearly about anything. I unworthily suspected her of taking money, or even sprigged muslins, from Richard Thurlby, Esq.—a different matter entirely from accepting gifts of pears from his orchard.

Dashing officers drove us to the event in open carriages, and we wore pretty dresses and wide hats with ribbons, and carried frilly parasols just like ladies of fashion. We dined under the shade of a marquee, flirting and chatting, as young men swatted balls about on the green field before us. Colonel Staffen attempted to keep any rivals away from Sunny, while I dumbfounded two lieutenants with my knowledge of pugilists and pugilism. Ben dumbfounded them even more by his description of how I foiled a robbery with a right to the jawbone, thus taking the stiffening out of my opponent. Meanwhile, Mama raised her eyebrows at him, quite futilely, in an attempt to warn him that other gentlemen might not admire female pugilistic skill quite as much as he did.

Before the match was over we left Mama and Mrs. Fitzherbert, with a major and two other of the more elderly gentlemen, in order to drive out to the raceground, where one of the officers intended to enter a horse in the approaching meet, then to drive back to Preston for tea, and finally to Xanadu, where we gathered on the terrace to sing to the accompaniment of Sunny's guitar.

The officers were charming, gay, attentive, and obliging, and one was most entertainingly foolish. "Always say, Miss Maudsley, that for the best accompaniment to a song, a guitar's the thing. So original! Wouldn't have a pianoforte for the world." For days afterward, Sunny fell into languishing airs, murmuring, "Wouldn't have a pianoforte for the world!" I can't say I didn't enjoy myself, but there wasn't a minute I was not missing Lord Breverton Dayne.

And then it began to rain the next day. The weather was so

stormy that we couldn't even give the infants and Charlotte their swimming lessons. Chaffinch had within a few days followed Dayne to London, and Lady Sarah was also gone; many of the officers were on summer maneuvers somewhere, and the wind and rain no doubt kept our more dandified admirers indoors. Ben's friend Dandy Rogers, who despite his name was not dandified at all, did brave the stormy weather to call. Usually, however, he just came to carry Ben off to spar in Mr. Chaffinch's temporary sparring parlor, and if not, he just sat around with Ben and Chunk reading sporting magazines, looking at Chunk's collections, or playing cribbage. Colonel Staffen also came to call, no matter what the weather, obviously still much taken with Sunny and replacing Jerry Richmondson, our foppish young neighbor from High Oak. Sunny has been the object of gentlemen's admiration since the cradle, although as I've said, she's too cranky to retain all of her admirers—including, thankfully, Jerry.

So in any event, we suddenly, after all the activity, found time on our hands—time enough to sit down again with the ciphered papers.

Dayne

"Well, what's the story?" Lady Sarah asked. She had demanded that her nephews report to her the *instant* they returned from Antwerp and their conference with Algernon, which—within reason—they had done. "Let's hear it from beginning to end." She folded her hands in her lap.

Walter leaned down to kiss his aunt's cheek, after which Dayne followed suit. "Well," the latter said as he seated himself, "Algernon's agreed to come back and settle his affairs. But he doesn't want the responsibilities of the title. His bargain was that he'd come back, provided we agreed to his abdication of the title. He also insists that the revenues of the estate go to me with the title. . . ."

Lady Sarah interrupted. "How's he been living all this time? Begging in the streets?"

Walter pulled off his gloves and sighed. He had found the

trip both tiring and trying. "No. His friend Lord Camelford was sending money to him through the Rothschild continental banking connections."

"Camelford! Well, there was another loony for you. Just as I've been saying."

"No, Aunt Sarah," Dayne said. "Camelford was not loony. Nor is Algernon. He's just enjoying wearing sack cloth and ashes."

"Insists that his flight was in fact his abdication. Now he wants to make it a legal abdication."

"He wouldn't have come back at all if Camelford had lived and been willing to continue sending him money. He asked a lot of friendship."

"Well . . ." Walter returned to the subject. "Brev told him he didn't want the title. . . . I'd be happy to take it; all the responsibility is mine, anyway, since Brev won't give up his career with the navy. In any event, Algernon wouldn't hear of it. He insists on orderly succession. However, my portion as a younger son was considerably increased, and it means I'm heir presumptive." He winked at his brother. "Until Brev opens his nursery, anyway."

Lady Sarah refused the bait. "Means petitioning the House of Lords. Ain't easy to abdicate a title. Then buying off Claudette; that'll cost a pretty penny. Suppose she'll sue on grounds of desertion. Ain't going to be much left when all that's done."

"We'll be able to scrape along quite nicely, all of us." Walter, who knew to a penny the yearly revenues from the Dayne properties—landed, funded, commercial, and industrial—controlled the amused twitch pulling at the corner of his mouth, and merely raised one eyebrow instead. "No fear of poverty for any of us, Aunt. I can't imagine what you may suppose the condition of our family to be, but I assure you, we are not about to be bankrupted. Brev can marry his poverty-stricken lady. . . ."

"Still determined, are you?" Lady Sarah fixed Dayne with an intent stare.

"Still determined. And you needn't look as though you were searching my soul to discover if the devil dwells therein.

I'm rational, sane, and—if I may use such a term with a worldly lady of your sensible generation—I am in love."

"Well. It's often been observed that young men will be fools. As Algernon has made abundantly clear."

Lady Sarah had no intention of confessing that an afternoon call from Lady Catherine deVandt and her elderly companion had quite cooled her enthusiasm for a liaison there. Lady Catherine had treated the companion, an impoverished cousin of her mother, with cold contempt. Lady Sarah, who admitted to being a little in years herself, had not liked such disrespect for grey heads. Nor had she liked the way Lady Catherine bullied her companion, a woman whose birth was quite as good as the girl's own mother's had been. Just because the poor lady's father had happened to be a fourth son rather than the firstborn . . . It never did to produce too many children; there were few estates that could provide a decent portion for the younger sons, as well as respectable dowries for the daughters. It meant that great families always had a bunch of impoverished relatives hanging about. . . . Lady Sarah had proceeded to state her opinion on the subject of irresponsible procreation among the governing and landed classes, apropos of nothing that her visitors had said—which, she speculated later, had no doubt given them the idea that she was wandering into her dotage. She also had a passing uneasy thought that she was rather given to bullying herself, but found no difficulty settling that with her conscience. Unlike the deVandt woman, she bullied everybody, rich and poor alike.

"Algernon wants to return to Dresden and his German mistress . . . wants to bring her here, in fact, while settling his affairs."

Lady Sarah realized that she had been woolgathering, another sign that her dotage might be creeping up on her. She raised her head higher and placed her hands on the arms of her chair. She would have been pleased if she'd known that her nephews thought she looked majestic. "Bring her here!" she said sharply. "Hope you didn't permit such nonsense."

Walter smiled faintly. "We convinced him to leave her in Antwerp. Even harder to buy off Claudette or to secure a divorce with a mistress in the background, we told him."

Lady Sarah snorted. "What's wrong with that wife of yours, Walter? A political wife keeps her ears open. Wasn't in town two days, myself, before I heard Claudette's got Lord Egletorne in her pocket."

"But enough in her pocket to stay there when she's divorced and not widowed?"

"Egletorne ain't a Papist. Ain't even Church of England. He's one of those odd-fangled Unitarians. They don't believe in anything. Don't you know he's been dragging Claudette along to that chapel they've got on Essex Street? You'll have to do better than that, my boy, if you think you're going to be any good as a politician. . . ."

"Yes, Aunt Sarah," Walter said, now smiling broadly.

"Take that smile off your face," Lady Sarah scolded. Her dinner was not sitting lightly, and she was feeling old. "Jackanapes, both of you. And don't expect any help from me with this coil. I'm going back to Brighton. None of my business what mess Algernon gets your family into."

Dayne was now smiling as broadly as Walter. "How nice that you'll be returning to Brighton, Aunt. I've got to get back myself to make a declaration in form to Miss Maudsley."

"Well, do what you want. Doesn't matter to me. But," she added, although without much conviction, "you'll be sorry."

Mr. Stuart Chaffinch had soon found himself in the unusual situation of having nothing to do. He had received an express from Dayne the day after his friend's departure, with a cryptic message to the effect that he would be delayed in London longer than expected; that the family business was indeed as urgent as his brother had stated, but that he would do his best to call in Bow Street for information about the Goodman woman. If anything else useful occurred to him to do, he would undertake to do it.

Chaffinch had made a restless call on the Maudsleys and had stayed the entire afternoon, wearing out his welcome, he was certain. The next evening he made a wet night of it with Colonel Staffen and lost twenty pounds at hazard. The condition of his head and his pocket the following morning convinced him that it was time to go to London. Although he was patience itself when there was a prospect of gaining information or apprehending a spy, he was not a man made for inactivity.

He made a hurried call on the Maudsleys, where he was received by Sunny. Lady Maudsley was resting, the infants were asleep, Ben and the children were off somewhere. Miss Maudsley was closeted with her man of business. He wondered uneasily what she was putting him up to this time. He passed by Henny's lodging to remind him to keep a close watch on the Maudsley house, particularly on Lia, and to be on the alert for any suspicious activity. Leaving instructions with Tilt to give Henny assistance if required, he packed a portmanteau and set out for London. He was soon driving at a spanking trot along the London road, one of the best in the kingdom, his headache diminishing and his spirits lifting with every mile.

He was not in Brighton, therefore, to receive the second express from Dayne, which informed him that Bow Street had uncovered Miss Goodman in Ireland, but that she would not be available for questioning for a week at least; and that, furthermore, "that fellow Price" had visited Bow Street to complain of a burglary—a burglary that from the method employed sounded very much like the same fellows who had burgled the Maudsleys. He'd seen Napean at the Admiralty, and the secretary was considering the next step. Claimed he didn't want to flush their bird too soon. Finally, Dayne advised Chaffinch to come to London immediately, since urgent family business was taking him to Antwerp.

So Chaffinch found himself in London covering already covered ground, which always made him feel choleric. Mumbo jumbo from the Admiralty worsened the condition, and a complaint to the Foreign Office came to nothing. He spent the next days at Gentleman Jackson's Boxing Saloon, sparring with Jackson and brushing up his skill with the foils with Angelo. At night he was at Jem Belcher's Jolly Brewer, in the thick of the plans for a match between Dutch Sam and Caleb Baldwin . . . and in between trying to forget that except for whatever might turn up at the Admiralty, he was no closer to the French spy ring—assuming it still existed—than he had been three months before. It was not a cheering thought. Miss Goodman was his next best hope.

He had gone around to Bow Street again, where he was told that it would be yet another week before Miss Goodman could be brought from Ireland, but where he encountered Jeremy Sturrock, Bow Street's top detection expert, with whom he spent a diverting hour. He returned to his London rooms in somewhat better humor, but without even the desire to seek out entertainment. He opened the door to discover a grinning Breverton Dayne.

"Brev! By all that's holy, I'm glad to see you! It's been deadly, waiting for the Goodman woman to be brought over from Ireland and not another scent to follow. . . . Admiralty fussing around . . . Bow Street has no clues to the burglary of Price's office; so it doesn't look like the runners will lead us to our quarry. Well . . . I must've been around to Walter's to see if you were back at least ten times. And what took you both to Antwerp? That is, if I may ask?"

"Algernon. He's returned."

"Algernon? You're not serious!"

"Would I joke about such a thing, Chaff?"

"No, no, of course not. But I can't believe it! I . . . Well, but have a cup of tea, or—or join me for supper and tell me about it. There's a quiet tavern just around the corner. Serves a good beefsteak. Algernon back! I can't believe it."

"Supper sounds just right. I've come from Aunt Sarah's. She was inclined to scold. Incidentally, Algernon kept himself afloat in France all these years with the aid of the unfortunate Baron Camelford and the Rothschild banking connections."

"So? An arrangement similar to the one by which the French paid Sir Whitney for spying?"

"Similar. No more. I'll tell you the entire tale at supper. How long before the runners have the Goodman woman in London?"

"Another week."

"The Admiralty?"

"They'll let us know."

"Gives me time to get down to Brighton; I can only hope Lia will receive me kindly. . . . I haven't even sent her a note to explain my delay in returning. Will you remain here?"

"No, I'll drive you down. Time I packed up my things, anyway. My work there is finished, and I'd like to take a proper leave of the Maudsley family. Never thought when we started this that there'd be pleasure in it."

"In this rain in your phaeton? Think I'll take the stage."

"Come now, that's not sporting at all. A musty stage . . . And you'll have to get out and walk up the hills, up to your knees in mud . . ."

Dayne looked thoughtfully at his leg. He patted it, then moved it back and forth. "It'll be clear tomorrow, according to my leg."

"You'll forgive me, but I'm getting tired of your leg."

Lia

So that rainy afternoon the three of us, Ben and Sunny and I, sat down to decipher Papa's papers. By the end of the day we were working with growing disbelief. It took us nearly fourteen hours over the course of three days to complete the task, and by the time we finished, we had a document the contents of which left us stunned, information so fantastic that we weren't even sure we should believe it.

I can't quote Papa's "letter"; it was too long and too detailed. However, he began it with some sententious advice on morals and manners for young people, such as he had been in the habit of occasionally bothering us with, before getting down to the more interesting information. But just as we began to yawn, the subject changed. He told us that he was writing only as a precaution in the event that some untoward incident should occur or evil rumors be connected with his name. He wanted to tell us, first, that the revolution in France had been the hope for a rebirth in the old world of Europe and England, and that despite the violence of the aftermath, he had been unable to accept that England would expend men and treasure to restore the old regime in France. And so he had openly declared, many times. Nor had he given up on badly needed reform in England and in Ireland, even when his radical friends like Mr. Coleridge and Mr. Wordsworth were beginning to talk like Tories . . . when people feared a Jacobin behind every tree and a republican under every bush, and when even religious dissent was thought by some to be equivalent to treason. He had openly declared his opinions on that score as well.

"Papa always could do and say the most outrageous things!" I exclaimed at that point. He had that wonderful talent for making people like him and trust him, no matter what he said or did. . . . How many times had he convinced a creditor that a few more months time would bring him the funds to pay a bill, and then—when no money was forthcoming—with another story convince the same gullible tailor (or jeweler, or blood horse breeder) that a few more months would *surely* put him in a position to pay, and that that particular creditor's bill would be the very first to be settled!

"He could say outrageous things because everyone knew he'd never do anything about it," Ben said cynically. "Papa was just all talk."

I had to admit that Ben was right, but as we continued on with the deciphering, we were forced to revise our disrespectful opinion.

Papa's letter went on to explain that his defense of the French Revolution and recommendations for reform at home, which did not prevent his being received in the "Best Circles" (we could almost hear his voice and the pride in it), and—lamentably—the appalling state of his finances, had encouraged French agents to approach him with offers of very generous reimbursement for information. In a word, they would pay him well to spy for them. He had always loved France and believed in the revolution, but he could not spy against his own country. He went to the Foreign Office. "Certain people" there welcomed the opportunity to use his talents (Papa was never modest) to penetrate a French spy ring for their own purposes. Papa became a double agent.

We knew so little of espionage at that time that Papa might

have been telling us he had become a frog, changed by the fairies on some long-ago midsummer night for witnessing a fairy dance.

"What's a double agent?" Sunny asked, a little fearfully.

"Well, from Papa's description," Ben answered, "it was all a hum on his part. It means he was really spying for England, but the French thought he was spying for them. . . . The French picked a troublesome customer in choosing Papa to spy for them!" he added proudly, with no trace of his former cynicism.

Papa used several pages to describe the means by which he accomplished his mission. But in the end it all came down to Papa's great charm and his ability to make the most fantastic lie seem plausible. People *liked* Papa, and they *wanted* to believe him. In fact, until the names of people Papa labeled as French agents began to appear, I had half suspected that he was making up another of his fantastic stories to amuse us.

In 1800, he began to suspect that he had been discovered, which led him to believe that there was a spy in the Admiralty or the Foreign Office who was also sending reports to France "by different channels," but reports at variance with his own. He was forced to carelessness in order to learn as much as he could before "retiring." At the very minute he wrote he was in danger of exposure and possibly of his life. Furthermore, his nerves were fraying. "I am not an iron man," he noted, with a kind of sad and uncharacteristic modesty.

The last page of his letter told us that he would deliver, on the following day, a memorandum to the Foreign Office, in which he would ask for an appointment to meet the Foreign Minister, and at which time he would expose what he knew of the network, names and all. And he hoped that we would all like the outposts of South America, where he would undoubtedly have to go to escape assassination.

"Assassination!" Sunny exclaimed. "Do you suppose he's serious?"

"I should think he was," I said. The idea had gradually come to me that the information in this letter was what my attacker in the garden had wanted and that the robbers had been seeking in our house. Had Papa not delivered the memorandum he spoke of? Had he died before the appointment he requested? Was it possible that the spies he named were still free to pursue their treacherous activities?

"Maybe we wouldn't have had to go to South America, though," Ben was saying, "but maybe to New York or to Canada." Ben has always wanted to travel in North America.

"Maybe we should lock the windows," I said.

Ben snorted derisively, but later he made a careful inspection of both the doors and windows.

The names of those Papa was accusing meant nothing to us, but thanks to Mr. Price, the banking house of Jarvis Brothers & Company did mean something. Papa's letter made everything clear—or almost everything—that Mr. Price had told me. "And," I said, "the wool business was just a story that Papa told Mr. Price. He doesn't say so, but I'm sure that's how the French paid him."

Ben began laughing, and Sunny and I looked at him inquiringly. We saw nothing so very funny. When he'd had his laugh out, he said, "Papa pulled the wool over Mr. Price's eyes. It was one of his jokes."

Ben was no doubt right. Papa never could resist a joke.

Chapter Seventeen

As soon as it was clear to us that the papers we were deciphering were not more of Papa's fantastic stories—that he was entrusting to us information of great importance to England's security—we knew that we had to tell Mama, and not only about the letter, but also about Mr. Price's investigations. We closeted ourselves with Mama in her dressing room, and then we told her.

The reader will remember how calmly she accepted Charlotte and Georgie as Papa's. When she read his letter, however, she began to tremble and then to weep. "And to think," she sobbed, "that all the time Whitney was risking his life! Just so we could have all the luxuries he thought we should have. And at any moment he could have been cut down in the street! And in the prime of his life! And it killed him in the end, for he says, doesn't he, that his nerves were too frayed to continue. . . ."

Mama went on in like manner, refusing all our attempts to soothe her, until Sunny lost patience. "Really, Mama!" she said. "Papa spent as much money on *horses* as he did on us!"

That wasn't quite true, but certainly Papa had never stinted himself in any luxury or diversion he desired, and when Mama began to accuse Sunny of not loving her father, Ben and I came to her defense.

"Papa spent lots of money on himself," Ben told her. "On horses and gambling and money he couldn't afford. Just on—on generosity. Lia and I found that out after he died. Mr. Price didn't even know where all the money went because he was so careless. It's not right to say that Sunny didn't love Papa."

"And it's not right to say that he spent all your fortune and his own just because he thought we should have luxuries!" I protested. "We could have had luxuries enough if Papa had had any sense of management at all. And we wouldn't have ended up nearly in the workhouse. We all loved Papa, but he was self-indulgent and—and *selfish!* But he wasn't dishonest. He never *ever* pretended that he did it all for us."

Mama had covered her ears and was shaking her head back and forth in denial, her eyes squeezed shut. "Leave me," she cried. "I can't bear any more!"

Sunny and I were in tears, but Ben said, with a grim set to his jaw, "It's time Mama admitted just what Papa was."

I suppose Ben was right. Mama had always been protected and indulged and spoiled—since childhood, our Great Aunt Edula says. Papa spoiled her, and we continued to spoil her after he died. But as Ben remarked once, Mama also had bottom, as we were soon to witness.

We passed two uncomfortable hours, during which Sunny and I periodically dissolved in tears, and Ben alternated between cracking his knuckles and clenching his jaw. Then, just as we'd decided to knock on Mama's door to see if she was all right, she entered the parlor. Her eyes were red with weeping, but her hair was arranged elegantly and she had put on a pretty dressing gown. "I have been speaking to Adam and Star," was her first statement, at which I nearly stood up and screamed. If I was going to hear that a dead brother and sister, seven and five respectively, had been defending Papa! . . .

But instead she merely said, "You will all be pleased to know that they are quite well and happy."

I refrained from commenting that I had not thought it possible to be anything else but well and happy in Heaven, as I might have on another occasion. I could find nothing at all to say, and Ben and Sunny sat equally mute.

Mama then said, reflectively, "I don't believe they will be visiting me again."

None of us was able to think of a reply to that statement, and Mama seemed not to expect one. She picked up the needlepoint tapestry she had begun working that morning, sat down in her chair by the Pembroke table, and turned up the lamp.

She bent her head over the work, and began setting her neat, careful stitches.

At last I said, very tentatively, "Mama . . ."

"Yes, dears. I know you're all sorry for the things you said about your dear Papa. I know you loved him, and I'm sure that since reading his letter you admire him greatly for his bravery and patriotism. Now we must decide what to do with the information he entrusted to us. Lia, please call for tea and some sandwiches."

We might not have told Lord Dayne and Mr. Chaffinch about Papa's letter had they not called on us the next day. They came unannounced, to find Colonel Staffen and Dandy Rogers and two other gentlemen with us—not to mention Richard Thurlby, Esq., who was in Brighton for two months with the militia encampment but who was just then apparently off duty, for he was sitting in a corner *tête à tête* with Mama. Mr. Thurlby—or I should say Colonel Thurlby, but I won't—was now openly courting Mama.

Ben and Sunny and I were on the terrace with the other gentlemen. Sunny was picking out the popular militia song "The Girl I Left Behind Me" on her guitar and we were all singing, when Jane announced our two old friends. They entered, each carrying an infant, to the immense and barely concealed amazement of our other masculine guests. It seems they had first visited the nursery to call on Georgie and Irene. Georgie, riding high above the world on Chaffinch's shoulders, his blond curls nearly brushing the ceilings, was obviously the lord of all he surveyed. Irene was swooning with happiness in Dayne's arms, babbling her incomprehensible pleasure at their reunion.

Except for such messages as eyes can convey, there was only a moment for other than polite conversation with my supposed lover. Ben's entrance with the announcement of a ship in the roads sent everyone to the front of the house. I would have followed, but Dayne caught my hand.

"I missed you, Lia," he said in a low voice.

I had no voice to reply with. I simply lowered my eyes—just

like any simpering female at Almacks.

"And did you miss me also?" he asked. "Tell me you missed me desperately."

"Mama and Mr. Thurlby will see us," I said, trying to pull my hand from his warm clasp.

"Tell me."

"Yes!" I whispered, pulling against his grasp.

"Yes, what?"

Although my breast was rising and falling like a maiden in one of Miss Fanny Burney's novels, I gathered my courage and my pride and turned to look at him. "I missed you desperately," I said, and then I watched his eyes, which had been full of teasing laughter, suddenly soften.

"My love," he whispered. "Sweetheart."

Such foolish things are said under the spell of the tender passion, but I was too much in the grip of it myself just then to think it at all foolish. Instead I felt faint, another foolishness engendered by love. Nonetheless, I had sufficient strength to withdraw my hand from his and to say, in a reasonably steady voice, that we should join the others. Before he left, however, we arranged to ride the following day, and I knew, quite surely, that somewhere out there on the Downs he would declare himself.

That we told Mr. Chaffinch and Lord Dayne about Papa's letter violated what I am sure must be a first rule of espionage: Do not trust anyone; suspect everyone. Particularly rich and fashionable young gentlemen who determinedly pursue an acquaintance with poor but proud families of deceased baronets. But because of our friendship, and what I believed was more than friendship with one of the gentlemen, we trusted them. . . .

Or we might not have done it had Mama not been so distressed at the thought of either me or Ben traveling on the stage to London with such a document. She wanted us to confide in Richard Thurlby, Esq., which I absolutely refused to do. So, in the end, after our guests departed and after another round of fruitless discussions, we sent a note to our two friends, asking them to call on us again that evening. Mr. Chaffinch, as Sunny pointed out, was a diplomatist, and that meant he was with the Foreign Office.

They both arrived promptly, looking concerned. "What is it?" Dayne asked immediately. "Have you had more trouble with intruders?"

Chaffinch pronounced emphatically that he would have Henny's head if there had been trouble.

We wasted no time in getting down to business. "No, it's not that," I told them. "We wanted to ask your advice about a message Papa wrote to us that we've just deciphered, and—"

"For God's sake, Brev," Chaff rudely interrupted me, "there were papers here, after all, and they didn't find them!"

Ben said, "No, Lia just said we found them."

"Why didn't you tell us you had them?" Dayne demanded, glaring at me as though he would have liked to give me a good shake.

"Why didn't you ask?" I demanded in my turn. "And, anyway, why should we tell you?"

"How did you know about them?" Sunny asked, going right to an essential point.

"Oh, damnation!" Dayne said.

We had all been talking at once, but with that exclamation, we all fell silent.

We stared accusingly at our former friends—even Mama. In those few seconds it had become clear to every one of us why our acquaintance had been so diligently sought by these two rich young men. They had been after those ciphered papers all the time, and every move they had made had been with the intent of worming themselves into our good graces and our confidence.

"Who are you?" I asked, while my mind raced. One hears of spies chewing up incriminating documents, but that didn't seem feasible—Papa always was terribly wordy—nor was it sensible, if the government was ever to be informed of the French spies in our midst.

Lord Dayne—or whoever he was—now directed his angry shafts at his friend, or supposed friend. "I told you we should have told them long ago!" He looked at me. "Lia, I beg you to hear our explanation. . . ." He must have sensed that my blood was firing, for he added, "Just please be calm."

"I am calm. Perfectly calm." I considered stuffing the papers down my bosom, but of course that wouldn't stop a determined man. . . .

"I've wanted to tell you for over a month now. Damn it, Chaff, tell them! You're in charge of this business."

Mr. Chaffinch said dutifully, "Lady Maudsley, Miss Maudsley . . . Miss Sunny, Ben, I can only offer my apologies. It's true . . . Brev has been at me to tell you our mission here for at least a month."

I felt, rather than saw, that Dayne was watching me closely, although after flicking one quick glance at him I refused to meet his gaze again.

"Our mission was to discover some clue to a group of French agents in England, and later, to appropriate if possible—and if such a document actually existed—some coded papers."

"They're in cipher, not code," I said idiotically.

"Yes, of course. Sir Whitney, as I suppose you now know, was what we call a double agent."

None of us said a word. Chaffinch looked helplessly at Dayne, who said, as though on cue, "Chaff's an intelligence officer with the Foreign Office. I was assigned by the Admiralty to work with him. I was . . . shall we say . . . available, and with a good reason to be in Brighton." His lips thinned with that touch of bitterness I remembered so well from the first days of our acquaintance, when the surgeons thought he would never walk again without the aid of a cane.

"We had nothing to go on at first but a memorandum Sir Whitney wrote to Lord Grenville, hinting at important information. A certain person—that is, a person at the Foreign Office—later told us he had hinted of information in code . . . uh . . . cipher. Actually, Sir Whitney said he was writing a book, but we guessed he might have been hinting at something more important and in safekeeping somewhere. We thought perhaps in a box at a bank, or the office of his man of business . . ."

"You!" I exclaimed. "The burglary of Mr. Price's office! It was you! You burgled our house! You—"

"No, no! Wait!" Chaff said, putting up his hand to

stop my flood of accusation.

"Let Chaff explain!" Dayne protested. "Please. We didn't break into your house. . . . We were with you. . . ."

"We now believe the French suspected that Brev and I were investigating Sir Whitney's affairs here in Brighton, and they searched your house as a precaution."

Ben was as offended as I. "But you broke into Mr. Price's office. . . ."

"And pried into our affairs!" I added. "How *could* you?" I looked at Dayne accusingly.

"Don't look so hard at me," he said. "We wanted to tell you. We couldn't."

"It had to be done," Chaffinch said. "It's true that Brev and I both went over all the papers in Price's office from the years before your father died, and then the cryptography people at the Foreign Office also. But we weren't interested in your affairs, only that there might be something . . . some clue. . . . And Brev didn't like it. He's a—a bit too nice for this business."

"Don't like it at all!" Dayne confirmed his friend's statement with emphasis. "Now tell them about the money, Chaff."

"We did discover that Sir Whitney had received payments through the banking house of Jarvis Brothers. Actually, by bills of exchange drawn on the account of a firm of merchants in America. We are told it's a firm established by French émigrés in Philadelphia. . . . But we believe they're agents of the French government, not émigrés. We've asked our ambassador in America and some gentlemen representing English commercial interests to investigate, but the last payments were made four years ago, and of course, America is a neutral. . . ."

We gave them the letter to read. We had made three copies—one to keep with us in Brighton, locked up at Wigney's bank; one copy for the Foreign Office; and one to put under lock and key with Mr. Price.

"By God, you were right, Brev!" Chaffinch exclaimed at one point, looking up from the page in his hand. "Here's your spy at the Admiralty! Been there since '83! Of all the!. . . Probably when we were trying to make a separate peace with the Americans during the rebellion . . ."

Suddenly, Dayne whistled, "Vanderstad at Jarvis Brothers!

A Dutchman! I've met him. Came over here when Bonaparte invaded Holland. Represented—what bank was it? One of the big Dutch banks. Can't remember the name."

"Who?"

"Sir Whitney claims here that Vanderstad at Jarvis Brothers is the head of French intelligence in England! *There's* the connection with the French agents in America. Merchants indeed!"

Chaffinch was on his feet. "But do you realize what we've got here, Brev?" he asked excitedly. "Intelligence rather than espionage."

"No. I hadn't realized. Remember, I'm just an amateur." He smiled at me. "Chaff's the expert."

I did not return his smile.

Chaffinch's excitement was at such high pitch that he was actually rubbing his hands together. "However inadvertent, Jarvis Brothers employs a spy! They'll balk at exposure. Perhaps we can also mention contraband cargoes. . . ."

"Smugglers?" Sunny and Ben and I chorused.

"The Gentlemen?" Mama asked, in a tone of disbelief.

Chaffinch regarded us with a warning frown. "I think it would be wise to forget I said that."

We all nodded. As I have remarked before, the smugglers have been known to take it unkindly when anyone pries into their affairs.

As he finished reading, Chaffinch said to Mama, "Ma'am, you have reason for great pride in your husband, but unfortunately, his accomplishments must be forever unknown. The nature of the work is clandestine, you know. . . ."

Dayne added his praises, and then said, "But who in the name of twenty *diablos* is Miss Goodman? Have you realized, Chaff, that Sir Whitney doesn't even mention her in this letter?"

"But she's the woman in Edinburgh," Sunny said. (I had resolved to never speak again to either of the gentlemen.) "Papa knew her. She's Georgie's mother. But how did you? . . ."

Once again we all turned accusing eyes on our two "friends," only to learn that they already knew about Miss Goodman and that Charlotte was French. Not only that, but they knew Charlotte's real name—Lucrèce Bonhomme, which was as ridiculous a name for Charlotte as that she was born French!

"But of course," Mama said. "Goodman. I can't think why it didn't occur to me before."

We all stared at Mama.

"Bonhomme . . ." Dayne smote his forehead—this time in earnest, not for melodramatic effect, as when he had played at plucking daisy petals with Charlotte and Angela. "But of course! *Bon homme* means 'good man' in English. Chaff, we're the most witless espionage agents in the kingdom!"

Chaffinch actually looked in pain. "I should resign my post!" he exclaimed. "Of all the thick-witted, simpleton blunders . . ."

More horrible thoughts were occurring to me. "Then the Goodman woman . . . she translated her name . . . she's Charlotte's . . . she must be some relative of Charlotte's father . . . that means she can take *both* of them away from us if she chooses!"

Dayne looked at Chaffinch and Chaffinch at Dayne, as the rest of us abandoned ourselves to a distressed babble.

"We might as well tell them," Dayne said. "They know everything else."

He rose from his chair to lay a hand on my shoulder. I jerked away.

Chaffinch threw his hands up. "We might as well have left the whole *business* up to them." He leaned over and took Mama's hands in his. "Miss Goodman has been apprehended in Ireland. She's being brought to London, where we intended to question her. We thought she was a member of the spy ring." He lifted Mama's hand to his lips. "We'll leave you now. . . . You must be tired. But I'd like to take Sir Whitney's letter and the copies, if I may. For your own safety, I'd prefer that you not have them in your possession any longer."

We all protested.

"Espionage records are destroyed. It's necessary. And I believe the Foreign Office would require it, in this case as in any other. However, perhaps we can arrange something. We'll call again tomorrow."

"You, Chaff, may call again tomorrow," Dayne said, "and

make any decisions you want about Sir Whitney's letter. I'm riding with Miss Maudsley."

I said I had discovered that I would be too busy and that it might rain again, anyway.

Mama looked at me disapprovingly. "It is impolite to break an engagement, Aurelia, and I have no need of you tomorrow afternoon. I'm sure that Sunny or Charlotte will be able to attend to whatever chore you might be thinking of."

Dayne said that his injured limb signified the same good weather we had been enjoying for two days.

"Oh, she's just mad," Ben explained to him, as if that weren't clear already. To me he said, "Come on, Lia, don't be missish."

"You don't have a thing to do that can't wait!" Sunny said.

It seemed that the rest of my family had forgiven Mr. Chaffinch and Lord Dayne for their underhanded motives in scraping an acquaintance with us, and making us all think that Dayne was courting me, and making me think that he was falling in love with me! It was just too shabby and I had no intention of forgiving him. At least, not right away. But in the face of family pressure, what was I to do? I agreed to honor my engagement to ride with him the following day.

Dayne

"Sorry that I've put you in bad with Miss Maudsley," Chaffinch said.

"Oh, she'll come around," Dayne answered, with what his friend thought was perhaps a touch of overconfidence.

"Let's hope so."

Mindful of the groom perched behind them, the rest of the journey was completed in silence. When they were back in their rooms, however, Chaffinch said thoughtfully, "You know, it's still possible that the Goodman woman could be a member of the ring."

"Just what I was thinking. Sir Whitney could have been protecting her. We still don't know what their relationship was."

"Exactly. We'll certainly want to question her closely."

"*You* will question her. *I* am resigning—in order to pursue one Miss Aurelia Maudsley. And once I have her promise of eternal love and devotion, and we've had some time together, I will pull every string I can find and every one that Walter can find to get another command."

Chaffinch didn't bother to argue. "Well, I wish you luck. Fortunate we don't have to confess to our intention to burgle their house as well as Price's office. One less difficulty for you."

"Yes. No need to confess to intentions, just deeds. Perhaps one day, when Lia and I are sitting in our rocking chairs with our latest grandchildren on our knees . . ."

"So I suppose this means that I'm going to London alone to confer with the Foreign Office on what measures to take, now we know who the spies are."

"Unless you need me."

"Not immediately. Stay and do your courting. I may want you later. I'll be off early tomorrow, but not so early as to arouse suspicion. We can't be certain that they feel safe just because their burglaries were unsuccessful . . . I'm going to have some strong words for Bow Street and the Foreign Office—that we didn't know about the second burglary of Price's office. . . . Unforgivable incompetence . . . But in any event, they may be watching us for an indication of whether they're discovered or not."

"You'll take Henny with you?"

"Yes, and a loaded pistol for each of us. Will you see to getting a copy put in a bank box here tomorrow? And I'd suggest that you send Tilt to guard the Maudsleys. Be careful yourself. And, of course, should anything untoward occur . . ."

"Of course. At your service."

Lia

We rode across the Downs, accompanied as before by our faithful young chaperon, Edgar. Dayne made no attempt at conversation, undoubtedly with some idea of letting me simmer in peace for an attack later. Once on the Downs, we spontaneously broke into a gallop. It was a glorious day. We stopped on a high ground from which we could see the sea. Dayne helped me dismount – Edgar was well versed in discreet chaperonage.

"Will you walk with me?" he asked, his hands lingering seductively about my waist.

"If you like," I answered coolly, stepping away from his embrace.

"I should like it very much," he replied with a smile. "Edgar, Miss Maudsley and I will be walking and enjoying the view. You may stay here with the horses."

"Yes, sir, m'lord," Edgar said, touching his cap. His expression was carefully and very circumspectly solemn.

The turf was soft and springy under our feet as we walked along the low ridge. The sea, shimmering under the morning sun, stretched away to the south, and to the north lay the undulating Downs. The wild herbs, which grow so profusely on the Downs, scented the air. Above us a hawk circled, and a flock of sheep grazed along a distant rise.

Neither of us spoke, until Dayne attempted to take my arm. I drew away. "I don't need help; I have two perfectly good limbs." And then, suddenly conscious of what I had just said, I hastily apologized. "I'm sorry, I – "

"Why should you apologize?"

"Because – because – Oh, because you know perfectly well why!"

"But I came to Brighton to recover the use of my limb, and I've done so. It's my heart that's suffered damage."

"If you're going to start that, I'm going to turn around and go right home."

"Start what?"

I was not going to permit him to put me on the defensive. "Make love to me," I answered.

"But how can I help it? I'm in love with you."

I stopped, dead still. All the speeches about rich young men who pretend admiration of innocent women in order to extract from them state secrets evaporated into the air, to mingle with the scents of wild herbs and midsummer grasses and sea. I simply stepped into his arms to be kissed most tenderly.

It wasn't at all proper, what we did out there on the Downs. He led me down the other side of the ridge, where a small grove of poplars, the only reminder of an abandoned cottage, made a little pool of shade. We sat down. He told me again that he loved me and extracted from me a similar admission. Then he lay back in the grass, his hands behind his head, and looked up at me with a beguiling smile. "Now, tell me how perfidious I am, and then I can tell you how I had no intention of falling in love with such an impertinent and vinegary young lady."

So I told him, without much conviction; and then he told me, with great conviction, that—defying all he would have believed only three months before—he had indeed fallen in love with a vinegary young lady.

"Why don't you take off your hat?" he asked. Then he said, "Will you kiss me?"

I bent over to kiss him, and he ran a hand over my hair, pulling at my braids. "Take down your hair, Lia."

The innocent bird, petrified by the snake, took down her braids and slowly loosened her hair. "So soft . . ." he murmured, and as he pulled my head down, his hands in my hair, I was kissed again, and then—I can't imagine how it came about—we were lying together in the soft grass, side by side.

I have no intention of describing further the most improper events that occurred there in the dappling shade of those trees, but at last he said, whispering into my hair, "I'm afraid that we must stop this."

"Yes," I whispered in return. "But not yet."

I was not an innocent girl, unaware of the pleasures of kissing. Girls who choose to do so can always find a way to be kissed without their chaperons seeing or knowing. I was just innocent about passion. My perfidious lover was not, and he was saving me from being ruined. He watched me braid up my hair, helped me set my hat straight, and adjusted the buckle under my chin. His fingers trembled slightly, and then I quite shamelessly asked to be kissed again, my hat falling off to dangle down my back. It was I, this time, who drew away.

When my hat was once again firmly on my head, we inspected each other for stray clinging grass or leaves, and he brushed my skirt. "There," he said. "Now, are you hungry?"

"Ravenous."

"Will you marry me tomorrow?"

I am afraid that my response to such an abrupt proposal was to gape idiotically at my lover. "Tomorrow?" I at last found wit to ask.

"Well, or as soon as the banns are read."

"I'm a Dissenter. . . ."

He began to laugh, really for no reason, and then I laughed with him, which was just what we needed to put us in a more proper frame of mind to face the public. He hugged me impulsively, then held me away from him. "But how will I ever put up with you for the rest of my life?" He released me, and we started back to Edgar and the horses. "Do you think now you could call me . . . ah . . . Breverton? For starters. Perhaps later, a shorter version."

"More abbreviated?"

"Yes, sauceboat."

"Breverton," I said experimentally.

"Ah, Aurelia," he said, and there we were again in each other's arms.

Breverton spoke to Mama that very afternoon, telling her all about his brother Algernon, his own prospects, and the legal complications that he could expect before assuming again the title of baron. Mama told him that he should communicate with Mr. Price, who would handle the settlements. Then she added, so Breverton told me, "I will speak to Adam and Star just once more. Lia's dear papa will be so happy." So my lover learned about Mama's communications with the Beyond and, I am happy to say, did not find it upsetting at all.

When I told Sunny, her first words were, "Oh, Lia, he's so *rich!*"

"Don't be vulgar, Sunny!" I expostulated. "I am not marrying him for his money!"

"Well," she retorted, "if he weren't rich you couldn't marry him, because Lady Sarah said it was our *duty* to marry rich men."

"I don't think she meant her nephew, though," I said, with just a slight stirring of uneasiness. Lady Sarah, I was certain, would not look kindly on the match.

"Lady Sarah will just have to learn to like it," Sunny pronounced with finality.

It was a week later that Chaffinch returned, with Miss Goodman's story, which—as he said—we were free to believe or not, as we chose. During that week I saw Breverton every day. He dined with us in the evenings and played with the infants in the afternoon. Together we walked on the beach and rode on the Downs, strolled in our garden and sat together on the curved veranda. We played casino with the children, their latest enthusiasm, and Breverton began to teach me chess. We talked and talked, but except for some careful and tender kisses, we were as decorous as any chaperon could wish.

Lady Sarah returned from London and came to call on Mama. She gave her grudging approval of the marriage. "Tried to talk the young fool out of it, but men will have their way."

I repressed a smile, but Mama bristled. "We have been friends these many years, Sarah, but—"

"Now, now, Tilly," Lady Sarah soothed, "don't get on the high ropes. Aurelia's a good girl, ain't saying she's not. Took hold when Whit died, I know that. Kept you all above water. And if Breverton's going back to sea . . . well, he needs a wife at home who can keep herself busy. Now, my sister Clara . . . or take Algernon's silly wife Claudette . . . Lying around on chaises all day with handkerchiefs soaked in rosewater on their foreheads."

Mama smiled sweetly. "But I thought, Sarah, that you had someone in mind for Breverton?"

As I've said, Mama is sometimes rather sly.

"Don't throw it in my face, Tilly. Such haughty impudence the woman showed that I'd never be able to have her in my house. Aurelia's impertinent, but she ain't impudent."

I leave the reader to divine that fine distinction.

We were all on the terrace later that day, when Breverton was announced, and Mr. Chaffinch with him. Angela and Charlotte were playing with the kittens, and Ben was reading a sporting magazine, occasionally stroking Mrs. Black Cat, who lay on his lap, purring benignly. Chunk sat at the table with his naturalist notebooks. Sunny and I were both reading, and Mama, her needlepoint laid aside, was also reading. Mama had always been interested in astrology, and she had lately begun regularly consulting *Moore's Almanac.*

"What a pleasant and leisurely family scene on a hot Sunday afternoon!" Chaffinch exclaimed. He greeted us all warmly, then took my hand. "Can't tell you how delighted I was to learn that Brev's suit was successful. I hope I may now address you as Lia and that you'll call me Chaff. Nobody I know, except my family, has ever called me Stuart."

I assured him that I would be honored to be addressed by my Christian name.

"And the babies?"

"Napping."

Mrs. Oliphant brought lemonade, in which floated a piece of very dearly bought ice, and a heaping basket of her molasses cakes. After our leisurely "tea," Mama shooed the children away, telling them that they could join us later for dinner, in honor of Mr. Chaffinch's return.

"Well," Chaff said as soon as they had reluctantly departed, "I know you're anxious to hear the results of my interview with Miss Goodman."

We all eagerly assented.

"Miss Goodman has confessed. . . ."

"Confessed?" we all chorused.

"Confessed that she isn't Miss Goodman."

"Not Miss Goodman?" we all chorused.

Chaff laughed. "It seems that Miss Goodman was one of those who escaped the guillotine; she was released with the fall of Robespierre in 1794. She walked out of prison with the Bonhomme baby—our Charlotte—in her arms." His expression sobered. "The baby had been wet-nursed by a woman whose own baby died and who was guillotined the day before Robespierre's fall. Life's many ironies . . ."

Breverton took my hand. "Charlotte and Miss Goodman are not related. She took the name and claimed to be the child's aunt, only as a means of escaping to England. She says she lost her own family in the Terror. She'd lived as a child in England, had an English governess, and was afraid of another imprisonment."

We all breathed a sigh. Charlotte, at least until some distant day, was ours. Then, when the war was over, we might venture to France to discover her French relatives. If any had survived.

"Georgie?" I asked.

Both gentlemen looked uncomfortable. "Well, Georgie . . ." Chaffinch said. "Forgive me, Lady Maudsley, if I cause you pain. The woman insists that Sir Whitney is his father. Frankly, you may believe it or not, as you choose. However, knowing that you wanted to keep him, I struck a bargain. The woman has signed a document stating not only that she has no blood relationship to Charlotte, but that she will forfeit all right to Georgie in favor of the Maudsley family, with the provision that you legally adopt him. Nor will she ever seek to see him. Your excellent man of business, Mr. Price, suggested that we not word the document in such a way that she give up the child to 'the father's family,' in case the woman decides some day to name a different father than Sir Whitney."

"You consulted Mr. Price?"

"We took him into our confidence when we discovered he'd attempted to hire a runner to search for Miss Goodman. And since he'd already discovered so much, it seemed best that he know it all."

Dayne smiled. "Chaff didn't want Price fishing in his pond and possibly disturbing the fish he was after." He frowned. "If you understand that somewhat awkward metaphor."

We all understood perfectly.

"You said a bargain . . ." I reminded Chaff.

"Yes. Miss Goodman and her guardsman were in some difficulty in Ireland . . . associated themselves, most unwisely, with another rebellion over there. We agreed not to prosecute either of them, provided they enter into no other plots against the government."

"But who paid Mrs. Clendenning for the children's care—after Papa died?"

Breverton frowned at me, and Chaff shifted uneasily in his chair. "Sir Whitney. He set aside a sum for Charlotte's maintenance from each of his payments for spying—and he was paid very well. An anonymous trust, Price calls it."

"But of course," Mama said. "He would have wanted French money to go to Charlotte."

When we all looked at her, she added, as though it were the most obvious thing in the world, "Charlotte was French, and the French paid Whitney for spying. It was the honest thing to do."

Chaff and Breverton looked mildly staggered by this logic, but Ben and Sunny and I understood Mama's reasoning, whether we agreed with it or not.

"Uh . . . yes. Quite so," Chaff said. "Well, to make short work of the story, just before Sir Whitney died, he arranged for the payments to go directly to Mrs. Clendenning. The bank paid until the money was gone. I think we can only guess at his motives."

I could have guessed very well at his motives—a rival in the form of an Irishman—but I preferred not to. Instead, I said, "And Mrs. Clendenning thought that she would be paid to care for Georgie, but she never was. It was just the fund for Charlotte's care. . . ."

"Miss Goodman did not strike me as dedicated to truth and verity."

"Her name?"

"Brottier. So she claims."

It only remained for Chaff to tell us whether or not the spies were caught. "You deserve to know the outcome," he said, "since it was Sir Whitney's letter that led to their discovery."

It seems that the spy in the Admiralty was apprehended attempting to flee England. In the seventeen years between 1783 and 1800, he had achieved a position of sufficient importance that he was privy to secret correspondence. Thus he had been in a position to destroy the copy of Papa's memorandum, which the Foreign Office had dutifully forwarded the day before Papa died, and to *not* discover a spy—that is, himself—when the warning of his existence was sent to the Admiralty by the mysterious gentleman-smuggler. He was also in a position to discover Papa's role as double agent, when he was notified by his superiors in France that one of his reports on naval plans differed from one of Papa's.

Finally, he had actually known of Breverton's search of Admiralty files for the missing copy of Papa's memorandum. Although Breverton had said nothing about the possible existence of ciphered papers or their possible content, the search had been enough to alert him and his colleagues to the danger of discovery, and to his own decision to attempt flight. *However,* as Chaff was quick to point out, the spies' mistake was the burglary of our house.

Sunny frowned. A beauty she may be and dear she is, but she is not awfully quick.

Chaffinch, noting the frown, explained. "The burglary told us that the French suspected what we were doing in Brighton."

"Oh," Sunny said. Later that evening, Ben and I explained it to her.

One of the spies whom Papa exposed in his letter was persuaded to reveal other names, among them my attacker in the garden, a young French émigré who had been assigned to lead all the burgling operations. His assistants were merely hired thieves and toughs.

The Dutchman, Vanderstad, probably alerted by the Admiralty spy, had fled to America, although purportedly to work with a Jarvis Brothers & Company correspondent bank in New York. This was what Chaff called a "cover story," meaning it was not true but merely the means by which Jarvis Brothers hoped to guard its reputation.

So except for the Admiralty spy, only the smaller fish were taken, after all. Smaller they may have been, but not unimportant, according to Chaff. And all in all, he was not disappointed by the outcome. He did blame the Admiralty for dillydallying, nearly losing a top spy by it and no doubt giving Vanderstad his opportunity to escape. However, by Vanderstad's flight the French lost a wily and wise head of intelligence in England. Any operations he might conduct from abroad would be watched, and although he might continue his nefarious activities, his value would be diminished. He even might be useful, for, as Breverton observed, counterespionage is quite as nefarious as espionage.

We were all silent when Chaff's account was finished, awed, I believe, by the significance of what Papa had done and our own glimpse into the hidden labyrinths of war. (Sunny later confessed she had come out all over with goose bumps.)

It was Chaff who broke the silence. "Well, to lighter subjects. Will you be attending the races this weekend?"

The prince was down from London, the Season was in full swing, and all Brighton was in anticipation of race week. . . .

Chapter Eighteen

Mama gave a dinner party one of those final days in July. As preparations went forward, it was obvious that the dinner would be sumptuous beyond our slender budget. Breverton had agreed, in the settlements with Mr. Price, to quarterly allowances for the children, for Sunny and Ben, and for Mama as long as she remained unmarried, all to be administered by Mr. Price. However, these allowances would begin only after our marriage. In other words, we were still poor.

The party would be large, with Chaff and Breverton, Colonel Staffen (still in Sunny's entourage), and Dandy Rogers, Ben's friend. Richard Thurlby, Esq., now a regular visitor at Xanadu, was of course invited, as well as Lady Sarah Pellett. Mr. Price had introduced a capitalist into our circle, a shy gentleman named Wiskitt, the son of an Indian nabob, with whom I had already begun discussing plans for a Maudsley Crescent. As Mr. Price explained it, my liaison with wealth had braced up the timid capitalists sufficiently that he had actually had to pick and choose among candidates. Mama included them also among her guests—after all, Mr. Wiskitt was a gentleman and Mr. Price was "deserving."

Mama had hired a young couple for the evening, he to serve and she to assist Mrs. Oliphant in the kitchen. The menu would be opulent, and Mrs. Oliphant, who had had no opportunity to exercise the full range of her talents that summer, was going about with stars in her eyes. (A few of the stars were perhaps due to Mr. Tilt, Breverton's manservant, who had called to escort her to church the Sunday after the robbery and had made it a regular habit since.) Mama seemed to feel that both Sunny and I should receive instruction in elegant dinners, and I was ordered to the dining room, where she was waiting with Mrs. Oliphant and Sunny to go over the menu and an extravagant wine list.

As I looked over the list, all the scraps of suspicion that had floated in and out of my mind suddenly came together. "Mama," I asked, "just where are we to get the money to pay for this?"

"Oh, I sold my Venetian lace shawl—I never wore it—and then I had a little left over from the jewelry I sold. To replace the lamp Ben and Chunk broke. Remember?"

"What Venetian lace shawl?" Sunny asked.

"Why, the one I've always had. Surely you remember . . ."

"We don't remember, because you never had such a shawl," I said. "Where are you getting the money, Mama?"

"Don't be inquisitorial, Lia." Mama raised her eyebrows slightly in a frown.

"You haven't been working very often lately on your new needlepoint tapestry," I remarked.

Sunny and Mrs. Oliphant were regarding Mama with considerable interest.

"I have been excessively busy recently, with everything . . ."

"I know where you got the money, Mama. You've been selling your needlepoint tapestries to that Mrs. Yewdall, haven't you?"

"Mama!" Sunny gasped, shocked. And then, as she remembered, she said, "The tapestry we saw in Mrs. Yewdall's shop . . ." She turned to me. "That was Mama's!"

"Yes. Oh, Mama! Your poor eyes!" I dropped on my knees beside her chair and hugged her. Sunny was hanging onto Mama's neck and Mrs. Oliphant was tush-tushing in the background—"Who would have ever thought!" etc.—when Ben came in.

"Girls, girls," Mama was saying, "let me breathe."

"What's all this?" Ben asked.

So we told him, then we all fussed over Mama, telling her how brave and how clever she was.

No doubt wearied by it all, she hushed us by saying, "I am

not at all clever, I know, and I could never learn how to cook or manage a house, so I couldn't do my share after your poor, dear Papa died. But I can sew"—then that sly gleam came into her eye—"and I'm sure Sunny would never have allowed me to take in sewing. . . ."

"Mama!" Sunny exclaimed, shocked again. When Sunny was small, Ben could always tease her, for she never learned that he only did it in order to get her into a fuss.

We were all a little ashamed that we had privately thought Mama so spoiled and . . . well, useless. However, it wasn't long before Sunny was back to scolding.

"I do hope, Mama, that you won't continue to sell your things," she said.

"But why not, my dear? I won't spend as much time on my needlework as I have been—if we are to have a little more money now—and I believe I'll begin going about in society more. But I do enjoy needlework, you know. And I rather like earning money. Although you should know that Mrs. Yewdall merely sold my tapestries for me." A note of smug pride had crept into Mama's voice, and her chin tilted up. "I paid her a commission for doing so."

"But it's so . . . Well, frankly, Mama, it's trade, isn't it?"

"And what if it is? I know several dukes and earls who sell the birds after a shoot."

Sunny frowned. "It's not the same thing."

"And why not?"

Indeed, why not?

Mama's dinner party was a grand success. The service was impeccable, the food exquisite, the wine superb, and the conversation stimulating. Our capitalist nabob owned race horses, and he insisted we all be his guests at the race ball and that we come to watch his prize horse sweep the field, as he fully expected it to do on the final day of the meet. Richard Thurlby, Esq. and Mr. Price spoke brilliantly of the political situation. Chaff and Ben discussed the proposed match between Mr. Baldwin and Dutch Sam of the iron fists, in words we could all understand and without one frown from Mama. Lady Sarah made pronouncements and ate far too much. Sunny kept Colonel Staffen and Dandy Rogers (who had apparently just noticed that evening what a pretty sister Ben had) in a state of begogglement (Charlotte's word). My lover and I made eyes at each other across the table.

As the last wine was served, Richard Thurlby, Esq. arose to state that he wished to make an announcement he hoped would make the rest of us at least half as happy as it had made him. Well, I suspected what was coming, as my readers undoubtedly do also. Mama sat there, glowing and blushing, as Mr. Thurlby told us that she had consented to be his bride. Romance was in the air that night, for in the kitchen Mrs. Oliphant was whipping sauces and dreaming of Mr. Tilt, as we were to learn some weeks later.

After our last guest departed, Mama said, "My dears, sit with me a minute. I want you to tell me that you're happy for me."

We assured her that we were, although just a little surprised. The truth was, of course, that we were all trying not to seem depressed.

"I know that you are not fond of Mr. Thurlby, but I believe that on closer acquaintance you will see his many good qualities. He can never replace your dear papa in my affections, but he is a good man. If you try . . ."

We assured her that we would and that we were happy for her, while Sunny, who happened to be standing behind her chair, rolled her eyes and lifted the corner of her lip in the vulgar way she had of doing sometimes. She is simply incorrigible. Nonetheless, we all did try and so did Mr. Thurlby, and although I don't believe any of us ever learned to love him, we managed not to dislike him and even to respect him. Mama's gentle hand and pliable disposition had an improving influence, and she was content if not gloriously happy in her second marriage. But she never spoke of Mr. Thurlby as "dear Richard" or—thank goodness—"your dear step-papa."

It was a warm night in August, and Breverton and I were to be married in two days, from the Dissenter's church in Brighton. Chaff would be Breverton's groomsman, and Sunny would attend me. It was to be a simple wedding. We would cruise for a week afterward on Colonel Staffen's yacht, then spend a month at the Dayne estate in Kent and some time in London. After that, Breverton would receive a new command and be gone to sea again. The Calcott relations were influential.

Lady Sarah had entertained Breverton's family and mine at a dinner to rival Mama's, but this day he and I had spent alone with his brother Walter and his wife—a pretty woman named Virginia—as well as the mysterious Algernon, who Lady Sarah continued to insist had a crack in his head. I was not of a mind to disagree, but I would have described it more delicately as eccentricity.

There was some artful joking between the brothers, Walter and Algernon, about the bachelor dinner the following night, at which Breverton would bid good-bye to his freedom—all of which we two females, the pretty Virginia and I, were expected to take in good part.

Truth to tell, I was the one who needed a bachelor dinner. The decision to marry and whom to marry is so terribly fateful for a woman, and I'd known Breverton for such a short time. Lady Sarah and Mama had both suggested that we wait, but neither of us would hear of it. Now I was wondering if perhaps my elders might not have been right.

As a matter of fact, Mama was the cause of my uneasiness. It was her duty, she no doubt felt, to counsel her daughter on the business of marriage, and one evening she called me into her dressing room. After what I presume is the usual advice from a fond and liberal parent relating to wifely duties, we spent a comfortable hour together chatting of nothing in particular. I suppose we both felt the approaching change in our relationship.

But then the conversation turned to more practical subjects. I wanted Sunny to live with me, after Breverton went back to sea, but Mama felt she and Mr. Thurlby should present her to society. (Mama and Mr. Thurlby were planning a simple wedding in the fall.) I also wanted Irene and Georgie to live with me, but that would mean we would have to separate Charlotte and Georgie, because Mama insisted that Angela stay with her and she wanted Charlotte with her as well. Charlotte still thought that Georgie was her little brother. So then we began to talk of when Charlotte should be told of her true parents . . . what to tell Georgie, once he was old enough . . .

"Why, we will tell him that he is my dear Whitney's child, of course," Mama said.

So fickle is the human mind, that once we knew that Miss Goodman—or Mlle. Brottier—had given up all claim to Georgie, we had reverted to our earlier indignation that she should have claimed he was Papa's. "Really, Mama," I said, with some annoyance, "the woman was so given to lies. . . ."

"But, my dear, I think she was telling the truth."

I looked at her in consternation.

"Lia, such *naïveté* is terribly dangerous. Innocence, my dear, can lead to great hurt. Whitney was often in the company of this Miss Goodman; both Mr. Chaffinch and Mr. Price have said so. But your dear papa was a gentleman of honor; he made very certain that neither I nor any among our acquaintance were aware . . ."

"But you don't know."

"I think I do. I doubted when we thought Miss Goodman was a Scot, but now we know she's French. . . . Well, the French perhaps aren't so frightfully clean, either, but so *very* elegant and charming."

"I simply refuse to believe it."

"My dear, try to learn a little wisdom . . . a little worldliness. You mustn't be hurt if you learn of some *affaire*. . . ."

Well, I think the reader can see why I should now be hesitating. To be required to consider one's husband's bits of muslin before one even has a husband is not likely to put one in a mood for tying the knot, as Ben would say.

I maintained my humor all that day with Breverton's family, and then through our dinner at the Old Ship, and through our parting glass afterward. I would not see them again until the wedding party assembled two days hence.

Breverton, who is somewhat more sentimental than I, suggested after we parted from them that, rather than return directly to Xanadu, we walk on the beach. "And we'll sit on the wharf where we met," he said. Darkness had fallen, after a lingering dusk. I carried a new cashmere shawl over my arm, a gift from my future sister-in-law, Virginia. It had been uncomfortably warm in Brighton for the past several days. Everyone was complaining about the heat—I believe the thermometer at noon stood at nearly ninety-two degrees!—and the shawl, which ordinarily would have been welcome around my shoulders, seemed hot and clinging draped over my arm. There was hardly a stir of air, which was even more unusual. It would be pleasant and cool on the wharf.

We were both silent, absorbed in our own thoughts—mine not very cheerful.

We greeted Mr. Scruggs at the fire cage at the bottom of West Street.

"Hot tonight," he said.

"Yes," we agreed.

"Never thought, did you, Miss Lia, when you went walking on the sands that night that you'd be meeting the man you'd marry?"

"No, I didn't. But you warned me, didn't you, Mr. Scruggs?"

Mr. Scruggs chortled in appreciation. "That's right, I did. Told you there was young gentlemen swimming that night . . ."

Mr. Scruggs wanted to talk it all over (I believe he had the idea that he was Cupid in disguise), so it was several minutes more before we could continue our walk.

As we finally set out along the beach, I said, "We didn't exactly meet on the wharf."

"True," my future husband answered.

A bathing machine with a broken wheel tilted derelict on the sand. A fishing boat had been pulled up on the wharf for repair, and we made our way around it. The light breeze off the sea brushed across our faces. We sat down, our legs dangling. It was low tide.

"Breverton," I said.

"Yes, my sweet?"

"I'm not sure I want to be married."

"What?" He turned to look at me, frowning quizzically. Perhaps he thought I was a little cross from all the joking about men getting "noosed" and "leg shackled."

"Mama says that she believes Georgie is Papa's."

"That's why you're telling me you don't want to be married? What do you want, then? That I set you up in a neat little house in Hampstead?" He laughed and pulled me against him. He kissed my hair. "If that's what you want, my sweet sauceboat, that's what you shall have, with a box at the opera as well, a new piece of jewelry every quarter day, and a neat cabriolet to drive about in."

I pulled away from him. "Why should women marry men, if they just go off and get themselves a mistress?"

"I could let you talk to Aunt Sarah. She can give you any number of sound reasons for sensible marriages and any number of sound reasons for dalliance. All from her own experience."

"You don't think I'm serious."

"Oh, but I do. You don't like the idea of a little Georgie popping up on your doorstep when you're your mama's age."

"Or before!"

"Lia, I'm in love with you. Do you think I'll stand for any little Georgies on *my* doorstep? I shall send you right back out into the snow—and the baby, too."

I couldn't help laughing and, of course, that meant an interlude of kissing, which always tends to distract one. After a time we stopped that, and I rested my head on his shoulder.

"How about the Harlein Miscellany?" he asked.

"Hmmm?"

"The Countess of Oxford's brood."

"Shocking."

"Lady Jersey?"

"Equally shocking."

"The Devonshire *ménage?*"

"Horrifying."

"And let's not forget Emma Hamilton. Now if you think that I, like the respective husbands of those ladies, will just sit by while a miscellaneous brood grows up around my knees, you are very much mistaken. If you *ever* . . ."

I submitted to being kissed again, but my mind wasn't truly on it. We all know that the world judges the escapades of men differently than it does those of women, but it didn't seem necessary to press the point. I believed that for the moment it had been made.

Breverton sensed that my mind was wandering. "I suppose now that you've decided to marry me after all . . ."

"Did I say that?"

He kissed me. "So I suppose, now that you've said yes, you're going to tell me that you're one of those terribly modern ladies who think it too vastly common to share a bed with one's husband?"

"No. Never have held with newfangled notions."

He kissed me again. "Nor have I."

After a time he observed, "You know, you were right. We didn't meet on the wharf. We met in the water."

I sat up to look closely at him. Something suspicious, and no doubt improper, was afoot.

"Let's swim," he said. He had all kind of arguments. We had met in the water, and sentiment required we go into the water again. There was that bathing machine with the wheel gone, or the fishing boat, for that matter, where we could leave our clothes. My hair would be wet? We could dry my hair with the shawl. . . . My family would want to see my gift and it would be all wet? He'd take it back to the hotel. . . . We would be unclothed. . . . The prologue to the play. Someone would see us. . . . It was the dark of the moon . . . . He lifted me to my feet.

Oh, well. A fig for propriety!

We undressed together in the crazily tilted bathing machine, bumping each other with our elbows, laughing and kissing and caressing in that deep black interior, but both of us careful to avoid an embrace. Our eyes were well accustomed to the dark, however, when we emerged, with the result that our arrival at the water's edge was a little breathless, as we kissed and parted and embraced again until we splashed into the sea. Or actually, we more or less tumbled in.

The ocean is warmer in August than in any other month of the year, but it was cold enough that we both gasped with the shock of it. We swam vigorously, side by side, until we were warm again. Then we clung to each other, bobbing with the incoming swells—in the embrace of Neptune, as Papa used to say.

It was by the narrowest margin that I was not ruined before my wedding night, but we discovered that even in the bathing machine, we shivered and came out with goose bumps. So we dressed, and we dried my hair as best we could, and I braided it up again.

Mr. Scruggs was busy replenishing the fire in the fire cage as we climbed the West Street Gap, so he only remarked that it had gone cooler now the sea breeze had sprung up. The villa was dark, except for the faint glimmer of one candle, but we said good-bye with only the lightest of kisses, although much lingering and anticipation.

I blew out the candle and picked my way up the stairs as quietly as possible. Sunny seemed to be asleep, and I was undressing quietly when she murmured, "You smell like the ocean."

"I've been swimming," I said.

She sat bolt upright. "Lia! You haven't! With Dayne?"

"Yes, love, but all very proper. So close your eyes and go to sleep. Mama will have us both sewing all day tomorrow, you know."

"Ugh," Sunny said. No doubt she was rolling her eyes and lifting her lip in that very vulgar expression.

Epilogue: 1814

Breverton Dayne leaned on his ship's rail and regarded the frigate that had just hailed him. She was three weeks out of England and was carrying a packet of mail.

There were two letters for him from Lia, and as soon as he could, he went to his cabin, called for a cup of coffee, and opened the one with the oldest date, a very thin communication, it appeared.

"Darling," Lia began. "I have bad news for you, about Aunt Sarah. She died, my dear, last week. She collapsed while eating her dinner and never regained consciousness. The doctor says it was an apoplexy. We comfort ourselves that she had not had a day of ill health, except for her occasional bouts of liver complaint."

Dayne wiped his eyes and for a time gazed out, unseeing, at sea and sky, hoping his Aunt Sarah had had time to reach the almond cheesecake before the apoplexy carried her off. He smiled, wiped away another tear, and returned to his letter and Lia's account of the funeral.

"And so, my dear, we are home again, greatly saddened, for we had all come to love her. I'll save such family news as I have until another letter, for indeed, I haven't the spirit or the heart to write more tonight. My love, good night."

He sat quietly for several minutes, the letter still in his hand, lost in memories of his Aunt Sarah. But at last he picked up the second letter and broke the seal.

"I have been down to Brighton," Lia wrote, "to attend to some business with the builder."

He paused to look at the date, and found that five weeks had intervened between the first letter and the last. Lia wrote faithfully once a week, and clearly five letters had gone astray, perhaps never to catch up with him. He would have to wait to discover what Lia and Walter had chosen to do about his Aunt Sarah's old servants, with her house in Brighton, and all the other duties attending a death. He returned to the letter in his hand.

"It's as well that we waited to begin building Maudsley Crescent, for the West Cliff has been much slower to develop than the East Cliff. However, Mr. Price and I expect a postwar expansion that will justify everything we are putting into the Crescent. . . . Darling, exciting news! Ben has just come in to tell me that Wellington has entered Paris!

"I finally take up my pen again, but a whole week later. Do forgive me for missing a week in our correspondence. But it was such an exciting week!

"Ben appears happy and satisfied with his life as a farmer and husband and father, and he is doing wonders at High Oak. He has even managed to purchase some of the land back. Much as we worried when Ben wanted to marry so young, it seems to have been the very best thing for him. Just imagine—his oldest is six now!

"Mama and Richard Thurlby, Esq. came the day after Ben and his family, with their own little darling. She's seven now and quite spoiled, although I'm sure that Angela and Charlotte and Richard have more to do with the spoiling than Mama. Mama reminds me of the mother cat we had, one of Mrs. Black Cat's numerous progeny, who could never seem to realize that those kittens were hers! Do you remember? Mama thinks the last of her babies is a dear child, but she's just another of many dear children who somehow turned out to be hers—or if not hers, Papa's.

"I had brought Sunny back from Brighton with me (scolding all the while about the destruction of Xanadu), and also her two little ones. You can imagine how full the house was! With Sunny's two, Ben's four, Mama's one, our three, and the two orphans, there were children underfoot everywhere."

"What orphans?" Dayne asked, running an exasperated

hand through his hair. What had Lia done now?

"I hope you won't be distressed about the orphans. I heard about them from Angela, who met their uncle at a ball in London. The poor young man (actually, I believe he's almost thirty) is their guardian, but hadn't the least idea how to go on with two children, and of course, his bachelor quarters were utterly inappropriate for two children. He's a bit of a Corinthian, too, Chaff tells me. (Chaff stops by often, and we keep introducing eligible ladies to him, but unsuccessfully. He's such a wonderful 'uncle,' though, that we'd almost be sorry if he should find a lady to his liking, for she might not find *us* to *her* liking.)

"They are just the sweetest little darlings, the orphans, and you will be delighted with them, I know. The poor little boy (he's seven) wets the bed and flies into terrible tempers, and the girl (eight) pouts and sulks terribly. They were sent home from India in the care of a governess who had absolutely no heart. And then to land in the bewildered hands of Henry Dawforth! (Henry is their uncle.) We devote a good deal of time to them, and I see signs of more sunshine ahead already!"

Commodore Lord Dayne sighed.

"When one thinks about it, how lucky Charlotte and George were to be given into the care of Mrs. Clendenning. They have just been on a visit to that worthy lady. George is supposed to be tutored all summer, preparing for Winchester, but you know his intellect is not strong (which convinces me he couldn't be Papa's—although, of course, Miss Goodman might have been lacking in wit), and I, for one, am determined to rescue him from the tutor. He's crazy for the Army, and I think it might be just the thing for him.

"Charlotte will come down with Angela as soon as the season ends, both to spend some time with me before going on to Mama and Richard in Lewes. As the war draws to an end, I begin thinking about Charlotte's French family. She's still such a practical girl and seems not at all interested. . . . Angela, Mama reports, is one of the season's belles, but Mama is always finding her *frowning* over piles of scribbles and with ink stains on her nose, and Mama just *utterly* despairs! Chunk escorts the two girls. He has been invited to join an exploring expedition as assistant to the ship's scientist. He'll be two years away from England, but it will be so exciting. . . .

"Your brother Algernon also called while Sunny and Ben and Mama were here. The crack in his head is still there, although I really don't believe it's wider. (You will remember that Aunt Sarah always thought it growing wider and permitting more air to enter, although by imperceptible degrees, each year.) He had two paintings in the Academy exhibit this year and quite good reviews. Walter and Virginia were with him—Virginia very proud, as she should be, about a recent speech Walter made in Parliament. They were of course in London when the news of Wellington and Paris arrived, and they say the illuminations were beautiful!

"Their two boys, ten and eight now, were a little stiff and shy with such a houseful of miscellaneous progeny (miscellaneous progenitors, too, my darling . . . every one of mine is yours). Irene took Walter junior in hand, he was so shy and lost she felt sorry for him. The youngest, Bobby, just simply disappeared in the whirlwind, to be extracted several hours later, identified by the color of his hair, which is a nice dull reddish gold like Virginia's.

"To top off the entire week, who should drive up but Great Aunt Edula! She's well on her way to four score and ten, as she warned Papa. She's eighty-five, and in vigorous health, and only stopped to deliver a birthday gift for our Chester, 'or whichever one it was with a birthday in May.'

"Do you recall, my darling, the wonderful lines by that unknown poet that ends . . . *'Christ, if my love were in my arms . . .'?"*

"And I in my bed again," he murmured. He folded the letter and put it away. Lia's letters always left him with an empty longing for her, and for the rackety family he'd married into, and for the rackety family they were making together.

He took paper and ink from the portable desk she had given him when last he was in England, trimmed his pen, and began a reply.

"My sweet sauceboat . . ."